Liz Evans was born in Highgate, went to school in Barnet and now lives in Hertfordshire. She has worked in all sorts of companies from plastic moulding manufacturers to Japanese banks through to film production and BBC Radio.

WHO KILLED
MARILYN MONROE?

Liz Evans

ORIEL

An Oriel Paperback
First published in Great Britain in 1997 by Oriel,
a division of Orion Books Ltd,
Orion House, 5 Upper St Martin's Lane,
London WC2H 9EA

A CIP catalogue record for this book
is available from the British Library.

Typeset at The Spartan Press Ltd,
Lymington, Hants
Printed and bound in Great Britain by
Clays Ltd, St Ives plc

TO MUM
in the hope that you're reading this somewhere

CHAPTER 1

Finding out who murdered Marilyn Monroe nearly got me killed as well.

Well it obviously didn't, did it, you're no doubt muttering, so why mention it? Mostly, I guess, because I have to start somewhere. And I don't suppose many of you will remember Tara Lloyd, although she did make a couple of paragraphs in the national papers, a brief mention on the local television news round, and five minutes at my dentist's as he scraped, drilled and polished.

'A girl, Miss Smith. One of them druggies I expect. Overdosed I daresay.'

'Aaaargh.'

'Or raped. Rape went up three per cent in this area last year, you know.'

'Ooo said?'

'Local paper. Day trippers probably. You seen what some of these girls wear? Asking for it.'

'Still against t' lor.'

'Daresay. But you've got to make allowances. Right little teases some of them. I get 'em in here. Forty D in a bit of lace that wouldn't make a decent table doily and all thrust in my nose while I'm trying to extract a nerve. Rinse.'

Gratefully I removed the disgustingly slurping saliva extractor from my bottom lip and took a mouthful of pink liquid. 'I missed the local news. My telly's bust. Where'd they find her?'

'Out along Halfpenny Lane by the cemeteries, I think. Open up.'

Puffs of air were squirted over my cringing enamel.

'Feel anything?'

'No.'

'You're done then. Don't eat for an hour.'

Reprieved for another six months I paid my money, signed my form and made my way down to the beach promenade. It would have been quicker to cut along the back streets to the office, but I liked walking by the sea.

It was, in theory, the beginning of the 'season'. But the streets were so quiet the local tourist officer was probably contactable via a ouija board.

The town's heyday had been in the nineteen twenties and thirties, when hundreds of Londoners flocked to this corner of the coast every weekend to enjoy two weeks of bracing winds sweeping over the North Sea and ruffling the crashing ice-cold breakers, until the landladies let them back into the boarding houses at five o'clock.

Nowadays their grandchildren opt for sun and chips on the Spanish costas and most of the boarding houses call themselves private hotels and exist on an intermittent stream of overnighters: pensioners, early-season bargain breaks, foreign language students and DSS claimants.

Leaning on the blue-painted iron balustrade that separated the promenade from the beach, I squinted against the light, watching the off-shore breeze rumpling frilly cream borders on the steel-grey sea. Here and there on the wide sands a striped windbreaker or solitary deckchair billowed and cracked as a counterpoint to the surf's booming *whooosh*.

A niggle at the back of my mind said the scene looked wrong; but I couldn't quite place why. At least trying to work out what was missing provided an excuse for a bit more time-wasting. I let my eyes drift.

A couple of kids were burying something in the sand; filling their hole in and patting it down with short plastic spades the colour of ripe tangerines. Fine powder grains flew up in swirls as they thumped with single-minded concentration. In the centre of their activity the sand heaved and buckled.

'Oi!' I vaulted the railings and landed in a soft drift that promptly poured into the sides of my shoes. 'Get out of there.'

Seeing me floundering towards them, both kids hesitated. They were in their early teens; chunky bodies underneath grey and yellow jersey shorts and T-shirts. Their arms and legs had a plump white softness that suggested a life of junk food and amusement arcades. I could see them assessing me as I got nearer.

I hoped they'd scarper before I got any closer. At a distance I look quite impressive if I do say so myself (and I usually have to). At five ten I could give them both six inches in height. The trouble is, according to those charts that assess your weight in relation to your height, I should be five foot three.

Whilst we're on my appearance, I've short blonde hair, brown eyes and a face that has been described as 'sensitive and aesthetic' (although I'll admit the usual reaction is 'You look pale, you reckon you got anaemia?'). My name is Grace Bernadette Smith.

The kids were standing shoulder to shoulder; a couple of solid little buckets of lard. I just hoped they weren't going to hit me. They looked like they could really hurt.

Luckily as I arrived they decided to back off. The spade they threw at my head came in handy for digging up the wriggling bundle they'd just covered up. It was an old pillowcase, twisted and knotted at the top to hold something in.

Wrestling with the tight mauve nylon cloth, I forced the material apart and tipped out a trembling tabby cat.

Crouching on the sand, it hugged the cold grains, claws flexing and retracting as it sought for a firm grip. I could see the violent thudding of its heart beneath the grey and black striped coat.

'Whoa, easy girl,' I soothed, running a hand lightly down its back. 'You're safe now.'

She turned a furry head to peer in my direction; her irises narrowed to ellipses in the bright sunlight. Gently I fondled the pricked ears. She nuzzled against the palm of my hand, rubbing her head into the hollow.

Then she sank her teeth into the ball of my thumb, bit a large lump out of the flesh and took off across the beach.

By the time I reached the office, the wound had pumped what looked like half a pint of blood into the grubby handkerchief I'd twisted round my wrist.

The premises of Vetch (International) Associates Inc. were located in a four-storey house (five if you counted the basement) in a street of similar buildings. Once they'd all been boarding houses. A couple still were. Others had been converted into flats. And some, like ours, were offices.

You couldn't really tell which was which until you mounted the flight of steps to the front door and found the rows of bell-pushes, name-plates or local tourist office awards.

Vetch's had a simple brass name-plate affixed next to the door. There was nothing to indicate the nature of the business. Those consulting private investigators didn't usually want the fact announced to the rest of the world.

There were six investigators working out of the premises. We were all self-employed. That was Vetch's idea. It gave us, he'd explained, the advantages of a 'corporate identity' and shared office facilities, whilst ensuring we retained our independence when it came to working methods and accountability.

In practice it meant he saved on National Insurance contributions and got to pinch all the best clients for himself.

Janice, our receptionist/typist, was just emerging from Vetch's office in the former residents' lounge when I entered the hall.

'Hi,' I said. 'Anyone been looking for me?'

'I shouldn't think so.'

She humped a pile of files over to the word processor behind the reception desk and slung them down. I took that as a 'no' and made my way up the flights of stairs to the top floor.

There were three doors leading off the square landing. The right-hand one had 'G. Smith' in wavering black paint on the white woodwork. The left had a brass name-plate engraved 'A. Smith'. I headed for the one straight ahead marked 'Bathroom'.

The boarding house had been left to Vetch by his gran. When he'd had it converted to offices, some of the original bathrooms remained in place. This one had cracked lino patterned in black and white diamonds; a white bathroom suite and real copper piping both stained with interesting designs in green rust and algae; an ancient geyser; and a framed notice informing guests:

> Baths are to be taken between four and
> six o'clock on Tuesdays and Thursdays only.
> An additional 1s.6d. to be paid in advance
> for each bath taken.

I washed off the bitten hand, splashed it with disinfectant and improvised a bandage with the loo roll.

That done, I stuck my head in my office, confirmed there were no messages, and knocked on the door opposite.

Just because we share the most common surname in the country, people tend to assume Annie and I are related. In practice all we have in common is that we both used to be in the police force.

Annie resigned for professional reasons. It was suggested I might care to leave for personal reasons. If this leads you to assume I'm bent – well, that's your opinion.

I make a point of keeping in with Annie; she's still got contacts in the force, including a brother in the local CID, which can come in very useful at times.

My own office has always been artistically challenged. Annie's, on the other hand, oozed soothing good taste. The plain walls were an unobtrusive blue-grey shade. The fitted carpet and curtains both had the same bluey tones, picked out with a damask pink. To the right of the room were her bank of filing cabinets and a small desk and padded chair. At the other end she'd installed a fatly cushioned two-seater sofa and armchair, both positioned round a long coffee table in pale wood. Tucked neatly in one corner was a unit in the same wood, which held her bone-china tea and coffee services, percolator, kettle and assorted goodies such as chocolate biscuits and cube demerara sugar. (She'd once told me that being betrayed makes some women ravenous.) Scattered throughout the room were various ceramic bowls containing both real and artificial plants.

The whole effect was of a suburban lounge; somewhere that girls could gather to enjoy a cosy heart-to-heart slagging off the men in (or recently departed from) their lives.

Additionally, if she wanted to totally obliterate all traces of 'office' from the effect, she had a folding bamboo screen that slid in front of the filing cabinets and a pink tablecloth with one of those lacy over-cloths that could be flicked over the desk.

She was folding this away when I walked in, so I guessed she'd just been interviewing a client. 'The same old he's-having-an-affair-with-my-best-friend-but-I-don't-want-to-accuse-her-without-proof routine,' she said in answer to my question.

'And is he?'

'Probably. I mean they usually know really. What she wants is for me to prove her wrong, not right.'

Annie's an expert on these things. She gets a lot of matrimonial work. And looking at her you can understand why. Not even the most humiliated wife would feel belittled confessing to Annie. Neither would she have any fear that, should her husband happen to come into contact with the PI, he'd add her to his trophies.

Annie's average height was padded out by two stone too much weight that had collected in all the wrong places. Her round face was framed by a lot of mousy hair and her very unremarkable features were hidden behind a pair of large, owl-like spectacle frames.

She peered at me now from a red-framed pair and asked what had happened to my hand. 'Enraged client?' she suggested.

'Demented cat.'

'She'd probably had a hard day.'

It wasn't worth explaining.

Annie flicked the tablecloth neatly into eight and returned it to the bottom drawer of the filing cabinet. 'Did you want something?' she asked.

I didn't really, beyond passing the time of day and establishing myself as a bona-fide pal *vis-à-vis* her brother's hot line to the CID computers.

I sought for something to say and recalled she'd had drinks last night with her latest boyfriend; a recently divorced computer something-or-other who'd originally employed her to get the dirt on his wife. 'How'd the date go?'

Annie pushed the monstrous glasses further up the bridge of her nose with one finger and dropped her voice to a confidential tone. 'You know that scene in the old films where the hero takes off the heroine's glasses, pulls the pins from her hair so it falls round her shoulders and murmurs in a husky voice throbbing with barely concealed passion, "My God, Miss Smith, you're beautiful"?'

I started to get interested. 'Yes?'

'Well, he didn't.' She sat down briskly. 'Did Vetch see you? He was looking for you earlier.'

'Janice never said.'

'I don't think they're on speaking terms again.'

7

'Did he say what he wanted?'

'Something about a case that might suit you.'

This wasn't good news because, as I've already said, Vetch kept all the best stuff for himself. So if he wanted to refer it to me it was probably some boring credit check or tracing job. However, beggars can't be cruisers, to mangle a phrase, so I trooped back down to the bottom floor again.

'Is he in?' I asked Janice.

She raised indifferent shoulders and continued to peer into the flickering processor screen.

The 'Engaged' sign wasn't across on his door. I knocked and went in without waiting for an invitation.

Vetch's appearance was at odds with his nickname of 'Vetch the Letch'. He was a short, fat beachball of a man with twinkling blue eyes set in a plump, line-free head that was as smooth as a billiard ball and sported a pair of ears that tapered to distinct points at the top. Cross-legged on a spotted toadstool dangling a fishing rod, he'd have made a belting garden gnome.

'Luscious thing,' he twittered as I went in. 'I came up to see you earlier.'

'I was out.'

'Do you know, I exercised my considerable powers of detection by opening your door and working that one out for myself. By the way, are you by any chance engaged in an investigation that requires some sort of biological experiment?'

'No. Why?'

'It's just that I couldn't help noticing that there's a cheese roll mutating into a new life form on your windowsill.'

I shrugged. Housework wasn't my strongest talent. 'Did you just come up to check on the dusting?'

'Not at all.' He hopped across the office and hitched himself up on his top-of-the-range, genuine calf leather executive easy chair.

Vetch's whole office was furnished in the 'public company,

8

executive chairman's boardroom' style. As a consequence, everything looked slightly too big for him. A psychiatrist would probably have had a field day in here.

'A case you might be interested in,' he said, picking up a folder. 'The client approached me this morning. Unfortunately, I'm rather tied up with other things at present. But as soon as I'd heard the details I said to Mr Drysdale, I know just the person for the job . . . Young, keen and, although naturally I didn't mention this to the client, a month behind with the rent and shared facilities payment for their office.'

'The work's been a bit slow recently.'

'Exactly. Which is why I just know you're going to take this case.'

There was something about his tone that suggested I might not go along with that idea. 'What is it?'

'Murder.'

I sat up straighter on the shiny chestnut leather of Vetch's *chaise-longue*. This sounded good. It sounded, to be accurate, like the kind of thing Vetch would normally gather to his fat little bosom. So how come he was passing it over? Was the client, for instance, solvent?

'Would I refer him if he wasn't?'

This made sense. If I didn't get paid, Vetch wouldn't get his rent. 'So what's the story?' I said warily. Vetch was still hanging on to the manila folder. 'Who got murdered?'

Vetch beamed, his shiny skin stretching even tighter, like a balloon that had just had another puff of air blown into it. 'Mr Drysdale would like you to discover who killed Marilyn Monroe.'

Visions of all-expenses-paid trips to California started to dance in front of my eyes. Half my mind was already trying to remember where I'd last seen bikinis and snorkelling gear. I realized Vetch was still speaking.

'Perhaps you'd like to see a photograph of the victim?' He extracted a print from the folder and passed it over.

I glanced down at the glossy black and white eight by ten. There was no mistaking the fair hair, huge brown eyes half covered by a sweep of seductive lashes, and soft velvet lips slightly parted over a row of gleaming white teeth.

It was a bloody donkey!

CHAPTER 2

I suspected a gag. But Vetch's face remained blandly business-like.

'It's a donkey,' I said.

'Yes.'

I tried again. 'Somebody wants us to find out who killed a donkey!'

'You've grasped the basics of the case admirably, dear thing. I've taken a few preliminary notes.' He passed the folder across to me. 'Mr Drysdale is expecting you to call. Oh, and don't forget to get an advance from him, will you?'

'You mean you didn't?'

'Mr Drysdale wanted to meet you and see if you were suitable before he parted with the fees.'

Drysdale, who I'd already begun to write off as some kind of eccentric, started to go up in my estimation. Normally Vetch has mugged the client's credit card before he's taken their name and address.

At least he'd managed to extract that information; it was in the folder, together with a brief statement outlining what the client expected from the investigation. Apparently Mr Drysdale wanted us to 'visit righteousness on the ungodly'.

An annotation from Vetch suggested we interpret this as providing sufficient information for the police to bring charges.

The aroma of freshly ground coffee was drifting appetizingly across my landing as I reached it. Either the cheese roll had mutated to a level of intelligence that enabled it to use simple electrical gadgets, or Annie was brewing up. My money was on Annie.

I knocked and opened at the same time. 'Have you heard what Vetch is trying to lumber me with?'

'I had heard, yes.' She poured a cup of coffee. One cup. I gave her my best little-girl-lost look. 'Make your own, you're always scrounging off me.'

'I'm out. I'll pay you back, honest.'

'You said that last time. Why don't you ever buy your own stuff?'

Basically, because I never paid for what I could scrounge. Which on this occasion was a mug of best arabica and a couple of chocolate digestives.

Annie sipped on a mug of black coffee and declined the biscuits. A sure sign that the computer-engineer affair was serious.

'Who is this Drysdale, d'you know?'

Before answering, Annie delicately licked her index finger and dabbed up the crumbs I'd just spluttered over her sofa. 'He's the donkey man. From the beach.'

A memory nudged at the corner of my mind. I remembered what had been wrong with the scene at the beach this morning. The rope corral of donkeys, patiently waiting to plod up and down the sands in a mini-caravan, had been missing.

I read the single sheet outlining Mr Drysdale's problem. Four nights ago someone had taken 'Marilyn' from her stable, led her to a deserted factory estate and slit her throat.

'Nasty,' I remarked. I thought back to the beach again and my two little lard buckets. Maybe some of their bigger brothers had graduated from cats to donkeys. 'Kids, you reckon?'

'Well, it's not the kind of thing you'd expect a normal, sane adult to go in for. On the other hand . . .'

She let the sentence hang. I knew what she meant. We'd both come across apparently rational, law-abiding citizens who hid perversions in their darker recesses that would have horrified their nearest and dearest. In fact, some of them *had*, which was when we'd been called in.

I scanned the rest of the file and found something else that made me sit up. Drysdale's first name was December!

'It was probably just the month he was born in,' Annie said.

She sounded huffy. I'd forgotten how sensitive she was on the subject of daft names. Her own parents were called John and Mary Smith. In an effort to raise their offspring above the commonplace, they'd given all their children unusual Christian names. Annie's full name was Anchoret – which is apparently Welsh for 'beloved' – and that was the best of the bunch.

'Do you think he's serious about this? I mean, how much is a donkey worth?'

'That's not really the point, is it? Some people become very attached to their animals. They're like surrogate children. I've been offered fortunes to find lost cats and dogs.'

So had I. And if Marilyn had simply gone walkabout I wouldn't have had any trouble in accepting Drysdale's money. But there was a problem with this case, which I could foresee was going to cause me no end of embarrassment.

On the other hand, I had nothing else in the offing that would cover the monthly expenses; so I telephoned Drysdale.

'Come now,' he offered.

'No rush,' I replied, hoping to postpone the inevitable.

'There is to me.'

'Yes. Right. I'll be with you in about . . .' I calculated the office's distance from Drysdale's address and added on a bit for lunchtime traffic '. . . twenty minutes.'

'And that's another thing,' Annie complained as I replaced the receiver. 'Half the calls on my itemized phone bill are down to you.'

'You'll get your reward in heaven.'

'I don't want to. I can't be certain that's my final destination.' She passed over a typed list. 'Those are the details. And the amount you owe me.'

I pushed it in the top pocket of my shirt. And it promptly tumbled through a hole, reminding me of something else. Critically I squinted downwards. I was wearing a checked brushed-cotton shirt, an old pair of jeans and black trainers with a mauve stripe. It looked OK to me, but . . .

'You know anything about Drysdale?' I asked Annie, who'd just retrieved my coffee cup. 'Apart from an emotional attachment to equines?'

'He's an elder of some alternative church. One of those secretive sects; outsiders aren't allowed in.'

'How'd you find out he's an elder, then?'

'One of the local CID is supposedly a member too. I'm not saying who.'

I filed this snippet away under 'Useful Info'.

'Do you think I ought to change?' I asked. 'Make myself respectable?'

'I don't think any client can wait that long.'

'Ha flaming ha. Don't give up the day job.'

I decided to spruce up the image anyway, since getting my hands on the advance depended on Drysdale's assessment. Observed by a herring gull, which had taken up residence on the ledge outside the window and was now eyeing my torso with a contemptuous curve of its beak, I unlocked the battered metal locker in my office and rapidly changed into my one and only business suit.

It's a grey pinstripe with a jacket and waistcoat and two possible bottoms: trousers or knee-length skirt. I'd intended to wear the skirt in deference to Drysdale's religious susceptibilities, but it turned out to have a splodge of unidentifiable goo in the lap, so I had to fall back on the trousers. I added a white shirt and, as an afterthought, a silk tie in a pattern of blacks and reds.

14

Finally I turned my attention to my hair. I keep it cut very short. It has two styles: casual, which involves sticking my head under the shower and letting it dry naturally; and formal. Which basically is the same technique, but I smooth gel through afterwards and comb it into what used to be termed 'short back and sides'. This occasion seemed to call for formal.

I observed the finished effect in the mirror tiles I'd stuck to the inside of the locker door. Eat your heart out, Demi Moore!

Weaving amongst the back streets, with the town on my left and the open fields to my right, it was possible to reach Drysdale's house in nine minutes.

The houses out here were smaller than those near the front, although they still displayed the almost obligatory signs propped in their front windows announcing 'Bed and Breakfast' and 'Vacancies'. Fresh coats of paint in predominantly pastel shades gleamed from the doors and frames, and bulbs were bursting into colourful life in flower urns and window boxes.

Drysdale's was at the end of the row. Unlike the rest of the street, which was red brick and brown tiles, this was a solid whitewashed structure with a slate-covered roof. It stood foursquare in its own patch of ground, separated from the front pavement by a low wall and a patch of gravel.

The door opened on my first ring; he must have been lurking behind the draught excluder of brightly coloured plastic strips. 'You said twenty minutes. It's been thirty.'

I swallowed an inclination to come back with a flip reply. 'Sorry.'

December Drysdale seemed vaguely aggrieved that I wasn't going to give him an argument. It was strange, I must have seen him thousands of times leading his donkey string along the beach; yet if I'd been pushed, there's no way I could have described him.

I looked him over as he led me down the hall and into a sitting room. He was probably in his sixties; medium height and weight with the deeply lined, walnut-coloured skin of a man who spends a lot of time out of doors. His thick, coarse hair touched his ears mid lobe and continued round in a straight fringe in a way that gave him a monastic look. Once it had presumably been the same dark brown as his eyebrows, but now it was a lead-grey shade.

'Take a seat,' Drysdale said. 'That pompous idiot in your front office tell you what I want?'

I started to warm to December. 'Mr Vetch did give me the file. But I gather you wanted to look me over before I got started. So let's get that bit out of the way, shall we? Otherwise we'll both be wasting our time.'

'Fair enough.' He hauled himself out of the plump armchair he'd just settled in and returned to the hall. It took me a couple of seconds to realize I was expected to follow. By the time I got out there, he'd disappeared.

I looked in the room opposite: dining room. The next one down was the kitchen, with a utility room off it. I tried the final door and discovered the downstairs bathroom.

'What are you doing? I thought you were a private detective, not an estate agent.'

'Er, just getting the feel of the place,' I lied. 'It helps if I have some background on the client.'

'I'm not your client yet. And I won't be if you keep snooping. This way.'

I let myself be led through the kitchen and out into the back yard. Along the left-hand side was a brick building with a set of large double doors. A similar structure stood opposite us across the yard, except that this one had a row of smaller, divided doors marking it out as the stables.

Drysdale walked briskly across the cobbled yard and slid the two bolts open on the end door. An excited whicker, accompanied by a Morse code of happiness tapped out by

16

impatient hooves, greeted him. A donkey the pale-gold colour of boiled toffee thrust its way past him and took a few steps into the yard. Twitching floppy ears, it raised its long face to the sun, wrinkled its muzzle and gave a resounding sneeze.

'Bless you,' I said automatically, before it occurred to me that I was calling down benedictions on a donkey.

It had the effect, however, of drawing the animal's attention to me. Ambling over, it nuzzled at my clothes, drooling saliva down the jacket pockets.

'Gerroff.' I raised a discreet knee and shoved. It seemed to take this as a gesture of affection and laid its head on my chest, bestowing loving looks in my face and half a pound of donkey hairs down the shirt front.

'Errol, leave off. Look.' With deft strokes, Drysdale was quartering an apple with a lethal pocket knife. My new friend swung away so fast he nearly knocked me off my feet with his swinging rump as he raced to gobble up this better offer. Most of my relationships end like that.

'Errol', I remarked, edging past the donkey and into the stables. 'That would be Errol Flynn, would it?'

It was dark in the stables after the brightness outside and I couldn't see Drysdale's face, but I sensed a change in the atmosphere that wasn't entirely due to the even more pungent evidence of the inhabitants. Mr Drysdale was starting to like me.

'I'd have thought he'd have been before your time. Like the old films, do you?'

'My dad's a fan. Got loads of them on video. He's always watching them.' I didn't tell Drysdale why. It wasn't any of his business.

'My wife loved 'em too. First in the queue for the late-night classics at the Odeon was my Jeannie. It was her idea to call the donkeys after film stars. My dad had had nature: Storm and Cloud, that sort of thing.'

17

'It's a family business then, is it? The donkey rides?'

'Been a Drysdale running the donkey string here for nearly a hundred and twenty years.' He seized a muzzle pushing eagerly for its share of the apples. 'This is Humphrey Bogart.' Humphrey was a gleaming chestnut and, in my opinion, rather better looking than his namesake.

As the donkeys jostled, pushed, whinnied and generally behaved like Members of Parliament at Question Time, I took stock of the stables. The row of doors had led me to expect eight separate loose boxes, but instead the interior was a long room divided into eight stalls by wooden partitions. A manger stretched along the back wall and a metal drinking trough stood at the side, where we'd just entered.

I glanced back and checked that there were no padlocks on any of the door bolts. At the other side of the yard a pair of wrought-iron metal gates with a simple latch fastening were blocking the side entrance between the left-hand wall of the house and the end of the other brick building. If donkey-napping was your particular fetish, you certainly wouldn't meet much resistance here.

Deciding I'd better look thorough, I investigated the other building. The far end contained bales of straw and hay and a couple of large bins that probably held the dry foodstuffs. Nearer to me were two rails with eight saddles slung over them and a bench laid with brushes, bottles and various other paraphernalia connected with donkey toiletry. The creak and whisper of metal and leather above my head made me look upwards to discover the eight bridles and headdresses suspended from the ceiling, each with a neatly lettered gold name gilded on to the head strap.

Returning to the main stable, I asked if the neighbours didn't mind having a load of donkeys living next door.

'All the same if they did,' Drysdale said, feeding a quarter of Miller's to a roan called Clark (Gable?). 'We were here first. Been a stable on this site for two hundred-odd years. Not this one, of course, My father had this built in the thirties. Same time as the houses went up.'

'Oh.' There didn't seem much else to say. To tell you the truth, I had only ever been involved in three suspicious deaths during my time in the force. And those had turned out to be natural causes or suicide.

On the rare occasions we'd had a murder case, the investigating officers had generally started off by questioning the body's nearest and dearest. But I could hardly start asking Clark how he and Marilyn had been getting along recently.

I noticed that one donkey wasn't joining in the general scuffle for titbits. A tall grey, he hung back at the other end of the stable morosely nibbling a morsel of hay. Stepping delicately over the trampled straw and other unmentionable things I'd rather not think about, I ran a tentative hand down the thick coat. 'Hello, boy. What's your name then?'

'That's Lana Turner.'

Lana obviously wasn't the modest type, otherwise he might have taken exception to where I was peering. 'Em, er . . . isn't this a boy?'

'Who are you?' Drysdale snapped. 'Gerald Durrell? They're *all* geldings.'

'But doesn't he mind being called Lana?' Even as I said this, I knew it was a ridiculous question.

Drysdale obviously thought it was too. He ignored it. 'He's Marilyn's brother. He's been pining something terrible since he got taken.'

Disentangling the genders in this sentence, I worked out that my victim was a 'he' too. 'When was that exactly? What time?'

'Dunno precisely. Police rang at midnight.'

'And you hadn't missed her, I mean him, until then?'

'If I had, I'd have called the coppers myself, wouldn't I?'

'What did you do after they called you?'

'Rang a bloke I know with a lorry.'

'Why?'

'To shift the body, of course.'

'But you didn't know it *was* Marilyn then.'

Drysdale raised impatient eyebrows. It was like watching a pair of flattened scouring pads jerking up and down. 'How many stray donkeys do you think were wandering around out there? I knew.'

During this conversation, I'd been idly tickling Lana's ears whilst he mumbled at my chest. Now I tried to step away; and discovered that the first three inches of my tie were clamped in his mouth.

Grabbing what was still visible; I jerked. Lana sucked. Another inch disappeared between his lips. The pulse under my ears was starting to sound like pounding surf inside my head. Twisting slightly sideways with difficulty, I looked across for Drysdale and discovered he'd disappeared.

Forcing a thumb into the tie knot, I tried to loosen it. No good. Lana's activities had already tightened it into a packed, unyielding ball. 'Gerroff,' I croaked. It was a mistake; the last of the oxygen hissed from my lungs and I couldn't suck any more in.

With half-closed eyes Lana braced his hooves against the floor and continued to suck with the blissful expression of an Italian matron enjoying the final delicious strand of spaghetti bolognese.

Drysdale's instruction to 'Hold still' was superfluous. What else could I do?

Through bulging eyes, I saw him advance on Lana with a pair of rusty shears. With deft precision, he snapped the blades together and made a grab for the material dangling from Lana's lips.

Lana beat him to it. The last morsel was sucked in with the *plop* of a vacuum cleaner turning off.

'Blast. Come here, you daft lump.' Grabbing the donkey's

mouth, Drysdale forced it open and peered between the large rows of yellow teeth. 'Looks like it's gone down. Had a pair of braces caught round the back teeth once. He'll eat anything, this one.'

I didn't care. I'd finally managed to wrench the tourniquet off my neck and was gulping in wonderful lungfuls of dung-laden air.

'We'd best go back to the house.'

I was expecting tea, aspirins or even a medicinal brandy. I got the one o'clock news. 'Do you think . . .' I croaked.

'Shhh! I want to hear the local reports.'

And I wanted a drink. I helped myself to a glass of water from the kitchen. Sipping to relieve the ache in my throat, I waited whilst an announcer tripped through the day's hot items: police were still trying to identify the dead girl found on Halfpenny Lane three days ago; a planning application for a by-pass extension had finally been given the go-ahead; an outbreak of food poisoning had been traced to a kebab takeaway (a shot of the closed business was interspersed with pictures of victims bravely smiling from their hospital beds); the local school choir had been placed joint second in a Three Counties contest.

Drysdale flipped the set off with a snort of disgust. 'See that?'

'What?'

'There was nothing about Marilyn. Local institution, those donkeys. Yet all we got was one quick mention three days ago. People just don't *care*. Including the coppers.'

Relieved that we seemed to be back on track, I asked who'd dealt with the incident.

'WPC Jane Mullins,' he said promptly. 'Nice enough lass, but she's not going to do anything. Good as told me so when I went up there yesterday. That's when I decided to hire you.'

'And am I?' I asked. 'Hired?'

'You'll do.'

I was afraid of that; it meant that there was no avoiding the part of this case I was dreading.

CHAPTER 3

It was nearly twenty past one when I left Drysdale's. If WPC Mullins had been on duty at twelve last week, then she was probably on earlies this week and due to go off at two. Nonetheless I decided to risk missing her and take a quick look at the scene of Marilyn's last moments.

The factory estate was located on the main road running south from the town. Someone had once designated this as a growth area for light industry. Light industry had been unimpressed and the farm fields now sported little clumps of disused, untenanted and unwanted warehousing.

Marilyn's graveyard was one of the oldest of these gulags; an enclave thrust into the fields and enclosed by wire fencing. The entrance gates sagged on their hinges, but swung open easily in response to a shoulder thrust. I drove the car in and got out to take a closer look at the dump.

Apparently the place had its fans. Mooching over the cracked and crumbling concrete forecourt with its meandering clumps of weeds, I came across assorted polystyrene food and drink containers plus half a dozen discarded johnnies (used) and one unused.

There were eight small one-storey buildings in all; four each side. The two nearest had had their windows and doors filled in with grey breeze-blocks. The estate agent's board informed me they were for sale or rent at 'extremely attractive rates'.

No. 3 appeared to be a different agent's headache. The board hanging by a thread from the brickwork was so cracked and blistered by the sun that it was hard to make out who or where to contact should you be in the market for a 'highly des. prop. with rm for impr'ment'. The windows were glass-less. I gave the iron bars an experimental tug and found that, despite appearances, they were firmly embedded and the doors were securely padlocked even if the chains had turned rusty with age.

The next four were the same: dirty, vandalized and covered in ancient graffiti. But all well bolted and barred against possible intruders.

What on earth *for*? I found myself asking. Who would want to intrude? An arsonist with manic depression?

The last building on the left-hand side had a barely legible blue and white sign over the door declaring it to be 'Turner's Engineering Ltd'. Mr Turner had left nearly ten years ago, I guessed, judging by the yellowed calendar and mildewing file cases I could see through the small dirt-encrusted window next to the main doors.

I gave the double doors a push. The padlock swung open and dropped on my toe. Cursing, I hopped inside.

The office I'd glimpsed from outside was just a glass cubby-hole. It was still furnished with a filing cabinet; dexion shelving holding black file boxes containing delivery notes, invoices and VAT returns; a large polished-wood desk and a couple of broken chairs. If I was laying bets, I'd have put my money on Mr Turner having been marched out by the bailiffs.

I did a quick scan and found that most of the room was well covered in layers of dust and grit, apart from the area under the desk where some attempt had been made to clean up.

The rest of the building was one long room. Holes in the floor showed where the heavy machinery had been ripped out, but apart from that there was nothing to distinguish it from the other seven dumps I'd just passed; except the smell.

It was unmistakable. Even after four days.

Just when I needed a bit of light, rent-a-yob incorporated had given the windows down the far end a reprieve. I did what any trained investigator would do in the circumstances: I broke one.

Disturbed by the sudden shaft of sunlight, a cloud of flies rose with the whine of an over-wound clockwork toy from one of the floor holes. I peered cautiously into the gap; it was about a foot square and six inches deep. And somebody had vomited into this natural bowl within the last few days.

Even though it had dried out, it still smelt pretty foul. Poor roof insulation plus the first of the spring sun was building up the temperature in here to sticky phug. I could feel my clothes starting to cling to my damp skin.

Marilyn had thrashed out his final moments in the far left-hand corner of the building. Even if the tide of blood, now dried to an ox-brown shade, hadn't marked out the spot, the scattering of overlapped hoof prints where he had slipped and slithered in his own gore painted its own pathetic little picture.

Squatting on my heels, I explored another machinery hole. The sawn-off remains of an end of rope were still looped round the rusting fixing bolts jutting from the concrete. Marilyn had been tethered here, probably with his head close to the floor to make it more difficult for him to lash out; then someone had run a knife across his windpipe, leaving him to kick and jerk in terror until he'd collapsed from shock.

Why down this end, I wondered, when there was nothing to choose between it and the front? The obvious answer was the rear fire door. I pushed it and discovered I hadn't needed to break the window after all. The door swung outwards on to a four-foot strip of concrete. On this side the wire fencing clung to one post by a single clip whilst the other end had already peeled away and disappeared amongst the rapidly growing weeds. It left a handy rat-run for anyone needing to make a fast get-away.

Stepping gratefully into the fresh air, I walked back down the side of the building to my car.

I was depressed; and it wasn't just down to the drop-dead ambience of the surroundings.

It was such a senseless, pointless, *mean* little crime. Not that most crimes aren't mean, but there is usually a sort of logic behind them: envy, greed, jealousy. Some basic human need that the perpetrator has to fulfil. But what was the point behind this one; who got their kicks from watching a donkey dying in agony?

A crackle from my inner pocket reminded me why I was going to find out. When I'd produced a list of my rates and pointed out that my minimum time was eight hours, Drysdale had taken an envelope from the sideboard and passed it over with a casual instruction to let him know when that lot had run out.

'I assumed you'd want cash,' he'd remarked.

I'd assured him old-fashioned money was always acceptable.

'And much harder to trace,' he'd responded, indicating a certain cynicism towards my relationship with the Inland Revenue. 'Mind, I want proper accounts from you. And regular reports.'

There was a thousand pounds in used tenners in the envelope; probably about ten times what Marilyn had been worth.

It was nearly five to two. Gunning the car engine, I raced back across town, weaving in and out of the short cuts, and arrived outside the police station just as the early shift were leaving.

I picked the first female leaving the yard. 'Hi, Jane left yet? I'm a bit late.'

'Jane who?'

'Mullins.'

The woman I'd stopped looked behind her and waved vaguely. 'No, you're OK. She's just coming out now.'

There were three females emerging: two tall brunettes and a shorter, mousy girl.

'Hey, Jane.'

Miss Mouse looked round. I waved from the open car window, keeping my head inside so that the sunlight reflected off the windscreen and hid my features. Jane Mullins hesitated, said something to the other women and walked over. I waited until she was opposite the car before I got out.

Jane paused, uncertain now she had a clear look at me. 'Sorry, have we met?'

'Not yet. I'm here on behalf of December Drysdale, he's . . .'

'The donkey man,' Jane finished, a smile of recognition lighting up her round face. In a superficial way she reminded me of Annie.

'That's him,' I agreed. 'It's about Marilyn. He's very upset, you know.'

'Oh, I know. It was dreadful.' Every emotion that WPC Mullins felt was etched across her face. At present it was guilt. From which I deduced that the hunt for Marilyn's killer wasn't top of the priority list around here. 'Are you a friend of Mr Drysdale's?'

'No. I'm a private detective.' I gave her a card and held open my car door. 'Look, have you got ten minutes, or do you have to be somewhere?'

'Only the section house.' She indicated the plastic carrier she was holding. 'I've got to wash out my spare blouses.'

This girl's social life sounded about as interesting as mine.

'I don't know,' she demurred. 'I mean, we're not really supposed . . .'

'Just a chat. General background stuff,' I said, taking charge before she could go coy on me about discussing cases. 'I'll park up and meet you in the Dog and Duck in . . . say . . . ten minutes?'

'Oh yes, that would be fine.' Her enthusiasm confirmed my first impression about her social life.

'See you there then.'

'Yes. Fine. 'Bye.'

The Dog and Duck stayed open all day; more because the landlord liked company than from any expectation of increasing its profits. We had the beer garden to ourselves.

Jane asked for a blackcurrant and lemonade. 'Can't drink at lunchtime, makes me sleepy.'

'Me too,' I lied, sticking to orange juice. 'So tell me about Marilyn. What time did you find him?'

I was relieved to be talking to Miss Mullins. She plainly saw nothing odd in December hiring a private detective to trace the killer. She was probably the only police officer in town who thought that way and I offered up a silent prayer of thanks. Because telling CID's finest that I was working on the murder of a donkey was the moment I'd been dreading.

Jane shook her head. 'I didn't find him.'

Don't tell me I was shelling out on drinks for the wrong girl. 'But Mr Drysdale told me you were handling the case.'

'Yes, no, well, I mean . . . I'm not exactly handling it. I mean, I gave it an incident number so he could, you know, claim the insurance, like in a motor accident. But I'm not really doing anything. I'd really like to, of course, only, well . . .' She was gabbling too fast and gulping at her drink at the same time. Blackcurrant dribbled down her chin. She wiped it away with the back of her hand.

'Only,' I finished for her, 'you were told not to waste time on a dead pet when there's more important things to be sorted.'

It was called prioritizing. With only so many man hours available within the monthly budget, the senior officers had to decide which cases got the lion's share of effort.

'Yes. We've put it on the computer and everything,' Jane said anxiously. 'And if it happens again, you know, to someone else . . .'

'You'll know you've got a serial donkey killer on the loose.' And it might get bumped a few more places up the priority list.

She giggled. It wiped away her resemblance to Annie. Or maybe Annie had looked like that when she was Jane's age. I suspected WPC Mullins wasn't long out of her probation.

I pressed her. 'So if you didn't find Marilyn, who did?'

'Rosco and Rawlins.'

'That would be Terry Rosco, would it?'

'You know him? You ex-job then?'

'Could say that. Can't say I ever came across a Rawlins though.'

'Gina transferred from the Met. I was talking to her when I came out the station, you might have seen her then.'

So Gina was a lithe, attractive brunette, was she? That would certainly make sense. Rosco liked tall, slim girls. I had the bruised bum and he had the loose tooth to prove it. 'How did you get involved in the case, Jane?'

She gulped the rest of her drink. 'Another?'

'I'll get them.'

'No, it's my round.'

I had to wait until she returned with two more glasses and a packet of crisps before she explained that she'd been told by the station to go up to the factory estate and relieve Rosco and Rawlins. 'There was trouble up the town centre: joyriders showing off. They wanted Terry up there in the Cosworth.'

'Must have been spooky. Up there by yourself.'

'Yes, it was a bit.' She blushed. 'I locked myself in the panda.'

'You didn't see anyone hanging around?'

'No. Not a soul. Until Mr Drysdale came.'

'OK, thanks for your help.' I drained my glass and swung my legs clear of the bench.

Jane looked disappointed. 'Oh, right, I suppose you have to get back to work.'

'No rest for the wicked.'

'No. Right. I guess I'd better go to the laundry.'

I looked Rosco up in the telephone directory. Fortunately, it's not a common name around here. He was listed as living in one of the roads that abutted on to the railway line just before it entered the station.

The girl who answered the door was so thin you could see the outline of her skeleton under the skimpy T-shirt and grubby white leggings. Exhaling a puff of smoke, she screwed her eyes up against the nicotine cloud and peered at my card. 'Sorry,' she said when I asked for Rosco. 'They left. About six months ago. We're just renting. Ask the landlord.'

'Haven't you got a forwarding address. For mail?'

'Sure. But I'm not going to give it out to just anybody. How'd I know who you really are?'

Full marks for theory in security consciousness; nil for practical work. I could see several bits of junk mail on the hall table, the original address crossed through and redirections added in ink.

It was a new housing estate to the east of the town, near the golf course. Expensive from what I could recall of the advertising splash that had appeared in the local press. The mortgage must be taking a good chunk out of Rosco's monthly pay cheque.

Since the lunchtime traffic had now cleared, I drove out along Marine Terrace, intending to follow the coast road round. The tide was out, leaving an expanse of wet, rippled sand that stretched almost to the horizon. Along the strip between the soft, powdery yellow drifts and the khaki-grey mud flats, a familiar string was plodding its normal path. Between the fourth and sixth donkey there was a larger gap; they'd left Marilyn's place free as if they were expecting him to rejoin them at any minute.

It made me feel a bit less reluctant to tackle Rosco. In fact I'd got quite a little speech prepared on the rights of all living things, etc. etc. It was a pity he wasn't there to hear it.

'Gone out with the missus,' a neighbour called across after

I'd been on Rosco's step for five minutes and he'd presumably realized I wasn't doing a bench-mark test on the door-bell.

'Any idea how long?'

''Fraid not.' He'd evidently got to a tricky point with the planting out and abandoned me for an alpine.

I decided to wait. Leaving the driver's door open, I stretched out across the front seat and read a paperback.

It was a very pleasant area: detached houses washed in pale beige, with Tudor gables and double glazing with leaded lights. Somehow I just knew the fully fitted kitchens would have a copper hood over the hob and bunches of dried flowers nailed to the mock-wooden beams.

It was nearly six before Rosco's estate car pulled into the drive. It was packed to the roof with carriers from the out-of-town hypermarket; a couple of squabbling kids; and a heavily pregnant Mrs Rosco.

Rosco ripped up the tail door and started dumping bags on the grass. Mrs Rosco levered herself from the front seat, opened the front door and waddled quickly inside. With more room to manoeuvre, the kids gave up screaming insults at each other and started slinging fists instead.

I waited until the boys had tumbled inside after their mother and then strolled over. 'Evening, Terry.'

Rosco looked up and scowled. He started poking amongst the carriers, sniffing audibly. 'Reckon something's broken in these bags. There's a bit of a whiff around here.'

'Not even original, Terry. But then original thinking isn't really your forte, is it? That last WPC you went over the side with used to get it in an empty office block, didn't she? And now you've moved upmarket to under a desk in an empty warehouse. I bet Gina Rawlins can hardly believe her luck.'

Rosco's square face flushed. He wasn't a bad-looking bloke, but up close like this you could see where the cracks were beginning to show. There was too much fat around the jowl and under the eyes, and not enough in the crease between nose and mouth.

'I don't know what you're talking about,' he snarled. (Told you he didn't go in for originality, didn't I?)

'Oh, come on.'

'Get lost, Smithie.'

He advanced menacingly. The effect was rather spoilt by the four carriers he'd picked up. What was he going to do? Hit me with a loo roll?

'Nice house,' I said, backing away round his car. 'Bet it's costing you a packet.'

'None of your business. Now beat it.'

'Mind you, by the time the CSA has taken you for the upkeep of this place and two, no, three kids, I reckon you'd be hard pushed to afford a cardboard box.'

'Listen, you cause me any grief with the wife . . .' He was still holding on to the carriers. We'd done a complete circuit of the car and were back where we started.

The older boy erupted from the front door. 'Mum says you bringing the shopping in or what? Can I have a Blue Riband?'

He grabbed a packet and ripped it open without waiting for an answer.

'Yeah, sure. Here, take these in to your mum.' Rosco pushed the bags at his son and heir. 'I just gotta show this lady something on her road map.'

'Now what's your game?' he demanded as soon as the kid was out of earshot. 'You asking to get thumped?'

'Not at all. I just want to know what happened that night. Did you see whoever attacked the donkey?'

'What you want to know that for?'

'I'm working for its owner. He's very distressed at the lack of police activity.' If I'd hoped the implied criticism was going to divert the scorn, I was wrong.

Rosco guffawed loudly. 'Oh God, that's priceless. Grace Smith, super sleuth. Dead donkeys a speciality.'

'Well, we know what yours is, don't we, Terry? And if you don't want anyone dropping a hint to Mrs Rosco . . .'

'Yeah, OK. It'll be worth it. Wait until I tell 'em down the station.'

'So what happened?'

'Nothing much, unfortunately. Me and Gina parked up and went in the front door. The padlock's busted.'

'I know. Did you see anyone?'

'Not right off. He saw us, though. Legged it out the back. We thought it was just some dosser at first. Until we walked down the other end. I nearly fell over the bloody donkey.'

'Was it dead?'

'I reckon. I wasn't about to start looking for its pulse.'

'What you do then?'

'We went after him. But it was too late.'

'Description?'

'Only got a glimpse of his back. White. Medium height. Medium build. Shortish hair.'

'Age?'

'Haven't a clue.'

Linda Rosco appeared in the front door. She looked like she couldn't expand any further without bursting. 'Terry, aren't you ever going to bring the rest of this stuff in?'

'Just coming, love. Now beat it, Smithie,' he added under his breath.

'You've not really been a lot of help, Terry,' I hissed back at him. 'Which way did he go when he legged it?'

For a second Terry had the grace to look guilty. 'He had a motor. Parked up behind the first factory place. Must have nipped back through the main gates.'

'And you didn't spot it when you drove in? Sloppy, Terry.'

'Yeah, well. Like I said. It was round the back.'

'I don't suppose you got the number?'

'No moon. And he didn't stick the lights on, did he? Just took off.'

'Make? Colour?'

'Van of some kind. Old. Dark colour.'

'And you didn't go after it?'

'For a dead donkey? Do me a favour. Now that's your lot.'

It was enough. And it meant there was an urgent question I had to put to December.

CHAPTER 4

I had to wait. When I drove back via the beach, the donkey string had gone. But when I reached Drysdale's place, there was no response to my ring.

I tried the side gate. It was secured with several yards of iron chain and a huge padlock. A classic case of locking the door after the donkey had bolted. Drysdale was probably *en route* from sand to stable. And I was fed up with sitting around in the car waiting for people.

I parked back at the office, intending to go for a quick run now the beach was emptying. Changing out of my day clothes, I pulled on a crumpled blue tracksuit. Taking a few notes from Drysdale's envelope, I pushed them in my pants pocket, then secured both the locker and office doors and hung the keys round my neck.

Annie's door was partially open, leaking the murmur of two voices. Presumably not a client, otherwise she'd have been more careful about possible eavesdropping. I gave a brisk knock and stepped in before she could answer.

A young man in his middle twenties with straw-coloured hair and a pale complexion was lounging on the sofa watching Annie entering data on her computer.

Annie's younger brother had been blessed with the name of Zebedee. His wide, innocent grey eyes always held the haunted expression of a man who'd spent most of his life being greeted by 'BOING!' every time he entered a room.

''Lo, Zeb. How's it going?'

'OK.'

'You really must try to control this impulse to chatter incessantly, Zeb.'

'If you're hoping to scrounge more coffee,' Annie interrupted, closing down her hard disk, 'we're just on our way to eat.'

'I wasn't. I came to pay you what I owe you on the phone bill.' I handed over a couple of Drysdale's notes.

'This is only half of it.'

'I have to eat too.'

'I want the rest by Friday. You ready, Zeb?'

'Yeah. Sure. Let's go somewhere we'll be served quickly. I have to get back.'

I hazarded a guess. 'Working on that girl's murder, Zeb?'

'Yeah.'

'Nasty business.'

Annie interrupted to tell me to quit fishing. Then added: 'Zeb doesn't want to talk about it.'

Zeb glared. He resented being cast in the role of the sensitive little brother who needed to be protected by his big, tough sister.

I was about to chip in with another provoking remark when she caught my eye and shook her head slightly.

'OK, I know when I'm not wanted.'

'Since when?' Zeb rallied slightly as I left.

The tide was nearly in again, leaving a narrow strip of firmer damp sand that I shared with the dog walkers and metal detectors.

It wasn't a happy combination. I did several laps whilst small, snappy mutts wove in and out of my ankles.

After half an hour I'd had enough. I was hungry and I needed a shower.

Hunger won. I visited my favourite greasy spoon: a backstreet café that was stuck in a sixties time warp of red and white formica chairs and tables adorned with huge plastic tomatoes filled with glutinous ketchup.

The food was better than the décor suggested. By the time I'd wiped up the last morsel of fried egg with a slice of bread and drained a mug of tea, I was ready to earn the money I'd already paid to Annie.

The office was empty by the time I got back. Throwing my jogging clothes on the floor, I grabbed a towel and made my way down to the bathroom. It didn't have a shower, but a quick splash in the bath would do as well; and it was quicker than going home.

I came out towelling my hair dry, and met Annie on the stairs. 'Listen, sorry if I upset Zeb earlier,' I said. 'Didn't know that business had shaken him up so badly.'

'Zeb still takes cases too personally. He's going to have to get his act together, otherwise he'll be totally twisted up.'

'Nasty one, is it? The girl?'

'They'd cut her about pretty badly. She's got impact injuries. Looks like whoever did it ran her over first then had some fun with a knife. You didn't hear it from me.'

'Fair enough. Sorry, must dash,' I said. 'Got to go and fill Drysdale in on my progress.'

'Have you made any?'

'Not a lot,' I admitted. Rather more than I'd expected, actually. But that was for the client's ears. And I still had my question to put to him.

This time the side gate was unchained. But when I stepped through it I was confronted by a slab of beef dressed in the mustard-coloured uniform of Mackenzie's, a local security company.

'What ya wan'?'

'Is this the elocution academy?'

'Ya wa'?'

'It's all right. She's a friend.' Drysdale had emerged from the stables, carrying two buckets. This time the top doors were folded back against the walls. Humphrey Bogart whickered a hello at me.

I gave him a wave. 'Here's looking at you, kid.'

'Go in,' Drysdale called. 'I'll be with you soon as I've settled the lads.'

I let myself in and wasted a bit of time indulging in one of my hobbies: sticking my nose in where it wasn't wanted.

I discovered Drysdale's reading tastes ran to the classics and books on financial management. His wife, I judged, had probably died some time back in the seventies. The photographs on top of the bookcase of a smiling, pleasant-faced woman with long brown hair stopped abruptly in the bell-bottom trousers and floaty chiffon top era. There was a boy in some of the pictures too: a kid with his mother's looks and Drysdale's expression in his eyes.

Drysdale came in, bringing with him an aura of eau-de-stable. 'Have you found out something?'

'Not much' doesn't induce a warm feeling in the client, I've found. So I temporized. 'I've made some progress. But there's something I need to ask you.'

'Can it wait while I clean up?'

'Sure.'

I nosed a bit further whilst water gurgled and banged down pipes that needed a flush-out. Drysdale re-emerged in brown trousers, grey shirt and tweed sports jacket. 'Fancy a drink?' he asked.

'Great. Thanks.'

I expected a can of lager. Instead Drysdale headed for the back door. 'Come on then. We'll go down the local.'

The slab of beef had disappeared. But in response to Drysdale's whistle he appeared from the back of the stables. 'Just sussing it out, sir. There's an 'ole round the back there, ya know?'

'I know. We're off for a drink. Be about an hour and a half.'

'Right-o, mate.'

'How long's he staying?' I asked.

'Till I figure out what kind of security system to get rigged up.'

I'd been heading instinctively towards the car whilst we spoke. Drysdale gave me a dirty look. 'Don't drink and drive, do you?'

'Just one. It won't take me over the limit.'

'It will with me. Come on. It's not far.'

Hands thrust in his pockets, he was already striding off in the direction of the sea front.

I'd pictured Drysdale's 'local' as somewhere dark and dingy, with a dart board in one corner, dominoes in another and a collection of real-ale buffs in pullovers and sandals raving about the warm draught bitter in the public bar.

Instead he managed to surprise me again by turning into the Electronic Daffodil.

The Daffodil (TED to the in-crowd) was *the* place to go clubbing. To be honest, it didn't have a lot of competition around here once you'd outgrown lager louts and football chants. But its gossip-column acreage had grown over the last few years and at weekends punters drove down from as far away as London for the privilege of being refused entry by the uniformed crowd control personnel (bouncers to you and me).

At this time of the evening we had the place practically to ourselves.

A couple of bored-looking CCPs were hovering by the entrance to the main dance floor; the polished tiles stretching and reflecting their black tuxedos and white shirts like distorted images in a hall of mirrors. I half expected them to challenge Drysdale; he hardly fitted in with their customer profile. But they made no move to stop him going up the side staircase that led to the main bar.

The first floor was effectively just a mezzanine that ran around the outside walls, leaving a large hole in the centre where the drinkers could look down at the gyrating dancers. The bar took up one side; it was long and wide with plenty of counter space for the bartenders to perform flashy hand acrobatics whilst they mixed brilliantly coloured cocktails.

A girl in black trousers, white shirt and yellow waistcoat smiled radiantly as we hitched ourselves up on the bar stools. 'Good evening, Mr Drysdale. The usual?'

'Please, Cindy. What are you having?'

'Draught lager. Half.'

It was cold and crisp and delicious. The pint Drysdale was sipping gave off the warm, yeasty smell of well-kept bitter.

'So,' he said when the first couple of inches had been drained, leaving a lacy pattern of foam over the gleaming glass, 'what did you want to ask me?'

'Is it possible for a donkey to ride in a car?'

'If he fastens his seat-belt.'

'Really?'

Drysdale's scouring-pad eyebrows rose in exasperation. 'No, not really. That was a joke. Why'd you want to know?'

I told him what I'd found out so far. 'You see, I'd rather been assuming that the killer was some yobbo who'd broken in, led Marilyn off and kept walking until he found somewhere to slit his throat.'

'And now you don't?'

'No. It sounds like whoever did it must have parked up by the factory then walked back here, taken Marilyn and led him back. That suggests a fair degree of planning. And more effort than I'd have expected from a yob who was just out to cause a bit of pain and grief. You sure he couldn't have got Marilyn in a car?'

'Even if you could, how are you going to drive with a panicking donkey trying to climb out the back window?'

'Drugged?'

'You ever tried lifting a dead-weight donkey?'

'What if it was a small van?'

Drysdale shook his head; small drops of bitter soared from his upper lip, spotting the black marble bar top. 'You'd have had to persuade him to walk in and lie down. And Marilyn wasn't keen on small spaces. I used to have a right job getting him in the horse box. He'd have bucked and squealed his head off if a stranger tried it.'

'Have you talked to the neighbours?'

'I asked around. But nobody saw anything. I'm the end of the line, see. All he had to do was go through the gate at the end of the road and there's footpaths over the fields.' He drained the rest of the glass in one comprehensive swallow and signalled Cindy for a refill. 'Can we have the telly on, love?'

'Of course.' She flicked a remote control at a small television set mounted on a bracket behind the bar.

The final bars of the signature tune for a hospital soap died away and were replaced by the strident opening chords of the news. We drank in companionable silence, nibbling peanuts and olives whilst famine, fire and natural disasters flashed over the screen.

Down below, the DJ was carrying out sound tests. In a control room somewhere else, an engineer was fiddling with the lights; plunging us into gloom one minute then filling the space with dazzling green or pink lights the next. A few more customers drifted in and spread out along the bar.

The main news finished and the local reports started. The food poisoning outbreak and the choir got a brief reprise but the big story of the moment was the murder.

'Police have now identified the girl's body found by Halfpenny Lane as that of Tara Lloyd, a known London prostitute. Tara's partially clothed body was discovered here three days ago,' a reporter announced to the camera, one hand clutching the microphone, the other fighting to sweep strands of hair out of her face whilst she gestured to an unremarkable tuft of grass. 'The hunt for her killer is being co-ordinated by Detective Chief Inspector Jackson . . . Inspector?'

41

The lollipop mike swung sideways.

Giving the camera his best side, Zeb's boss confirmed the girl's identity. 'We believe Miss Lloyd was killed elsewhere and her body dumped here.'

'Is it true that she was tortured before she was killed?'

The lolly was in danger of jamming in Jackson's nostrils.

'I really can't comment on that. But we do need to trace her movements before her death and we are particularly anxious to speak to anyone who was using this road on Friday evening. If anyone believes they have any information we would ask them to ring the police on . . .'

A number was flashed on to the screen, superimposed over a photograph of a heavy-featured girl with a cloud of dark hair. It was probably a mug shot.

A derisive whistle echoed from further down the bar. 'What a dog. She'd have had to pay *me* for a fuck.'

'Oi, that's enough of that language.'

Drysdale had got up. My heart sank. There were two of them: bullet heads, tattooed fingers, shared brain cell. 'What's it to do with you, Grandad?'

They weren't drunk enough to want to fight a bloke of Drysdale's age. If he'd been eighteen I'd no doubt they'd have bundled in.

'Leave it, Griffo,' his mate advised, pulling at his elbow. 'It's just some tart. What do you care?'

'Yeah. Right,' Griffo agreed, seizing on his face-saving escape route. 'Who gives a toss about the bitch? Give us a refill here, darling.'

Cindy swept down the bar with her ever-present smile on her face. Out of the corner of my eye, I could see the bouncers strolling up the stairs and making a casual sweep around the mezzanine. She must have pressed a hidden alarm bell.

'It was just talk,' I said to Drysdale.

'I don't care. They'd no call to speak about her like that whatever she did. She was a nice enough little lass in her way.'

'You knew her?' Wild ideas about Drysdale's spare-time activities started whizzing through my mind. And he plainly read every one of them.

'Not like that. She used to come round and have a chat with the lads sometimes. Always had a chocolate peppermint cream for 'em.'

'But it said on the news she was a London girl.'

'What do they know? Couldn't even get her name right. It was Tina, not Tara.'

'And she lived near you?'

There was no reason for the two cases to be connected. But it was just the association of ideas: two deaths; two cases of mutilation with knives.

'She visited,' Drysdale was saying. 'Place over the back. Her aunt and uncle.'

'When did you last see her? Recently?'

'No, it would have been months back. Last year. End of the season.'

'Did you know what she . . . you know?'

'Did I know she was on the game, you mean? Sort of. Didn't say as much, but she told the lads things. You didn't have to be a genius to figure out how she lived.'

His tone had softened slightly. I realized that for Drysdale the world was divided into two species: those who got on with the 'lads', and those who didn't.

My suspicious little imagination was kicking in. I can't help it. Why think the best of people when thinking the worst is so much more fun? And generally saves a lot of time in the long run? Why had it taken so long to identify Tina if her aunt and uncle lived locally? Had they been involved in her death in some way? And if not, why were they keeping their heads down?

When I put the question to Drysdale, he shrugged. 'Maybe they didn't know Tina was missing. She didn't live with them, more's the pity. Tina's mum and dad were killed, road accident, when she was thirteen. But her aunt wouldn't take her in; reckoned she'd got enough on her hands looking after the uncle. So they stuck Tina in one of them council places. Well, you read about what happens to girls in those homes, don't you?'

'What was wrong with the uncle?'

'In a wheelchair. And he'd gone a bit . . .' Drysdale tapped the side of his forehead. 'Been attacked. You know, what d'they call it nowadays . . . mugged.'

'Tough.'

'On everybody.' He frowned into his empty glass, then asked me if I thought he ought to contact the police.

'Don't see why. I mean, you haven't seen her over the past week. Her aunt will do the identification.'

'If you think that's best.'

I did. It suited me because there were a couple of things I wanted to check out before the police started prowling. Which meant that, assuming Tina's aunt had seen the same television news, I hadn't much time to waste.

Nonetheless, there was something I simply *had* to ask Drysdale. 'How come your name's December?'

'Because me dad's name was November.' It wasn't a gag this time. The eyebrows remained still. 'Family tradition again,' Drysdale said. 'Oldest boy gets christened the next month. I'm the end of the year. Had the whole lot from January now.'

I blinked, working out that not only had Drysdale's great-great-great-great-great-grandaddy been called April, but he must have saddled *his* eldest with May.

I recalled the photographs in Drysdale's lounge and couldn't resist it. 'So, em, what's your son called?'

'Kevin.'

Chapter 5

The human bulldog was staring wistfully out at the street when I returned to Drysdale's.

His name was Colin and beneath the straining security uniform lurked the soul of a fork-lift truck driver.

'I worked up the 'olesale ware'ouse,' he confided, trotting along behind me as I made my way down the yard. 'Got laid off, though. They're all going over ter France for their booze now.'

'Bad luck.'

'Yeah. Me and me mate got laid orf same time. Nuffing down the job centre 'cept this. He reckoned it was a poxy job. Said he'd rather go on the social. But not me.'

'I see.' I wanted to snoop on my own but Colin appeared to take his duties very seriously. He followd me round the corner of the stables. There was a donkey cart parked in the small square formed by the end walls of the stable and the feed and tack store. The stable itself ran behind the gardens of the last three houses in the road backing on to Drysdale's. There was a beaten mud path about two feet wide between the rear wall of the stable and the bushes bordering the house gardens.

I ran a speculative eye over the bushes. They looked densely packed and at least several feet wide. Too thick for anyone to force their way through. I dropped to my knees and squinted under the prickly growth. In the twilight I could just make out the barer trunks of two of the bushes. For some reason their branches started a couple of feet above the earth, leaving a natural tunnel between into the far garden. Over the years it had become clogged with an accumulation of empty crisp packets, chocolate wrappers, ripped envelopes, dirty carriers and other wind-blown debris.

'I found that,' Colin wheezed in my ear. He was on his knees too, panting in a way that suggested asthmatic tendencies. 'They give ya a manual when ya join, ya know? Says to check the perimeter. I done that.'

'I can see you've got a great future in security ahead of you, Colin.' Climbing to my feet I brushed down my knees.

'Tell ya the truth, I don't really fancy it,' Colin admitted, escorting me back to the gate again. 'Me mate's right about the dosh, it's crap. Two quid an hour.'

I left the car parked in Drysdale's road and walked round the block to the street that ran behind his. A row of two-storey bow-fronted houses displaying 'Bed and Breakfast' and 'Vacancies' signs stretched along either side.

The end house opposite Drysdale's stood out even in the dimming evening light. It had an air of neglect that hung over it like a creeping mould. The paintwork was peeling on the wood, hanging like sloughed-off snakeskin; the water pipes and guttering were rusting and the pointing had crumpled in a dozen places, giving the brickwork the appearance of acne pitting.

It was in darkness: the curtains undrawn and no sign of a light inside. The bell chimes echoed hollowly amongst the silent rooms, confirming the evidence of the two pints of milk standing by the step and the local paper half protruding from the letter box. I went round the back.

The door was wider than normal, with a wheelchair ramp and a single metal handrail leading up to it. Drysdale had said Tina/Tara's uncle was disabled, so I guessed I was snooping in the right back yard.

I had skeleton keys and a glass-cutter hidden in a concealed compartment in the car. But I preferred to leave them there whenever possible, since the police tend to take a dim view of anyone caught in possession of same. Luckily it's difficult to prove that carrying a pair of rubber gloves constitutes 'going equipped', so at least I wouldn't need to leave fingerprints. On the off-chance I tried the back door. It opened.

The back door led directly into the kitchen. In the lambent light from outside I could make out the utility room to the right. I moved forward and heard the sticky squeak as my feet stuck to the floor tiles. I couldn't put the lights on, but I guessed the inside was no cleaner than the exterior.

The units were old-fashioned; wood not laminate. There was no table but a breakfast bar had been built along the far wall. It had a peculiar step design, with the right half slightly higher than the left. One chair-height, one wheelchair-height, I surmised. There was a tupperware container and an empty thermos flask in the centre of the lower drop. I opened the box and found neatly cut tuna sandwiches, an apple and a mini chocolate roll. A picnic for one which – I gave a cautious sniff at the tuna – had been sitting waiting for a couple of days.

Once I was in the hall, I risked using my pencil torch. The mail on the front mat was addressed to Mr and Mrs Parker: bills, junk brochures and an envelope franked with the stamp of a well-known chocolate company. The chocolate company had posted theirs first-class last Friday. The rest were second-class and bore dates ranging from last Wednesday to the Friday again. Which all suggested that nobody had picked up the mail since Saturday; the day after Tara/Tina was murdered.

I checked out the downstairs rooms, sliding back doors that rolled noisily along fluff-choked runnels. There was no challenging shout from upstairs, or telltale creak of floorboards as someone crept to a phone extension. Nothing of interest down here. Just well-worn furniture, pushed back against the walls to allow a turning circle for the wheelchair, and wooden floors that bore the scuff marks of the chair's tyres.

The stairs had been fitted with one of those electric chairs that glide up the banister. Something reached out and touched the base of my spine. An uneasy reminder of parts of my life I don't like to think about. I shook it off and climbed the scuffed stair treads.

Three of the five bedrooms were furnished. The wardrobe in the front double held a woman's clothes; old-fashioned chain-store bits and pieces plus a few flashy items in shiny polyester – tight ruffled blouses and short skirts in vivid blues and pinks. The drawers in the dressing table were stuffed with half-used make-up and partially empty perfume bottles. They smelt wonderful and looked disgusting.

The next two doubles were empty except for the bare bed frames, but the last held a single bed and wardrobe and a commode marked 'Property of the Red Cross'. The mattress in here had been stripped off and the interior of the wardrobe yielded nothing more than a couple of wire coat-hangers. My imagination started going into overdrive: maybe Auntie had buried hubby in the back garden, and murdered Tina when she found out.

There was one other bedroom left.

It was a small boxroom tucked into the corner of the house. A mattress and folded blankets were stacked on the single bed. The wardrobe and dressing table were those cheap self-assembly affairs that warp and distort as soon as you put more than a nylon shirt and folded hanky into them. And both were empty.

The bathroom and loo were equally unproductive. Finally, I let down the attic steps and flashed a torch beam around the sloping rafters. It wasn't until I'd replaced the self-locating steps that I realized I'd been holding my breath, and let it out with a convulsive sigh.

I'd been half expecting to discover Auntie and Uncle sliced up somewhere, and *not* finding them was something of an anti-climax. Now what?

The police had said they wanted to trace Tina's movements prior to her death. I'm not proud. If I hear a good idea, I pinch it.

Dropping back down to the hall telephone table, I flicked my way through the velvet-covered numbers books, showering loose slips of advertisements for double glazing, takeaway food and taxi companies all over the floor. Tina was listed under 'T'. Two dozen or more numbers had been crossed through and a new one inserted underneath. Tina got around a lot.

I jotted down the last three numbers on the back of one of the leaflets and pocketed it. That done, I remembered the utility room. It was the one place I hadn't searched.

There wasn't much to see. An old twin-tub-style washer/spin dryer, a chest freezer (full of food, not dismembered bodies, I was relieved to discover), ironing board, plastic bowls, airing frame, mops, brushes and economy packets of cleaning materials. It was almost as an afterthought that I poked amongst the boxes and plastic containers.

A bunch of keys slid from its perch on the fabric softener with a soft click. I twisted the key-ring in the light. The Yale looked new. The other key was for a Union lock. Neither fitted the Parkers' back door.

Returning the key-ring to where I'd found it, I crawled over the floor, paying more attention this time. The red leather purse was under the broom cupboard; a couple of five pence pieces had spilt out and winked in the torchlight as I quartered the ground systematically. There was a partially used lipstick by the side of the freezer, and eyeshadow, in the same brand, in a flower pot on the windowsill. A rape alarm, a packet of condoms and a grubby brush full of blonde hairs had fallen between the plastic bowls, and the return half of a train ticket from London was nestling in the floor cloth.

Years ago I'd had to arrest a girl in a pub fight. She'd been using her handbag like a flail, whirling it round her head by the

49

straps until the clasp had finally come undone and showered the contents over most of the drinkers. My guess was that someone, either Tina or her aunt, had done the same in here. The fact that the train ticket was from London suggested it was probably Tina.

In which case, where were the Parkers?

I was still sitting back on my heels, trying to make some sort of reasonable theory from the facts I'd uncovered, when the door bell shrilled into the empty house and nearly gave me a heart attack. I stayed low, expecting the caller to go away when they realized they weren't going to get an answer.

Time ticked on: by my watch it was five minutes. I'd half risen, deciding it was safe to leave, when the back-door handle rattled. A couple of tea-towels on the drying rack fluttered in the draught.

Edging to the utility room entrance, I half crouched, ready to fight or run. Run was definitely the favourite option.

The visitor was barely more than a silhouette in this light. Long legs in tight jeans, a high bottom, neat waist, long rippling hair that hung heavily over wide shoulders. For a terrible moment I was afraid Drysdale and I had got it wrong. Perhaps Tina was just an untidy slut who was returning after an innocuous day out.

Still moving warily, she turned slightly, allowing the window and the lighter blue of the night sky to form a frame around her profile, and I realized I'd jumped to a conclusion based on the Michelle Pfeiffer hair-do. 'She' was a bloke.

I stayed where I was. He moved forward again, his body held stiffly, hands partially extended. A stranger moving across a terrain with which he wasn't familiar and frightened of stumbling into the furniture. There were light switches both inside the back door and by the internal one leading to the hall. They wouldn't have been hard to locate, even in the dark, but he didn't try.

I could follow his progress by the creaks and squeaks of

doors and stair treads. Occasionally I caught the protesting whine of sticking wood as he tried to pull out warped drawers.

The best way to discover what he was looking for was to let him find it. It took an hour of searching, and by the time he returned to the kitchen, it was pretty obvious he'd been unsuccessful so far.

He'd become bolder, moving with more assurance as his eyes became accustomed to the dark and no bogeymen leapt out of the cupboards to challenge him.

I let him pull out drawers, swirl a hand around the tea and sugar canisters and empty out the kettle and teapot. The rest of the store cupboard got the same treatment. He'd still come up with zilch. There was only one place left for him to go: the utility room.

To keep the initiative, I stepped out, flicked the torch on and demanded to know what he was doing here.

The circle of light caught him full in the face, blinding him temporarily. It gave me a chance to do a quick stock-take: about eighteen, five nine, a cloud of hair the colour of those sun-bleached red roof tiles you see in Tuscany; pale, almost translucent skin stretched over a long, pointed face with arched eyebrows and a nose so thin you could have cut cheese with it. He looked like he'd stepped straight out of a Botticelli painting.

After the first gasp of alarm, he recovered himself quickly.

The pointed chin went up defiantly and the hands were thrust into his jeans pockets in a deliberately arrogant stance. 'I'm looking for Mrs Parker. Who are you?'

'Expecting to find her in the tea canister, were you?'

'No. I said, who are you?'

'I'm asking the questions.'

'Why?'

That one was a bit of facer. How come interrogation suspects never say that in all the best gumshoe novels? I decided to try another approach. 'Look, I don't mean to hassle you. But you *are* prowling around where you've no right to be.'

'And how'd you know I shouldn't be here?'

It was a good performance, but I caught the barest shake in his voice. He'd been caught out all right, but he didn't intend to relinquish the high ground until he was certain I had the advantage.

I tried a little more manoeuvring. 'You've been here an hour and you haven't put a single light on. Either you've got a healthy consideration for your friends' leccy bills or you don't want anyone to know you're here.'

That wasn't exactly the brightest statement in the world. In order to show his blameless intentions, he promptly stepped back and snapped the light on. It was the last thing I needed. Now I was on full view to anyone who cared to look through the uncurtained windows.

'You don't look too happy,' he said coolly. 'You sure *you* should be here? Maybe we're looking for the same thing.'

'Maybe we are,' I agreed, repocketing the torch. 'Might be easier if we looked together.' I gave what I hoped was a winning smile.

'Maybe. Maybe not.' As I moved forward a couple of paces, he retreated, keeping the same four feet between us.

'Look, come on,' I urged. 'It'll be much easier with two of us.'

It certainly would for me; for a start, I might find out what *it* was.

He looked me up and down, chewing his bottom lip. 'Fifty-fifty split?'

'Goes without saying.'

'OK.' Relaxing the aggressive posture, he extended a palm. 'Give me some skin, partner.'

I matched his gesture, slapping palm on palm to seal the deal. At least, that was the initial plan.

It wasn't until I was flying forward and an excruciating pain

52

exploded in my stomach as it came into contact with a viciously applied knee that I realized I might have made a tactical mistake here.

The kitchen plunged into darkness again. I made a futile grab at his leg as he shot past me, and was rewarded by an elbow in the eye.

By the time I'd recovered my breath and got out into the back garden, he'd disappeared. Hobbling into the front, I drew shallow breaths between clenched teeth, trying to minimize my own body noises so that I could detect the sound of running feet on the pavements.

There were none as far as I could tell.

He could have turned the other way and gone over the fields. And if he had, I decided, examining the miles of flat countryside and water-filled ditches, there was no way I was going to catch him up now.

Since the neighbours were such an incurious bunch, I risked returning to the house and making a more thorough search of the utility room: unloading frozen packets from the freezer, peering inside the twin-tub and checking all the containers to see if any had been dummied up. As far as I could see this room was as unproductive as the rest of the house had obviously been for my red-headed friend. Reshutting the back door, I slipped out again. Now when the police finally caught up with Tina's local address, they'd be starting from the same baseline that I had.

Collecting my car, I drove back towards the front. The multicoloured strings of lights outlining the promenade were in fierce competition to outglare the fluid neon tubes flashing out the names of the games arcades and pubs that lined this section of the front.

Even through the car windows, I could hear the deep bass thump of music systems and the squeals of laser games, interspersed with occasional rumbles of charging ride cars and terrified shrieks from the amusement park.

I got a bag of chips and ate them one-handed as I drove back to the office. It was late but I had a policy of never using my home phone for business if it could be avoided.

Mind, I didn't use my office one either very often if I could help it. On this occasion I was out of luck.

'There's an electronic block on this phone,' the note on Annie's receiver read. 'Use your own.'

Some people are so suspicious. Fishing my own phone from my office drawer, I dialled the last number Mrs Parker had listed for Tina.

It was answered on the tenth ring. I could hear reggae music blasting away in the background and the sound of someone shouting; not angry, just bawling to make themselves heard.

'Yeah?' It was a female voice, but deep and full-throated and, at present, turned to full volume.

If it was a working number, maybe she used her working name. 'That Tara?'

'She ain't here right now.'

'Are you a friend?'

'Who wants to know?'

I made a quick decision. This wasn't the sort of news you broke on the telephone. 'My name's Smith. Look, I'm coming up to London tomorrow. Can I drop round? We need to talk.'

'We do? Why?'

'I can't explain over the phone. Can you give me the address?'

The silence went on for so long I thought the connection had been cut. 'Hello? You still there?'

'Yes.'

'So how about the address?'

'I don't know.'

'Listen, I'm a private detective. I think something bad may have happened to Tara. But I need to speak to you to check it out. I mean, maybe I've got it all wrong and I'm going to stir everybody up for nothing. Now can you at least tell me your name?'

'Bella.'

'So how about your address, Bella? Believe me, this is really important.'

She gave it reluctantly. I scribbled the information down on the back of the taxi leaflet I'd purloined from the Parkers'.

She sounded nice. I just hoped she and Tina hadn't been real close.

CHAPTER 6

There was a fast train to London at 10.10 a.m., which gave me a couple of hours to spare. I wandered round to the Parkers' place again to see if there was any sign of police activity.

There was no activity of *any* kind. The milk and paper were still as I'd left them.

The Parkers' next-door neighbour had the ubiquitous 'Vacancies' board in the window and a polished wooden name-plate with curlicued black letters denoting it as 'Magnolia Blossoms'. The woman who answered the door could have been the model for a seaside landlady in those old joke postcards: billowy folds of flesh caught in a tight dress and the wide-eyed face of a china doll framed by hair the colour of full-fat butter.

'Morning. I'm trying to trace someone who stays next door sometimes. I was wondering if I could have a quick word.'

'You'd better come in, dear.' She stood back, allowing me to squeeze past her into the hall. It was overly supplied with brass ornaments, shell boxes and dried flower arrangements, but the effect was welcoming and suited her somehow.

'My hubby's little joke that,' she chuckled when I queried the lack of magnolia trees in the garden. 'It's my name, you see: Magnolia. And he always reckoned I blossomed after he brought me to the seaside. Don't mind talking in the kitchen do you, love? Only I've got me breakfasts to see to.'

'Not a bit. I'm sorry to bother you this early.'

'No trouble.' A deft flick of her plump wrist spun a slice of bacon over and pinned it to the grill pan again. As we talked she prodded sizzling brown sausages, darkening mushrooms and tomatoes that were gently charring round the edges as they released some of their juices into the spitting fat. 'Now who did you say you were looking for?'

'Either of the Parkers would do.'

She shook her head regretfully, sending a halo of yellow curls bobbing and dancing around her shiny face. 'You're too late if it's Des you're after. He died a couple of months back. Probably a blessing. He wasn't right, you know.'

'Handicapped, wasn't he?'

'Couldn't walk far. But it wasn't just that. He was, you know . . .' She banged the bowl of a teaspoon against her skull. 'Doo-lally.'

'I heard. What about Mrs Parker? I can't seem to find her either.'

'Judy? She should be there. Maybe you just missed her.'

'I don't think so.' I told her about the milk and papers.

A defensive note crept into her voice. 'I've got two lots of regulars in, I don't have time to be watching the neighbours.'

'What about the others in the street? Is she close to anyone in particular?'

'Well, no, not what you'd call close.' Colour stained her cheeks as she ladled hot fat over the eggs.

I'd hit on a sensitive subject. I waited. Through the dining hatch, I could hear the rustle of cereal packets, followed by the whoosh of cornflakes shooting into bowls.

'They'll be ready for this in a minute. I must get on.'

'I don't like to press, but it really is important. Would Mrs Parker have told anyone around here if she was planning to go away?'

'No. I wouldn't think so. I was the closest thing to a friend she had in this street. And she'd worn her welcome thin here.'

'Oh?'

I could tell she didn't like this line of questioning and wanted me to go, but she was too nice to throw me out. I'm not nice; if she wanted rid of me, she was going to have to sling me out.

Magnolia pulled a stack of plates from the warmer. 'Thing is,' she burst out suddenly, 'she took advantage. I mean, everyone was sorry for her, of course. But you've got your own lives to lead, haven't you?'

'Absolutely.'

Her elbow was flashing up and down like a steam hammer as food was scooped from pans and slid on to the waiting plates. 'Yes, well, I helped out. Ask anybody.'

'But Mrs Parker expected more?'

'*Took* more. I mean, she'd ask you to keep an eye on Des for an hour while she went up the shops, and then she'd be gone all afternoon.'

'Not on, that, is it? Especially in the season.'

'Well, exactly.' Magnolia relaxed, pleased to get it off her well-upholstered chest. 'She'd done it to everyone along here. It got so people didn't like to go round the house. I mean, soon as you set foot in the door, she'd be grabbing her coat and rushing out. And what could you do? Couldn't just leave Des on his own, could you?'

'Not in his condition.' I was beginning to get seriously worried about the full breakfasts that she was waving around to emphasise her point.

'I said to her, I said, there's the social services. That's what they're there for, if you can't manage.' She was really getting into this complaint. It was plainly a grievance that had been festering for months and now she was going to let rip. 'Know what she did once? Went off for the whole weekend. Just stuck a note through my door on Friday night asking me to look in on Des.'

'There was always the social services,' I couldn't resist murmuring.

'I tried them. There was just this duty girl. Said it didn't count as an emergency. Well, it was an emergency to me, let me tell you. I had three bedrooms to turn out that Saturday.'

'She came back though? Mrs Parker?'

'Turned up Sunday evening bold as brass. Said she'd just fancied a break. Well, that was the end of it as far as I was concerned. Hire a proper nurse I said to her; that's what the compensation money was for.'

'After the mugging, would that be?'

Magnolia registered the plates she was still clasping. 'Just a minute, love, or these will be stone cold.' I had to wait while the breakfasts were delivered and the teapot collected before she answered me, 'I don't know that you'd call it a mugging exactly. I mean, he was driving the taxi.'

'What happened? Argument with the fare?'

'The fare?'

'The passenger,' I elaborated, assuming Des Parker had had the misfortune to pick up a drunk or a nutter.

'Oh no. He was killed, poor man. They thought Des was going too. In hospital for weeks he was.'

'When did all this happen?' It wasn't ringing any bells at all with me. 'Recently?'

'Must have been . . .' She frowned through the window, automatically swirling hot water round the teapot. 'It was our second season, so that would be . . . about twelve years ago.'

'Did they get anyone for it?'

'One of them.' She added tea bags to the pot. 'Mind, I can't see what this has got to do with Judy being missing now. She's probably gone off somewhere and forgotten to cancel the milk.' She sounded as if she was trying to convince herself.

'Probably,' I agreed basely.

'Anyhow, I thought you said you was looking for somebody who stopped next door. Judy never took in paying visitors.'

'I doubt if she paid. It's her niece, Tina, I'm interested in.'

'She lives in London.'

'I know. But I heard she might be down here. You haven't seen her?'

'No. Mind, she's a funny girl. Off-hand. Cross the road rather than say good morning. And she hardly ever comes anyway. Tell you the truth, I'm not sure I'd know her if I passed her in the street.'

Or saw her flashed all over your TV screen, I thought silently.

But a heartening idea had occurred to Magnolia. 'I expect that's where Judy's gone. Stopping up in London a few days now she don't have to fret about Des no more.'

It was a good theory if you didn't know about the abandoned picnic and the unlocked back door.

'Perhaps.' I stood up. There was nothing else to be learnt here. 'Look, I'll leave my card. And if Mrs Parker does show up, could you ask her to get in touch?'

Wiping greasy fingers on a tea-towel, Magnolia accepted the square of cardboard and propped it against her toaster. 'Private investigations. Like on the telly?' she enquired, reading the printing.

'Not nearly as exciting.'

'Their Tina's not in any trouble, is she?'

'No,' I said with perfect truthfulness. 'Tina has nothing to worry about. I won't hold you up any longer.'

My stomach was screaming for cooked breakfast and Magnolia had not proved to be the soft touch she looked. I was going to have to abandon my principles and spend money.

Magnolia showed me out the front door. At the last moment, she caught at my jacket sleeve. 'If you do find Judy, could you let me know? I mean, I'm sure she's all right, but you know . . .'

I promised to ring if I heard anything.

I went into one of the private hotels that advertised 'Open to Non-Residents'. In return for a view of the sea, turning from grey to aquamarine as the clouds skidded over the sun, they charged me three times Magnolia's rates. And the sausages weren't a patch on hers.

Mid-week and outside the rush hour, the station was virtually deserted. The 10.10 to Victoria fitted itself into the curve of the platform, collected three passengers, gathered speed and rushed across the Medway towards London.

By the time we drew into Victoria another possible line of investigation had occurred to me. I had to splash out on a packet of mints in order to get change for the phones.

Feeding a ten-pence piece into the slot, I dialled a number back home. The receiver was lifted immediately, choking off the first ring. The display started counting down, nine, eight, seven . . .'

'Hello . . . hello . . .?'

'Hang on, Ruby, I'll be with you in a minute.' I fed a handful of coins into the machine.

'Oh, it's you, is it, Grace dear? Got something for me?'

'Yeah. Got a pen?'

'Pencil.' I heard the spit down the phone as she wetted the point. 'Ready when you are.'

I gave her the details of Des Parker's robbery. 'Photostat anything you can get.'

'Any time limit?'

'Say seven hours. Drop any copies off at the office.'

'Will do, lovely.'

Listen to Ruby's honey tones on the telephone line and you'd picture a luscious twenty-year-old with curves to give Claudia Schiffer an inferiority complex. In actual fact she was a pensioner who spent a large part of her time saving on heating bills in the local reference library. For four pounds an hour she'd wade through years of newspaper back issues for you.

I figured a bit of background on Tina's uncle was a reasonable use of twenty-eight quid of Drysdale's money. Let's hope he did too.

Replacing the receiver, I made my way back across the concourse and dropped down the stairs into the underground system and onwards to my appointment with Bella.

Chapter 7

The area of London to the north of King's Cross in which Bella lived was a curious hybrid; a Rubik cube of various architectural styles where some streets had turned full circle to show their best sides whilst others were still in a shabby transience. Grubby, narrow Victorian buildings of yellow London brick abutted on to concrete and glass blocks of flats built in the sixties and then suddenly gave way to dark, solid, square blocks of red brick and grey slate constructed in the thirties.

The later stuff seemed to be fighting a losing battle against obsolescence, whereas the original houses, having reached their lowest point, were now on the up: steam-blasted brickwork, brass carriage lamps and tubs of bay trees announced their upwardly mobile pretensions.

The whole area smelt of car exhaust and rotting food.

The address Bella had given me was one of the older roads, built at the beginning of the century when the middle class had maids to occupy the attics and cooks to slave away in the basement kitchens.

When the servants had left forty years ago the houses had been subdivided into bedsits and let to transitory tenants who didn't give a damn that the brickwork was crumbling, the window frames were warping and the paint hadn't been renewed for two decades.

Making my way along to number twenty-one, I was aware of being watched. In the basement area of number three, a guy with Rastafarian dreadlocks sat against the wall, aimlessly playing a mouth organ. When I glanced down he gave no sign that he knew I was there, but I caught the flash of white as his eyes rolled and the jauntier note to the tune as I passed on.

The front doors to all the houses were approached by steep flights of steps guarded by six-foot pillars. Number seven's was being propped up by a skinhead in denim jeans and a T-shirt that didn't conceal the roll of flesh around his waistband. I was raked by a considering glance as I passed.

Evidently I didn't rate a pick-up. I was piqued: in preparation for my visit to the big city, I'd pressed my jeans and used the free sample of eyeshadow that had come through the door, and even the low-life didn't fancy me.

About half the houses were, officially at any rate, unoccupied. Their windows and doors had been covered by honeycomb-coloured hardboard shutters, embellished by the more artistically minded inhabitants with the aid of spray paint and felt tips. One was girded with scaffolding and gift-wrapped in sheets of green polythene. The whole street had an air of impermanence; a suggestion not so much of menace, more of indifference.

Number twenty-one had a brand new Yale lock on the door, with the shiny, just-fitted gleam of the key on the ring in the Parkers' kitchen.

There was a pad of bells to one side of the porch. But no names. I leant on all of them. After a few seconds, the door opened a crack then stopped, the heavy security chain still in place.

'Yeah?'

'Bella in?'

'Yow expected?'

'I phoned.'

Through the partially closed door, I caught the murmur of another voice followed by the chain being dragged loose.

He looked about fourteen. All legs and arms, with sloe-eyed good looks and skin the colour of dark honey. Behind him a young woman had paused halfway down the staircase.

64

'You the private detective?'

'Yep.'

'Come on up.'

She was no more than five foot two. But solidly built. The thighs that jutted from the tiny red skirt looked like they'd been sawn from the legs of a twenty-seater mahogany dining table. It wasn't fat, it was muscle. I could see the flat tautness of her midriff beneath the black cotton lace top that confined her heavy breasts.

Her hair had been pulled back in dozens of tiny plaits. They jiggled round a face that seemed to have been made up from a paint-by-numbers kit: full deep-pink lips, lines of solid buttercup and sapphire shadow in her eye sockets and two sweeps of metallic bronze blusher flowing over ebony cheekbones. It ought to have looked odd, but it didn't. Somehow it seemed to hold out the promise that she might be fun.

As I moved forward to follow her up the stairs, I was aware of a reduction in the light spilling in from the open door. I found the exit blocked by six foot of muscle with a West Indian origin.

'Who's this?'

'It ain't no problem, Amos. She's looking for Tara.'

Amos back-heeled the door shut, making the kid who'd opened it jump back and collide with the pay-phone fixed to the wall. 'She back?'

'No. Ain't no problem,' Bella repeated. He seemed prepared to take her word for it. I wondered what problem he imagined I might have toted in with me.

Over the banisters, I watched Amos fling an arm round the kid's shoulders and lead him towards the back of the house. 'Thought I told you not to open the door.'

'Sorry, Amos. I forgot.'

'Yeah. Well don't forget again, you hear?' Amos tucked the kid's head under his arm and aimed a punch at his forehead. It was half playful, half serious.

'I won't. Honest.' He pulled free, flushing slightly and lowering his head in a shy gesture.

'We got problems with the council,' Bella said, seeing my interest. 'They've been trying to get us out. Amos don't like strangers in the place. In here.'

She opened one of the first-floor doors and ushered me in. It was furnished with a convertible bed/sofa covered by a patchwork quilt that would have cost a couple of hundred in a twee 'craft shoppe'; a full-length wardrobe and dressing table in a pale clotted-cream shade edged in swirling curls of gilt; and an ottoman in a deeper gold velvet that blended with the bold patterns in the curtains and carpet. One corner was partitioned off by a screen painted with abstract patterns in vibrant glosses; through the joint gaps I caught a glimpse of a sink, cooker and fridge.

She'd added personal touches with small ornaments, a few framed prints and jewellery hung as wall decorations rather than stashed away out of sight.

'Great room. Whenever I try to do that interior decoration stuff it just ends up looking like I'm too lazy to put the junk away. Where'd you learn it?'

She cut straight through my attempts at social niceties. 'I just picked it up. What's happened to Tara? You said bad. How bad?'

I told her.

She made a small mewing sound deep within her throat. For a horrible moment I thought she was about to throw up and ruin a few hundred hours of quilting.

'It was on the local news, southern. You didn't get it up here?'

She shook her head, sending the plaits bobbing like tide-washed seaweed. 'We get London. There wasn't anything in the papers.'

I pointed out that there probably had been before the body had been identified, then decided I'd better check we were both talking about the same person. 'Did Tara call herself Tina sometimes?'

'That was her real name: Tina Bottle. She hated it. Wanted something classier. Started off calling herself Charlotte de Valier. Can you believe that? Had a couple of others too. I forget what. Finally she settles on Tara Lloyd.'

Bella had flopped on to the bed as we talked, hunching her legs and hugging her knees for comfort. Now she rested her chin on the gleaming kneecaps and frowned up at me. 'What d'you say your name was?'

'Grace Smith.'

'I don't get this. How come you're investigating Tina? Why ain't the police doing it?'

'I'm not investigating Tina. Matter of fact, I'm investigating a donkey called Marilyn Monroe.'

I was calculating that the truth (or at least part of it) would catch her interest. And I was right.

'I know about them donkeys! Tina told me. She's a real animal lover, you know.'

'Must help in her business.'

'Yeah, you said it.'

'When'd you last see her?'

'Friday.'

'Where'd she go?'

'I don't really know. She just split. Amos was mad.'

'How come?'

'He figures if she's living with us, she ought to be earning her keep.'

I remembered the string of telephone numbers in the Parkers' address book. 'How long's Tina been living here?'

'Few weeks maybe. She was sharing a place in Ealing with a couple of Scotties. They went back to Glasgow. So she turns up on the doorstep with her things. I always looked out for her since we was in the home together.'

'I heard about her parents. Must have been tough. Especially when her aunt couldn't take her in.'

'Yeah. She was really pissed off with her aunt, you know?' Bouncing into a more comfortable position, she fished a packet of cigarettes from beneath the pillow and offered it.

I shook my head. 'She kept in touch with her though, didn't she?'

'Yeah, well . . .' Bella shrugged. Tipping a match from the fag packet, she clamped it between her thumb and forefinger and flicked a scarlet nail over the tip. It ignited in a hiss of blue flame. 'Family, wasn't it? I mean, you need someone out there to notice, don't you? Me, I got a gran in Trinidad. Writes to me sometimes. Me and Amos's going back soon as we save up enough. Thought maybe I'd open myself an aromatherapy place. They do courses at the local tech.'

There was nothing of the Caribbean in her accent; it was flat north London. I had to guess she'd never set foot in Trinidad.

Bella exhaled a cloud of blue smoke. 'I met her once, Tina's aunt. About a year back. She came up one weekend. Wanted to do the clubs. It was dead embarrassing.'

'How come?'

'Well, she was wearing these gross clothes. Like all frills down to here.' Bella poked a lethal nail into the gorge between her own breasts. 'And this short skirt, so's you could see her bum.'

She was chattering on in a normal tone of voice. Just a couple of girlies, together giggling over a friend's weird relatives. The fact that I'd just announced her best friend was dead had been shunted into the area of her brain marked 'Hold'. Pretty soon it was going to push its way to the 'Immediate Attention' section. I played along with her until that happened.

'What'd you do with her?'

'Took her round some places. She got totally rat-arsed. Started trying to pull blokes young enough to be her son. I mean, like, me and Tina didn't know where to put ourselves. In the end she passed out. We let her sleep it off on the floor then stuck her on a train home next day.'

Without warning she stubbed her glowing cigarette viciously into the quilt. A spark sizzled in a fizz of charred cotton. 'Sod it.' She slapped her fingers down on the blaze, beating out the flames in a series of vicious open-handed whacks.

'Sod her, sod her, sod her.'

I understood. She was mad at Tina for checking off Planet Earth without notice.

I waited until she'd finished beating the soft furnishings to death and then said: 'Look, maybe they made a mistake or something. Have you got a picture of Tina?'

I didn't really believe that; but she wasn't going to be any use to me if she went into shock.

A spark ignited inside the black eyes. Scrambling off the bed, she rummaged in the dressing table and unearthed a Polaroid.

'Here you are, that's Tina.'

It was the girls' night out. Bella was on the left of the trio, her earth mother figure squeezing out of a short dress in some kind of metallic fabric. She had one arm linked into an older blonde's. I recognized the satin blouse and skirt from Judy Parker's wardrobe. The girl on the right I didn't know at all.

Bella leant on my arm, her breast lolling over like a fat watermelon. She touched the third girl's face. 'That's Tina.'

My initial reaction was that the police had got it wrong. The news picture that had drawn such scorn from the customers at the Electronic Daffodil had shown an overweight, heavy-featured girl with scruffy brown shoulder-length hair. The young woman leaning against Judy Parker's other arm was slim, with white-blonde hair cropped to an inch's length, framing a face dominated by huge eyes that held a vaguely bemused expression.

Bella had been reading my reactions. 'It's not her, is it?' she demanded. 'They screwed up, didn't they?'

I turned the print, trying to put three-dimensional planes on to a two-dimensional print. 'I don't know. The TV picture was different. She looked much fatter. And her hair was longer and darker. It looked like it might have been a mug shot. Did she ever look like that? Maybe a few years back?'

'Maybe.' She said 'maybe' in a way that meant 'yes'.

The tears started then. I put an arm round her shoulder, letting her cry it out.

I'm no good at this empathizing business. I wasn't when I was in the force. If there was bad news to be broken, I usually tried to make sure I was out of sight when the short straw was being dealt.

When she seemed to be calming down, I tried again. 'Look, I really need some help here, Bella. You feel up to talking?'

She used an elbow to lever me away. 'Who gives a stuff about a dead donkey?'

'I do. And Tina probably would have too.'

Bella considered this; the effort of holding back the last of her tears gave a sulky pout to her heavy mouth. Abruptly she said: 'What happened? To Tina. How'd she . . . I mean, how did they . . .?'

'Knifed, I think. The police aren't giving out much at the moment. They're trying to trace her last movements.'

'Think they'll come round here?'

'Probably. Any reason they shouldn't?'

'Amos won't like it.'

Tough. I bet that would really bother the investigating team. Bella gnawed her bottom lip. 'She skipped from her last place. The others did too.'

'You mean they owed rent?'

'And some other stuff. From catalogues.'

In which case it was unlikely any of her recent neighbours had Tina's forwarding address. So it could take a while to track down all her known associates. But sooner or later they were going to arrive at her old pal Bella.

Sitting beside her I said gently, 'Look, why not call them yourself? I mean, if all you've got to tell is that she went off somewhere on Friday, what's the harm?'

'Amos won't like it.'

'Come on. Amos is big enough to look after himself.'

Bella still looked dubious. 'I don't know anything.'

'What about the others in the house?'

'There ain't really anyone now, except me and Amos. And Warren.'

For the first time the quietness struck me. There were none of the irritations usually associated with communal living: fights, tuneless singers, ghetto blasters, noisy plumbing and the DIY fanatic with the blunt drill. Instead the place had the echoing quality of rooms devoid of furniture and furnishings to absorb the acoustics.

'So what's the story? Where'd everybody go?'

'Council rehoused them. They want to renovate this street.'

'Would Tina have said anything to Warren? Or Amos?'

'Shouldn't think so. Tina, she didn't talk much, you know?' She made circular motions with her hands, as if she was shuffling cards across a desk. 'Leastways, that's not exactly right. She talked, but she didn't . . .'

'Confide?' I suggested.

'Yeah. That's it. She kept things to herself. Inside, like. She acted tough; like she didn't care about nothing. But she did. I mean, she was really choked about her aunt not having her to live with them. She hated being stuck in the homes. She wanted a place of her own where she could keep animals. Cats and dogs and things. She used to talk about having her own horse. She liked animals better than people.'

No wonder she'd got on with Drysdale. I asked Bella what time Tina had left on Friday.

'About half three. I'd gone up the market. She was leaving as I come back.'

'Did she have a case?'

'No. All her stuff's still upstairs.'

'Weren't you worried when she didn't come back?'

'Not really. This was just supposed to be temporary until she got herself sorted out. I figured she'd found somewhere else and she'd come back for her things when she was ready. Tell you the truth, I was mad at her for leaving me to square it with Amos.' She displayed a sudden flash of insight that surprised me. 'You think whoever did in the donkey got Tina too, don't you?'

'Perhaps. But I'd appreciate it if you didn't mention that to the police if they come calling.'

'Why not?'

'Because they're getting a big enough laugh out of this donkey business as it is.' (And, I failed to add, if they get involved with Marilyn's death, Drysdale might ask for his money back.)

She let me take a look at Tina's room. It was empty of furniture apart from a mattress on the floor.

Tina didn't travel light. Six plastic sacks proved to contain clothes, most of them cheap but up-to-date. Thirty pairs of shoes were ranged along one side of the room. Another corner had a CD player, video, television and stacks of boxed CDs. Other boxes holding heated rollers, hot brush, cassette recorder, clock radio and assorted ornaments mostly of the crystal animal variety were pushed behind the door.

I went back downstairs. Bella was still huddled on the bed where I'd left her.

'She was a spender, wasn't she?' I remarked.

'Yeah. Money burned holes in Tina's pockets. Couldn't save it. Maybe it's best she went now, eh? I mean, she weren't ever gonna get that place in the country, was she?'

'Probably not. Barring divine intervention. I guess I'll be going now. If you think of anything, will you give me a ring?'

'Sure.' She stood up. The top of her head came to the bottom of my chin. Tilting back, she stared into my face. I could see the beginning of more tears welling in her bottom lids and spilling in salty droplets that clung like rain to mascara-encrusted lashes. 'Who's going to bury her? Her aunt?'

'I wouldn't know. The police will probably hang on to the body for a while.'

I didn't mention Judy Parker's disappearance.

'Will you let me know?'

'Sure.' She showed me downstairs. A whisper of shadow slid over the hall plaster on the second-floor landing.

'Hi, Warren.'

Somewhat sheepishly he shuffled into sight, leaning with pretend nonchalance on the banister. 'Yow going then?'

'That's the general idea.'

Hands thrust in jeans pockets, he slouched down the stairs. His feet, in scuffed trainers, barely fitted on the treads.

'Might see yow around then.'

'Might.' On an impulse I said: 'Don't happen to know where Tina went, do you?'

'Who?'

'Tara,' Bella interjected. 'She means Tara.'

'She split. Friday. Had a phone call.'

Bella had been drawing off the security chain. Now she stopped, the Yale half turned. 'You never said nothing about a phone call.'

Warren dropped off the bottom stair, a jangle of loose limbs, awkward movements. 'Why should I?'

'Do you know who called her?'

My eagerness spooked him. I caught the flash of white in the dark hall as he rolled his eyes towards Bella.

'Well, do you?' she demanded.

'Some woman.'

'You didn't happen to hear what they talked about?'

'Not sure 'xactly.' Despite his size he was still a kid. And he was a kid who thought he'd been caught out doing something he shouldn't.

73

'Listen, you'd really be helping me out if you could remember anything, Warren.'

'The other woman was trying to get Tara to go somewhere. First she said why should she, the one who'd rung had never done nothing for her when she was a kid. Then I guess the other one talked her into it, 'cos then she said OK she'd go, but it was going to cost plenty. I guess the other one said OK, 'cos finally Tara says: half and half, roight?'

'You didn't hear where she was going?'

'No. She wrote something down. Like an address or something. Didn't see it. I was up there.' He jerked backwards to indicate the landing. 'She was going to catch a train.'

'How'd you know that?'

'She rang up, didn't she? I heard her talking about times and if they were stoppers or straight through.'

'But you didn't hear where she was going?'

He shook his head. 'It weren't local, though. She turned out her pockets. Didn't have enough for the fare first off. She was going all through the kitchen drawers and things looking for coins.'

Given Tina's remark about doing nothing for her when she was a kid, and the area where her body had been found, it was a reasonable guess that it had been Judy Parker who'd rung and that Tina had been catching the train to Seatoun. And now Tina was dead. And Judy Parker was missing.

CHAPTER 8

It was gone seven by the time I got back to the office. I still get a kick out of going to the seaside. Even though I live at the coast, there's the same old buzz when the scenery outside the train window changes from suburbs, to farm fields, to scrubby flats of marsh and gorse, and finally melts into a lightness that's too substantial to be sky. Something shining in a gun-metal gleam of brightness. The ocean.

It was a lift that lasted until I got into the office and saw what was waiting for me.

None of us keep regular hours so there's generally someone in the building. Letting myself into the deserted reception area, I gave an exploratory whistle.

There was no answering shout. Whipping open a dummy wall clock, I punched in the disabling code before a silent alarm alerted the security company.

Relocking the front door, I checked the answerphone under Janice's desk. It was showing no messages.

Janice had a pass key to all the offices, and if anything had come in during the day, she'd have left a written message on my desk. Taking the stairs two at a time, I inserted my own key, flung the door back and entered.

Beneath a banner asking 'HAVE YOU SEEN THESE SUSPECTS?' someone had plastered the walls with photographs, newspaper shots and film posters. The whole equine range was there: every four-legged star from Champion the Wonder Horse and Muffin the Mule to Shergar and Red Rum.

It wasn't just professional work; a lot of them looked like

holiday snaps. In fact, I was pretty certain I could recognize Linda Rosco in the background of a row of grinning donkeys in Spanish-style sombrero hats. The whole flaming station must have contributed.

No doubt they'd also chipped in for the several tubes of superglue it had taken to get this lot up. After a few futile minutes of ripping, which resulted in a confetti drift over the floor and several scraped nails, I gave up.

There were two messages from Drysdale, both asking for an update; and one from a solicitor who occasionally placed work with me.

The solicitor would be closed. I tried Drysdale's number, but gave up after the phone had rung fruitlessly for several minutes. He was probably tucking the 'lads' up under hay duvets.

I rang Magnolia to see if there had been any sightings of Judy Parker.

'Nothing,' she said, sounding flustered. 'I knocked and rang several times. And she's left the back door open. That's not like her. Do you think I ought to call the police?'

'That's up to you.'

'Yes.' I could hear the heavy panting as indecision chewed its way around her brain. 'I think maybe I'll leave it. For a day. I mean, she's probably just gone up to town like we said.'

'Probably,' I agreed without a blush.

Remembering my visit to the Parkers' house brought to mind something I should have asked Bella. The phone was picked up on the third ring.

'Yoa!'

'Hi, Warren. What's with the American accent?'

'Who's this?'

'Grace Smith. We met this afternoon.'

'Oh, right. Yow're the private detective. Bella told me. That sounds really neat.'

'Mostly it's really boring.'

76

'Yeah?' I heard the doubt. He didn't believe me. Few people do. They think I zoom from one exotic case to the next in designer clothes and an upmarket sports car, effortlessly righting wrongs with the aid of an (illegal) handgun and a black belt in karate. I wish!

Warren interrupted my flight into the realms of wish-fulfilment. 'Hey, is it true, what Bella said? About Tara being killed?'

'Yes. It's true.'

'Wow.' I heard the small intake of breath. Then he confided diffidently: 'I've never known anyone who died before. It's sort of weird, isn't it?'

'I guess weird covers it as well as anything. Is Bella there?'

'She's upstairs. Hang on.'

Her voice was breathy and disjointed, as if she'd been crying. In answer to my question about red-headed blokes, she denied ever having met my late-night wrestling partner.

'Mind, I don't know everyone Tina knew. Only it don't ring any bells here.'

'OK, thanks. Keep in touch.'

As a final thought, I checked the metal mailbox clamped to the back of the front door. We used to have letters on the mat like common folk, but ever since the husband of an ex-client had reciprocated our attentions with a bottle of petrol and a match, anything coming through the slot was held in a heatproof cage.

This evening it was a single brown envelope addressed to yours truly. Ruffling out the half a dozen sheets of paper inside, I scanned the top one. Fuzzy newsprint, dated 11 March thirteen years previously. The headline screamed:

LOCAL MAN KILLED IN HORRIFIC ROBBERY

Good old Ruby had come up trumps on the Parker robbery.

Resetting the alarms, I retreated to the greasy spoon to see what she'd managed to unearth.

Dusk was leaching out the day colours from the streets and sea. The jewel shades of neon signs and coloured lightbulbs twinkled and glowed like exotic fireflies as I wound my way along the front. The sea was black and calm, low waves rippling across each other like heavy oil. Out on the horizon the running lights of an oil tanker slid silently into the rapidly approaching night.

It was all unusually calm for this early in the season.

The greasy spoon was called Pepi's. Who Pepi was (and if he'd ever existed) was a mystery to everyone, including the present owner, who'd been christened Hubert but now answered to Shane.

Thirty years ago Shane had been the lead singer in a minor pop group. There were black and white shots of the group framed on the wall behind the serving counter. A dark-haired Shane, his lean frame hunched into a moody swagger inside a white T-shirt and blue jeans, glowered out at the world.

The hair had gone and so had the lean figure. The T-shirt and jeans had stayed. They were straining at the seams as Shane performed an impromptu cabaret behind the bar.

His musical tastes have been marooned in a time-warp too. The huge jukebox only contains forty-fives from the nineteen fifties and sixties. It even takes pre-decimal coins. You can buy a couple of shillings from Shane if you're daft enough to want to play something. Otherwise he feeds the thing himself.

With one thumb hooked over his waistband and the other hand waggling in a royal wave, he sashayed crabwise, his eyes closed as he sung along to Elvis berating that hound dog.

A couple of girls at the nearest table giggled. Opening one eye, Shane gave them a friendly wink, then swayed back the other way, his hips grinding in what was supposedly a sexy wriggle.

'Any chance of some food?' I yelled over the King.

'What ya want?'

'What's in the rolls?'

Shane did a few pelvic gyrations on the spot whilst he examined the cling-film-wrapped lumps in the glass case. 'Beats me,' he admitted. 'The missus made them. And she's gone home now. Want me to give her a bell?'

'Don't bother. Fry me something.'

'My pleasure.' Waving two cast-iron frying pans as if he were signalling-in a 747, Shane howled mournfully that I weren't no friend of his.

Collecting a coffee, I slid into my usual two-seater by the window and started to sort out Ruby's clippings.

The first one was from the local *Herald*. They must have got lucky: the robbery had happened the day before they went to print.

Beneath an uninteresting shot of an unmade country lane bordered by a high hedge and roped off by police marker tape, the reporter had done her best to obscure the fact that very little information had been released to the press at that point:

Early yesterday morning retired army major Edwin Woolley was brutally battered to death in Easter Lane. Major Woolley (58) was apparently being driven to the local station when his mini-cab was stopped and the Major and his driver were viciously attacked.

The report waffled on for several more paragraphs, via crime statistics, quotes from representatives of the British Legion and Conservative Club, and noncommittal remarks from police and hospital spokesmen, before the reporter provided the only other facts that she'd managed to glean:

The Major was dead on arrival at hospital. The cab driver, Mr Desmond Parker (35), is in intensive care. His condition was described by a hospital spokesperson as 'very poorly'.

Police believe that the motive for the attack was robbery.

A loaded plate was dumped in front of me, together with a knife and fork wrapped in a paper napkin.

'There you go. Anything else? Fancy something special on the jukebox?'

'How about a mute?'

He paid me back with a rendition of 'Have I the Right?', complete with drum accompaniment smashed out with two spoons on the metal tea urn.

He'd taken me at my word and fried everything. Fishing out a blackened pineapple ring, I sliced into it with my fork and continued to browse amongst the purple prose.

A couple of the nationals had picked up the story in their next editions. Basically their reports were just rehashes of the *Herald*'s. One had a shot of the Major's wife and son leaving the hospital.

She had her face buried in a handkerchief. The son looked to be in his late thirties. One arm was round his mother's shoulder and his head was bent towards hers. Strands of black hair had been whipped by the wind, revealing the bald spot on the crown. There wasn't much else to see: his coat collar was bundled up to his chin and thick-framed glasses hid his eyes.

I scanned the next paragraphs.

Major Woolley's son, Roger, said today that the people who had killed his father were the scum of the earth. 'I appeal to anyone who has any information to come forward before these monsters strike again,' Mr Woolley told our reporter.

Mr Woolley (35) is a teacher at St Aethelred's secondary school. The headmaster said that the whole school was shocked by this outrage and extended their deepest sympathy to Roger and his mother.

Police are anxious to trace two men seen working on a blue car in Easter Lane shortly before the incident. The car, which was possibly a Ford Escort, had apparently broken down and the men were attempting to push-start it.

The next photostat was a stop-press item from the same daily, but dated ten days later.

DRAMATIC DEVELOPMENT IN 'TAXI' MURDER
A man is under police guard in Seatoun General Hospital, believed to be arrested in connection with 'taxi' murder of Major Edwin Woolley.

I'd finished the fry-up by the simple expedient of holding the paper between myself and the plate, fishing blindly and eating whatever I managed to spear. It's a system I've always found works for me. Deprived of the sense of sight, most things taste OK.

Shane whipped the plate away and dumped a pudding dish down.

'What's this?'

'Spotted dick and custard.'

'Did you fry them too?'

'Nope. Just the custard.' Having won that round, he sauntered off and left me to the remaining clippings.

The next one provided more details on the arrest.

The apprehended man is believed to be Mr Alan Kersey. Mr Kersey has been a teacher at St Aethelred's school for the past two years.

The headmaster said Mr Kersey was a well-liked and respected member of staff and he would prefer not to offer further comments until the whole story was known.

Pupils at St Aethelred's told our reporter that Mr Kersey was a friend of Roger Woolley, the dead man's son. Neighbours confirmed that Alan Kersey drives a blue Ford Escort.

Mr Kersey was taken to Seatoun hospital four days ago with serious head wounds. A hospital spokesman stated that his condition was 'serious but improving'.

(Medi-speak for 'We don't expect him to snuff it, folks.')

There was a fuzzy, slightly out-of-focus photograph included with this report. It looked as though it had been clipped from a larger shot of a boys' sports team. Alan Kersey was half hidden behind the kids in striped jerseys, a printed circle outlining his head like a transparent football.

It was a spectacularly unmemorable mug: narrow-jawed and standard-featured, with dark hair parted on one side and curling round the lobes of longish ears.

The final cutting was just a couple of paragraphs topped by a picture of Alan Kersey's house and car. The copy indicated that police were still looking for a second man, described as 'short, stocky and in his thirties' in connection with the murder.

A final sentence, almost an afterthought, told its readers that Des Parker was 'out of danger'.

I checked the envelope to see if I'd missed anything. A library reservation card was caught in the seam. Ruby had written in the 'Author' box: '7 hours × £4 – drop it through the letter-box.'

There was nothing else. I made a few calculations. Given Kersey's reported condition, it was probable that it would have been weeks before he'd been in any state to appear at the initial committal. And probably months before the case came to trial. (Always assuming it had gone the distance.)

I fanned out the sheets. Was I on the wrong track? I was being paid to investigate the death of a donkey. Why should Des Parker's robbery and his niece's murder have any connection?

It seemed fair (and smart) to check back with Drysdale. It

was his money. I didn't want any arguments about the bill later.

The house was in darkness again, but Colin, the human bulldog, greeted me like an old friend.

He'd set up an ancient deckchair in the yard. An open lunch box and a thermos stood on the cobbles.

'Tried eating in the stable. But them donkeys scoff anything.'

'I know. Drysdale in?'

'Gone out. Church council or something. Back about midnight. You want to wait? I got some cards. We could have a game.'

He sounded wistful. I guessed that, after the social whirl of the ''olesale ware'ouse', donkey-guarding was proving to be on the lonely side.

I had to turn his attractive offer down. 'Can you tell Drysdale I was just checking in? I'll catch up with him tomorrow.'

I couldn't think of anything further to do on the case, so I headed home to type up my notes.

'Home' is a basement flat. Originally it was the kitchen and storage quarters of the ubiquitous four-storey Edwardian boarding house. The windows are barred; the floors are cold stone, polished by the shuffling feet of the kitchen skivvies; and the whole place has a permanent chill no matter how high the temperature outside climbs.

From my point of view, however, it has one feature that makes it more attractive than a thousand luxurious penthouses (well, one penthouse at any rate): it's rent-free.

It was empty the first time I noticed it (drunk, locked-out and in search of a safe place to pass the night in if you must know). A few months later, when I was in urgent need of a new address, I happened to pass the house again. The basement was still unoccupied. Two days later I'd changed the locks and moved in.

At the time I'd assumed the other tenants were legitimate. However, over the past couple of years, I've discovered we're all in the same boat: squatters in a house that appears to have no owner.

My section is definitely the pits in more ways than one, but at least it has a separate entrance.

I have four rooms to call my own. The largest was the former kitchen; it still has the gaps where the cooking ranges stood. I do most things in here: cook, eat, sleep, worry and workout.

There's a smaller room just off it that was probably a pantry. I've got that rigged out as a walk-in wardrobe. The old scullery at the back of the house is now a bathroom. There's another smaller, stone-flagged room just opposite it whose purpose I've never been able to work out. It has an outside wall, but no windows. Since I felt a pressing compulsion to stamp my ownership on the whole territory, I stuck a fold-up bed in there and christened it 'the guest room'.

Now I drew the ceiling-to-floor red velvet curtains I'd picked up in a car boot sale across the window wall in the kitchen, turned the gas fire on and hauled my manual typewriter on to the table.

I don't like the administration side of the job, but it has to be done. Shuffling together top sheet, carbon paper and a flimsy, I rolled them into the platen and commenced to thump down on the keys like a demented concert pianist. I put in the date and the case number I'd allocated to Marilyn's murder, and headed it up 'File Note No. 01'.

Having got the preliminaries out of the way, I started turning out my bag and pockets. I've a habit of scrawling information on assorted scraps of paper. I use them as memory joggers when I'm setting up reports and expense claims.

I assembled what I'd accumulated to date. The receipt for my snack at Victoria Station plus a rail-excursion leaflet with details of train and tube fares founded the 'Expenses' pile. I hesitated over the three-star breakfast, then thought what the hell – Drysdale could only throw it out.

The Polaroid that Bella had let me hang on to went in with 'File Notes', together with a list of Tina's last phone numbers that I had copied from Judy Parker's house.

It was the sight of that list that pulled me up short. I'd written it on the back of a flyer for a mini-cab firm. Had I been missing the obvious?

The dispatcher picked up on the first ring. 'Forbes Cabs. Miriam speaking. So what can we do for you?'

There was an antipodean twang to the tail end of her words.

'Hello, Miriam. My name's Grace Smith. I was rather hoping you might be able to help me out with something.'

'Well, I'll sure give it a shot if I can, Grace.'

'The thing is, I'm worried about a friend of mine, Judy Parker.' I gave her the Parkers' address, and explained that no one had seen Judy since the previous Friday. 'It occurred to me she might have gone somewhere by cab. And I was wondering if you could check your records for that day. You do keep records of fares?'

'We sure do. Thing is, though, I don't know I should give out information on our customers.'

I assured her I understood that. 'But see, I was thinking maybe I ought to report her as missing to the police. Only if she's just gone off on a razzle, she's not going to be too pleased with me.'

'I can see that.'

She was weakening. I pressed on. 'Couldn't you just take a look and see if you picked up a fare from that address on Friday? I mean, you don't have to tell me where you took her. Just so long as I know she's OK.'

'Well . . . I guess I could do that.'

'Thanks, Miriam. I really appreciate this.' I reeled off my phone number before she could change her mind.

She promised to ring me back 'in a few hours'.

She must have had a busy night. It was gone seven a.m. before the phone bell dragged me out of a warm, fuzzy dream of golden beaches and tropical seas.

CHAPTER 9

It was so obvious that I was ashamed of myself for not thinking of it.

Miriam explained that, in the circumstances, she was breaking the company's rule and telling me the fare's destination.

'Circumstances?' I'd mumbled, struggling to keep the duvet round me with one hand whilst I extended the phone aerial with my teeth. 'Wa' cir'stances?'

'We took Mrs Parker to the hospital. I spoke to the driver who picked up the fare. He said she looked crook.'

'When was this?'

'Friday afternoon. The booking was called in at fifteen twenty.'

Judy must have rung the cab company just after she called Tina.

'Do you know what was wrong with her?'

'No idea. The driver's got a degree in geography, not medicine. I thought, seeing she was a mate, you'd want to get round there right off.'

Unless she's already dead, I thought. Thanking Miriam, I rang off and stumbled out of bed, dragging the duvet with me.

I needed the local directory. I eventually ran it to earth in the washing machine.

Since I'd no idea what Judy Parker had been admitted for (always assuming she *had* been admitted), I ended up being transferred from ward to ward.

'Look, don't you have some sort of central admission

records?' I asked the operator mid switch between Female Orthopaedic and Psychiatric.

'We do. But the office staff don't start until nine a.m. Would you like to call back then?'

The hands on the large enamelled clock (rescued from a skip), said it was ten to eight. Judy had waited for nearly a week. If she hadn't died yet, she probably wouldn't in the next seventy minutes. 'I'll do that, thanks.'

They eventually managed to track her down at 9.20 a.m. Judy Parker had been admitted to CCU on Friday.

'What's CCU?'

'The Coronary Care Unit. Would you like to be put through?'

'Please.'

The nurse in charge of the CCU confessed that they had had a Judy Parker but she had now been transferred down to Nightingale Ward.

'Is she OK?'

Mrs Parker was 'comfortable'. That could mean anything from dancing round the day room to being immobilized in traction, but since I wasn't a relative, that was all the information I was getting over the phone.

'Can I see her?'

'Visiting hours are two to eight.'

Pulling on jeans and sweater, I unearthed a towel and a bottle of shampoo, rolled a bread-wrapper round some cold toast and headed for the office.

Janice was already at her desk but denied having let anyone into my office yesterday.

'Well, somebody with a tacky line in interior decorating got in. You're supposed to vet callers. Not let any pond life who feels like it wander around the building.'

Bridling, Janice informed me that most of my clients looked (and smelt) like pond life. 'And if one of the others brings them in, I can't stop them.'

She flushed, realizing what she'd said.

'Thanks.'

Taking the stairs two at a time, I knocked on Annie's door and opened it before she could stop me.

'Did you let anyone into my office yesterday?'

She was wearing a beige suit today, with matching plastic-rimmed glasses. Without even pausing on the keyboard, she said: 'No.'

I waited for more. She typed.

'Did Zeb come by?'

'Yes.'

'Loaned him a byte of vocabulary, did you? Only I can't help noticing you don't seem to have a full directory this morning.'

She hit the 'save' key with vehemence, dropped her hands to her lap and swung to face me.

'Zeb came to see me. The others told Janice they were with him. I had to go out just after Zeb. I assume they hid in your office until I left. I didn't know anything about it until this morning. OK?'

She was daring me to call her a liar. Actually I believed her. Frivolous practical jokes weren't really her style. Frivolous anything wasn't really Annie's style. She did everything with a single-minded gravity that was quite frightening at times.

'OK,' I agreed. Searching for some way to restore normal relations, I asked her how things were going with the computer buff.

'He's taking me out for a drink this evening.'

'Great. Well, have a good one.'

I retreated to the bathroom, locked the door and washed my hair, using a glass to bale lukewarm water from the taps.

Whilst the damp tendrils dried around my face and chilled the back of my neck, I rang the solicitor who'd tried to get in touch yesterday.

He wanted me to track down a witness who was due to appear in court next week.

'Nothing suspicious,' he said cheerfully. 'She's got a permanent address, if you can call a caravan permanent, but she tends to go walkabout sometimes. I just want to know where to lay hands on her in the next few days.'

'OK. Fax me the details.' I was about to hang up when it occurred to me to ask about the Woolley case. 'It was about thirteen years ago. The papers said an Alan Kersey was arrested in connection with the incident. Do you remember the case?'

'I do, as a matter of fact. One of the partners in my last firm represented Kersey.'

'Did it go to trial?'

'Most definitely. Kersey got life. What's your interest?'

I admitted I didn't really know. 'His name came up in connection with another case. I'm not sure it has any bearing really. Is his solicitor still around?'

'He retired. He still lives locally, though. George Spinnaker. He's in the book.'

'Thanks.' I hung up and dialled Drysdale's number. The phone trilled fruitlessly for several minutes. Collecting my bread-wrapper, I headed for the beach.

Business was slow. Drysdale was seated on a fold-up canvas seat reading the *Financial Times*, whilst the 'lads' stood placidly in their rope corral dreaming donkey thoughts.

He refolded the paper and thrust it into the pocket of a padded body-warmer as I flopped down on the sand beside him.

'I've been trying to get in touch,' I said.

'Colin said. You got anything yet?'

'I'm not sure.' I told him about my visit to Magnolia, the trip to London and what I'd gleaned so far about Des Parker's connection with the Woolley robbery. 'Tara Lloyd is definitely the Parkers' niece, Tina. The police should be told. The longer it takes them to identify her, the colder the trail is going to go.'

'I phoned them yesterday. Said I reckoned they'd got the name wrong. I thought they'd send somebody round. But so far I haven't heard a dicky bird.'

'They've probably had a lot of cra—' I bit off the word. But he got my drift.

'Think I'm a police case groupie, you mean?'

'Something like that. They'll be working through the leads, checking all the possibilities. They'll get round to you soon. I'd be grateful if you could keep me out of it as much as possible. The police and I don't have what you'd call a positive relationship.'

'I heard.'

That threw me a bit. Had he heard recently – or before he decided to employ me? Was I for the chop? And if so, how much of his thousand quid could I legitimately hang on to?

Worry puts a lot of people off their food. It has the opposite effect on me. Unrolling my bread-wrapper, I chomped cold butter and stiff toast, sending out a shower of crumbs that caught in the downy hairs of my jumper.

The noise attracted a hopeful snort from Errol.

'Do they eat toast?'

'They eat anything that isn't nailed down.'

Stumbling to my feet in powdery drifts, I walked across to the donkey. Errol's ears flicked back and forth like a couple of beer-pump handles. He accepted my offering with an 'I suppose this is better than nothing' snort, and then gave my hand a thorough tongue wash just in case he'd missed a millimetre of butter.

Drysdale waited until I'd rejoined him, drying my hands on the back of my jeans, before he spoke again. 'You really think whoever killed Tina got Marilyn too?'

'I don't know,' I admitted. 'Maybe it *was* a local sicko. I could start checking out the video shops if you like. See if anyone's into snuff flicks with four-legged players.'

'You mean they stock that sort of thing?'

'Not out front, no,' I admitted. 'But I expect I could find someone who could lay their hands on it. Most perversions are catered for if you know where to look.'

'They want locking up. The law's too soft. Always has been. So taken up with the criminals' rights, they don't give a toss about the victims.'

I half expected this conversation to go down the well-worn path of bringing back National Service and/or the birch. But Drysdale had lapsed into a brooding silence.

Resting my forearms on my knees, I watched the scene in front of me.

The morning mist still took a while to burn off this early in the year, but the promise of last night's calm sea had started to materialize.

The sun was breaking through the clouds, changing the colour of the waves from grey to turquoise where it dabbled across them in impressionist splodges. The sand underneath my bottom still held winter's dampness, but it didn't deter the amateur builders and excavators. Several sand castles and a couple of holes were already under construction.

Along the length of the beach the steady banging of knobbly lumps of white rock on the wooden posts of wind-breakers formed a bass section to the tinny music of a small carousel.

A tiny girl dressed in pink leggings and a Winnie-the-Pooh T-shirt skipped over to Drysdale and offered a handful of silver. Evidently she was a regular.

'Hello, Beth, which one do you want to ride?'

Beth studied the corral with all the seriousness of a bloodstock agent considering the thoroughbreds in the selling ring. Eventually she settled on Lana. Drysdale lifted her up and set off. With a bit of good-natured shoving and jostling the rest of the string fell into line and trotted after him.

At an unseen marker they all wheeled, and started the trek back. Marilyn's place in the string was still being maintained, I noticed. I mentioned it to Drysdale, after he'd hitched Beth from the high saddle and sent her scampering back to her mother, where she could clearly be heard whining for 'Just one more ride, p-l-e-a-s-e.'

'They're very loyal,' Drysdale agreed, looping the rope barrier back in place. 'They miss him.'

'Will you get another one?'

'Perhaps. It's not as easy as you'd think. They have to have the right temperament.'

'To fit in?'

'To stop my insurance company wriggling out under the small-print clauses,' he snorted. 'They've already got so many escape routes in their policy it might as well have been written by Ronnie Biggs.'

'What are you insured for?'

'Public liability. That's why it's important to get the right beast. I had one once, few years back, seemed as sweet as a new-born lamb. First time some lout cracked him in the ribs and yelled "Get up, Red Rum", he took off like someone had stuck a lighted fuse up his backside.'

'What happened?'

'Chucked the kid in the sea.' The reminiscent grin playing round Drysdale's mouth made it clear whose side he'd been on.

'So you got rid of him?'

'Unfortunately not. Some interfering lifeguard fished him out.'

'No. I meant . . .' Too late I caught the twinkle in Drysdale's eye.

'The donkey is living the life of Riley on a mate's farm. The rest of them go out to pasture there at the end of the season.' A slight shadow darkened his eyes. 'Or when they die.'

Abruptly he looked me straight in the face. For the first time I became aware of a much sharper intellect hidden under the eccentricity. It was a strange feeling; rather like finding a triffid lurking amongst the busy lizzies.

'You think I'm daft, don't you? Getting this wound up about a donkey?'

'I did,' I admitted. 'Only now I've had a chance to think about it, why shouldn't you? I mean, some people shell out for fancy cars or golf lessons, because those things are important to them. Donkeys are what goes with you. Why not? It's your cash.'

'The cash is what counts with you, isn't it?'

'Sure.'

I'd been down this conversational road before. I just hoped he wasn't going to push it. Luckily at the moment he had a mini-boom in customers. When the business slackened, he came back to the stool, but didn't mention my motivation again.

'So,' I asked when it became clear he considered the conversation at a close, 'do you want me to go on poking around for a connection with Tina's death? Or check out the video angle?'

'Do what you think best. That's what I'm paying you for. But keep in closer touch. I don't like having to chase you.'

'Fair enough.'

I left him at one o'clock to make my way round to the hospital.

CHAPTER 10

The legend 'Sea Bathing Hospital' was still clearly visible above the open first-floor terraces of our local hospital; an establishment that had been erected at a time when cold salt-water baths and bracing north winds were considered ideal treatment for the chronically sick.

Nowadays they've moved to more conventional medicine, but the grim, grey, uncompromising building still radiated the governors' basic belief that the inmates should pull themselves together. It wasn't the kind of place you'd want to be ill in.

Nightingale Ward was on the ground floor. It was a long, narrow room holding about thirty beds. The cream-painted walls and ceiling were clean and undecorated. The grey floor reflected the scuff tracks of numerous wheeled trolleys, gurneys, drug carts and drip stands. It was functional, sterile and depressing.

None of the three nurses sitting at a wooden table in the centre of the ward took any notice of me as I walked through the nearly silent room. But when I asked for Judy Parker, the staff nurse looked up.

'Sure, and you must be Tina.'

That answered one question. Tina's death hadn't penetrated this far yet.

'No. Sorry.'

'Not to worry. She's been expecting her niece to visit. I thought you must be her. Judy's down there in bed three. Although I shouldn't by rights be letting you in yet.'

I followed the direction of the pointing biro, but the garishly patterned orange bed curtains were partially drawn.

'Look, I've got some news for her. It's not good. I mean, is it OK to tell her? What's she in for?'

She hesitated. 'Are you a relative?'

'No. We've never met.'

'In that case, I think it would be best if you were to be speaking to the doctor.'

'You could well be right.'

She directed me to a day room opposite Nightingale Ward. The ubiquitous cream paint was heavily in evidence again. The chairs were covered in tangerine vinyl. Sitting in one caused dirty yellow foam to bulge out of a ripped seam.

A heavy, old-fashioned television was on in one corner, but only one of the occupants of the room was paying it any attention. The other half-dozen were grouped round a balding bloke in plaid pyjamas and a tartan dressing gown who was busily scrawling on a large yellow pad with a thick-nibbed marker pen.

There was something vaguely familiar about their faces, but I couldn't pin the elusive memory down.

'How about this then,' Baldy said loudly. 'This gross negligence on the part of the Public Health Department not only seriously blighted the quality of life that we had been enjoying but caused severe financial hardship. Underline "severe",' he muttered, heavily underscoring that word. 'What do you think, Mr Mouldar?'

The man who'd been leaning forward, trying to hear the television commentary, reluctantly drew back at this appeal. 'I'm not sure it really applies to me. It hasn't caused me any hardship. I wasn't working anyway.'

'We've got to stick together. Compensation, that's what we're entitled to. Those bloody kebabs nearly killed us. God knows what damage they've done to our guts.'

My memories finally connected. I was looking at the survivors of the Great Food Poisoning Disaster.

'Whatever you think best, Albert,' Mouldar said.

I caught his eye and winked. He took it as an invitation to join me.

'His heart's in the right place, miss,' he whispered.

'But his mouth's occupying too much space?'

'Spot on, miss. I thought I was safe, hiding out in the day room. But he tracked me down.'

Our socializing was cut short by the arrival of the doctor.

'Are you the lady who's visiting Mrs Parker?'

'That's me.'

'Raj Patel. I'm the senior registrar. We can talk in the office.'

A half-drunk cup of tea and an untouched chocolate bar were already on the desk. He ripped the plastic wrapping off with his teeth and ate quickly as we talked.

Judy Parker had been admitted following a coronary thrombosis.

'A heart attack?'

'By any other name.'

'But she came by herself. In a taxi. I thought heart attacks just clutched their chests and keeled over on the spot?'

'Not necessarily. The early symptoms can be coming on for weeks. Mrs Parker showed great presence of mind in coming here. A crash team got to her in seconds when she did keel over in A and E.'

'How would she take bad news?'

'How bad?'

'The worst.'

He gulped several mouthfuls of tea before he answered. Allowing me time to assimilate the facts that (a) he was rather dishy and (b) he was wearing a wedding ring.

'She's stable now. But once a patient has had one attack, well . . .' He lifted his shoulders. 'No one can ever say for sure that there will never be another. Does she have to be told this bad news now?'

'No. But she's going to find out pretty soon. And if she is going to have another attack . . .'

'She's in the best place for it,' he finished for me, jettisoning the crumpled wrapper into the bin. 'OK. But I'll tell Nurse Connell to keep an eye open for any signs of stress.'

I was duly escorted down the ward. Nurse Connell's shoes squeaked.

'Here's a visitor for you, Judy.'

It was the face from Bella's Polaroid, but thinner and greyer. Devoid of make-up her lips looked thin and mean, and the shadows around the eyes gave them a skeletal look. Nonetheless, for a moment they flashed with a spark of excitement. Then the flame died and they became cold and grey; pebbles rather than crystals. I wasn't the visitor she wanted to see.

'Hi, my name's Smith. I'd like to talk to you about Tina, if you don't mind?'

Hope ignited inside the washed-out face again. 'Are you a friend of hers?'

'I talked to Bella yesterday,' I temporized. 'You remember Bella?'

'The black.' She was wriggling her shoulders against the pillows as she spoke, using them and her heels to lever herself into a sitting position. 'Sit down.'

I manoeuvred the heavy chair, sliding the wheeled bed-tray out of the way.

'I thought you'd be all wired up to bleepers and flashing machines.'

'I was for the first couple of days. Till they moved me down here.'

'How are you feeling now?'

'Tired. But I'm used to that. I've been nothing but bloody tired for the past twelve years.'

'I know.'

98

'Do you?'

'My dad's in a wheelchair.'

'You take care of him?'

'No. My mum does.'

'Poor cow,' Judy said with feeling. 'Accident, was it?'

'He was attacked. Like your husband.'

Now that we'd established some kind of rapport, a trace of animation was creeping into the wan face. Pulling down a flap on her locker, she fished out a brush and started dragging it through the coarse blonde hair.

'It's natural, you know,' she said, struggling with a knotted tangle. 'Didn't come out of a bottle. Des, my hubby, couldn't believe it first time he saw me starkers. Yours natural?'

'No, 'fraid not.'

Judy preened; she'd just put herself above me in the trichology department. This could be the beginning of a very brief friendship.

It ended again when Judy asked: 'You another prozzie?'

'No. I'm a private detective. I'm working for a Mr December Drysdale. He owns the house at the rear of yours.'

'I know. Bloody donkeys. Stink the place out some summers. What's this got to do with Tina?'

This was hopeless. I was no better at this breaking-the-bad-news lark now than I had been when I was in uniform. There was nothing for it but to dive in head-first. 'Have you see the telly in the last few days?'

'Telly? No. There's one over the day room. Can't seem to be bothered somehow.'

I could believe that. I'd been in hospital. Within a few hours the outside world fades into insignificance; the progress of the drug and food trolleys the highlights of the day.

'What about the papers?'

'Don't get 'em unless someone brings 'em in for you. Anyway, what's this got to do with the price of fish? Listen, whatever your name is, do you bloody know my niece or not?'

'No.' I took a deep breath. 'But there's been a body found. The police say it's a Tara Lloyd. She'd been murdered. Knifed.'

Judy sat up with a strangled moan. The brisk squeak of Nurse Connell's shoes announced her approach behind me.

'I think you should be going now.'

'Just a couple more minutes.'

'She needs to rest. Should I be fetching the doctor to you, Judy?'

Judy directed her shock at the unfortunate Nurse Connell, who was told to 'Bugger off.'

As soon as she was out of earshot, Judy fixed thin bony fingers round my wrist. 'Who did it?'

'I've no idea. And neither do the police as far as I know. As of last night, they still hadn't worked out she was your Tina. Mr Drysdale had rather assumed you'd call the police,' I lied glibly. 'Nobody knew you were in hospital.'

'There was nobody to tell. Nobody was interested. They made that pretty clear, the selfish, smug sods!'

She broke off in a fit of dry-throated coughing. I heard the squeaking shoes take several paces in our direction, then think better of it.

The glass of water I poured was accepted without thanks. Her locker top was bare except for the plastic jug and glass. There was none of the usual paraphernalia of flowers, cards, sweets and fruit that cluttered the other lockers.

'What happened?' she asked once she'd regained control of her voice.

I outlined the little I knew about Tina's murder.

'Has this Drysdale hired you to find out who killed Tina then? What's in it for him?'

'My client wants to know who slit one of his donkey's throats.' It was on the tip of my tongue to say I thought it was probably the very person who'd performed the self-same operation on Tina. But caution stopped me. The police were undoubtedly going to be speaking to Judy very shortly. I'd rather she didn't pass on that particular piece of information. 'Tina spent a lot of time with the donkeys, I gather.'

'Well, she's hardly going to go slitting their throats, is she? Can't you find anything better to do?'

'We all have to earn a living.'

Judy seemed to have lost interest in me. Her fingers restlessly pleated the edge of the turned-back sheet as she looked around the ward. More visitors were streaming in now and the level of noise was rising.

'Mrs Parker, Judy, I really need to ask you this. Why did you phone Tina on Friday? Did you send her somewhere?'

I wasn't making contact here. Judy seemed fascinated by a toddler who was crawling over the opposite bed, making hopeful lunges at the fruit bowl.

'Judy?'

'I won Ernie.'

'Sorry?'

'Ernie. Me premium bond came up. Not the jackpot or nothing. But enough, see? More than we'd ever 'ad at one time before.'

'Well, that's terrific, but what I really want—'

Judy couldn't give a toss what I wanted. She was going to talk. I could listen or not, as I pleased.

'Been together since we was fourteen, me and Des. Best-looking boy in the block. All the other girls was after him, but I got him. Didn't see beyond a pretty face then, that's the problem. Well you don't, not at that age. Couldn't see it was all talk. Full of daft schemes, he was. Always going to be rich next year. Never was. Never had two pennies to rub together half the time. It was always me left to hold things together.' Tears started to run down her cheeks in glistening rivulets. 'When Ernie come up, I put me foot down; bought the boarding house. It was going to be our fresh start, see? He was only doing the mini-cabbing until I got the place on its feet.'

The tears were in full flood now. I cast a nervous look over my shoulder, but Nurse Connell had disappeared.

Reaching over, I took one of Judy Parker's hands. Her fingers closed convulsively round mine. 'We were going to have kids. Before it was too late. Well, I got one, didn't I? Des was like a kid after what they done to him. Take your eyes off him for a minute and he'd be into trouble.'

'I thought he couldn't walk?'

'Be easier if he couldn't have. I had to listen out, day and night. I was so bloody tired. All I wanted was to just *sit* somewhere for a few hours. Not have to keep looking at my watch, seeing if it was time to rush back. You know?'

'Yes, I know.'

'They wouldn't let me, though: "You will be back by four o'clock, won't you, Judy?"; "Only half an hour, Judy"; "Might be able to spare two hours Tuesday night, Judy. Only if there's nothing decent on telly, mind." Always rush, sodding rush.'

I was beginning to get seriously alarmed. She was getting distinctly wound up here.

'I never used to swear. Wouldn't let Des do it neither. Now I hear the words coming out of my mouth. Why'd you think that is?'

'I read somewhere it was a symptom of depression.' Or was it some other disorder? I couldn't exactly remember. But it hardly mattered since Judy wasn't listening to me anyway.

'Did Des ever talk about the robbery?'

'What?'

I repeated the question.

'Couldn't remember nothing about it. Anyway, what's it got to do with you?'

Nurse Connell had re-emerged from the sluice room, her progress charted once again by the shriek of her soles. I needed to establish a connection with Judy – fast.

'Did you get compensation?' I asked quickly. 'My dad did. Mind, it took five years. And then it was peanuts.'

Money. It's a subject most people can't resist. And Judy was no exception. 'You're lucky,' she snorted. 'Took me six years. Didn't even cover what I owed the loan company.'

She moved restlessly on her pillows. 'How old d'you think I am?'

Probably the same age as her husband would have been. But I charitably deducted a few years and suggested: 'Forty-five?'

She didn't contradict me. Instead she addressed the ceiling. 'I'm not old. I can't be old. I haven't done anything yet.'

Quite. I hadn't got time for this. 'Listen, Judy. I really need to know what you said to Tina on Friday. Where did you send her?'

She denied sending Tina anywhere. 'What have they done with her things?'

'The police will have them.'

'They're mine by rights. I'm the next of kin. Tell them that.'

'Sure. OK.' I was getting fed up with the evasions. 'But I think you'd better think this through, Judy. Somebody slit Tina's throat. Maybe they'll do the same for you once you're out of here. The more of us that know what's going on, the safer you are.'

She was rattled. But not frightened enough to give up whatever she was protecting.

'I don't have to answer your questions.'

'No. You don't. But you might be smart to do so. Think about it.' I placed a card on her locker. 'That's my number. Call me. Is there anyone you want me to ring for you?'

'No. There's no one gives a toss now.'

Nurse Connell looked relieved as I made for the door. And dismayed as I wheeled round and headed back to the bed.

'By the way, Judy, do you happen to know a boy, late teens, thin-faced, red hair down to his shoulders?'

'No. Why?'

She was telling the truth this time, I was sure of it.

'Just wondered.'

I left her mulling that over and skedaddled before the shriek from Connell's shoes reached teeth-itching overdrive.

Turning left, I headed for the entrance nearest the car park.

'Miss?'

Correctly assuming this was me, I searched for the location of the sound, and found Mr Mouldar lurking in the corner between the snack-vending machine and the internal wall.

He jerked a thumb in the direction of the day room and accompanied it with a raise of thin eyebrows.

'Coast's clear.' I inserted a few coins and collected lunch: cheese biscuits and a Kitkat.

It wasn't until the poor bloke turned a pale chartreuse shade and turned away that it occurred to me I might be being a trifle insensitive here.

'Sorry.' I thrust them out of sight in my pocket. 'Still feeling queasy?'

'Not too bad now, thanks, miss. Bit shaky on my pins. But a lot better than I was. I thought I was going to meet my maker a few days back.'

'Nasty. Er . . . would you mind if we changed places?'

'Pardon, miss?'

'I want to lurk in that corner while you stand here holding my change,' I elaborated.

I do love people who don't always have to know why. Without another word, he shuffled from his hiding-place and let me take it.

In a half-crouching position behind Mouldar's rough-weave dressing gown, I watched Zeb and his boss stroll down the corridor and turn into Nightingale Ward. The police had finally identified Tina. And they'd found Judy a lot faster than I had.

But I'd found her first. It seemed prudent to let any ruffled feathers settle before my next encounter with CID.

'Can I move now, miss?'

'Give it a sec, could you? Unless you're feeling dizzy?'

'Not in the slightest, miss. How was your friend? Mrs Parker, wasn't it?'

'Coming on.'

'It's always pleasant to have a visitor in hospital. Makes the time go quicker. Unfortunately I know no one in the area.'

'Not local then?' No enraged plain-clothes officer had re-erupted from the ward. I eased my way out of the corner.

'No, miss. Londoner, born and bred. Lived there all my life. Until I lost my job.'

'Redundant?'

'No such luck. Firm went bankrupt. A familiar story these days, I fear.'

'Sorry to hear it.'

I was backing up the corridor, but Mouldar seemed determined to hang on to me.

'Extremely kind of you to say so. Much appreciated.' He shuffled along in ancient slippers trodden down at the back. Every few steps one shoe shot forward and he was forced to grope for it with bony toes.

'I'm renting a small caravan down here now, miss. Always wanted to live by the sea.'

'Oh yes?'

'Luckily my needs are modest. I don't require much to live on.'

'Oh, er, yes . . .' I found a few coins.

'Oh *no*, miss. I don't want charity. I want a job. Perhaps there might be a position where you work? I was a book-keeper but I'm quite willing to turn my hand to anything.'

Embarrassed at my *faux pas*, I found myself apologizing for Vetch's. 'It's a very small company. And the owner's a tight-wad. There's really nothing.'

'How unfortunate. I do hope you didn't mind my asking, miss? Only they say at the Job Club that we should chase any possible lead. Nothing ventured, you know?'

'No. I didn't mind.'

The light coming from the entrance behind me fell full on him, cruelly highlighting the thinning grey hair, scraggy legs and skin mottled with brown age spots. I put him in his fifties. Did he really expect to ever work again?

I felt guilty because I was young (ish) and employed (mostly).

'Look,' I said, 'I think a local security company are taking on staff. Mackenzies. Try them. The money's not much, but the job opportunities are interesting. Friend of mine's baby-sitting a load of donkeys at present.'

He was still inking the address on his wrist when Zeb appeared in the corridor behind him and I legged it out to the car park.

CHAPTER 11

I borrowed a paint scraper from Shane on the way back to the office and spent a few hours working off my frustrations by removing the additional decoration from my office walls.

It was therapeutic watching the slivers of paper drop to the bare floorboards. The damn stuff had bonded to the plaster with the tenacity of dried instant porridge.

Vetch stuck his head in in mid scrape and expressed a hope that I intended to make good.

'Why should I do it? It's not down to me. Bill those jokers at the station.'

'I think not, luscious thing. Lash out a smidgen of Drysdale's advance on a tin of emulsion.'

'How do you know Drysdale gave me an advance?'

'You've just told me.'

'Shoot.'

'Rent up to date by Monday, if you please, sweet thing.'

I was still kicking myself (metaphorically) and the drifts of paper shavings (literally) when Annie came in with two china mugs in her hands and a large shiny carrier dangling by its silken rope handles over one forearm.

'I thought you might like a cup of coffee.'

'Cheers.'

Thrusting my chair back, I crossed my ankles on the desk and waited.

Annie put the bag on the desk top. Everything about it, from the thick stiffness of its plastic sides to the bold blocks of its primary colours, screamed 'expensive'. My comments were plainly invited.

I was in a bitchy mood. I ignored the damn bag. One lousy mug of coffee and cream wasn't enough to bribe me into the role of girlish confidante.

Annie perched on the visitor's chair and sipped at her own black coffee. 'How are you getting on with the donkey business?'

I filled her in up to date.

'Are you sure it was Judy that phoned Tina?'

'Her body turned up here. That's a bit too close for coincidence.'

Annie took another mouthful of coffee and winced. She really hates it black. 'I'm not saying she didn't come down to Judy's house. She almost certainly did, given the stuff you found scattered over the utility room floor. But are you sure it was *Judy* asked her to come? Your redhead was plainly searching for something in that house. Isn't it possible that somebody who knew Tina was related to Judy asked her to go down and do the same?'

It was. And I hadn't thought of it. So I argued. 'What could the Parkers have that's worth killing for? Their house looks like it's been hit by a blitz squad from the Salvation Army.'

'I would have thought Judy Parker was the best person to answer that one. Did you ask her where she was going that Friday?'

'No. I couldn't. Not without admitting I'd been snooping around her kitchen and seen the sandwiches.'

'Suppose not.' Apparently thinking of something else, Annie casually moved the carrier a fraction with one finger. 'So where do you go from here?'

'I left a message on George Spinnaker's answerphone asking if he'll see me.'

'Who?'

'Alan Kersey's solicitor. The bloke they put away for the Des

Parker job. Well, Edwin Woolley job to be exact,' I corrected myself. 'Parker's assault seems to have been the also-ran on the charge sheet. Which I suppose seemed fair enough at the time, since it was Woolley who ended up dead; although I'm not sure he got the worst of the deal in the end.'

Our minds shot off on the same tangent. A phenomenon confirmed by Annie's next question. 'How is your father?'

'All right. I guess. Haven't been over lately.' And wouldn't be welcome if I went, I nearly added. Instead I bounced a question back at her. 'How's your computer bod? Tonight still on?'

She abandoned the coffee immediately and scrabbled in the carrier. From layers of tissue, she dragged out a blouse and shook it out for my inspection. 'What do you think? Be honest.'

If someone says 'Be honest', it's a pretty fair bet they really want me to lie like hell. 'It's lovely.'

It was, actually: black voile heavily encrusted with jet beads in swirling patterns.

Annie held it to her shoulders. 'How do I look?'

Like a short, plump, mousy woman in an expensive top.

'Terrific,' I said.

It's amazing how easily even the most hard-headed of us can persuade our normally logical brains to accept the lies we want to hear.

With something that might have been a blush, Annie refolded the blouse. 'Thanks, I wasn't quite sure. I didn't want to look like mutton dressed as lamb.'

'You're not mutton,' I protested. 'You're not that much older than me. I sure haven't finished my gambolling and frisking phase yet.'

'I don't suppose you ever will. Anyway, I'm thirty-two.'

'How old's what's-his-face?'

'Jonathon. He's forty-one.'

'Who divorced who?'

'She dumped him. Said he was boring.'

'Is he?'

The indignant denial that she was about to spit at me was forestalled by the trill of the phone.

'I'll leave you to it.'

'See you, Annie. And good luck for tonight. Vetch's International, Grace Smith speaking.'

It was George Spinnaker. He'd see me now. 'If that is convenient to you?'

'Very convenient. Thanks.'

Why I should expect a retired solicitor to be tall, silver-haired and distinguished, I don't know. Media brainwashing, I guess.

George was short and broad-shouldered with the hair-cut and muscles of a boxer.

'Deed-poll job,' he said when I asked about his unusual surname. 'My father had some unpronounceable Estonian name. Changed it so us kids could grow up to be proper little English gentlemen.'

'And did you?' I asked. I was perched on a stool in his out-house watching as he heaved barrels of semi-fermented beer mush around.

'Not so's you'd notice. We didn't sound posh enough, you see. At school we learnt to speak like everyone else; which, unfortunately for Dad, meant dead common. Then we'd go home and be surrounded by aunties and uncles all babbling away like half-baked extras from *Rasputin*. Accent still counts in this country, however much they try to tell you class barriers have been stormed. That's how Alan Kersey managed to get by.'

'How's that?'

Drawing up a barrel, he sat opposite me. I could smell sweat and peppermints.

'He was a teacher, local school. Taught history and a bit of physical education. But he did it with modulated vowels and chisel-sharp consonants. A real class act, in fact. If you'd have met him, you'd have put him down as minor public school; second degree at a good university; undistinguished academic career since. Bit of a plodder.'

'And?'

'And you'd be right. But what you wouldn't have picked up is the two prison sentences.'

'For?'

'Passing dodgy cheques the first time. Some scam involving fake insurance claims the next.'

'And the school employed him!'

'Passed the time off as working overseas. Right accent, see? You don't call an accent like that a liar. It's just not cricket. Basically he was a loser who wanted to be rich with as little effort as possible on his part.'

'So how did he graduate to murder?'

'I've no idea.'

'He didn't tell you?'

'If he had it would count as client confidence. But he didn't. Fact is, he pleaded not guilty.'

'Were you expecting the guilty verdict?'

'Do you expect the toast to fall butter side down?'

'That obvious?'

'Our best chance would have been if the jury had consisted of twelve lobotomy victims.'

I had the distinct impression George was enjoying himself. At my expense.

He relented. 'Come inside the house. It's Jo's baking day. Gingerbread and fresh scones if we're in luck.'

I followed him through to a lounge where the scent of lemon polish was competing with the warm aroma of a bakery in overdrive. Bliss.

'Take a seat,' George invited. Raising his voice, he yelled, 'Any chance of tea, Jo?'

From this angle I had a clearer view of the back garden. It

looked like a feature from *Homes and Gardens*: all smooth turf, mature flowerbeds and cunningly placed sundials and fountains in aged stone.

'Nice place,' I said admiringly. 'You the gardener?'

'No, that's Jo's territory too. Jo's the artistic one in this partnership. I'm the intellectual slob.'

Demanding growls were issuing from my stomach as my nose detected sugar, spices and white flour. Hog heaven was approaching!

To cover the noise, I said quickly: 'Tell me about the Woolley robbery. I've only seen a few newspaper cuttings. He was in a taxi, right?'

'Local mini-cab. He'd been picked up at home and was on his way to the station to catch the London train. He was intending to call in at one of the London auction houses.'

'Buying?'

'No. He wanted a valuation on a statue.'

'Valuable?'

'According to Mrs Woolley the Major expected to receive in the neighbourhood of a hundred grand for it at auction.'

'Nice neighbourhood! I take it that was what Kersey was after?'

'Since he never confided in me, I couldn't say with any truthfulness what my client's intentions were that day.'

'Solicitor-speak.'

'One is required to acquire a smattering,' he said in a non-apologetic tone.

'Did your client know about the statue?'

'He certainly knew it existed. Indeed, it was he who drew the Major's attention to the possible value. A fact that the prosecution made much of at the time of the trial, I'm afraid. You wonderful creature . . .'

The last remark was directed at the pusher of the laden tea trolley that was now gliding across the carpet towards us.

'This is Jo. Jo, Miss Smith.'

'Grace.' I extended a hand. 'Does that lot taste as good as it looks?'

'So they tell me. Never touch refined food myself. Got to keep this in trim.' Two palms slapped over a stomach that was flat as a board. 'I cook for this fat slob. Don't I, lover?'

They exchanged a look; a low, lazy, complacent smile between those who knew they were loved.

I don't do many tea-parties, so I wasn't quite sure of the etiquette. Picking up the flower-patterned pot, I said brightly: 'Shall I be mother?'

'Please do. After all, you're the only one of us qualified,' Jo murmured. 'Give me a shout if you need any more hot water.'

The jeans-clad bottom was as flat as the stomach, I noted with envy as it sauntered out of the room.

I dragged my eyes away. And found George's eyes fixed on me. 'Gorgeous, isn't he?'

'I'll say.' A Tom Cruise lookalike, but six inches taller.

'Help yourself,' George invited, passing me a plate to make it clear that this invitation was restricted to the pastries.

I'd been properly brought up. 'Bread and butter first; cake second,' my mother's voice whispered in my head.

'Kersey,' George said, by-passing bread and heaving the largest slab of gingerbread on to his own plate, 'was undoubtedly involved in the robbery, although whether he killed Edwin Woolley is open to debate.'

'Debate,' I invited. 'What put him in the frame?'

George touched thumb to little finger:

'One: a car the same model and colour as Kersey's was seen at the murder spot ten minutes prior to the time of the murder.'

The thumb nudged the ring finger:

'Two: two men, one resembling Kersey, were fiddling with the car, apparently trying to fix it.

'Three: Kersey was originally thought to have been the victim of a bungled house-breaking. He'd been beaten senseless with one of those gadgets that they use to immobilize car steering wheels and his house had been thoroughly turned over. However, when they got him to hospital some bright copper checked his record and found out about the porridge. Then they do a forensic check on Kersey's car, and lo and behold, they've got a blood and tissue match for Woolley and Parker from traces in the boot.'

'The murder weapon?' I interrupted.

'Seems likely. It's probable that they threw it into the boot after the robbery and then disposed of it as soon as they were safely away from the crime scene. It was never found.

'Four: other items were taken from both victims: watches, wallets, a gold bracelet from Parker and the Major's wedding ring. The last item was found under the carpet in Kersey's car. Having been dropped there when he gave the Major a lift a few days earlier, according to my client's explanation.

'Five: Kersey had booked a cabin on the ferry sailing for Santander in northern Spain that Saturday. This was news to the school since he'd just sent in a doctor's certificate laying him off with stress and depression.

'Six.' He waggled a thick thumb at me. 'And this one was the real killer. The prosecution turned up some expert from a Madrid dealers who'd had a long telephone conversation with a guy on sixteenth-century West African bronzes a week before Woolley was killed. Guess what a check on Kersey's telephone calls turned up?'

'The Madrid number. Couldn't he have been calling on Woolley's behalf? Getting another valuation?'

'That was his story. "Testing the waters in an international market" I think were his exact words. But the Madrid angle was too much for the jury to swallow. Why Spain, for heaven's sake? Woolley had no Spanish connections. A New York or Tokyo dealer would have made more sense for price comparisons.'

'So how'd Kersey talk his way out of that one?'

'He didn't. In fact he more or less implied he wouldn't

expect a suburban jury to understand the subtle niceties of the antique trade. Frankly Kersey didn't make a good impression on the jury. He was arrogant. Too arrogant to take counsel's advice and stay off the stand.'

'How did he explain the blood traces in the car?'

'He said he'd suspected the car had been moved the morning of the robbery. But since it was back in the garage when he went to get it for work, he hadn't bothered to report the matter to the police.'

'Was that feasible?'

'Just about, I suppose. He rented a place in Pound Lane; it's not there now. They built over it a few years back when they put up the new supermarket. Anyhow, Kersey garaged his car in a shed a short distance from the cottage. If he was a heavy sleeper I suppose it was possible the car could have been moved without waking him. But the jury didn't buy it.'

'Did you?'

'I'm required to believe what my client tells me.'

'Did Kersey live with anyone?'

'No. He was divorced. Wife went back to Australia years ago. A couple of one-night stands came forward after the case. You know the type: "My Night with the Taxi Murderer". But no one able to provide a convincing alibi for the time of the murder.'

Abandoning the bread and butter, I started making inroads on the scones, using my tongue tip to scoop up oozes of cream and jam.

'Who found Kersey?'

'Someone from the school went round to get a cupboard key and discovered him. According to medical myth, no one expected him to last the night.'

'Was it his own car lock they used to beat him unconscious?'

Deep in another slice of gingerbread, George grunted: 'Hh . . . hh.'

So it probably hadn't been premeditated. Whoever had belted Kersey had grabbed up a weapon from the spot.

'I take it it was assumed to be a case of thieves falling out?'

'Hh . . . hh.'

'Who was the other bloke?'

George broke surface. 'That, my dear Miss Smith, is the sixty-four-thousand-ecu question.'

'Kersey refused to grass?'

'Kersey claimed to be entirely ignorant of the whole sordid business, if you'll recall. Stupid tactic. Partial culpability would have been far more astute.'

'How'd you mean?'

George shrugged. 'We'd have fallen back on the time-honoured tradition in such cases and tried to dump everything in the other party's lap. Of course *his* counsel would have been trying to do exactly the same to Kersey.'

'What do you think Kersey's motive for holding back was? Loyalty or fear?'

George considered, masticating a scone top before replying. 'To be honest, I don't know. Had you asked me at the time of the trial, I'd have said a combination of fear and greed. The statue was never found. And the consensus of opinion was that Kersey was keeping his mouth shut in return for a share of the spoils.'

'What do you think now?'

He gave me an odd look, then said obliquely, 'Now, Miss Smith, I think you should reconsider your involvement in this matter.'

'Why?'

'Because Kersey was motivated by hatred. It fed on him for years, gnawing and sucking out every shred of decent emotion that might have been left. It sustained him, Miss Smith. Gave him hope, a future, a reason to survive.'

A large lump of scone dough had stuck fast in my chest. Determined not to be rattled, I poured us both a refill.

'You've seen him since his conviction?'

'Yes.' He swirled a teaspoon, sending eddies of brown liquid into the saucer. 'Kersey was released on parole four months ago.'

Unconsciously, I looked over my shoulder.

'He's not lurking in my sideboard, Miss Smith. He was released to the care of a hospice.' The tea slid down his muscular gullet in one smooth movement. 'Alan Kersey is dying. Stomach cancer.'

'How long?'

'Days.'

'What did he ask you to do?'

'How did you know he . . .'

George trailed off as he realized he'd been suckered. Vetch wasn't the only one who could stoop to that one.

'It can't be client confidence now. You're retired.'

'There are worse things than being struck off.' He clasped his knees. 'Do you believe in hell?'

'I'm not sure.'

'Neither was I at your age. But I'll tell you something. The older you get, the more you'll believe. You have to. Because you don't want to believe this is all there is. You want to consider the probability that there's something beyond. And if you embrace the idea of heaven, then you have to let the other side have its place in the scheme of things.'

'So?'

'Alan Kersey is going to hell. But he assures me he'll find some way of coming back to deal with anyone who attempts to interfere with his revenge. And I believe him, Miss Smith. Oh yes, I believe him.'

I'm not often silenced. But this was one occasion when I couldn't think of a single flip reply.

Whatever I said wasn't going to change George's mind. I didn't have much option really. 'Do you think Kersey would talk to me?'

'He may. Excuse me.'

Lifting the gently trilling telephone, he said: 'Spinnaker.'

A tinny, disjointed, sexless voice crackled on the other end of the receiver.

'I see. Thank you for letting me know.' Replacing the phone, he turned back to me. 'If you want to speak to Alan Kersey, Miss Smith, I suggest you hurry. He's just been given the last rites.'

CHAPTER 12

At least George's car lived up to my fantasies regarding the lifestyle of retired solicitors.

He drove a Jaguar XJ6. Not new, but still sleek and powerful enough to create the subliminal impression that we were sticking two fingers up at the drivers we swept past.

'Is it far?'

'Ten minutes at this speed.'

'Wouldn't velocity be a better word?'

'You sound like Jo. He's always giving me grief about my driving. But a man should have one vice in his life, don't you think?'

'At least,' I agreed. 'Preferably more.'

'Why are you shouting?'

'Am I? Sorry.' I was used to riding in rattletraps where serious lung-power was needed to carry over the engine noise.

'How come you're still involved with Kersey if you're retired?'

'Alan didn't want to "break in" a new brief, as he put it. He wrote to me from prison, asked me if I'd tidy up a couple of loose ends before he died.'

'Why'd you agree if he puts the wind up you?'

The car dropped smoothly into third gear. 'Vanity,' George said. 'It got up my nose that I had never managed to get to the bottom of the Woolley business. I think I was hoping for some kind of death-bed confession. And to be blunt, I didn't know he was loony-tunes until it was too late.'

He turned the car inland, gliding past flat green fields still flooded with pools of low-lying water and entangled with twists of overflowing drainage canals. There was no sign of life out here beyond the odd huddle of stoic sheep.

The Peace Hospice had been built around the nucleus of a substantial farmhouse. The original turn-of-the-century red-brick building now fronted a discreet complex of modern one-storey wings.

George was known. With a nod at the receptionist he made his way through the house and down the left-hand wing.

I trotted after him along a corridor flanked on the outer side by single rooms and on the inner by arched windows giving on to an internal courtyard of lawns, fountains and flowerbeds. The whole place had the quiet, well-maintained air of an efficiently run hotel.

'Is this private?' I asked George's hurrying back.

'It's a charity. Why?'

'It seems a bit on the plush side for the NHS.'

'Too good for a convicted murderer, you mean?'

Well, it was certainly a better deal than Judy Parker had got in Nightingale Ward.

'Do they know about him in here?'

'The administration and medical staff do. They take a certain number of prison referrals in return for a small amount of government funding. As to the rest . . . only if he chose to tell them. This is it.'

The lightest rap brought a patter of footsteps across the carpet.

A charge nurse opened the door and stood back. 'Come in, Mr Spinnaker. And . . .?'

'This is Miss Smith. An acquaintance.'

'Is it OK to . . .' I nodded at the cot-style bed.

'Of course. Although I'm afraid you won't find him very lucid. He's pretty much in a morphine sleep most of the time now.'

Death had started with colours; draining them from him like

water pouring from a bucket. He was grey: skin, eyebrows, hair had taken on a uniform tone. The only movement was the barely perceptible lift of the crisp white sheet over his chest.

'Mr Kersey?'

There was no flicker beneath the eyelids.

Bending near the bedhead, the nurse said coaxingly, 'Alan, you've visitors. Come on, mate, don't you want to say hi?'

Slowly the eyes opened and slid across their sockets to focus on me. It was like watching a clockwork toy whose spring had barely enough power left to sustain movement.

'Hi. My name's Grace Smith. Some people call me Smithie.'

I caught George's eye and signalled for help. I didn't know what else to say. What I was doing felt like a terrible intrusion.

Moving a collection of local guidebooks and maps out of the way, George moved into Kersey's sight line. 'Good afternoon, Alan. I've brought someone to meet you. Hope you don't mind? Miss Smith is a private detective. She's investigating a death.'

Something flickered within Kersey. A fire that had nearly died flared in one final, brief burst of life. A hand closed round my wrist like a steel handcuff.

It was all I could do to stop myself wrenching it free. The flesh was already cold and dead, as if it had spent a few hours road-testing its eventual resting place.

'Dead? Tell me. Tell me.'

He didn't seem to have enough time left for the full story, so I gave him the abridged version: 'Someone slit the throat of a donkey called Marilyn Monroe on the night a girl called Tina got the same treatment. Tina was Des Parker's niece. He was the taxi driver who you supposedly smashed over the skull. I think you know what's going on. I'd like to know too.'

His grip was tightening. My fingers were growing numb. The other hand scrabbled claw-like at his stomach as a spash of pain contorted his features. It brought into sudden relief a tracery of old white scar tissue that stretched across the left-hand side of his face. Without warning, he started to giggle.

'It's started. Oh yes, it's started.'

The laughter became higher and shriller; like a girl's. Icy water trickled down my spine. George Spinnaker was right. The man was quite mad.

His breath took on a rasping sound as pain gripped him again. The nurse gently checked the connection on the IV drip in his other arm and adjusted something. 'I think it might be best if you both left now.'

'You go on,' George instructed me. 'I'll meet you outside.'

I didn't argue. There was nothing to be gained here. Alan Kersey was beyond persuasion, reason, bribes or threats. Whatever it was he'd set in motion had gathered momentum and taken on a life of its own whilst Kersey's slipped away.

Stepping through a set of French doors into the garden, I perched myself on the edge of a pool, where I could contemplate the bare bottom of a mock-marble Aphrodite. Against her carved cheek she was cradling a large conch shell that sent a gentle trickle of water into the dish at her feet.

Within the splashing water, plump golden fish darted and rippled between waving weeds. Three-fingered, I flicked small waves across the surface, watching them breaking and turning on transparent fins as the vibrations reached them.

A shoal of mouths broke the surface, pursed lips opening and closing on alien air.

'You're not supposed to feed them, you know.'

Snatching my hand back with a quick denial, I faced the owner of the schoolmistress voice. And blinked.

She was about my height, with paper-white skin and a pair of pale-blue eyes recessed on either side of a nose that would have given a bald eagle an inferiority complex.

Dressed from throat to ankle in a flowing robe patterned in a riot of colours, she was leaning on a seven-foot wooden staff, topped with a carved skull. As she moved, the sunlight caught the silky material in the dress, causing the patterns to change shape like a kaleidoscope. The whole lot was topped off by a huge turban in the same shades.

'I call it my ethnic psychedelic look. What do you think?'

'Armani eat your heart out!'

'Right on.'

Using the staff for support, she eased herself down beside me.

Close up I could see that the shaft was decorated with a mélange of elongated faces: high-cheek-boned and large-toothed skulls with slyly secretive eyes.

'Where'd you get it?' I asked, touching the polished stem.

'Car boot sale. One previous owner: a very careful voodoo priest.' She rested it against the stone coping. 'Probably mass-produced in Birmingham if the truth were known. But it suits me. Can't make an individual statement with a Zimmer frame, can you? What do you think I used to do for a living?'

I hadn't the foggiest idea. But to humour her, I fell back on my first impression. 'Headmistress?'

'Oh blast. What gave me away?'

'Your voice.'

'How very depressing.'

'Sorry.'

'Hardly your fault, my dear. I shall have to redouble my efforts to embrace eccentricity before I die. I'm Dorothea Springle, by the way.'

'Grace Smith. Some people call me Smithie.'

'Do they? Oh, well done. Nobody ever showed the slightest inclination to call me "Springy" or even "Dotty". My life has been a paean to twin-sets, tweed suits and not shocking the horses. So I've decided to make up for lost time.'

Whilst we were talking she'd extracted a twist of paper from a slit in her robe and unscrewed it. Leaning back over the water, she shook out a cloud of breadcrumbs.

'I thought you weren't supposed—' I began. 'Oh right, power to the revolution.'

'A small gesture each day. Now what else can I do to rock the Establishment?'

There didn't seem to be a lot of scope around here. 'Pick the flowers?' I suggested.

'Did that last week.'

I was stumped. For a few moments we both sat in silence, contemplating the garden. Seduced by the sheltered warmth, the early tulips had spread their petals out so far they looked like exotic daisies.

Dorothea stroked a curling bloom the colour of ripe peaches. 'Wonderful the way they hang on. Just when you think they must fall off today, they close up and survive to see another sunrise. A bit like the rest of us, really.'

'How long have you been here?'

'Eight months, off and on.'

A male voice yelled from the open French door, its owner unseen behind the sparkling glass: 'Dorothea, you old bat, you're keeping us waiting!'

'Dear me, the cocktail hour already. Will you join us?'

She struggled to her feet, using the staff for leverage. There was still no sign of George, so I followed her back through the French doors and into a lounge in the main building.

A woman, plump and elderly with frizzy clumps of ginger hair, was seated at a card table. As Dorothea and I made our way across the room, a wheelchair shot through the opposite doorway.

'Name your poison,' called the driver, manoeuvring with one hand whilst the other held a tray in place over the handles.

Without waiting for a reply, he picked up the first glass and handed it over. 'Double tomato juice, Dorothea.'

'Cheers.'

I was amused to see that the glass was decorated with a

cherry tomato on a cocktail stick and a small paper parasol. Dorothea made the introductions:

'This is Edna and Jules. This is Smithie.'

'Pleased to meet you,' Jules smiled, bobbing a head as smooth as a boiled egg. 'Can I fix you something? Tomato? Carrot? Apple juice on the rocks, shaken not stirred?'

'I'll take a rain-check, thanks.'

'Who are you visiting?' Edna asked, cutting and shuffling a pack of cards.

'Alan Kersey.'

'He's popular all of a sudden,' Jules commented, edging his chair up to the table. 'Are you family?'

'No.' I found a business card and passed it over. 'I was hoping to ask him some questions about a case. But it looks like I'm too late.'

Dorothea plucked the card from his fingers. 'A private detective. How wonderful. I think that's what I'll come back as next time.'

'Oh, Dorothea, you were wanting to be a trapeze artist last week,' Edna commented, 'with a young, virile Latin-American lover with skin the texture of warm silk, wasn't it?'

'I've changed my mind. This sounds more fun. What are you investigating and can we help?'

I told them about Marilyn, glossing over the more unpleasant details. 'I know Kersey's connected, but I don't know how. You could help best by telling me about him.'

'Not much to tell really,' Dorothea said. 'And I saw that card come off the bottom, Edna.'

'Just testing, my lovely,' Edna said calmly, collecting in the hands and reshuffling. 'Keeps himself to himself, does Alan. You thought he was a teacher, didn't you, Dorothea?'

'Mmm, educated but dull with it. He used to go out a fair bit when he first came; bus stops down the lane every hour if you can believe the timetable. Hired a car once, and Jules gave him a lift into town a couple of times.'

'When was that?'

Jules wrinkled his forehead, sending wave patterns over the tightly stretched skin. They were the only lines on his face; he was probably younger than me. 'First time must have been about six weeks ago. I was on my way home; I only come in here for respite care, give my mum a break, and Alan asked me to drop him in town. It was cold enough to freeze the bum off a baboon, so I guess he didn't fancy hanging around the bus stop.'

'You didn't see where he went?'

'No. He just asked me to drop him by the post office. Said he'd get a mini-cab back. He had some letters to post, I remember that.'

'What about the second time?'

'Monday, three weeks back. He wasn't getting about too good by then. I wanted to go along, but he blew me out, told me to stay put in the car. Came back about quarter of an hour later. Seemed pretty pleased with himself over something. Can't say why, though. Like Edna said, he's a closed-arsed tyke.'

'Don't be so disgusting. I'd never use such language,' Edna protested, rearranging her cards. Her hands were brownspotted and swollen with age, the gold wedding ring embedded in the skin of her sausage-like fingers. 'I daresay he was looking forward to seeing his friends.'

'Kersey has friends?' I queried. It was the first I'd heard of any.

'Surprised us too,' Jules agreed. 'But he seemed very keen to see them. Even paid the ward maid to fix tea for them in the patients' kitchen.'

'Did they come by car?'

'Well the old girl did, certainly,' Dorothea said. 'She could hardly have walked from the bus stop with those legs. Varicose veins,' she informed me. 'Terrible case. Must spend a fortune on elasticated stockings.'

'Did you catch a name?'

No one had. 'They went straight through to his room. All together.'

'Except the girl,' Edna chipped in. 'She was late. Came flying in just after they'd gone through.'

'Twenties, short blonde hair, anorexic-thin?' I hazarded.

'That's her.'

'And you've never seen her since?'

Three heads shook.

There was a large television set standing in the corner of the lounge, and several of the rooms we'd passed on the way to Kersey's had had portables on bedside tables. Why the police had bothered putting out that early picture of Tina was beyond me. They might as well have transmitted a shot of Minnie Mouse.

'Are we helping?' Dorothea enquired.

'Yes. You are.' At least I now knew why Tina had come down from London. And I was damn certain Judy had sent her here, whatever denials she might be flinging around. 'Tell me about the others. The woman, how old?'

Estimates varied between 'ancient' and mid seventies. 'And overweight,' Edna chipped in. 'You'd think she'd have more sense with those legs.'

'What about the blokes?'

'One medium, the other shortish but chunky. Both oldish,' Jules offered.

Down her beak Dorothea shot him a look that must have turned many a first-year pupil to a pillar of salt. 'They were younger than me, you cheeky devil. No more than mid fifties.'

'I don't suppose you heard any names there either?'

They hadn't. Nor had they noticed what cars the visitors were driving.

'Friday's a popular day for visiting,' Edna explained. 'The car park was packed.'

'Doesn't mess up our nearest and dearest's weekends if they

can combine the duty call with late-night shopping at the hypermarket,' Dorothea remarked.

'How long were they here?'

'Hour. Hour and a half?' It was Jules who had spoken; now he looked round for confirmation. The other two nodded.

'They left about half past seven,' Dorothea said.

'Oh, it's lovely to have friends visiting when you're a bit low. Makes all the difference.' Edna was drifting. 'Seemed to cheer Alan up no end, didn't it, having his friends all making a special effort to come visit like that?'

'You don't know they were friends,' Dorothea interrupted. 'Could have been creditors for all you know, come to make sure he wasn't going to try taking it with him.'

Edna had a very literal mind. 'That's silly, Dorothea. What would he be doing giving little presents to creditors?'

The other two turned glimmering eyes on the unfortunate Edna.

'Presents?' Dorothea said, her voice as silkily smooth as the scalp her rapidly descending turban was revealing.

'*Little* presents?' Jules repeated.

A tide of colour swept up from the neck of Edna's padded nylon housecoat. 'I was just, you know, taking a bit of a walk before supper.'

'Outside Alan's window?' Dorothea asked, her elegant eyebrows lifted in a sceptical arch. 'Along that very narrow pathway? The one that's so wet and slimy at this time of year?'

'The one,' Jules added, 'that's so overhung with bushes one positively expects to come across a lost tribe in there?'

'Oh, don't exaggerate,' the unfortunate Edna protested. 'It's not that bad, you know it's not.'

'And you looked in Alan Kersey's window, did you?' I broke in.

'Not looked. Glanced.'

'And he was dishing out presents, was he? What kind of presents?'

'Little ones,' Jules murmured, *sotto voce*.

'Yes. Well they were little. Little boxes, wrapped up in shiny paper and that gold curly ribbon. He had them on his bedside table and they were all to choose. Like a lucky dip, see.'

'Long glance,' Jules hissed.

'It was *not*.' A suspicion of moisture was forming in Edna's protuberant eyes and running along the black-pencilled line on the inner lid. Edna was bottom of the pecking order in this pack.

Sliding an arm round her shoulder, I gave her a squeeze and planted a quick kiss on the rounded cheek. 'Cheers, Edna. You're a darling.'

Edna shot a triumphant smirk at her card partners. But they'd already lost interest. Their attention was fixed on the hall that we'd crossed to enter the lounge.

During our talk I'd been vaguely aware of people coming and going across this space. At first the traffic had been two-way, but over the past few minutes it had become concentrated in one direction. Staff were being drawn down Kersey's corridor like balls of fluff being sucked into a vacuum cleaner nozzle.

Several other patients had joined us in the lounge. Now they gave up any pretence of reading, embroidering or whatever, and sat in silence watching the entrance to the corridor.

A few seconds later George emerged. Catching my eye through the open lounge door, he gave a slight nod.

The room let out its breath in one collective sigh.

'Game over,' Jules said.

CHAPTER 13

Alan Kersey died thirty minutes later.

Before they'd let me go, the card-playing trio made me promise to call again.

'It's not that we like your company,' Jules said frankly. 'It's just that we're all incurably nosy.'

The sky had turned a dull grey by the time George and I stepped outside; as if someone had dipped a paintbrush in dirty water and swept it from horizon to horizon.

The day's warmth hadn't gone from the air yet, but I was aware of feeling cold somewhere deep down inside my bones. George must have felt the same way. Whilst I struggled with my seat-belt, he flipped the car heater to 'full'.

'What will happen now?' I asked. 'About Kersey?'

'The usual. He'd already made the funeral arrangements. It won't be fancy.'

'What happens to his estate?'

'I can't discuss my client's affairs.'

'Why the hell not? Who's going to complain? There's only us in here, unless you've got squatters in the boot. I won't tell if you don't. Is there something iffy about the will?'

'No. It's quite straightforward. He left everything to the hospice. There's not much, a few hundred pounds probably, if I waive my fee.'

'Nothing to his family?'

'He had no one. Apart from the ex-wife who dumped him years back.'

'What about friends?'

'Not that I'm aware of. He is – was – a bit of a loner.'

'He had four visitors last week. Even gave them presents.'

'Then obviously I am mistaken.'

Had he always had that iron control of his features? Or had years of being 'economical with the truth' in magistrates' courts, in accordance with his clients' instructions, eradicated all the nervous tics and muscle spasms that give most of us away?

He knew who the four were. *I* knew he knew. He knew I knew.

'Oh come *on*, George. You can't really believe Kersey is going to pop back from Hades to put the frighteners on if you tell me.'

'I gave my word.'

'He's dead. It doesn't count any more.'

Some idiot in a black Porsche was trying to mate with our exhaust pipe. With two wheels over the central line and his headlights in our rear-view mirror, he was indicating that he found George's habit of driving a mere thirty miles above the speed limit an unreasonable obstacle to his ambition to break the land speed record.

For the next few minutes George was occupied in steering along the twisting road, trying to avoid a rear-end collision. Finally we came to a few hundred yards of straight tarmac, giving our road-hog the chance to blast past.

'I always hope I'll find the pillock wrapped around a tree on the next bend,' George remarked. 'But I never do.'

'I have noted your attempt to change the subject. Now please can we get back to Kersey's four visitors? Who were they?'

'Why should I tell you?'

'Why shouldn't you?'

He considered this one whilst we waited to turn right on to the main road.

'You understand I have no way of knowing who Kersey's

visitors were,' George said, tucking in between a white transit van and a Mercedes.

'But you can make an educated guess?'

'When I agreed to represent Kersey again, he asked me to trace four people for him. "Trace" as in locate their current addresses. I never made contact with any of these people.'

'Judy Parker being one of these traces, I take it?'

'Desmond Parker actually,' George corrected me.

'He's dead.'

'So I understand. However, Kersey's request was made approximately four months ago when he was granted parole, and at that time Desmond Parker was still alive. And living in the same house the Parkers had occupied at the time of the murd— At the time of Major Woolley's death.'

That made sense, I suppose. Any correspondence Kersey sent to Des would have been opened by Judy. 'What about the other three?'

'Two. He changed his mind on the last one. Said not to bother, Barken had already been in touch. As far as the other two go: one was Major Woolley's widow; Simla. She's living in an old people's home now. Or residential care complex, as we must learn to call them.'

The sky artist had redipped his brush and was now painting the heavens a deeper shade of grey. In front of us, towards the east, it was already night, the darkness broken by scattered town lights that looked like broken jewellery on scrunched black velvet.

'What about the last address?'

'Olly Colville. Works in a garage in High Wycombe.'

'What was he to Kersey?'

'I didn't ask.'

Prising that much out of him had taken the rest of the ride to his house. As we pulled in, a motorbike suddenly roared from the side of the house. Jo slowed briefly, raised four fingers in our direction, then sped away.

'I hate it when he rides that thing. It's so dangerous,' George remarked, dousing the ignition and headlights simultaneously. 'And he looks so tasty in those leathers it's a pity to waste them on the philistines at the Red Hen.'

The Hen was a pretentious eatery about a mile from town, which specialized in 'food-speak' menus that promised a gastronomic treat and delivered portions that wouldn't have satisfied a slightly peckish gerbil.

'Jo work there then?' I asked. More because I was reluctant to leave all this plush luxury and get back into my own rattletrap than from any real interest in Jo's career.

'Part-time. At least it's supposed to be part-time. He's off tonight. They must have given him a call. The chef's out of it most of the time.'

'Drink?'

'Wacky baccy. Or worse if you ask me. Take a tip: don't eat there.'

'I can't afford to.' Reluctantly I pushed the heavy door open. It swung out, letting the rapidly chilling night air flow over my face. 'Can I have a copy of those addresses?'

George sighed heavily. 'If you must.'

'I must,' I confirmed.

'Wait here.'

He left me in the Jag whilst he went into the house. Sliding into the driver's seat, I held the wheel at arm's-length and waggled it like a kid on the dodgems. Oh yes, I could definitely get used to being rich.

I tried the glove compartment and found a metal case containing half a dozen of George's business cards. I'd just pocketed a couple when he returned with a single sheet of paper.

'Here. If there's any comeback, I'd prefer to be kept out of it.'

'Wouldn't everybody?' I reflected, climbing back into my own rust-bucket. 'This Barken bloke. Didn't catch a first name, did you?'

Stooping to the partially open window, George winced visibly as the engine jolted and ground into life. 'Billy. "Trust Billy to scent the trough first" were Kersey's exact words.'

Bumping back towards the sea front, the noise inside my own jalopy seemed to have magnified a thousand times since I was last in it: everything rattled, banged, squeaked or vibrated.

I felt low. All those reminders of my mortality had depressed me. It's generally accepted that at times like these one reflects on how little one has done for the world. But I found myself musing on how little the world had done for *me*. Not very altruistic, I know, but much more satisfying. Who wants to be the next Mother Theresa anyway? Fantasizing on the possibilities of being the next Ivana Trump can work up a perfectly wonderful glow of envy and greed.

In this spirit of maudlin self-pity, I parked up in a side street and wandered down to Marine Terrace.

The breeze blowing in from the sea was more noticeable over here. Resting my arms on the top of the balustrade, I leant there staring out into the blackness and listening to the hungry rush of water against the shingle. It was a large, flat beach this, the sand gently sloping for miles beneath the cold, yellowing sea. There was none of the spectacular booming and crashing you get in rockier coastal waters.

With my chin on my forearms, I let my eyes become accustomed to the dark. After a while I could pick out individual features: the lumpy square of tarpaulin-covered deckchairs, the low rock wall of the oblong paddling pool filled with glinting sea-water that would be swept out and cleaned at the next high tide, the pegs of the corral where the donkey chain stood each day.

Below my feet I caught a sudden muffled groan followed by a suppressed cry of triumph coming from one of the canvas beach huts.

A claw of loneliness clutched at my heart and twisted hard. Normally I can manage quite well on my own; in fact, I prefer it. But tonight, I wanted company. A quick review of my options revealed I didn't have any. Normally I go round to Annie's place at times like this; when she is otherwise engaged I'm friendless. I guess I really should do something about that one of these days.

I was just toying with the idea of going round to Pepi's when the pungent whiff of fish drifted past my nostrils: battered, deep-fried and swimming in salt and vinegar.

I tracked it to one of the wooden shelters thoughtfully provided by the local council for those who wish to sit and contemplate the sea, the traffic, the clock tower or the roundabout (dependent on which side of the shelter had been chosen).

When I appeared in the open entrance, one hand tightened possessively over the handle of the supermarket shopping trolley containing assorted bags and old newspapers, whilst the other prodded at the open package of chips on her lap.

Sitting on the slatted bench, I remarked that it was growing colder.

'Piss off.'

'Those chips smell good.'

'You can't have none.'

The fingers poking through the holey woollen gloves were black. I'm not noted as a gourmet, but even I have my standards. 'I don't want any, thanks.'

Dragging on the trolley handle, she pulled it sideways, blocking off part of the bench. 'This is my place.'

'Very nice. Did you select it for the view? Or the avant-garde décor?'

'Sod off.'

I can take a hint: this woman did not want to be my bosom chum. Which, judging by the state of the grubby anorak over her drooping chest, was a lucky break. 'Well, this has been nice. We must do it again some time.'

Ducking across the road, I made my way back to the side

road where I'd parked the car, intending to drive it round to Pepi's. But the scent of hot fat and sizzling vinegar was even stronger here where the Chinese takeaway had diversified into English cuisine.

On impulse I went in and ordered cod and chips twice.

'You want sart? Vinegar? Warries?'

'Salt and vinegar. Hold the gherkins.'

'Hokay.'

Stowing the two warm parcels on the passenger seat, I drove round to Drysdale's.

I half expected him to be out living it up at the Electronic Daffodil again, but the house lights were blazing and there was no sign of Colin on duty in the yard.

Drysdale answered on my third ring. He'd changed into brown slacks and a matching tweed waistcoat over a beige shirt. The odour of damp skin and wet hair suggested he'd just got out of the bath.

'You said to report regularly,' I said in answer to the levitation of the wire-brush eyebrows. 'I brought supper,' I added, proffering the parcel.

He stood back, letting me pass him whilst he relocked the door. Things, I reflected, were getting desperate, if I was prepared to spend good money bribing a man twice my age to spend time with me.

'Do you want a plate?'

'Not unless you do.'

'Don't bother.'

We sat in the lounge in companionable silence, scrunching batter and licking greasy fingers. Despite the warm spell, he'd lit a fire in the small grate. A dry log cracked and spat burning fragments on to the tiled hearth. I wriggled my bottom back into the soft depths of the huge armchair. It was a comfortable place: good, solid, well-worn furniture and enough papers and clothing strewn around to make me feel relaxed.

'Want tea?' Drysdale asked when we finally rolled up the polystyrene containers and fat-stained papers.

'Love some.'

He came back two minutes later. There were no china cups and home-made scones here. Two huge mugs of dark liquid were dumped on the hearth.

One mug said: I LOVE DONKEYS; the other had a picture of a donkey's head, grinning with a set of teeth that looked like they'd fit a cart-horse.

'My grandchildren,' Drysdale explained. 'I get a new cup every birthday.'

'How many?'

'Two grandsons; sixty-two birthdays. How old are you?'

'Twenty-eight.'

'Time to be thinking about what you're going to do with your life then.'

'I am doing something with it, thanks very much. I'm a private investigator, remember?'

I hadn't meant to sound snappy, but I was beginning to get feelings of *déjà vu* here. He sounded like my mum agonizing over my failure to snare a 'proper' career and/or suitable husband.

'You won't retire on what that pays.'

Coming from someone whose income relied on four-footed hay processors, I thought that was a bit rich.

'I do OK.'

'If you were doing OK, you'd be sitting in the posh downstairs office in that place of yours, dumping the unpromising cases on someone else and clipping off part of their fee, 'stead of that pint-sized smart aleck with the Mr Spock ears.'

I bristled. 'Who the hell asked you? A donkey string is hardly a flaming Newmarket stud, is it?' I was mad because I knew he was right. For a horrid second after the words left my big mouth, I thought I'd just blown myself off the case.

Draining half his mug, Drysdale said calmly, 'Matier, though. What you got for me? Did you see Tina's aunt?'

I gave him a brief summary of my conversation with Judy and the subsequent visit to the hospice.

'God rest his soul,' Drysdale said quietly when I'd finished.

It took me a minute to click that he was referring to Kersey. I suppose you have to take the charitable viewpoint if you're religious.

'So how does all this fit in with my Marilyn's murder?'

I had to admit I still didn't know. 'I'm certain it *was* Judy who telephoned Tina, whatever she's saying now. She was planning to take that trip to the hospice.'

The evidence had been on the table: sandwiches and a drink. Over the years Judy had grown used to scrimping and saving. Even on this short journey she'd planned to take her own refreshments rather than risk being stuck somewhere and having to spend money in a restaurant or vending machine.

But the symptoms of her approaching heart attack had become sufficiently strong to frighten her into calling a cab to take her to the hospital.

'She could have just passed on the Kersey visit,' I said, drawing my legs up into Drysdale's armchair and rearranging my thoughts out loud. 'But she didn't. In fact, according to Warren, the kid who lives at Tina's last place, Judy was actually prepared to split something fifty-fifty, with her niece, she was so desperate for *someone* to keep that appointment with Kersey.'

Kersey had given them something. 'Little presents', Edna had said.

'Blood money?' Drysdale suggested when I told him about the packages. 'For the widows of two blokes he'd wronged: Parker and this Woolley bloke.'

'He hadn't much to leave, according to his solicitor. A few hundred at most. And I didn't get the impression he'd repented of his sins or any rubbish like that.'

Mentally I was travelling that last journey with Tina. She could have picked up a mini-cab from the station, but she'd barely managed to scrape the train fare together, so my guess was that she'd taken the bus, which would have dropped her on the main road, leaving her to walk the last few hundred yards to the hospice. Hence she'd been later than those who'd come by car.

And after the visit, she'd have made the same journey in reverse. Why had she gone to the house rather than the hospital? Judy must have told her what she intended to do. Perhaps she'd planned to pick up some bits and pieces, nightclothes or something, for Judy.

At any rate she'd gone in through the back door and somebody had pounced, dragging her into the utility room. No, wrong, I corrected myself. They hadn't dragged her. She'd been free enough to swing the handbag as a flail and keep them off. Perhaps they'd made a sound as she came in the back door, giving her just sufficient warning to lash out.

He must have managed to overpower her somehow and . . . and what? I'd come across no sign of blood in my perfunctory examination of the Parker house. He could have knocked her unconscious and carried her out to a car. Wouldn't the neighbours have seen something? Probably not, given the fact that even Judy's closest neighbour hadn't noticed she was missing.

Guilt gave me an admonitory kick up the backside. 'Can I use your phone?'

'It's in the hall.'

Drysdale collected up greasy papers and dirty mugs and conveyed them to the kitchen, whilst I telephoned Magnolia and told her about Judy.

By the time I'd put the receiver down on her flood of self-recriminations and exclamations of horror, the kitchen was empty and the back door was standing open.

He was in the stable, surrounded by a press of ever-hopeful

donkeys. 'No more apples tonight, lads. Sleep tight, eh, don't let the bedding bugs bite.'

Scratching behind Lana's ears, he drew forth a blissful sigh of contentment.

Lounging against the door frame, I watched whilst he repeated the whole performance with the other six.

None of them seemed to mind the audience. In fact, Errol even wandered over and nuzzled a private good night into my chest.

I ran a palm over the warm silkiness of the questing muzzle and received a gummed kiss in return. 'I'd best be going then, Mr Drysdale. I'll try and get back to you again tomorrow. Good night.'

Following me out, he rebolted the stable door. 'You can call us December if you like. Good night then . . .?'

'Smithie,' I reminded him.

'I'm not calling you that. It doesn't sit right. What's wrong with your given name?'

'It doesn't suit me.'

'What is it?'

'Grace.'

'God's favour.'

'Sorry?'

'That's what your name means.'

Did it? I'd always associated it with elegance and style, and felt awkward lugging it around as a totally inappropriate label.

'Who chose it?'

'My dad,' I said hurriedly, not wanting to go down this particular highway. ''Night.'

The road outside my house isn't yellow-lined, so sometimes it's possible to park right outside. More often than not, though, it's used as an overflow car park by those who don't want to risk parking in the controlled zone along the terrace. This proved to be one of those nights. I had to cruise the parallel roads until I found a slot three streets away.

Wandering back, my head full of Kersey's visitors, I took no notice of the darkened streets beyond the fact that it was pretty well deserted as usual at this time of night. Maybe I subconsciously saw them sitting in the car; I don't recall now.

At any rate, my conscious mind didn't register their presence until I set one foot on the iron staircase leading down to the basement.

'Oi!' I couldn't turn in time. Hands grabbed my coat and dragged me backwards.

CHAPTER 14

They threatened to throw away the key.

'On what charge?'

The DS suggested that perverting the course of justice would do for a start.

'Fine. Charge me then. And I want a solicitor.'

'When I say.'

Shrugging, I folded my arms, hunched my shoulders and closed my mouth.

Deep down I knew it wasn't a smart move. Getting bolshie with the police wasn't going to hurt anyone but me. But the way they'd just bundled me into the police car without so much as a 'd'ya mind?' had got right up my nose.

Fortunately, at that moment Chief Inspector Jackson entered the interview room. He thanked me for coming. I pointed out I hadn't been given much choice in the matter.

'I'm sorry if the sergeant failed to make it clear that your presence here is entirely voluntary, Grace. May I call you Grace, by the way?'

He always did, every time we spoke. But he never failed to ask permission each time.

'Whichever you like.'

'Grace then. Have they offered you tea, coffee?'

'No. Coffee. White. No sugar.'

'Three spoonfuls in mine, thanks, Sergeant.'

The look the DS shot at the back of Jackson's head as he slouched out spoke volumes.

Sitting opposite me, Jackson dropped his right eyelid in

what could almost have been a wink. The whole performance had so obviously been staged to create the illusion that Jackson and I were united as a matey team that I nearly laughed out loud.

However, discretion being the better part of cowardice, I gave him my best winning smile and waited to be told what he wanted.

It was quite simple: having seen my business card on Judy Parker's beside locker, they wanted to know what she had told me.

'Why not ask her?'

'Mrs Parker hasn't much time for the police. She cut up rough. We got slung out of the ward. Can't really press it in the circumstances.'

'Police brutality gives grieving widow heart attack, you mean?'

'That sort of bullshit,' he agreed. 'We'd appreciate your co-operation, Grace.'

So I co-operated. Which didn't do him much good, because let's face it, Judy hadn't really told me anything.

When I'd finished, Jackson said: 'How does this tie in to December Drysdale's dead donkey? That's what you were hired to dig into, isn't it?'

It occurred to me that perhaps Jackson was the CID officer who, according to Annie's information, belonged to the same secretive church sect as Drysdale.

'I don't know that it does. It just seemed to be connected. You know: same night; two deaths, two knifings.'

'Hardly conclusive. You should have tipped us off on the Lloyd girl's identity earlier, you know.'

'I didn't know for sure until Wednesday. I told Mr Drysdale to contact you.' ("Liar," my conscience hissed.) 'I can't help it if you didn't follow up. The picture you released to the press wasn't exactly spot-on for likeness, was it?'

He raised a pair of elegantly chiselled eyebrows in deprecating dismissal of somebody's goof-up. 'Mistake that, in hindsight. Had all sorts of so-called sightings of Tara or Tina or whatever she called herself.'

'She called herself Tara because she thought it gave her a bit of class. Everyone else called her Tina, so I guess she never got to be that classy.'

The DS returned with two plastic cups of coffee, then, in response to a jerk of Jackson's head, made himself scarce again. The parting rattle that he gave the handle ensured that it just failed to catch, leaving the door fractionally ajar. Jackson didn't intend to risk my shrieking molestation if I started feeling stroppy.

Not that I would have; I quite like Jackson. And I've always had the feeling he had a soft spot for me. I wondered whether he'd recommended our firm to Drysdale.

Surprisingly Jackson volunteered the information that they'd traced Tina's London address. 'From a number at the aunt's place. Pay-phone job in one of them bedsit places. DC Smith went up this after. Seems Tina took off on the Friday. Friends didn't know where she was going. Don't suppose you can help with that?'

I made a few calculations. It didn't sound like Bella had mentioned my visit. But on the other hand, she'd probably handed over an up-to-date photo of Tina. As soon as that hit the television screens, the occupants of the Peace Hospice were going to contact the police.

I told Jackson about Tina's Friday-evening appointment. And was piqued to find he wasn't as surprised as I expected him to be.

'Did you know Kersey was back in circulation?'

'He's out on parole. Of course we knew. Although in his case circulation is hardly the right word. Stomach cancer, isn't it?'

'It was.'

'We're not talking miraculous remission here, are we?'

'Nope.'

'I'll cross him off the Old Lags' Christmas Party list then.'

'Did you know him? Personally.'

'Before my time.' He took another swallow of coffee. He had a strange habit of cupping his fingers over the top like a mini mechanical grab and sipping through the gap between thumb and forefinger. 'So what did Kersey want with the Lloyd girl?'

I saw no reason why I should do all the police legwork. They had, after all, terminated my employment with them some time ago. Jackson could find out about Kersey's four visitors in his own time, not mine.

'No idea. Ask her Auntie Judy.'

He made a note, as if he were grateful for a suggestion. 'Anything else you could help us out with, Grace?'

There wasn't. But there was something I wanted to ask him.

'Do you think Kersey did it? Killed this Major Woolley?'

'The jury said he did.'

'Juries can get it wrong.'

'True. But if you're asking for my gut reaction, I think this one got it right.'

'So who belted Kersey? Did they ever trace the second man? The one who was trying to push-start the car with Kersey?'

'If they did, they didn't tell me.'

I caught the ironic note in Jackson's voice. He was beginning to close down. Now that I'd told him as much as he figured I could, he wanted me out of here. Which was fine by me, until I discovered they weren't planning to offer me a lift.

'No way. You got me here, now you get me home again. If your officers had asked for my help in a civilized manner, I could have followed them down in my own car. Be Safe, Not Sorry, isn't that police advice to lone women?'

I was trying it on really. It wasn't that dangerous a place, and anyway I could look after myself. I had to; there were no other volunteers for the job. But to my surprise, Jackson offered to drive me back himself.

'I'm heading out now anyway,' he remarked, leading me round to his Vauxhall. 'Overtime budget's just about knackered for this month.'

He didn't say anything else until we drew up outside the flat and I was unbuckling my seat-belt whilst nudging the door with my other elbow. Abruptly Jackson leant across me and pulled the door shut again.

The combination of the unexpected action plus the sudden mixture of aftershave and soft hair tickling across my mouth and nose caused me to jerk back with an involuntary tightening of my stomach muscles. Jackson was reputedly happily married with one kid and the second under starter's orders. He was the last bloke I'd have expected to try it on.

I was just weighing up whether the offer merited a tactful refusal or a fast elbow under his nose, when he disillusioned me by saying: 'Stay out of the Tina business, Grace. Whoever chopped her up enjoyed themselves. I don't want you ending up as prime cuts as well.'

'It's nice of you to care, Inspector. But I'm investigating the death of a donkey, remember?'

'No you aren't. You're fishing in dangerous waters.' He'd settled back in his own seat. Now he reached behind his back and opened the driver's door sufficiently for the interior light to activate, bathing us both in a feeble glow. 'You're still narked that they kicked you out, aren't you, Grace? Still trying to prove we were wrong?'

I raised my shoulders. 'I do OK. And you can't stop me asking questions if I want to. No one's forced to answer them and I don't use threats or trespass.' A vision of my nightly prowl round the Parkers' empty house was ruthlessly sat upon by my cowed conscience.

His elbow was over the back of the car seat. Without moving it, he gripped my shoulder lightly and said quietly: 'Leave it alone, Grace. Believe me, getting one over on the force isn't worth what Tina went through.'

If anyone else had said that to me I'd have snapped back some flip retort. But something about his expression stopped me. He really did care what happened to me. In the end, I just muttered that I'd be careful and scrambled out of the car.

He waited until I'd let myself into the flat and switched the lights on before he drove away.

I was cold, tired and depressed. Falling into bed, I pulled the duvet round my head, expecting to collapse into a dead sleep. It didn't work.

As the hours ticked by, the small sounds of the night world filtered in through the barred window high above my head: shuffling feet accompanied by the squeak of an unoiled trolley wheel; the sharp rat-tat of stilettos, followed a few seconds later by the heavy thud of running trainers; the patter of soft pads and spiteful ripping teeth as an urban fox prowled amongst the heaps of black plastic rubbish bags in next-door's basement.

After the fox had gone three falls and a knock-out with the local cats, I gave up and got up again.

Fuelled by a mug of black coffee, I rolled paper into the typewriter's platen and brought my notes up to date:

Item 1: Why was Judy Parker so reluctant to tell me about her appointment with Kersey? Was it in some way connected with the "little present" Edna had seen Kersey dishing out to his visitors?

(Even as I typed that, I realized it was pretty unlikely. George Spinnaker had said Kersey had very little to leave. But perhaps Judy hadn't known that?)

Item 2: Who were Kersey's two male visitors? Given that he'd chosen to give presents to the widows of the men he'd supposedly killed and maimed, could the men have been victims of his earlier frauds?

Item 3: What time was Tina killed? Was it possible the killer had threatened Marilyn in order to make Tina talk? About what?

Item 4: Was the red-headed bloke searching Judy's place connected to all this, or was he just an opportunist thief who'd noticed the place had been empty for a couple of days?

Item 5:

I stared at Item 5 for a long time, until the chill penetrated through the sweater I'd pulled on over my pyjamas, making me aware of a stiff back and freezing feet. I couldn't think of Item 5. I wasn't even sure there was a fifth item.

In the end I scrawled: "Phone Olly (High Wycombe) and Mjr Woolley's widow" on a Post-It, slapped it on the kettle and fell back into bed.

Curled into a ball, hugging two blocks of ice where my feet had once been, I resolved to get up early, take a bracing run along the beach and spring into Friday imbued with a new and blinding initiative.

I woke up at eleven o'clock. It was too late for the beach run unless I wanted to do it to a chorus of cat-calls, inane comments and whinging kids crying that I'd kicked over their sand castles.

I probed my subconscious for any signs of a burgeoning initiative. In the end I gave up, shifted the Post-It from the kettle to the front of my jumper and hunted around for the makings of breakfast.

After ten minutes, I was forced to admit it was either going to be tinned rice pudding and pickles or a Pepi's All-Day Special.

The warm spell was holding sufficiently to tempt even more day-trippers and early weekenders on to the sands. The trampolining business had opened for the first time this year and beyond it the boat-shaped swings were soaring back and forth propelled by vigorous tugs on the candy-striped ropes.

I gave December a wave from the promenade and could have sworn Errol brayed back his own "good morning". I was going to have to watch myself; I was getting as daft as Drysdale about the stupid beasts.

Shane was in a modernist mood – fried bread and runny eggs were served to the accompaniment of the Stones belting out "Satisfaction" and "Little Red Rooster", which was just about as up to date as his musical tastes got.

Instead of my usual table, I'd chosen to perch on a high stool at the counter. During a lull in customers, I asked Shane if he remembered the Woolley case.

'Can't say I do. Give us a clue.'

I gave him a brief outline of the basic facts.

'Oh yeah, course I remember now. That cabbie got bashed over the bonce, didn't he? They used to come in here, you know. The drivers. Office used to be just up the road.'

'I don't remember any cabbing business around here.'

Shane applied a wet rag to the counter with vigour, releasing a cloud of pine-scented disinfectant into the air. 'Closed down years ago. What's your connection? Thought you were down for the donkey that turned up its hooves.'

'How'd you hear about that?'

'All over town, ain't it, love? 'Ad a reporter from the local bog-sheet in here last night. Reckoned they might do an interview with you. Give everyone a bit of a laugh.'

'Oh *hell*!'

'Could be a nice little earner, that,' Shane pointed out. 'Bit of free advertising.'

'Not a chance. Tell him I've emigrated if you see him again. Did you know Des Parker?'

'No. Why? Did they do a piece on him?'

'He was the cab driver. The one who got . . .' I whacked my own skull with an eggy fork.

'Oh, that poor sod. Can't say I *knew* him, no. He come in a couple of times, I reckon. Had the gift of the gab as I recall. Full of big plans.' Shane twisted the dishcloth into a pole shape, crooning into his makeshift microphone the news that he couldn't get no "sat-is-fac-shun".

'You and me both,' his other half yelled through the open hatch. 'Two egg and chips.'

Shane jigged the orders to the waiting customers.

When he returned I asked him if he could remember whether Des Parker had had any particular friends amongst the other drivers.

'Not so's you'd notice, no. Mind, like I said, he only come in a few times. Want a refill?'

'OK.'

I pushed my cup across. Shane hefted up the huge stainless-steel teapot. 'Tell you what, though,' he said suddenly, 'there was a bit of trouble, I just remembered . . . they switched the collection.'

'Sorry?'

The jukebox had exploded into 'Great Balls of Fire'. Eyes half closed in rocking bliss, Shane started to finger the formica counter like a piano, as he explained that the cab drivers had set up a collection for Des Parker after the attack. 'They asked me if they could put a box in here. Got quite a bit in it too. I reckon they must have had a couple of hundred out of my place alone. Then about a fortnight later, they suddenly changed the poster to "Holiday Fund for Handicapped Kids" or something. Couple of customers complained. Reckoned it weren't rightly legit, that. But you can't ask for it back, can you? Not when it's kids.'

'Thanks, Shane.'

He'd started off an interesting train of thought, which I mulled over whilst I made my way back to the office, availed myself of Vetch's lukewarm water to take a bath and checked Annie's office to see whether the block was still on her phone.

It was. And she caught me coming out.

'Hi. How's Jonathon?'

'Very well, thank you.'

It was the pale-beige suit today, with gold-rimmed spectacles to match. I hovered in the doorway, whilst she drew screens around the filing cabinets and shrouded the desk in pink linen and lace. 'That's it? Just "very well". Not great, terrific, twelve out of ten? Where'd you go?'

Inserting a paper filter into the coffee machine, Annie said tartly: 'I don't see it's any of your business.'

'Oh go on. You know you're dying to tell me.'

Annie informed me she wasn't. Then added quickly, before I could disappear, 'If you must know, we had dinner at the Red Hen.'

'Bloke I know works there. Reckons the service is a bit moody.'

Annie spun the top off a bottle of water and filled the machine's reservoir. 'It is a bit slow, I must admit. Jonathon complained, as a matter of fact. He can be very forceful when he wants to be. But the food was very acceptable when it finally came.'

'Did he take you home?'

'No, he left me to hitch back.'

'There's no need to be sarky. I'm just trying to take an interest.'

'You're just trying to find out whether I slept with him.'

'So? Did you?'

Annie drew a loud breath and asked if anyone had ever told me I was a nosy cow.

'I have an honours degree in nosiness. I take it that means yes?'

'It means get lost. I've got a client coming in . . .' She flicked a quick glance at the neat gold watch. 'Ten minutes. Why don't you go to lunch?'

'I've just had breakfast. Listen, that dead girl, did Zeb happen to mention the time of death?'

'I can't remember. Why?'

'Just an idea I'm working on. See you.'

Everybody seemed to be in for once. As a consequence, I had to use my own phone to ring Zeb.

'Listen,' I said as soon as we'd gone through the 'how you doing?' preliminaries. 'Are you free for lunch?'

'*You* want to buy me lunch?'

No, I didn't, actually. But then I wasn't going to: Drysdale was, although he wouldn't know it until I presented my expense claim.

'So how about it?' I pressed Zeb.

'I'm kind of busy.'

'You can't be too busy to eat. BHS restaurant. One o'clock, OK?'

I put the receiver down before he could tell me it wasn't.

By the time Zeb arrived, I'd already bagged a window seat overlooking the boating pond. My initial triumph at seeing his lanky frame was rather dampened by the sight of a second figure collecting utensils and paper serviettes from the corner table.

Warily I watched as they wove between the packed tables, elbows bent and held high to clear waving hands and bobbing heads.

'So we meet again, Grace,' Inspector Jackson remarked, sliding a plate of cod and chips, cutlery and a pot of tea for one on to the table.

'And so soon,' I agreed, shooting a look at Zeb that hopefully conveyed 'traitor'.

'Don't blame DC Smith,' Jackson mumbled through clenched teeth that were currently tearing open a sachet of tomato ketchup. 'I was at his desk when you called. Thought I'd join you. Perhaps you've remembered something else Mrs Parker told you?'

'No.'

'No? Pity. Got any vinegar there, Zeb? So why'd you offer the DC lunch then? Don't tell me you fancy him?'

'Don't you reckon he's fanciable then?' I asked, playing along whilst I dredged around for a believable story.

'Not to me, at any rate.'

'I'm glad to hear it, sir,' Zeb said, fitting in half a piece of haddock sideways and scrunching with obvious satisfaction.

'So, Grace?'

'I want to pick Zeb's brains,' I admitted.

'Abou' wha'?' Jackson mumbled, inserting half a dozen chips.

'The time of Tina's death.'

'Why?'

The rate at which they were both shovelling in food was beginning to make me dizzy. Jackson caught my eye and explained: 'Have to be in court. So speed up the dialogue, will you, Grace? Why'd you want the time of death?'

I explained my theory about someone threatening the donkey in order to get Tina to talk.

'Talk about what?'

I had to admit I didn't really know. 'It's just the only motive that seems to make sense. For slicing up Marilyn, I mean.'

'What timc'd the donkey go missing?'

'December's not sure. But he says Marilyn was OK when he went out to the stable at eleven. Factory's about a mile and a half across the fields, so assuming normal walking speed and adding in the donkey-drag factor, sometime between then and midnight.'

Pushing the cleared plate away, Jackson demolished his dessert of lime jelly and cream in one wrist-flick of his spoon. 'Doesn't fit. Doc says Tina was dead by ten; probably a bit earlier.'

'Sod it.'

'Right. So now take my advice and keep your nose out of it, Grace.'

'It's my job.'

'No it's not. Your job is getting the dirt on straying other halves, finding lost dogs and uncovering dodgy insurance claims. Investigating violent deaths is no career for amateurs. You're a good-looker. I'm sure we'd all prefer you to stay that way. Wouldn't we, Zeb?'

'Yes. No. I mean . . .'

'Anything else you want to share with us, Grace?'

'No.' I don't know why I did it. Perhaps, like Jackson had suggested, my main motive for pressing on was a deep-seated ever-present desire to stick it to my former employers.

'So when'd they discover Des Parker was in on the job?'

Jackson had stood up, preparatory to returning his tray to a wheeled collection trolley. Now he paused and asked who'd said he was.

I told him about the aborted collection at Shane's café. 'Word got round pretty fast, didn't it.'

Jackson shrugged. 'Yes, well, you know how these things leak out.'

And he hadn't even bothered to try and deny it! One up to Grace Smith investigations! I nearly gave way to a reckless impulse and kissed DCI Jackson.

CHAPTER 15

Jackson dropped his voice and murmured beneath the general chatter of the other diners, 'Of course Parker was in on it. It took the investigating officers about two seconds to work that one out, Grace.'

'Parker and Kersey were in the same open nick a few years previous,' Zeb chipped in, before being told to shift it by Jackson or they'd be late for court.

'I know about Kersey's fraud convictions; what was Parker inside for?'

I thought Jackson wasn't going to answer. Technically speaking, he shouldn't discuss convictions with me. But since it was a dead man's record, I guess he decided to stretch a point and offered the news that Parker had been convicted of handling stolen property. 'Dodgy car spares. Not exactly a virgin to the business, was our Des.'

'Judy said he was full of get-rich-quick schemes.'

'Yes, well, in Des's case they were generally get-nicked-even-quicker schemes.'

'So how come Des ended up a cabbage if he was in on it?'

Buttoning his overcoat, Jackson shrugged. 'Ask Judy.'

'There were no charges brought against him, were there?'

'It wasn't considered appropriate. Let's face it, the CPS weren't going to get far prosecuting a virtual cabbage. But perhaps you should take a close look at the way Parker ended up, Grace. Leave the villains to the professionals. Amateurs can get hurt. Isn't one member of your family in a wheelchair enough?'

That last crack was so below the belt, and so unlike Jackson, that I was still groping for a response when he and Zeb left the restaurant.

I wanted to run, yell, punch and kick something. I tried to jog off the excess burst of rage-driven energy on the way back to the office. Weaving past three-abreast pensioners in plastic macs that still showed their folding creases, and gaggles of foreign students babbling away in every language but the one they'd come here to learn, I pounded out of the shopping area, down past the harbour and out along Marine Terrace.

I had to pass the hospital to get back to the office. I was half tempted to shoot straight in there and give Judy Parker a piece of my mind, but common sense just managed to win over injured pride in the end.

There was, after all, absolutely no reason why Judy should have told a nosy investigator who was hassling her in her sickbed that her old man was an ex-villain.

So I channelled my bile into a burst of efficiency, peeled the Post-It off my jumper and dialled Kersey's two visitors.

The garage in High Wycombe turned out to be one of those places where they fit tyres, exhausts and batteries. An obsequious receptionist informed me her name was Lisa and wanted to know how she may help me. When I asked for Olly Colville her desire to assist slipped a few notches down the scale.

'May I ask if there's a problem?'

'No problem. I'd just like a word.'

'Is this a personal call?'

'It's business.'

'Then if I could take the details, our manager will be pleased to ring you back and discuss your requirements.'

'My requirement is to speak to Mr Colville.'

'The fitters aren't allowed to take personal calls.'

'This is not . . . Oh look, forget it. Can you take my number and get him to call me back?'

I reeled off the office number before she could say "not a chance".

'Got that?'

'Yes thank you. Could I take your address as well?'

'What on earth for?'

'I'll put you on our mailing list. We run special offers throughout the year.'

'Oh, I don't think that will be necessary, thanks. The BMW's still under warranty. And my husband is thinking of trading the Alfa Romeo in for one of those Jaguar convertibles. I think that new silver shade is just dinky, don't you?'

I hung up on her excited paper-rustling.

The retirement home was more helpful. They were quite happy for me to speak to Mrs Woolley. However, having agreed to fetch her to the phone, the speaker then disappeared for so long that I nearly had a heart attack envisaging the units mounting on my BT bill.

Eventually a scuffling indicated that the receiver was being picked up again.

'Mrs Woolley?'

'Yes. This isn't Elaine, is it?'

The voice had an upper-middle-class timbre overlaid with a husky panting, as if the owner had just finished a strenuous work-out.

I denied I'd ever been called Elaine.

'The girl said it was my daughter-in-law. Such a silly mistake. Elaine has quite a cultured voice.'

Well bully for Elaine, I reflected, repressing a desire to explode into a cod-cockney dialect of the "cor luv a duck" variety.

'My name is Grace Smith. I was hoping I might talk to you about Alan Kersey.'

'Are you a reporter?'

'No.'

'Police then?'

'No, nothing like that. I'm a private investigator.'

'And why do you wish to speak to me? Is it Miss or Mrs Smith?'

'I'm not married, if that's what you're asking. I wanted to talk about your visit to Alan Kersey last Friday.'

'I really fail to see what business that is of yours, Miss Smith.'

At least that confirmed I'd got the right woman.

I just wasn't up to going into the whole Marilyn Monroe saga again. It was hard enough face to face; over the phone, to a woman who plainly regarded me as dead common, I couldn't hack it.

So I bent the truth a bit. 'It's connected with the death of Des Parker's niece. He was the—'

'I know who Mr Parker was,' she interrupted sharply. I wondered whether the extent of his involvement in her husband's death had been generally known at the time. 'By his niece, I assume you're referring to the girl who called at the Peace Hospice last Friday?'

'Tina. That's her.'

'And you say she's dead?'

'Murdered.'

Her tone became less self-assured. 'I had no idea. And Mrs Parker? Is she also . . .?'

'In hospital. Recovering from a heart attack.'

'Ahh.' Through the earpiece I could hear someone else moving around in the background. Something was placed over the mouthpiece as Mrs Woolley spoke to whoever had interrupted her.

'Look,' I said as soon as a clearer reception indicated that she'd taken the muffler off the receiver. 'This is really difficult over the phone. Is it OK if I come round and see you?'

I was going to anyway, whatever she might say. But as it turned out, I got a reluctant invitation to come that evening.

'Now would be better.'

'That's not possible. My son, Roger, is calling shortly. I would prefer it if he were not involved in this matter. I shall expect you at six o'clock, prompt.'

'Cheers.'

I'd hardly put down my own receiver when it gave three quick buzzes, Janice's signal for "pick up".

'Yes, Jan?'

'Some woman called Magnolia's been trying to call you. I said you'd ring back. And there's a bloke down here to see you.'

'What bloke?'

'Didn't ask.'

There was no point in complaining. The only person around here who received anything like an efficient service from our receptionist was Vetch the Letch. Janice knew darn well the rest of us would never get organized enough to agree on her dismissal.

My acquaintance from the hospital, Mr Mouldar, was perched on a plastic chair against the hall wall. Ankles together and raincoat neatly folded over his legs, he was watching Janice's fingers flashing over the processor's keyboard.

As I came down the last stair flight, he rose and smiled. 'Good afternoon, miss. I hope you don't mind my calling at your work.'

'No. Of course not. When did they let you out?'

'First thing this morning, miss. They don't hang around these days. Need the beds, I suppose. Not that I'm complaining. There's too many people complaining about the NHS in my opinion. Those doctors work miracles, miss. Miracles. They saved my life, I'm sure of that.'

'Well, I'm glad you're feeling better.' He didn't look it. The thin face was pale and pinched and the watery blue eyes didn't exactly suggest robust health.

'Kind of you to say so I'm sure, miss. I bought you this.'

From beneath the folded raincoat, he drew out a flowered paper bag containing a small box of chocolate flakes.

'It's just a small thank you for putting me in the way of employment. I telephoned the security company this morning. And they were quite encouraging. In fact I have a definite interview. I'm most grateful.'

I couldn't see that the prospect of twelve hours patrolling some deserted building site was anything to get excited about, but obviously it all depended on your expectations. Mr Mouldar's were plainly lower than mine. I wished him luck.

'Thank you, miss. I told them your little joke about the donkey guard. But unfortunately it seems that that position is not currently available. Which is a pity, because I've always been rather partial to donkeys.'

Seeing him out, I suggested he introduce himself to December. 'He likes people who like donkeys.'

His face lit up. 'Perhaps I might do that, miss. It's difficult, making friends, when you're new to the area. And you must feel free to call on me for a cup of tea too, miss. Or even something a bit stronger. Any time. I have one of those caravans in Cliff Park. Ask anyone for William Mouldar, they'll point you in the right direction.'

'I'll remember.'

Behind his back, Janice was pulling a series of sarcastic faces; the last degenerated into a giggle as he turned and caught sight of her expression.

Taking pity on his embarrassed blush, I advised him not to mind her and eased him gently out of the door. Whipping back upstairs, I dialled Magnolia's number.

'She's out,' Magnolia said without preamble, when I'd identified myself. 'Judy. Came home in a taxi this morning.'

'So why are you telling me?'

'She won't let me in. I mean, she shouldn't be on her own. I wondered, did you manage to find her niece? She's flesh and blood, isn't she? She ought to be looking out for her auntie.'

I couldn't see why. After all, Judy hadn't looked out for Tina during the years she needed her most. Still, the argument was academic now. 'Tina's dead,' I said baldly. 'Somebody killed her.'

'Oh, lord. Oh, poor Judy. There were men all over the house yesterday. I thought they were gas board, but one of my regulars said they looked like coppers to him. You don't mean Tina . . . I mean, she hasn't been *in* there. Next door. All this time?'

'No. She died . . . elsewhere. Look, I'm a bit busy, Magnolia. I'll catch up with you later.'

'Yes. All right.'

She let me go with reluctance and I guessed she'd be back on Judy's step with chicken soup and bottles of Lucozade within a short space of time. Had she been a little less nice, she'd have spared herself an awful lot of guilt.

I busied myself tidying up the office and sorting out the stubs on my chequebook until it was time to call on Mrs Edwin Woolley.

The car was still parked where I'd left it the previous night just before my encounter with CID. The nearside wheel was flat. Closer examination revealed several large gashes, probably made with a chisel. I suspected I'd parked on someone's cherished patch. Whatever the motive, by the time I'd lugged the spare from the boot, located the wheel brace and jack and got myself hot, mad and greasy, I was well and truly late for my appointment.

St Theresa's Retirement Home (Grant Maintained) was located on the farthest edges of the neighbouring town. It looked turn of the century: a grim, double-fronted building, constructed in a heavy grey granite that was unusual in this part of the world. The lintel stone over the double doors still had the discernible word 'Rectory' engraved in its lighter material.

Parking at the side of the building, next to a minibus that

displayed the legend 'Donated by the Round Table', I scrunched back over the gravel drive to the front. The door was flung open before I could reach the bell, and a gangling middle-aged man pushed past me and ran across to a yellow Metro parked directly in front of the 'No Parking' sign.

'You see?' he shouted, kicking the rear. 'You can hardly claim that is a "mere scratch".'

Several occupants of the home had joined me on the step. We all duly looked at the smashed tail-light and dented metal.

'I can't afford to lose my no-claims bonus. If you can't take more care I shall have to insist you return the key.'

Banging the car door closed, he screamed away in a bow wave of loose gravel chippings.

Above our heads, half a dozen gulls rose shrieking from the roof in sympathy. One of the spectators cackled with amusement. She looked quite refined: silky, long-sleeved dress, grey tights, polished shoes, discreet make-up and white hair swept into a French pleat. Personally I thought the navy knickers round her ankles were an interesting touch.

A woman in a green checked overall that I assumed was some kind of staff uniform placed firm hands on the refined one's shoulders and steered her back indoors. It gave me a clear view of the third person standing in the doorway.

She'd shrunk since the newspaper photograph had been taken just after her husband's death. I put her height at under five feet. Leaning heavily on two metal walking sticks, she was glaring in the direction that the car had taken in a way that made me certain the abuse had been intended for her.

'Mrs Woolley?'

'Yes.' Two currant-bun eyes swivelled right.

'Hi. I'm Grace Smith. I phoned. Sorry I'm late. Car trouble.'

'I dislike a lack of punctuality. I was always taught it was rude.' Whilst she scolded, she was manoeuvring round on the sticks until she faced the hall. 'I suppose you'd better come in.'

'Thanks.'

The hall was covered in a bilious-green lino. A paler-green emulsion on the walls was decorated by unframed childish crayon drawings. The whole place stank of cabbage, mashed potatoes and urine.

Mrs Woolley made her way by painful inches to a door in the hall corridor. Nudging it open with a stick she said: 'I'm in here. Lock the door after you.'

The room was adequately furnished, to put it politely, with heavy wooden bedroom furniture and a white china hand-basin. Even from across the room I could see that the pink candlewick bedspread had seen better days. Ditto the curtains around the bay window and the well-trodden beige carpet.

She was using the sticks again, to pat a footstool into position. With a grunt of relief, she lowered herself into a high-backed chair and put her heavily bandaged legs up on the stool.

Dragging a padded seat from under the dressing table, I perched on it.

'Thanks for seeing me.'

'You are very late.'

'Car trouble,' I apologized again. 'Must be the day for it. Me and Roger, you know. That was your son, wasn't it?'

'Yes, that was Roger.' Her tone didn't invite me to continue with the subject of her offspring.

'Simla? That's Indian, isn't it?'

She seemed surprised to find that I could recognize any-where beyond Dover. 'Yes. It was a hill station. Mummy and I always went there in the summer. We all did. All the women and children, I mean. The men had to stay behind and work, of course.'

'Is that where you met your husband? India?'

'Yes.'

'When did you come home?'

A smile at my ignorance crossed her small wet lips. 'India was home. We returned to England after Independence.'

'You must have travelled around a bit though – army postings.'

'Edwin had a few overseas postings, yes. I did not accompany him. In any event, it was only for a few years.'

'Oh? Sorry, I'd rather got the impression he'd only retired from the army shortly before his death. The rank and all that.'

'I don't know who told you that, Miss Smith. Edwin retained the rank as a courtesy title. He resigned his commission many years before. Although to be blunt, I can't see that my husband's employment record is any concern of yours.'

'No. Sorry. I was just trying to get the overall picture.'

There was an aggression in her attitude that went beyond a natural resentment at some nosy cow barging into her life and asking personal questions about a painful subject.

There was a collection of framed photographs on the dressing table. Picking one at random, I said: 'Is this your husband? He was a good-looking man, wasn't he?'

'He thought so.'

'And you didn't?'

Simla Woolley linked her hands over her stomach and remarked that she daresay she had once. 'A uniform can be very seductive. In my day, Miss Smith, you didn't have live-in lovers or life partners. You had a husband. And once you were married, you made the best of it. Particularly if you had children.'

'You've others then, besides Roger?'

Simla admitted to two middle-aged daughters, pointing out the relevant photos with the rubber-tipped stick. Both had lived in Canada since their twenties.

'And Elaine is so good to me, I just feel like she's my own girl.'

'Elaine doesn't have a car?'

'She doesn't drive, no. Why do you ask?'

'It's just that I couldn't help hearing that you'd borrowed Roger's motor.'

'And why shouldn't I? My son is a useless, ineffectual . . .'

Running out of adjectives, Simla squeezed her stick, kneading and twisting it in a way that suggested she wished it was Roger's neck.

Since the photographs had proved a useful method of unlocking her mouth, I shifted a few more around and discovered several of a young woman with Roger and two toddlers. And later pictures of the same female with the boys now older and in school uniforms.

Simla confirmed that that was indeed Elaine with her two boys.

Something about the images nagged me, stirring a worm in my mind. Before I could pin down the elusive memory, Simla exploded in another rage of resentment against the unfortunate Roger. It seemed he'd refused to replace her last car when it finally went to rust in peace.

'He claimed it wasn't a priority. Well, it certainly wasn't to him, of course. But what sort of man can work for thirty-odd years and not be able to raise the price of a second-hand car, tell me that, Miss Smith?'

Even if I had been able to tell her, there wasn't much point in trying, since now she'd got her second wind, Simla had every intention of running through her full list of grievances against good old Rog.

'Ridiculous. Roger cannot manage even the simplest household accounts. Heaven knows what state they'd be in if it weren't for Elaine.'

The radiator under the bay window gurgled and thumped, emphasizing her words with a series of hollow bangs. They were followed a second later by a sharp rap on the door and a rattle of the handle.

'Simla, dear, dinner in ten minutes. Can you open the door, please. You know we don't like them locked.'

'I have a visitor.'

'All right, dear. But key out when they go. Shepherd's pie

tonight. Our favourite. Mmm, yummy.'

The whole conversation had been shouted in an archly high-pitched voice, as if the speaker felt that Simla was either deaf and/or half-witted.

I saw the tight-lipped glare of frustration she shot at the closed door and understood. Thanks to Roger's inability to manage money, his mother was trapped in a cut-price old people's home. No wonder she despised him.

'Look, I'm sorry to bring up a painful subject, but I really would like to talk about Alan Kersey. It's important.'

'To whom, Miss Smith?'

I had to give her a resumé of the donkey saga again. And follow it up with a brief run-down on Tina's murder.

'You said Mrs Parker is in hospital?'

'She apparently came home this morning.'

'I shall write to offer my sympathies on her niece's death. I remember how distressing the aftermath of these things can be: the identification of the body; sorting out the personal effects. I suppose she'll have to do that?'

'I suppose so.'

Simla "tssk-tssked", murmuring, 'So difficult. So much.'

'I think Tina's death is in some way connected to her visit to Alan Kersey last Friday. Could you tell me about it? What did he want?'

'He wished to ask my forgiveness for his part in Edwin's murder. To apologize for abusing our trust and hospitality.'

She was lying. I just knew it. A self-conscious flush swept up from her neck.

'He was a friend of your son's, wasn't he?'

The flush receded now she was on safer ground. 'Perhaps friend is too strong a word. He had visited out home several times. Indeed it was he who drew Edwin's attention to the possible value of the bronze. He had a degree in history, you see.'

'Did you have any suspicion he was involved in the robbery?'

166

'Of course not! It came as a complete shock. In fact, he even called to offer his condolences. I shall never forgive him for that piece of insensitivity.'

'Is that what you told him?'

She looked at me blankly. I had to remind her that forgiveness was the supposed reason for her visit to Kersey's bedside.

'Oh. Yes. I said I would try to pray for him. It seemed charitable in the circumstances.'

'More than charitable. What about the other three? Were they going to pray for him too?'

'That was a matter for their own consciences.'

'Who were they? I mean, I know who Tina was, but what about the two men?'

'We were not formally introduced. I believe they were other acquaintances of Alan's.'

Well, obviously they were. I asked her what they'd talked about.

'Very little. Alan was not lucid for some part of the time. Conversation was difficult.'

'But you must have said something? Between yourselves?'

'We spoke of general topics. The weather. Institutional care, that sort of thing.'

I just couldn't swallow this picture of total disinterest. After thirteen years she's summoned to the bedside of her husband's murderer and she sits there discussing the possibility of rain! Oh yeah!

'What else?'

'I really don't remember, Miss Smith. And I should like you to leave. Dinner will be served shortly, as you heard.'

She was already struggling to her feet. I was beginning to wonder why she'd agreed to see me. 'Was there anything else?' I asked, supporting her under one elbow.

'Else? No. Would you unlock the door, please.' In accordance with her directions, I relocked it once we were outside and dropped the key into her pocket. 'Otherwise they'll take it.'

I made one last stab at getting the truth out of her. 'Did Alan Kersey give you anything?'

'No. What did he have that I could possibly want?'

Good question. I wished she'd tell me. But she plainly had no intention of doing so.

The refined one had rehitched her knickers and was now sitting on the outside step, humming away to herself as I pushed past.

'G'night,' I said. 'Better go in or you'll miss the shepherd's pie.'

Clasping her knees, she swayed even harder and sang tunelessly. With an effort I recognized, "You Must Have Been a Beautiful Baby."

The words stirred that little worm that had niggled at me in Simla's room. I'd seen something important, but what?'

CHAPTER 16

There were Post-Its from Janice plastered all over my office.

4.15 p.m. Mr Drysdale called. Ring him back *urgent*.

5.00 p.m. Drysdale rang again. He really needs to talk. (I don't think he believes you're not here).

5.20 p.m. Tell that donkey bloke I don't lie (well, not for you anyway).

5.30 p.m. Same as above – with knobs on!

From which I gathered December wanted a word – yesterday for preference.

It was already late. Since I was out in the car, I'd made a detour via the Cliff Park Caravan Park to find the wandering witness my solicitor customer had wanted pinned down.

I didn't find her. But I did run into the ubiquitous Mr Mouldar, who seemed pathetically pleased that I'd taken up his invitation.

'I've only just got back from a little errand in town myself, miss. A minute earlier and you'd have missed me altogether.'

Rather than disillusion him, I enlisted his help in the search.

The park was still half deserted at this time of year, the power-point connections springing from the grass like bizarre crops and the empty swimming pool full of wind-blown rubbish.

Most of the resident caravans seemed unoccupied. Those who answered were fed up that we'd interrupted their meals/ TV-viewing/nookie. The whole exercise was carried out to the accompaniment of a pirate radio station blaring from the tattiest van on the site and the frantic barking of an evil-looking mutt tethered by a piece of string to the van's steps.

When I asked Mouldar why someone didn't complain, he explained that it was the caretaker's nephew's van. 'He just turns the radio up louder if anyone says anything. Still, the rent is very reasonable this time of year. I suppose one must count one's blessings.'

The dog was eyeing us with the anticipatory gleam of a gourmet who can see a cordon bleu ankle approaching. I got Mouldar to distract him whilst I banged on the door.

The window shot up. 'Yeah? What ya wan'?'

'I'm looking for someone. An old woman. She lives here, wanders around quite a bit.'

I was yelling to make myself heard over the mind-numbing blast of acid house vibrating from the interior. The dog howled with even more vigour.

'There, there, boy. It's all right. Yooow!'

My head jerked round. Mouldar was frantically trying to shake off the dog as it clung grimly to his hand, its stumpy legs paddling furiously in mid-air.

'Yeh! Go to it, Prickle. Stuff the bastard!'

Balling my fists, I thumped down two-handed on the beast's nose. It dropped with an indignant yelp then lunged forward again.

We ran.

'You should get that hand seen to,' I panted when we paused for breath at the other end of the field, leaning breathlessly against an apparently abandoned and rusting van. 'Tetanus shot.'

'Oh, it's not too bad, miss. Gloves are pretty thick. It's hardly nicked, see. Let's just finish off down this end then I'll bandage it.'

Eventually we gleaned enough information for me to recognize my friend with the supermarket trolley from the seaside shelter.

'A gentleman in the end caravan says that she frequently moves along the coast, often for several weeks at a time,' Mr Mouldar explained, watching the cold water splash over his punctured hand and swirl in a pink tide round his stainless-steel sink.

I poured disinfectant liberally over the wound and applied a clumsy sticking plaster. 'I'm sorry about this.'

'Hardly your fault, miss. Could you just sprinkle some cleaning powder in the sink for me?'

'Where is it?'

'Top cupboard.'

He was using it as a makeshift book end to prop up assorted maps, local guides, DSS booklets, newspapers and other paraphernalia related to his job search.

I sprinkled, he scoured and wiped out neatly. 'There. I do find it pays to keep things clean on a regular basis, don't you, miss?'

I couldn't actually remember when I'd last cleaned the flat, but I hadn't the front to admit to such gross slovenliness, so I retreated into moaning about my perambulating witness. 'How am I supposed to keep her under tabs until the magistrates' court next week?'

I didn't really expect an answer. But Mouldar seemed to take my disappointment personally. 'They say she just goes from town to town. Collecting things in her trolley. Quite a little magpie, apparently. I could find her each day and then report back and tell you where she is. After all, she can hardly proceed at a very great speed.'

'I couldn't ask you to do that.'

'Oh, it would be a pleasure, miss. It's so encouraging to be finally making friends. They're a standoffish lot on this site.'

I didn't really fancy keeping Mouldar as a long-term buddy, if I was truthful. But if he didn't keep an eye on Supermarket Sal, then I'd have to. And it occurred to me I could probably bill the solicitor for mileage.

Since Mouldar didn't seem to expect any payment, I accepted his offer with thanks and drove home.

It was only after I'd settled down with a black coffee to bring my notes up to date that I'd recalled the message I'd left for Olly Colville. After a brief tussle with my resolve, which really wanted to snuggle up on the sofa, under the duvet, and gorge chocolate flakes dipped in coffee, I'd unrolled myself, climbed into the car, driven round to the office and found Drysdale's messages.

There was no sign that Olly Colville had returned my call. Assuming that the ban on receiving personal calls during working hours also applied to making them, I dropped back downstairs and checked the answerphone under Janice's desk for late callers.

There was nothing from Colville. But December had rung every half an hour until eight thirty.

I dialled his home number and let the distant phone trill for two minutes before digging out the car keys again and driving round to his house.

'You've missed 'im by twenty minutes,' Colin said, peering at me through the barred side gate. He reminded me of a picture I'd seen once of a gorilla at London Zoo.

'I don't suppose he said why he wanted to see me?'

'Can't say he did. Wanna come in and wait? I got the cards.'

'Sorry, Col. Duty calls.' Or, at the very least, central heating. The temperature had dropped noticeably over the past few hours. 'Do you know where December went?'

'Dunno.'

'Thanks, Col. You've been a big help.'

'*Have* I?'

'No. I was being sarcastic.'

'Me gran reckons that's the lowest form of wit.'

'That's me all right, Col. The original low-life. See ya.'

'Yeah. See ya.'

Eight or nine messages would seem to indicate that whatever December wanted, he wanted in a hurry. I was torn between going home and ringing in every few minutes, or trying to track him down.

The second option wasn't a sensible course of action. I knew little about December's life outside donkeys, beyond the facts that he belonged to an obscure sect and drank in the Electronic Daffodil. Going home and phoning him was the sensible choice.

I opted for tracking him down. Nobody had ever accused me of being sensible.

The church was out. I had absolutely no idea where it was located. (Or if, indeed, this sect had a formal church building. For all I knew they went in for aluminium pyramids aligned to ley lines.)

That left TED. I figured I'd charge the entrance fee to expenses.

Scuffed jeans, even more scuffed trainers and a jumper that had fluff balls the size of marbles were not going to get me into TED. I had to make another trip back to the flat and dig something suitable out of the pantry-wardrobe.

I opted for a black slip dress I'd picked up in a car boot sale and lace-up ankle boots. As an afterthought I looped a green silk scarf several times round my hips to appease the style police on the door; on Fridays and Saturdays TED can afford to be selective about its customers.

The queue outside testified to the fact that the inside had already reached the capacity allowed by its fire and safety certificates.

No one was drunk enough to mind yet. The crocodile giggled, joked and occasionally shuffled forward in a feint at the bouncers' solid shirt fronts. It was all very good-natured. Until I sauntered up the stairs. A murmur of resentment jabbed at my already chilly back.

One of the shirt fronts blocked my vision. 'Sorry, love. We're full at present. There's a queue if you'd like to wait.'

'I'm meeting someone inside.' (Hopefully.)

'You'll still have to wait. We'll send a message in to your friends if you'd like. Get someone to come out to you.'

I looked him up and down whilst he performed the same operation on me. We both recognized that I'd met the original immovable object.

'If you'd like to give us a name, love, we'll put it out over the speakers. Who's the lucky bloke?'

'Mr Drysdale.'

A 'Y' appeared between his eyebrows. 'Mr Drysdale's expecting you?'

'He's been trying to get in touch with me all evening.'

A jerk of my shirt front's head brought the other shirt front over. Heads touching, they murmured in conference.

Another jerk summoned a third bouncer, who must have been standing behind the mirrored doors. After a quick consultation, he took up guard on the front step. My shirt front beckoned me into the lobby.

'What's your name, miss?'

I was interested to see I wasn't his love any more. 'Tell him Smithie. No. On second thoughts, say it's Grace. He'll know. We're old friends.'

'Stop here.'

I stopped. There were no chairs, so I occupied myself investigating the urns and troughs of greenery, trying to second-guess which were real and which artificial.

I'd just ripped a leaf off a yellow and green specimen which seemed to fall between two stools when the automatic inner door hissed open, releasing a brain-numbing blast of dance music and a vision.

'Good evening, I'm the manager. I hear we're old friends.'

Well, I certainly wouldn't complain, was the thought that sprang to mind while I struggled to thrust the evidence of plant vandalism out of sight.

Late thirties; brown hair, brown eyes; square face; six feet tall; blue silk shirt; Italian designer trousers and jacket; the sort of winter tan that's acquired in swish ski resorts.

My hormones did a quick victory roll and signalled "jackpot".

Leaning casually against the mirrored wall, he folded his arms across his chest and waited.

I became aware of two things simultaneously. One: his wedding ring. Two: I was gaping.

'Sorry,' I apologized, ordering the hormones back to base and trying for my best cool-collected-career-girl look. 'I think there's been a mistake. I asked for Mr Drysdale.'

'That's me.'

'It is?'

Something about the amused brown eyes triggered a memory. 'You're Kevin!'

'Guilty!'

'Well, that explains that. I thought it was a weird place for your dad to drink.'

'I think I get the picture. You're meeting Dad here, are you?'

'I'm not sure about meeting. He wants to talk to me urgently. But we keep missing each other. Is he in there?'

On cue the doors slid open again and another few decibels of eardrum assault thudded out. A drunken foursome swayed out and across to the coat-check.

'Coats, darling.'

The girl in the kiosk was wearing the same black trousers and yellow waistcoat as the bartenders. Shaking a curtain of blue-black oriental hair, she reached under the counter and passed over a breathalyser. I expected a complaint but the recipient blew meekly into the bag and even managed a sheepish grin at the cheers of derision when he failed.

'Let me. I'm not as pissed as him.'

Another bag went across the counter. Lips thick with gloss lipstick were clamped round it. She looked pretty pissed to me, but she must have been under the limit. The bloke made a half-hearted snatch at the key ring, which she foiled by dropping it down her cleavage.

Kevin had been watching this exchange with a relaxed smile. I reclaimed his attention by asking what happened if someone refused to be tested.

'We ask them to wait in the back office while we call the police to arbitrate. There are very few takers. Normally they let us call them a cab. You said you were looking for Dad. Are you something to do with the church?'

'Me? No! Do I look like I might be?' Somehow I'd been picturing this sect as all thermal underwear and scrubbed faces.

'Hard to say,' Kevin informed me. 'They come in all shapes and sizes. It's just that most of Dad's acquaintances are in that lot.'

'I'm a private detective. He employed me to . . .'

'Sort out Marilyn Monroe. He did tell me, but the name didn't click. You don't look like a private dick.'

'I'm not. I haven't the anatomy.'

'Sorry. I was weaned on a diet of American movies. Look, Dad's not in at the moment, but he might look in later. Why don't you come up to the office? I'll ring round, see if I can track him down.'

He used an electronic key card to open a side door and led me up a steep carpeted staircase. At the top another key let him into a room off a narrow landing. As soon as he shut the heavy door, the sounds of dance music which had been filtering into the stairwell stopped as if cut off by a guillotine.

It seemed to be half-office, half-lounge. The part we'd stepped into contained the desk and filing cabinets. The farther end had the easy chairs, coffee table and bar. Leading me across the thick grey carpeting, Kevin indicated a chair.

'Have a seat. Drink?'

I elected for vodka and tonic, he had bitter lemon. Both were served up in heavy crystal glasses that weighed half a pound apiece.

'Cheers.'

I couldn't resist it. 'Here's looking at you, kid.'

'I see Dad's got to you already.'

'He didn't have to. My dad's a fan too.'

We clinked rims in celebration of parental eccentricity.

Kevin flicked a remote control in the direction of the desk, and the floor-to-ceiling venetian blinds that lined the left-hand wall of the office twisted open. Cindy, the blonde bartender, was standing two inches from the glass wall, grimacing in at us.

After a second's disorientation, I realized I was looking through the back wall of the bar December and I had sat at a few days previously. Instinctively, I hitched up a slipping dress strap.

'It's OK. The mirror's one-way. They can't see you.'

There is something quite irresistible about voyeurism. From up here I had a clear view of all of the mezzanine and about half the dance floor below.

Fascinated, I carried my drink over to the window and watched as they grimaced, gestured and swayed. There was no sound at all; the whole thing was like viewing a silent film.

Behind me Kevin had picked up a handset and was punching in a series of numbers.

Three calls later, he'd located his father.

'One of the congregation has been taken ill,' he explained, sliding the aerial down with his chin. 'Dad's hanging on for the doctor. He says to keep you pinned down till he gets here.'

It was an idea I wouldn't have been averse to, if it hadn't been for the perspex-framed photos of two boys and what was presumably Mrs Kevin Drysdale that I'd glimpsed on the desk as we came in.

'I could wait out there if I'm in the way,' I suggested, waving an empty glass at the eerily silent nightclub.

'Whichever you prefer. You're OK here if you want. Excuse me.'

This time the caller was reporting some kind of administrative problem. Excusing himself, Kevin left to sort it out.

I went back to my contemplation of the pantomime beyond the wall. It was remarkable how daft people appear with the sound turned down. Hands waved, mouths jerked up and down, eyes rolled and tics appeared in all sorts of unsuspected places.

The music must have changed to a slower number. Down on the floor everyone was swaying in slow motion. With closed eyes and expressions of apparent agony, they shuffled and dipped in some kind of mating dance.

The flickering lights illuminated a circle of females, weaving and bobbing at each other. I recognized WPC Jane Mullins; her plump figure squeezed into a short black skirt and metallic-striped waistcoat. Beyond her Terry Rosco was clamped to Gina Rawlins, his hands caressing her bottom through her brown silk trousers. A switch of lights silhouetted the WPC who'd pointed out Mullins for me. Scanning with more attention this time, I spotted the other brunette who'd been leaving the police station with Mullins and Gina. It must be the local nick's night out.

I took another look and tried to find Zeb or DCI Jackson. But CID seemed to be unrepresented.

However, I did chalk up another familiar face. Annie was weaving her way between the mezzanine tables towards two empty seats. In her wake she was trailing a slimmish bloke in his early forties. Presumably the famous Jonathon.

I watched as they performed a little ritual of 'You take this chair'; 'No, it's OK, you have that one'; 'Look, I think you'd be better in this one.'

It was like being invisible. The temptation was too strong. Sticking my tongue out, I waggled my fingers in my ears.

'Of course, the security cameras can still pick you up,' Kevin remarked.

Embarrassed, I swung round. He'd slipped in without my noticing him. Searching for something to say, I pointed to Annie. 'That's my best friend. And her boyfriend.'

'Did you want to say hello?'

'In a sec.'

Fascinated, I watched them. Annie was waving her hands around, emphasizing a point.

'Can you lip-read?' I asked Kevin.

'A bit. They're tossing up between glasses or a bottle of white wine.' He lifted the phone again.

Cindy lifted a wall receiver next to the optics.

Kevin told her to take across a bottle of champagne and two glasses to the couple at table nine. 'Say it's with the compliments of Miss Grace Smith.'

'You didn't have to do that,' I protested.

'Pleasure.'

The ice bucket and glasses were duly delivered. I grinned, watching Annie swivelling this way and that trying to find me.

Kevin was pouring himself a refill. He raised the vodka bottle with an enquiring look.

'Please.' I took my glass across. 'Are you teetotal? Or is it a case of "not on duty"?'

'Neither. It's just I have to drive home tonight.'

'Your dad's got a thing about drink-driving as well, hasn't he?'

'He didn't tell you why?'

'I'd sort of assumed it was the religious thing again.'

'No.' Hitching up his trousers at the knee, Kevin perched on a chair arm. 'It was Mum. She was killed by a drunk driver. Dad was driving our car at the time. He's never driven anything but the donkey cart since.'

I sat down opposite him, cradling my glass. The icy bottom froze my knees. I was caught in another of those sticky emotional moments when I had to say something, but I hadn't the faintest idea what.

I fell back on the detail my detective's mind had registered and stored. 'It was a while ago, wasn't it? I'm going on the age of the photos in your dad's place.'

'Twenty years. The bloke ran a red light, smashed into Dad's car; passenger side. Dad got off with whiplash. Mum died three days later. The bloke got a suspended sentence. Previous good character, the judge said.'

'I'm sorry. That's shitty. How old were you?'

'Eighteen. And I thought I knew all the answers. I was no use at all to Dad. That's when he took up with the donkeys. I mean, he'd always run the string, of course, but they were just sort of pets, like cats or dogs. After Mum, he started treating them like they were kids. He's not daft, though. Far from it.'

'I didn't imagine he was. I like your dad.'

'Good. What about your old man? Did he teach you this detective business?'

'No. He *was* a policeman.'

Our career paths had crossed; Dad had come out of the force just about the time I was being sworn in. Had he listened to Mum he'd have been a bored but healthy store manager for a frozen-food shop. But the police had always been Dad's ambition. So once we kids had reached the ages where we'd left home and were fully – if not always gainfully – employed, Dad had become the force's oldest recruit.

Two years later colleagues answering his emergency call had found him slumped in an alley behind some empty garages.

'He'd been stabbed through the spine with a sharpened metal pole. He's been paralysed from the waist down ever since.'

It was Kevin's turn to murmur awkward condolences. 'Did they catch whoever did it?'

'Not exactly.'

Everyone knew who'd done it. In fact he'd even jogged past our house a few times when Dad came out of hospital; making a special point of running on the spot outside our gate.

'Three of his mates gave him an alibi. Said he was in a card game at the time. And Dad never got a clear look. They'd got him from behind, see. So that was that. No prosecution.'

'Why'd he do it?'

I shrugged. 'He'd been boasting he was going to stick a pig for months. He's got a legitimate business now. And all the trimmings: company car, detached house, trophy wife. My dad got a pittance in compensation and my mum looks after him and works part-time too because they need the money. Although we all have to pretend it's because she wants an outside interest for the sake of Dad's pride.'

While I'd been talking, Kevin had eased from the arm to the seat of his own chair. Now he leant towards mine and clasped my bare forearm. Goose pimples shot down my back. 'I'm not surprised you left the police yourself.'

Obviously Drysdale Senior hadn't passed on the rumours about my inglorious career. 'It didn't put me off the job. It just made me realize how important it is to have money. Plenty of it. I don't intend to ever be poor.'

I knew I sounded self-pitying. I didn't realize I also sounded tearful, until Kevin passed me his handkerchief.

'Sorry. I hate women who snivel.'

'You don't snivel. You cry very attractively.'

By some process of which I'd been unconscious, he seemed to have eased himself on to my chair arm and his arm was round my shoulder.

It was at this point that December arrived and delivered the message that he'd been trying to share with me since four o'clock.

I was fired.

CHAPTER 17

'You can't do that!'

'Yes I can.' December opened his son's mini-fridge, helped himself to a bottle of lager and poured it slowly into a straight glass. The action left me glaring at the back of his tweed jacket.

He was quite right. He was the customer. He could dispense with my services any time he felt like it; in the same way I could pull out of a case whenever I chose. There was no obligation on either side beyond the settlement of legitimate fees and expenses and the surrendering of any relevant material I'd collected in the course of the investigation.

'Look,' I tried again, pitching my voice lower and trying to sound reasonable, 'I realize it may not look as if things are moving very fast, but it takes a bit of time to—'

'It's not that,' December interrupted, taking his son's vacated seat. Kevin had found something to occupy him at the desk.

'I want the whole thing laid to rest. Marilyn's gone to a better place. I'd rather you didn't join him.'

Comprehension didn't so much dawn as explode into a full sun-burst: 'Oh, I get it. Jackson's told you to dump me!'

December sipped calmly and informed me that Detective Chief Inspector Jackson was in no position to "tell" him to do anything.

'Perhaps not. But he's behind this, isn't he?'

'He did point out the danger you could be in, yes. When I hired you, Grace, I imagined we were facing an Assyrian who'd come down on the fold, so to speak. If I'd known that this one wasn't so much a wolf as a headhunter for the Angel of Death, I would never have started. You can keep the cash advance. But no more investigation.'

'I don't want the cash advance!'

What was I saying? The shock of such blasphemy stunned me into silence.

'Give it back then,' December said calmly.

'No. I mean . . . I'll have to work out your account.'

'Fair enough.'

I wanted to argue, but in the short time I'd known December, I'd formed the distinct impression that he could be as stubborn as his precious donkeys when he felt like it. And tonight he plainly felt like it.

'Fine. If that's what you want, I'll go.'

Kevin returned from his tactful self-exile at the desk. Dropping a file on the table, he retrieved the remote control and clicked the venetian blinds shut again. 'There's no need to rush off, is there?'

'Up to me now, isn't it? My time's my own.'

Why did I always manage to sound petulant when I wanted to sound indifferent?

'Stay and enjoy the club for a while,' Kevin suggested. 'Join your friends. I'll send more drinks across.'

'I suppose I might as well,' I said off-handedly.

'Good.'

'I'll be in touch,' I said to December, keeping my chin up and stalking towards the door that led to the front stairs.

It was a performance that was somewhat marred when Kevin took my elbow, turned me one hundred and eighty degrees and ushered me to the other end of the office.

December had opened the file his son had flung down and was rifling through the papers inside. He didn't look up as I repassed his chair, but I could have sworn he chuckled under his breath.

The stairwell at the other end of the office was identical,

except that the steep flight of stairs led to the back of the building rather than the front lobby. And an additional door on the landing led into the mezzanine bar.

Attuned to the silence of the office, my senses received an auditory shock as a confused blend of formless sound swept over them. After a few seconds, they started to sort themselves into music, laughter and individual voices.

'I'll fix the drinks,' Kevin shouted into my ear, his breath tickling the tiny filaments in my ear canals. 'Are you sticking to vodka? Or champagne?'

'Champagne.' I knew how to freeload with the best of them.

The bar area was packed. Shuffling crabwise and putting my elbows and shoulders to good use, I managed to fight my way to Annie's table by the mezzanine rail. She had her back to me and didn't react until I tapped her shoulder.

'Hi! I was looking for you. Thanks for . . .' She touched the empty bottle lolling in its ice bucket. 'This is Grace. She's the one who sent us . . .' The introductions were bawled across the table. I had to lean right over to hear that Jonathon was pleased to meet me.

'Same here. Heard a lot about you.'

Actually I'd heard precious little, so I looked him over now. He was the original Mr Average: pale complexion, pale-blue eyes, pale-brown hair professionally styled to hide the bald spot. His clothes were expensive, mind you: little designer motifs peeped from under his dark-blue shirt's collar, smirked from his linen jacket's inner pocket and peeked up from behind the hand-tooled leather trouser belt. Even his socks had Lacoste crocodiles hugging the ankle-bones.

Annie was wearing the embroidered black chiffon number over a gold dress. Her legs gleamed whitely beneath shiny black tights.

Leaning closer, so that I could see a convex distortion of my face reflected in her shaded spectacles, Annie shouted: 'If you can afford champagne, how come you can't pay my telephone bill?'

'Don't be so plebeian,' I yelled back. 'Anyway, I didn't pay for it. The manager's a friend of mine.'

This news didn't impress Annie one jot. Although Jonathon shot me a look of respect when Cindy arrived with a fresh bottle, three glasses and dishes of peanuts, olives and unidentifiable balls covered in breadcrumbs.

Uncovered food attracts pests, our food technology teacher had preached. This lot certainly had that effect.

Terry Rosco materialized out of the wreaths of drifting cigarette smoke and strobe lighting. One arm was still clamped possessively around Gina, although I noticed she'd moved it a few inches further up her anatomy.

''Lo, Annie. Good to see you.'

He pointedly ignored me. So I introduced myself to Gina. Noting the wedding ring, I asked: 'Is your husband here, Gina? I hear he's fun.'

'Dunno who told you that. Any'ow, it's job only. No uvver 'alves. 'Ere, they got champers, Terr. I could really go a glass of that.'

Her voice was a shock. It was like hearing a beautiful, sleek leopard open its jaws and emit a pig's grunt.

'What's the occasion?'

'Janie's birfday. Been trying to keep shtoom about it, 'adn't she, Terr?'

She waved a hand tipped with blood-red nails in the direction of the bar. Squinting against the stinging smoke, I made out WPC Mullins handing over a sheaf of notes.

She must have caught Gina's gesture in the mirror. Leaving one of the other girls to carry the round of drinks, she made her way across to our table.

'Sorry, couldn't find you, Gina,' she said. 'My shout.'

She was standing at my shoulder, and slightly behind me. Before Gina could respond, I smiled up into her nostrils and said loudly: 'It's OK, Jane, Gina fancies champagne. Terry was just going to get a bottle in. Take a seat and have a glass.'

I grabbed the dripping bottle from its bucket and waved it at Cindy, semaphoring another one and three more glasses.

'Ooh, lovely, Terr.' Gina planted the impression of her red lips on his cheek, and slipped me a broad wink as she dragged another seat to the table.

Jane Mullins perched on the edge of her own seat, displaying plump knees and a few inches of bosom where the top button of her waistcoat had come undone. 'Hello. Grace, isn't it? I didn't recognize you all dressed up. How's Mr Drysdale? Have you found out who killed his donkey yet?'

'No. Not yet.'

I wasn't going to admit in front of this audience that I'd been given the push.

'Bit too much of an intellectual challenge, was it?' Terry was leaning back against the mezzanine rail. Now he bent forward, scooped up a fistful of peanuts and flicked one into his tilted mouth.

'Terry,' I squealed in mock admiration, 'I didn't know you'd graduated to words of five syllables. Can you do joined-up writing yet?'

Terry scowled, flicked and snatched another nut with his teeth.

Before he could think of a smart reply, Cindy took his breath away by telling him the price of the champagne.

'Ooh, Terr. You're a mate. I just love a bloke 'oo knows 'ow to splash owt.'

Gina slid the geranium nails up Terry's thigh, which was at her cheek level.

I was beginning to warm to Gina. She was evidently a woman who knew her own worth and was going to make sure Terry paid it to the last ecu.

Jonathon took a handful of stuffed olives and imitated Terry's thumb flick. Unfortunately he miscalculated and the descending black globe disappeared down his open shirt. We all pretended not to notice.

The music mercifully changed to a caressing tempo, the new mood reflected by the lighting. Brilliant bursts of eye-aching primary light no longer stabbed across the dance floor. Instead the whole area was bathed in washes of violet, azure, indigo and aquamarine. Up above, the roof had darkened to velvet black and instead of spotlights, star constellations twinkled against the dome.

For a moment I imagined the ceiling was retractable. But the temperature remained constant, signalling that it was all done with lights.

'Oooh, ain't that somefing else, Terr? Sor' of puts you in the mood for it, don' it?'

'Yeah? Want to dance then?'

'Nah, let's finish the drink first.'

Annie didn't want to dance either. So the six of us were stuck with each other until we'd all polished off our fair share of the champagne.

Another handful of snacks disappeared down Terry's gob. 'What line you in then, Jon? Not another private snooper, are you?'

'Me! No. I'm in computers.'

At least four of us started to exhibit the glazed expression that words such as 'modem', 'software' and 'rom' can bring on faster than tranquillizers.

'Gawd, are you? I'd be bored stiff stuck in front o' one of them screens all day.' Gina experimented with one of the breadcrumbed balls, nibbling with lipstick-smeared teeth.

'Me too,' Terry agreed. 'Can't stand desk work meself. Miss the action too much.' He mimed an upward punch.

There was an awkward pause which was eventually filled by Jane contributing that she quite liked those computer game things. 'Although I'm not very good at them. I bet you're terrific.'

'I don't play, I'm afraid. The software for those can be quite sophisticated, I suppose. But of course I was referring to the leading edge of the art,' Jonathon said. 'Laser technology; star wars; operations performed by robots. You name it, it's probably controlled by a computer. Or will be in the near future. I feel sorry for the techno-illiterates. Really, if you don't understand the basics, you'll be as handicapped as, well . . . a medieval peasant trying to drive a car.'

Terry was back on safer ground. 'What sort of motor you got, Jon?'

Tilting back and crossing his ankles, Jon included the whole table in his reply. 'Porsche.' He managed the olive-flicking trick this time before continuing, 'You want a bit of power under the bonnet. How about you, Terry? What sort of wheels you go for?'

'Volvo. Estate.'

'Really?' Jon's supercilious smirk invited us all to note that he'd come off best in that round.

'It's for the missus,' Terry said, a defensive note creeping into his cocky tone. 'Needs something roomy for the shopping and kids, you know?'

'Sympathize.' Jon nodded. 'Sympathize. Had the same problem myself. The wife insisted on a Fiesta. Not my thing, but there you are; can't expect a woman to handle the big boys, can you? Different now I've dumped her, of course.'

Annie had told me Jonathon's wife had gone off with his best friend. I flicked a quick look to see how she was taking this metaphorical chest-thumping. She was nibbling and sipping with an indulgent smile.

'Wha' you reckon them balls are?' Gina asked, licking each fingertip thoroughly.

'Fried couscous I think,' Annie said, sampling another.

'Taste a bit naff, don' they? Give us yer glass, Terr, I gotta get this taste out me mowf.' The last of Terry's champagne went down in one swallow. 'That's betta. I feel like a dance now.' Standing up, she slid her palms over her stomach, flattening the brown silk trousers. 'Fancy a bop then, Jonnie?'

'Heh, what's the idea? You're with me.'

'Oh, lighten up, Terr. It's a party, ain't it? Put yourself around a bit. Come on, Jon.'

Dragged from his seat, Jon let himself be pulled down the stairs on to the dance floor. From where I was sitting, he didn't put up much resistance.

Terry's next move was transparently obvious. He needed a partner to dance with, or more accurately, grope to music, in order to demonstrate to Gina her dispensability. Annie's expression was not inviting. Not even rampant sexual jealousy was going to make him ask me. That left one alternative.

Jane had just discovered the open waistcoat button, refastened it and was unsuccessfully wriggling her skirt down over her knees when she was hauled up by one wrist and dragged off with a grunted, 'Come on.'

Shifting round to take the empty seat next to Annie, I remarked: 'How'd you think she got past the selection tests? Not exactly assertive, is she?'

'Perhaps she has hidden depths.' Annie slewed round in her own seat until she could look me full in the face. 'What's up?'

'How'd you mean?'

'Oh, come on. I know you. Something's bugging you. And it's not Terry Rosco. I got puncture wounds from the raised prickles soon as you sat down.'

'I've been sacked.'

'You're self-employed.'

'From the job. The Marilyn Monroe thing. December's given me the elbow. Thanks to your pals in CID. Jackson fed him a load of guff about me being in danger.'

'Well, you might be.'

'Thanks. Whose side are you on?'

'Don't get shirty with me. It's not my fault. He's not trying to get out of the fee, is he?'

'No.'

'There you are, then.'

'There I am, where?' I demanded. 'Un-em-bloody-ployed, that's where. Apart from keeping dibs on Supermarket Sal, the wandering witness.'

'Who?'

'Never mind.'

'I could use some help on these divorce surveillance jobs if you're at a loose end.'

'No thanks. I don't need hand-outs.'

'Please yourself, you moody ratbag.'

Edging her seat nearer the rail, Annie watched the dancers below. Having killed off the conversation, I joined her.

It was hard to tell where Jon ended and Gina began. Entwined in a knot of limbs, they were swaying in closed-eyed oblivion while Terry orbited them like a jealous comet, hauling a red-faced Jane around like a sack of potatoes.

'Is it serious? You and Jonathon?'

'Bit early to say.'

'Translation: it is with me but he hasn't made up his mind yet?'

'You might think that. I couldn't possibly comment.'

'I see.' My already sinking spirits headed for the seabed. No more cosy girlie evenings chez Annie. The idea of cosy evenings chez Jon-and-Annie was just too horrible to contemplate. But how do you point out to your best friend that her fellow is a pretentious prat?

Annie managed to read my mind again. 'He's not really like that, you know. It's just what his wife said, about him being boring, it hurt.'

For once I exercised some tact, and bit my tongue rather than point out that the truth often did.

Instead I determinedly concentrated on the dancers.

Which was just as well, because I'd probably glanced over him half a dozen times already without connecting.

He was alone as far as I could tell. Lost in the music, he moved in slow motion to Whitney Houston's impassioned assurance that she'd always love him. Indigo light bathed the Botticelli face in an eerie luminescence and darkened the red hair to the shade achieved by a henna rinse that had gone badly awry.

'Annie, centre left. Ponytail, five ten, dark trousers, white shirt, dark waistcoat.'

'Got him. What about him?'

'It's *him*. The bloke who was searching Judy Parker's house that night I took a look round.'

'So? You're off the case, remember?'

'I'm not being paid to work on it any more. That doesn't mean I can't ask questions on my own account.'

'Hang on. Let me tip off Terry. Get you some back-up.'

'Don't you dare,' I hissed in her face. 'This is nothing to do with the police.'

Without any clear idea of what I was going to do when I got there, I sauntered casually down on to the dance floor.

Using the engrossed couples as cover, I edged closer to my quarry.

I was almost within spitting distance when his unfocused eyes made contact with mine, snapped back into focus and registered alarm.

Wheeling on one heel, he barged off the floor and headed for the front door.

Trying not to attract undue attention, I followed.

He'd disappeared by the time I walked briskly into the lobby. Approaching the Chinese girl at the coat-check, I asked if my boyfriend had left yet.

'Five ten-ish. Red ponytail.'

'He just went out. Second ago,' she assured me.

'Thanks.'

The wind had whipped up. It felt like an icy sponge bath across my bare arms and back. Shivering theatrically for the benefit of the doorkeepers, I started to run for the car park.

The barriers were down. I went through the same missing boyfriend routine with a parking attendant.

'Went that way, love,' he said, indicating the right-hand corner of the asphalt rectangle.

'Cheers.'

I couldn't do anything about the boots clicking on the hard surface. Warned of my approach, he'd got the car into gear and was already pulling away by the time I reached the Metro.

Planting myself in the headlights, I mimed "switch off" and jerked a thumb: "Out."

My weight was on the balls of my feet, ready to spring sideways if he decided to hit the accelerator. But I guess he was as conscious as I was of the security cameras.

Leaving the engine running, he stepped out, cradling his arm along the half-open door. 'What's your problem?'

I raised warning eyebrows in the direction of the camera monitor. 'Smile, you never know, Beadle might be about.'

He saw the sense of that instruction. With a friendly beam he murmured: 'Get out the way, you bitch.'

With a carefree laugh, I told him no chance. 'Not until you tell me what you were looking for at the Parkers'.'

'Chill out, I'm not telling you zilch.'

'Darling,' I cooed, blowing a kiss, 'did you know the place is just jam-packed with police officers this evening?'

'So call them, babe. What they going to do about a bit of trespass? Now f**k off.' He accompanied this advice with a regretful shrug of his shoulders, presumably indicating to the watching cameras that I'd refused a lift. Stepping back into the car, he gunned the engine.

Another pair of headlights, sweeping round to approach the exit, momentarily dazzled me. Instinctively I looked away and shifted my position slightly. It gave my intruder just the extra few inches he needed to shoot past me.

The approach was so close, the wing mirror caught me a glancing blow in the stomach. With an "oof" of surprise, I reeled backwards and sat down heavily between two parked vehicles.

Running feet sped across the car park.

'Are you OK?'

Leaning against somebody's tyre, I peered up at Annie's anxious face.

'Just fine,' I managed to gasp.

'I got that maniac's number. Let's hope the car wasn't nicked.'

'Don't worry.' Shifting a bare shoulder against the chilly metal, I tried to regain my breath. 'It wasn't. Leastways, I'm not sure his dad knows he's got it. But I don't suppose he and his gran consider it stealing.'

'I thought you didn't know him.'

'He's grown up since his last portrait sitting.'

Then both his height and his hair had been at least a foot shorter. But as soon as I'd seen that busted tail-light, the memories had clicked into place.

'That,' I informed Annie, panting noisily, 'is the saintly Elaine's eldest.'

'Who?'

'Mrs Edwin Woolley's grandson.'

CHAPTER 18

I failed the rotten breathalyser test and had to get a cab home.

The weekend lived up to its promise. Rain tipped down in a series of lashing squalls, leaving all those who'd booked mini-breaks on the strength of the recent hot spell to throng the amusement arcades and shops.

I spent a frustrating forty-eight hours trying to talk to people who didn't want to speak to me.

Chief amongst them was Olly Colville.

Having walked round and retrieved my car from TED's car park, I'd dropped into the office for a couple of hours on Saturday morning to give Olly the chance to call. By eleven o'clock I'd acknowledged he wasn't going to ring me. I dialled the garage again.

Colville wasn't there.

'He's not turned in. Claims he's sick.'

This time I'd got as far as the manager. 'How d'you mean, claims?' I asked.

'Are you a friend?'

Honesty seemed the best policy in this case. 'I'm a private investigator. I've been trying to trace him. Why'd you say claims to be ill?'

'I mean Colville's symptoms have a habit of getting worse at the weekend, which is our busiest time. He pulled the same stroke last week. If you do find him, tell him he's fired.'

'Have you got a home number?'

'We've already tried it. He moved a couple of months back. Don't know where his new gaff is. Best of luck, love.'

'Thanks,' I murmured as the dialling tone hummed back along the disconnected line. Judging by that crack about Colville skiving at weekends, I guessed he must have pretended to be sick on the Friday he'd taken off to keep his appointment at Alan Kersey's hospice.

My mind jumped from Kersey to his solicitor. If Spinnaker had traced Olly Colville for his client, then he must have the new address.

Easy-peasy.

Spinnaker's answerphone picked up the call; neither he nor Jo were available to speak to me at present, but I was invited to leave a message after the tone.

'Hi. It's Grace. The message is that I hate talking to these things.'

I tried the restaurant where Jo worked. He was "orf", according to the woman who answered the phone. 'A dirty weekend in Amsterdam, the lucky sod.'

'I don't suppose he left a phone number?'

'Would you?'

'Probably not.'

Hanging up, I wallowed in a wave of self-pity. The fates were against me.

The office was cold and the radiators were even colder. Vetch never switched the boiler on at the weekend unless he had clients himself.

Thrusting my hands into my jumper sleeves, I leant back in the chair, crossed my ankles on the desk and watched the rain flinging itself against the window panes.

After a while that got boring, so I hauled up the jumper, unfastened a few shirt buttons and admired the purple and red design of the bruises left by the wing mirror last night.

Why was I giving myself all this hassle? Even my client no longer required my services. Perhaps I should just take Annie's parting advice last night and forget the whole thing.

I could work out December's account, add a few generously

calculated expenses and let the boys in blue and/or divine justice catch up with Marilyn's killer.

'I'll do it. Sod them all!' I informed the empty office. Returning the chair upright, I decided on a comfort splurge of coffee and biscuits first to warm myself up. And then Marilyn and her ungrateful owner would be consigned to my "case closed" drawer.

I was out of coffee. Annie's door was locked. I tried other offices on my scrounge for a teaspoonful of instant granules. Every single one was tightly shut up for the weekend.

'Paranoid lot,' I growled at the deserted reception area. My lock-picking tools were in the car outside. But by the time I'd fiddled around in here, I could be at Pepi's.

Pepi's won. Resetting the security system, I drove back along the nearly deserted front. Everything on the beach was lashed down: blue tarpaulins covered the deckchair stacks and trampolining areas, and the hatches of the ice-cream and snack bars were closed and bolted over the serving areas. In the paddling pool the yellow-grey water was speeding along and slopping over the pitted walls as the wind created the illusion of a tide.

There was no sign of December or the lads.

Pepi's was delightfully fugged up, the windows dripping condensation and obscuring the customers unless they'd rubbed themselves a personal porthole in the steamy glass.

Inside, a delicious aroma of frying onions, coffee and toast combined with a not-so-delicious whiff of damp clothes.

It was also packed with other lost souls trying to keep out of the rain. Squeezing soaked hair back off my face, I made for the only empty seat and plumped myself down.

'Is this seat . . . Oh, hi, Annie.'

'Hi yourself. How're your bruises?'

'Getting bruises of their own. Wanna see?'

'No thanks. People are eating.'

'You aren't,' I remarked, wrinkling my nose at the black coffee.

'I'm dieting.'

'Can't Jonathon accept you as you are?'

'Of course he can! This is for my benefit, not his.'

'Oh yeah? Where is Sonic today? He's not meeting you here, is he?'

'It's his weekend for the kids. And there's no need to be so bitchy about him.'

'I feel bitchy. So I've come in for a spot of comfort gorging. What's your excuse for hanging out in a greasy spoon?'

'I'm working.' As proof, she tilted the shoulder bag hanging from her chair back so I could see the camera.

'Where's the target?'

'By the window. Second from the door. She's supposed to be at her sister's place in Rochester.'

Under the pretence of trying to attract some service, I looked across. Passion comes in all shapes and sizes. These two were rumpled, middle-aged and instantly forgettable.

'You'll have trouble getting any decent pictures in this weather.'

'I know, I was hoping for some excuses to get off a shot in here.'

'Buy us some elevenses and I'll get you one. You can put it on your expenses.'

'Deal.'

I gave my order: large white coffee with three sugars and a mega-sized toasted tea-cake with lashings of strawberry jam.

'Sadist,' Annie hissed. She tensed suddenly, staring over my shoulder.

'They going?'

'Could be. No, it's OK.'

Mr Rumpled brushed past us on his way to the counter. Collecting a shilling from Shane, he made his way over to the jukebox and fed the monster.

Marty Wilde's mournful tones rose above the general chatter; his baby wanted him to join her 'Endless Sleep'.

'Bloody hell!' I hissed at Annie. 'You don't think they're planning to chuck themselves off the harbour, do you?'

'Shouldn't think so. They look fine to me. Take a peek.'

Hands clasped, they were gazing into each other's eyes in blissful enjoyment whilst Marty's "baby" drowned herself in the deep.

The tea-cake arrived, sliding down Shane's hairy forearm as the last of a four-plate delivery. 'So what d'you reckon to this number, Shane?'

'Lovely performer, Marty. Knew how to really reach in an' grab yer guts with a song. We played the same bill with him once.'

I'll say one thing for Shane, he knew how to feed his cues. Even if he was unaware he was doing it.

'Shane used to be a famous rock star, you know,' I informed Annie loudly.

'Pardon?' Annie looked blank. Mainly at my choice of the word "famous", I imagine.

'He played with all the big ones, didn't you, Shane?' Grabbing his arm, I snuggled up to his T-shirt. 'Would you give me your autograph?'

'Leave off.'

Assuming it was a wind-up, he tried to head back behind the counter. I hung on.

'Oh, go on. Give him the napkin, Annie.'

This time I managed to tip him a broad wink.

Puzzled, but game to join in, Shane duly scrawled the napkin to "Smithie with love".

'How about a picture together?' Annie suggested.

'Ooh, *yes*. Is this all right?' I thrust a hip into Shane's and beamed fatuously.

'Move a bit left, I'm getting the tea urn in.'

Arms round each other's waists, Shane and I shuffled first left, then right, as Annie lined us up. Finally, she pronounced herself satisfied and squeezed. The automatic motor fired off half a dozen flash shots. Only we saw the lens slide on to its new targets after the first two pictures.

'Thanks,' Annie whispered, re-storing the camera as Shane shot off in response to a bellowed "Sausage, chips, peas. Two cod".

'My pleasure. I aim to please.'

'You miss the target a lot.'

'Ungrateful bitch,' I mumbled, masticating large lumps of toasted tea-cake and jam.

'I believe in telling my friends the truth.'

'Take my tip: lie. You'll keep them longer.'

Thrusting up her jumper sleeves, Annie leant her elbows on the table and rested her chin in her hands. 'Have you decided what to do about this donkey case yet?'

'Yep. I'm taking your advice and ditching the whole mess.'

'I'm glad. It's for the best, Grace. We both know that all these stories of the talented amateur swanning in and uncovering the murderer under the noses of the dumb coppers are just a load of balls. Leave it to the police. They've got the back-up if things get nasty. Less chance of said murderer ploughing over them with a transit truck when they get too close to the evidence.'

'Nicely put, Annie.'

'What? Oh, sorry. I was forgetting about . . .'

'My inglorious departure from the job?'

'Well, yes.'

'I suppose I should be glad someone has.'

One of the reasons for my departure from the police was linked to the injury of another officer for which I was held indirectly (although not officially) responsible. But let's not get into that now.

For the present I was making up my mind to abandon Marilyn's murder and – by association – Tina's as well, and return to tracing lost pets, straying spouses and wandering kids.

In a haze of virtuous resolution, something Annie was saying connected in my brain.

'What did you say?'

Swilling out the last dregs of black coffee, Annie repeated: 'I said I'm glad I'm out of the job myself on days like this. I don't envy Zeb and the rest of the team freezing their assets off searching that factory site in this weather.'

'When you say "factory", you mean the one where they found Marilyn's body?'

'Well of course I do.'

The penny dropped. Tina had, according to news reports, been murdered elsewhere and dumped by the roadside. And what's the best way to hide a murder? Under another one, that's where. Particularly one that wouldn't attract much of a police investigation. Faced with a dead donkey and a building splattered in donkey blood, who'd have bothered to check for forensic evidence of another crime?

'Do you mean to say Jackson has pinched my theory that Marilyn and Tina were killed by the same person? After he had the nerve to junk it yesterday!'

'There's no need to get so shirty. Maybe you could ask for a credit on the final report. You know, "We gratefully acknowledge the assistance of . . ." sort of thing . . . Where are you going?'

'To get back on my case, that's where!'

'You've packed it in.'

'I've just rehired myself.'

CHAPTER 19

Simla Woolley was out as well. The sainted Elaine had taken her shopping. Thereby frustrating my plan to ask a few pertinent questions *vis-à-vis* her grandson's nocturnal search of the Parkers' house.

I spent the afternoon in the St Theresa's residents' lounge, watching the rain cascading down the bay windows in solid sheets and wondering if the half-dozen ladies nodding around the walls were asleep or dead.

Just before three o'clock an assistant appeared, spread plastic sheeting over a side table and silently laid out disposable cups, a jug of milk, a bowl of sugar and plates of biscuits. A second trip produced two metal teapots.

The activity had woken some of the sleepers. I could sense a frisson of excitement crackling beneath the paper-thin skins.

The grandfather clock in the hall started chiming the hour. The first 'bong' released them from their chairs like greyhounds out of the traps. At the same time the refined female with the gravitationally-challenged knickers shot in from the hall.

She won the table race by a short head, seized a handful of biscuits and thrust them into her dress top.

Ignoring the rebellious mutterings of 'Chocolate bourbons', 'Not fair, my turn' and 'Report her to the office', she poured half a dozen teas by the simple expedient of tilting the pot and scything the spout around in a wide arc. The milk jug got the same treatment.

A waterfall of milky tea poured down the sides of the

sheeting and spread over the wooden floor. Ignoring it all, she picked up a cup and carried it across to the chair next to me.

'I've seen you before.'

'That's right. I came to see Mrs Woolley.'

'Thought so.' Peering down her bodice, she fished out a bourbon, dunked it in the tea and sucked vigorously.

'Do you know Mrs Woolley's grandson?'

'It's free, you know.'

'Sorry?'

'Inclusive price. Afternoon refreshments.'

'Sounds like the bargain of the century. About Mrs Woolley's grandson . . .'

'Heating too. Heating's included.'

Included where? I wondered. It didn't seem to be included in this room.

'I had a garden, you know. He said I had vermin.'

'Did you?'

'Gives herself airs. Just a fancy rat-catcher, that's all he was. My father gave them half a crown to clear the barn. Not surprised he lost his money. Takes them likes that sometimes. My cousin Rose's boy would wager on two raindrops sliding down a window. They lost him in Malaya.'

'About Mrs Woolley's grandson. Do you know him? Tallish, red-headed boy?'

'He's a headmaster.'

I took a flying leap into the random thought processes that seemed to be going on in her head, and hazarded a guess. 'Roger Woolley, you mean?'

'He taught my third cousin Henry's girls. Hopeless. Couldn't keep discipline. The children know. Like wild animals; they scent blood, go in for the kill. None of this protecting-the-weak nonsense. Have more honesty, young children. I expect that's why they promoted him.'

'More than likely. About his son . . .'

The biscuit was sagging towards the carpet. Extending

a blue-tinged tongue, she fished for the drooping end. 'They nearly sacked him. Wouldn't think he had it in him, would you? Had a girl like that in my class. Mad for the German teacher. Sent her away. TB sanatorium, they said. 'Course, we all knew where she'd really gone. She'd left the school, though. Suppose they decided she was old enough to know her own mind.'

Something told me we were into the realms of Roger and Elaine's marriage. Which was all very interesting, but I really needed a handle on the grandson. 'Does Roger's son visit Mrs Woolley very often?'

With a cluck of annoyance, she poked with one finger at the bourbon which was now bobbing in the tea like a wrecked raft.

A chat about Master Woolley was obviously out. I got a teaspoon and helped her fish out the soggy lumps.

Around the walls, the other occupants drank and ate with a silent concentration. The only time they reacted to my presence was to growl. "Residents only" when I helped myself to a broken Rich Tea.

At half-three the assistant reappeared and cleared the table, by the simple expedient of gathering up all four corners of the plastic sheeting, dragging the mess into the hall and swabbing the floor with a disinfectant mop.

The refined one thanked me for visiting her and shuffled out again. The other lounge residents displayed their facility for lapsing into self-induced catatonic trances. I went back to contemplating the distorted world beyond the water-streaked windows.

It was undoubtedly one of the most depressing afternoons I had ever spent in my life. By the time Simla Woolley returned, I was almost prepared to like her.

The car that bumped slowly over the gravel drive, its windscreen wipers hardly coping with the lashing rain, had a large aerial on the roof indicating a CB radio inside. Mini-cab, I decided, trying to make out the occupants.

The woman who climbed out was muffled in scarf and raincoat. She'd dropped the metal sticks in the porch and returned to the car by the time I reached the front door.

Pulling on both arms, she and the driver tried to extract Simla. Simla wriggled and lunged, edging forward an inch at a time. Eventually a final determined yank hauled her out. Half lifting her, they ran her into the porch.

'Oh, thanks. Thanks a lot,' Elaine said breathlessly, as I proffered the sticks. Propping them under her mother-in-law's forearms, she gasped her goodbyes. 'Meter's running, I'll ring.'

She was gone. I held open the inner door. Simla shuffled inside and, for the first time, looked at me.

'What are you doing here?'

'It's nice to see you too.'

'If you have come to visit me, Miss Smith, you are wasting your time. I have nothing more to say to you.'

'That's OK. You can just listen. Allow me.' Taking the key from her fingers, I opened her bedroom door.

Simla stayed where she was. And since she had a butt a battleship would envy, I couldn't get inside either without manually dragging her to one side.

'What do you want, Miss Smith?'

Good question. What I really wanted was a simple, one-syllable explanation of the reasons behind her visit to Alan Kersey, rather than the rubbish she'd fed me last time about Kersey's sudden attack of conscience. And then I wanted to know about her grandson's unannounced call on the Parkers.

I tried the second question first. She denied knowing anything about the visit.

'Oh, come on. I saw him myself.'

'Indeed? Then why have you not reported the matter to the police, Miss Smith?'

The half-sly glance told me she already knew: because I had no more business being in there than what's-his-name.

What *was* his name, come to that?

'Eddie,' she said when I asked. 'He was named after my husband. His grandfather.'

I decided to go for the moral high ground. 'Does Roger know you loan his car key to Eddie?'

'I have absolutely no idea. And frankly I do not care.'

'Bit dodgy, isn't it? Supposing Rog reports it stolen?'

'Roger wouldn't prosecute. He knows perfectly well that if he wasn't such a useless specimen he could afford to buy his son a car.'

'Moral blackmail?'

'A proper allocation of responsibilities. Like his father, Roger is often unable to see where his true duty lies. Now I must wish you good afternoon.'

She'd managed to turn herself in the doorway, using the sticks to obstruct my entrance. Now she started to nudge the door closed again.

I stuck a foot against the jamb. 'Hang on.'

A metal bar hit my knee with enough force to make me yelp. 'You old . . . '

By the time I'd bitten off the expletive, I found myself snarling at the closed door.

It is hard to hold a dignified conversation when you're crouched on your knees talking into a keyhole.

'Look,' I coaxed, 'Judy Parker's niece was murdered. Possibly because of something Alan Kersey gave her or told her. Now use your brains, Simla. I'm not the police. I'm not going to split on you, whatever it is you're up to. Let's talk.'

I applied my eye to the keyhole to see if I had her attention.

A black orb glittered back from the other end of the short tunnel.

'Open up,' I whispered.

'Go *away*.'

'No.'

'I'll call for the supervisor.'

'Go ahead.'

This childish tit-for-tat might have gone on indefinitely if I hadn't glanced behind me.

The occupants of the lounge, plus two care assistants and a stern-faced female in a grey suit sporting a 'Supervisor' badge, were ranged around me in a half-circle, staring silently.

'Just saying goodbye,' I murmured, climbing to my feet and brushing off my knees. Both actions sent a stab of pain through the patella that Simla had just whacked.

Fishing in my back pocket, I found a tattered business card and fed it through the door crack whilst wishing Simla a breezy goodbye. 'Ring me if you think of anything else,' I called.

Gritting my teeth, I limped out into the downpour.

I'd left my lights on. The battery was as dead as Terry Rosco's brain cell. I had to wait through two hours and ten more visitors before one finally produced a set of leads from his boot and gave me a jump-start.

So much for Saturday, I decided, shedding my clothes and climbing under the duvet. Sunday could hardly be worse.

Sunday proved me wrong by waking me at seven with a thumping head, sore throat and raging temperature.

Deciding I wanted to die in my own bed or, at the very least, my own couch, I crawled back under the duvet and listened to the rain pouring off the streets and into the basement yard.

After a while the splash, splash, splash started to drive me mad. Balling lumps of tissue paper, I stuffed them in my ears and stuck my head under the pillow.

I was vaguely aware of the day's passing. Each time I slipped into a doze, the moody light outside had become a little denser and greyer by the time I awoke.

The last time it was pitch black and that damn splashing had stopped.

Curled into a ball, I made little forays with my senses, trying to determine whether I'd gone deaf or blind.

Blind was out: I could just make out the shape of the table and shelves materializing from the heavier shadows as my eyes became accustomed to the dark.

I checked out deaf and found I could distinguish the distant squeal of car tyres outside and the monotonous click-click of the wall clock in here. The rain seemed to have stopped.

Relieved, I eased myself into a sitting position. I'd got cramp in my leg where I'd been lying awkwardly, and it still hurt a bit to swallow, but the head was better and my skin didn't feel like it was on fire any more.

Groping my way to the wall, I drew the curtains and flicked on a few lights.

Stripping off the T-shirt and pants which my nose was telling me had soaked up several pints of sweat, I padded into the bathroom. The wall heater took an age to fill the bath.

Eventually I was able to sink into blissful steamy heat and lay back comparing the purple bruise on my stomach with the black and yellow job swelling on my knee.

It was delicious to be warm. I never wanted to get out.

After an hour, I reluctantly heaved myself into the chill air again. Dried and freshly T-shirted, I checked the time, and discovered it was quarter to ten. So much for Sunday.

An angry rumble from my stomach reminded me that I hadn't eaten since yesterday.

It was ages since I'd shopped and the cupboards were more or less bare. Tipping the last of the coffee grains into a mug, I added boiling water and a slug of Spanish brandy. There were a few cream crackers left in the bottom of the tin, so I carried that back to the couch as well.

On the off-chance I switched the telly on as I passed. It's been busted for days, but occasionally it bursts into life for no apparent reason. Tonight my luck finally changed.

With a crackle, the picture flickered then settled into the opening captions of the ten o'clock news.

Thrilled at this sign that the fates were no longer against me, I sipped, nibbled and luxuriated in a bit of voyeuristic suffering. All that death, scandal and misery was so much easier to take when it was dished up in three-minute slots and didn't affect you one jot.

Tomorrow, I decided, dipping my cracker and sucking off the boozy coffee, I'd drive up to High Wycombe and track down Olly Colville. Perhaps he'd be less coy about the reason behind Kersey's last tea-party.

Fate had one more little sock in the jaw lined up for me that night.

The 'also-rans' were crammed into the final couple of minutes. Items which hadn't made a full slot got a quick ten- or fifteen-second mention each. I was half dozing again as the newscaster galloped through the last report . . .

'. . . Police are treating as suspicious a fire in a flat in High Wycombe. One body was recovered from the building. It is believed to be that of the tenant, Mr Oliver Colville, a garage fitter of High Wycombe. And now for a look at the weather . . .'

CHAPTER 20

I have never, in the words of the song, hated Mondays. In fact, I generally quite like them. Perhaps that says something about my weekends.

By the time I swam back to consciousness on Monday morning, the Sunday bug had more or less disappeared, apart from a slight wobbliness in the legs and a tickle in the back of the throat.

The weather was smiling on the world too. When I flicked back the curtains I found a square of sky the colour of robins' eggs washed by streaks of milky clouds.

I wanted air, and light, and human contact.

Pulling on my training clothes I set off at a gentle jog for the town square. The promenade steamed gently as the heat dried the soaked pavements. I was running into the sun, and the light glinting off the gently swelling sea was almost too much to bear.

Swinging back in again at the clock tower, I abandoned the front with reluctance and jogged through the side streets to our concrete-ugly shopping centre.

Marilyn was on hold until I'd restocked my larder. Since I was now working for myself, I figured I could give myself an hour off without feeling guilty. And if I was truthful, Olly Colville's death had brought me up against another dead end. I needed a bit of thinking time to figure out where to go next.

Wrestling a trolley free I headed down the supermarket aisles with the fervour of a born-again shopper.

The trolley was suffering from a political crisis. The off-side front wheel was a Tory and favoured the right, whilst the other three wheels insisted on going left. The trolley and I had just completed our fourth *pas de deux* pirouette down the frozen-food aisle when we came to a crashing halt, horns locked with another trolley.

'Sorry,' I apologized, trying to disentangle us both.

'That's OK. I weren't looking where I was . . . Heh, it's you!'

You know that sensation when you see a familiar face outside its normal context and you just can't place it? For a moment I was totally flummoxed.

Then a gangling shape shambled across and dumped half a dozen loo rolls into her trolley and my mind jumped back to the half-boarded-up street in north London.

'Warren. Bella. What on earth are you doing down here? It's great to see you again.'

Bella's face split into a grin. 'Same here. Surprise, eh?'

'I'll say. How come?'

Heaving her wire monster free, Bella fell into step with me. Warren shambled behind us, occasionally adding packets of biscuits, savoury snacks and soft drinks to her trolley.

'I come down to do the identification.'

'Tina's?'

'How many corpses you think I know, honey?'

'Sorry. But I mean, shouldn't her aunt have done it?'

'Wouldn't do it. The police asked me.'

She'd exchanged the brilliant make-up and tight clothes for a pair of grey stirrup pants and a baggy man's jumper in the same shade. Perhaps it was her attempt at mourning clothes.

'Have you seen Judy?'

'Sure.' She flung a frozen pizza on top of her pile. 'Warren and me's stopping round here. She discharged herself from hospital, you know? Didn't ought to be on her own in that state. Suppose she has another attack? Anyway,' she added candidly, 'it's better than stopping with Amos's mum. The old cow don't like me. Really gives me hassle, you know.'

'What happened to your place?'

'Bailiffs slung us out. Council's tarting the area up.'

'Can they do that?'

Bella shrugged. 'Amos bought the rent book. Council said we was trespassing an' they didn't have to rehouse us.'

We'd reached the check-outs. Under cover of unloading, I was able to get my head close to Bella's and ask if she'd mentioned my visit to the police.

'Nope. You said not, so we didn't. You found out who topped the donkey yet?'

'Not exactly. But I'm pretty certain it was the same person who topped Tina. So you watch yourself, you hear?'

She looked startled. 'You think he's coming after me?'

'Not you exactly . . .' We'd finished packing by this time. 'Want to share a cab?'

'OK. Warren, get a hold of these bags.'

Further conversation was out until we'd staggered to the taxi rank in the main square.

'I'm splitting,' Warren announced as soon as we'd found a cab. 'See yawl latta.'

Swinging his baseball cap back to front, he slouched off.

'Arcades,' Bella remarked. 'Can't stay out of them. It's like he's a machine junkie, you know?'

'What's the story with Warren? Is he a relative?'

I caught the slightest pause before she claimed him as Amos's cousin. The cab swung into traffic at that moment, banging us together on the back seat. By the time we'd regained the upright, Bella had changed the subject back to Tina.

'Why should I watch out? You think this crazy's coming for me?'

'Judy perhaps.'

I was conscious of the taxi driver straining to hear as I

told her about Olly Colville's unexpected launch into the underworld.

'That's two members of Kersey's tea-party dead. Bit too strong for coincidence.'

Bella clasped the slippery carriers to her bosoms. 'Judy never went to see this Kersey bloke.'

'No. But she was meant to. Perhaps that counts. Watch yourself anyway. Don't let any strangers into the house, OK?'

'OK.'

We were nearly at my corner. To get back to Judy Parker's house, the driver was going to have to recircle the town. It will give you some idea of how worried I was when I tell you I actually paid my half of the fare.

'Listen,' I said, heaving my own carriers on to the pavement. 'I might drop round later.'

'Great. I'll cook the pizza.'

Leaving my own shopping in the flat, I walked round to the office.

After the solitude of Saturday, the place was positively buzzing. Janice sat in the centre of the web, a spider in thick black opaque tights and a crocheted mini-dress in four-ply ebony wool.

'Who died?'

She lifted her head then and I saw the split lip for the first time. 'Me nearly,' she snapped. 'Some stupid sods were messing around behind me on the crossing Friday night. Shoved me right off the kerb. It's lucky the bloody bus driver had good brakes. You should see my bruises.'

'No thanks. I'm growing my own. Any messages?'

Janice jerked a finger upwards.

'Cheers.'

Annie's door was partially open. I put my head round it to say, 'Morning.'

She was thrusting papers in a briefcase. Without looking round she mumbled: 'Morning. Got to go.'

There was a suspicious quaver in her voice.

'You been crying?'

'No.'

'Are you sure?'

'Yes, I'm damn well sure.'

'OK. Sorry I asked.'

There were two messages on my desk.

One was a phone call taken by Janice:

Ms Dorothy Springle rang 9.30 a.m. Says she has more info re "the little presents" (said you'd understand this). She's not there this a.m. but said to call after 3 p.m.

The other was Mr Mouldar's reports on Supermarket Sal.

Two cheap sheets of paper were headed respectively 'Saturday' and 'Sunday'. In neat, cramped printing he'd detailed her progress on each day, even to the extent of providing mileage estimates along each stretch.

Never one to look a gift horse in the mouth, I faxed copies to the solicitor, together with an interim bill.

That done, I telephoned a news service that I knew Vetch had connections with and did a passable imitation of Janice's voice. As 'Mr Vetch's personal assistant' I got the low-down on the High Wycombe fire.

Basically it was little more than the television had reported. Colville was thought to have been killed some time on Saturday afternoon. Probably with the ubiquitous 'blunt instrument'. It wasn't certain whether the fire had been an accident or deliberately started to destroy the evidence. If the latter, it had failed: after smouldering quietly for several hours, it had been spotted almost immediately when it finally roared into life, and Colville's body had been retrieved more or less intact for forensic examination. There were no known witnesses. Almost as an afterthought, the reporter asked if I wanted Colville's previous.

'Is there much?'

'Not recently. Looks like he's been clean for about twelve years. But I got a few whispers on past stuff. Mostly burglary, house-breaking, receiving. Haven't checked it out yet. Tell Vetch I'll fax him chapter and verse if it comes in.'

That'll surprise him, I thought, replacing the receiver with my thanks.

Where to now?

I didn't seem to have much choice. If Simla Woolley wouldn't talk to me, then my next best source of information about that tea-party was Judy Parker.

My first plan had been to collect the car and drive over to the Parkers'. It was frustrated when the motor gave one painful cough and expired. I tried again. Shorter cough, same result.

If it wasn't out of petrol – and it wasn't – then I was stumped.

When I tried to turn it over for the third time, a passer-by gave me the benefit of his expert knowledge.

'Starter motor's knackered, love,' he shouted from across the road.

Terrific. Taking a few warm-up breaths, I set off again at a steady running pace.

Rather than go back along the promenade and through the side streets, I went out the back of the town, cut across the fields, dropped down by the old town cemetery and crossed the main road a few hundred yards down from the factory site where Marilyn/Tina had met their respective ends. There was no sign of any police activity, although a few strands of blue and white tape fluttered forlornly from the fencing and gates. Presumably they'd completed the forensic examination over the weekend.

The Sunday bug and the lack of training had caught up with me by this time. Clambering up one side of the road, I slowed to a walk as I crossed and scrambled down to the opposite field.

The land was ploughed here, the furrows already showing the beginnings of a sparse green carpet. A flattened footpath meandered round the edges of the fields, crossing another A road before following the railway tracks for several hundred yards and terminating in a footbridge over the lines.

It occurred to me I was now following the same route as Marilyn's killer, only in reverse. Slogging up the metal staircase with my breath burning the inside of my lungs, it also occurred to me that this was a ridiculous performance for the killer to have gone through in order to cover up the site of Tina's murder.

Why a donkey, for heaven's sake? The fields might have been dark at that time of night, but he'd have been plainly visible when crossing the roads and positively conspicuous up here to any train passenger who'd happened to glance up.

Why hadn't he – or she – kidnapped a couple of friendly dogs and killed them in the warehouse? The chances of anyone remembering a late-night dog-walker were minimal. On the other hand, a midnight donkey-walker is going to stick in the mind. So why take the risk?

Perhaps it was because I was brooding on donkeys. But by the time I looked up again, I found I'd overshot Judy's road and was at the boundary fence opposite December's.

Excited whinnies and hee-haws greeted me from the yard. Errol and Clark were scuffling for the best position at the barred gate. Behind them, I made out four more furry ears milling around.

The chain was still wrapped round the gates. Using the curling ironwork for footholds, I scrambled over the top.

'Col! December! Anybody here?'

'What you doing up there, lass?'

Halfway down the far side, with my heel wedged fast in an ornate scroll and Errol giving me encouraging nips in the butt, I glared over my shoulder at December.

'Where's Col?'

'Day off. No sense us both being here. Do you want a hand there?'

'No, I like hanging around like an uncoordinated bat.'

'That's all right then.'

He left me there. I eventually managed to get free by unlacing the trainer with my teeth and wriggling my foot out.

Hopping into the feed and tack store, I flopped down on a straw bale and glared. December continued to anoint a bridle.

'Why aren't you on the beach?' I demanded, relacing the shoe.

'Monday's the lads' day off.'

'What about Saturday? You weren't out then.'

'Too wet.'

'Sunday?'

'Same.'

'Not exactly cost-effective, is it? As businesses go.'

'The Lord provides for those who ask.'

Religion makes me uncomfortable. So I changed the subject again. 'I'm still working on Marilyn's murder.'

'Thought you might be.'

'Does it bother you?'

'Can't stop you, can I?'

'No.' After a pause, I told him that the police thought Tina had been killed up at the warehouse too.

'I know.'

I'd forgotten he had the inside track when it came to the CID.

Suspicious that they might be missing out, the donkeys had abandoned the gate to huddle round the open door. Lana ventured in a few steps.

'Whoa. Go on, out. You know that's not allowed.'

Head lowered, Lana obediently backed out again.

'Want to help me groom them?'

'I wouldn't know where to start.'

'At the end the feed goes in, lass. Work your way back to where it comes out. I'll show you.'

And he did. For the next three hours we brushed, combed and sponged. I discovered donkeys suffered from bad breath; at both ends.

Occasionally my eyes were drawn over the top of the stable to the roof of the Parkers' house. I ought to be round there, asking pertinent and searching questions. So why wasn't I? A spot of rudimentary self-analysis came up with the worrying suggestion that I felt safe and warm here with December and the lads.

I was going soft. Alarmed, I flung myself into the brushing with renewed vigour.

'God,' I said, collapsing with an aching back whilst December applied the hoof oil. 'Do you do this every day?'

'Couple of girls come in every morning to muck out and groom. Monday's their day off too.'

Exhausted, I sat on an upturned bucket and watched him sluicing and brushing down the yard.

I just couldn't figure out how he was making any profit at all out of this business. 'You got the time?'

December dug a pocket watch from his shirt pocket. 'Just gone two.'

'Can I use your phone?'

'You know where it is.'

The hospice declined to let me speak to Dorothea.

'But she asked me to call.'

'I'm sorry. Miss Springle had treatment this morning. She's sleeping now. We don't wish to wake her.'

I had no choice but to leave it.

I'd been sitting on the floor. As I stood up, I had the sudden sensation that the walls were retreating and the tide was crashing into the passage. Inexplicably I seemed to be looking at the ceiling.

December was bending over me as I came round, his frowning face a few inches from mine.

'What happened?' I asked.

'You tell me. Are you ill?'

'I had a bug yesterday. But it's gone now.'

'What have you eaten today?'

I tried to remember. I hadn't fancied the chocolate flakes for breakfast. And I hadn't bothered when I returned from the supermarket, thinking I could scrounge coffee and biscuits from Annie. 'Nothing,' I admitted.

'God help us,' December muttered, sending the pot-scourers shooting up into his hair line. 'The lads have more sense.' He grasped me under the armpits, hauled me bodily into the lounge and dumped me on the sofa. 'Stop there.'

Ten minutes later, he came back with a bowl of tomato soup and toast cut into fingers. 'Eat that.'

A terrible sensation of *déjà vu* swept over me. The shock was so intense it took all my will-power to regain control of my shaking hands. Skimming up a spoonful of soup, I sipped. Something rolled down my cheek and plopped into the bowl, pitting the soup with tiny tidal pools. Horrified, I watched the spreading circles.

Without comment, December handed me his handkerchief. It smelt heavily of oil and liniment.

Blowling noisily, I gulped my thanks.

'What's the matter?'

'Nothing. I'm just a bit wobbly from the bug, that's all.'

We both knew I was lying.

CHAPTER 21

'I ought to go,' I said, when I'd finished eating. 'I've got to see someone out at the hospice.'

I'd decided while I was finishing the soup that it was probably more sensible to find out what Dorothea had discovered about the "little presents" before I tackled Judy. The more I appeared to know about Kersey's tea-party, the more I figured I could rattle her into revealing.

I wondered just how far she'd recovered from the heart attack, and asked December if he'd seen her in the past two days.

'I never saw her before Tina died, and she's got even less reason to come by now, hasn't she?' he pointed out. 'She got the funeral fixed up yet?'

'Tina's friend Bella's staying round there. Expect she'll be taking care of that. Shall I tell her to let you know the arrangements?'

'You do that. Me and the lads will pay our respects.'

I had a mental image of the lads decked out with black plumes on their heads, like horses pulling a Victorian funeral carriage.

"Bye then. Thanks for lunch.'

Standing up, I caught a glimpse of myself in the heavy gilt mirror over the sideboard. It wasn't a pretty sight.

Apart from wisps of hay and straw tangled in my hair and tracksuit top, I had pink-rimmed eyes from the snivelling and a bright-orange moustache courtesy of the tomato soup.

'Bloody hell,' I said, scrubbing at my top lip with the back of my hand. 'You were going to let me walk out like this, weren't you?'

'None of my business.'

I threw him a glare whilst I used my fingers as a makeshift comb.

'I'd use the bathroom if I were you, lass. You look like you need a good grooming.'

I paid him back by whipping off the tracksuit top and giving it a vigorous shake over his bathroom carpet. After splashing cold water over my face and warm over my hair, I returned downstairs and found him washing up in the kitchen.

'Can I borrow a couple of quid?' I asked. 'I spent up at the supermarket this morning.'

'No.'

'I'll pay you back.'

December shook water off the dishes and stacked them in the drying rack. 'I don't lend money, it causes bad feeling.'

'Well, you're not exactly giving me a good feeling here at the moment. I won't leave the country for the sake of a couple of lousy quid. You can hold my watch as security if you like.'

We both looked at the tatty bit of plastic clasped round my wrist. Perhaps two pounds was rather overvaluing it.

'Look, my car's knackered. I only want the bus fare out to the hospice. Save me going back to the flat for cash.'

'I'll give you a lift.'

'What about leaving the place unguarded?'

'I'll fix up something.'

He made a quick call, then led the way into the back yard again. The lads barged and nudged at him eagerly. Errol ducked his head and spun round the yard in a tight circle, looking rather like a carousel horse.

'Is he all right?'

'Don't like being cooped up. None of them do. Hold this.'

'This' was a harness he'd taken from the tack area.

Padlocking the door, he gave a sharp whistle through his front teeth: 'Come on, boy.'

Lana barged his way out of the herd and trotted after December.

'Where are we going? I thought you were giving me a lift.'

'That's right. This way.'

It wasn't until we'd rounded the corner of the stable that I belatedly remembered: December didn't drive any more.

Or, to be accurate, he didn't drive motor cars any more.

'You're joking,' I said faintly as he hitched Lana into the donkey cart harness.

'No. Very fashionable these days. Eco-friendly – isn't that what they call it?'

That wasn't what my acquaintances would call it. I was a private investigtor. We sped through cases in an open-topped sports car, the wind in our hair and funky music pounding through our quadraphonic stereo system. It said so in all the gumshoe novels. How could I retain my street cred if anyone saw me being pulled by one-horse (ish) power?

'Are you sure he can manage both of us?'

'Course he can. Go on, open the gates.'

We were perched outside, Lana rattling his head with impatience, when a BMW drew up and Kevin climbed out. Evidently Monday was his day off too: he'd abandoned the club manager's gear for jeans, pale-blue shirt and leather jacket.

All right, so he was spoken for. But a girl has her pride.

'Hi, Grace. Good to see you again.'

'Hello.' I picked a few more bits of hay off my trouser knees and dismissed the horrid suspicion that I was blushing.

'Are you OK? We caught that maniac in the car park on the security video if you want to press charges.'

'No need. All sorted out. Can we go, please?'

Releasing the brake, December flicked the reins. 'Girrup, boy.'

Lana 'girrupped' with an enthusiasm that nearly shot me off the seat.

For the first few minutes, I concentrated on gripping the metal side bar until my knuckles turned white.

'Relax,' December advised. 'Go with the movement. You won't come out.'

Cautiously I let go. 'Goes at a fair old clip, doesn't he?' I remarked as Lana, ears pricked and legs raised with the precision of pistons, trotted out briskly.

'He's fresh after being shut in for the past three days. He'll settle down in a mile or so.'

'Why'd you have all male donkeys?' I asked when I grew tired of watching the tarmac whizzing between the bobbing ears.

'Geldings are stronger. And they don't come into season. See, *I* know they've had the chop, but sometimes the lads forget if there's a jenny around. Gets a bit tricky to explain that sort of thing on the beach. Like our Kevin, do you?'

The juxtaposition of sex and Kevin was pretty pointed. But I wasn't about to fall for that one. 'He seems OK.'

Instead of going out the back of the town and through the back lanes as I'd expected, Drysdale had chosen to go via the sea front and take the main road Spinnaker and I had driven back along the other night. When I queried the route, he said briefly: 'Wider roads. Lets the drivers get past. Pedestrians like donkeys. Motorists don't.'

Which was true enough. Waves and smiles followed us along the promenade.

The sunny weather had held over into the afternoon. Together with a slight offshore breeze, it had dried and freshened the sea front like a brisk rub-down with scented towels after a sauna. I was almost enjoying myself. Until December asked me why the tomato soup had upset me.

'It didn't.'

'Yes it did.'

'Are you calling me a liar?'

'Yes.'

'That's bloody presumptuous, considering you hardly know me.'

'Stop wriggling, lass, and answer the question.'

He was totally relaxed, scarcely moving the reins now that Lana had settled into a steadier pace.

I didn't have to tell him anything. But I did.

I told him that my dad had brought me tomato soup and toast fingers when I was a little girl.

'I got terrible nightmares when I was a kid. He'd chase the monsters away for me and then we'd have midnight feasts. Mum used to go spare when she smelt it next morning.'

'He makes you face your own monsters now, eh?' December said, steering Lana right and along the cliff road past the wide greens and sunken gardens of the town suburbs.

'He doesn't talk to me at all. He hasn't since I left the force. You could say that I've fallen from Grace,' I remarked with a bitter laugh.

And it had all been done with the best of intentions.

I'd had a call to a house with a history of domestic violence. A minor villain who smacked his wife around regularly. On plenty of occasions we'd taken statements at the hospital only to have her withdraw the complaint at the station.

'She said she was too scared to press charges in case he got off. Reckoned he'd kill her,' I explained to December.

On this particular night I'd arrived to find the front door open and her sitting at the bottom of the staircase, her nose broken and blood pouring from her mouth.

'She said he'd just left. Begged me to say I'd seen him do it. Promised she'd go the full distance, have him charged, if I'd back her up and testify in court.'

It had seemed so simple at the time. Not strictly legal, perhaps, but definitely just. So I'd written up my report, detailing the assault I'd supposedly witnessed.

The next day, news had filtered through of a bungled drugs seizure further along the coast. Some of the gang had got away, mowing down a plain-clothes police officer in the process. One of his colleagues had thought they'd recognized the van driver.

'It was the wife-beater. And I'd put him fifty miles away.'

I looked sideways at December to see how he was taking this news. But all I could see was a quarter-profile. He was apparently absorbed in the bays to our right. From up here we looked down into each little mouth-shaped bite in the cliff bordered at its foot by a concrete promenade and a frill of brightly coloured beach huts.

Workmen were dragging new rubbish bins from a lorry the size of a Dinky toy and fastening them to the promenade rails. One fell with a clatter that rolled upwards and set Lana skittering sideways.

'Pack it in, you daft lump,' December shouted, getting a firmer grip on the reins and steering the cart back on course. 'Confess?'

I'd become sufficiently used to December's abrupt conversational style to recognize this as a question to me rather than an instruction to Lana to repent his donkey sins.

'No,' I said.

At the time the officer's injuries were said to be slight. So I'd stood by my report rather than land myself in it. Later, when they'd turned out to be far more serious than first supposed, it had been too late to change my mind because I was well and truly in it up to my eyebrows.

'So you gave this villain an alibi?'

'Yes.'

'Is that what he planned?'

'I don't know.'

I'd often asked myself that. Had they set it up between them; a bit of extra insurance because they'd been expecting trouble on the drugs job? Or had the wife been seeing someone else and viewed it as a chance to put her husband out of the way for a while? I don't suppose I'll ever know now.

'Did they send him to prison? For the assault on his missus?'

'She refused to testify. The Crown Prosecution Service wouldn't proceed on my evidence alone.'

At about the same time I'd received a bookmaker's slip detailing a racing accumulator that added up to a two-thousand-pound win. When I checked my bank statement I found that a comparable amount had been deposited in my current account.

They hadn't been able to prove anything. Not officially, anyway. But I'd been called in and silently handed a type-written resignation and a pen. I signed.

'You're the first person I've ever told,' I informed December.

I sounded whiny even to my own ears. A little-girl-lost seeking absolution.

I didn't get it.

'What did you do with the money?'

'Kept it.'

Well why the hell not? I'd earned it.

It was tea-time by the time we reached the hospice. Most of the mobile inhabitants were grouped around tables in the lounge. Unfortunately that didn't include Dorothea.

Edna was clad in the same quilted nylon housecoat as last time. She fluttered across the carpet at us like an animated teapot cover. 'Oooh, isn't this nice now? Jules has just gone to fetch our teas. You sit down now, dear, and I'll tell him to bring more cups. And is this your father?'

She'd darted away before I could disabuse her of that idea. She returned chattering to Jules nineteen to the dozen, getting under his wheels as he tried to manoeuvre his chair, and creating total confusion as she collected up magazines, knitting and needles she'd used to reserve the seats.

'Let me,' December said, taking the loaded tray from where it was balanced on the chair arms.

'Thanks, mate.' Sweeping away all the junk Edna had just deposited on the table, Jules cleared a space for the tray.

'I was hoping to see Dorothea. Is she around?' I asked whilst Jules measured milk into the cups.

'Oh no, dear. She's asleep.' Edna finally twittered to a halt. 'They've got the "Do Not Disturb" sign across, I'm afraid. Was that you in the donkey cart?'

'It's December's. My car's out of action.'

'I love donkeys,' Edna exclaimed. 'Hours the children and I spent on the beach watching the donkeys. Could I give him a biscuit?'

Approval radiated from December as he remarked that Lana was very partial to orange creams.

Personally I felt Lana would probably have scoffed the china plate given half a chance, but Edna was led off quite happily, clutching a plate of biscuits in one hand and December's tweed jacket sleeve in the other.

'Are you still sleuthing?' Jules asked once they'd gone.

'Sure am. In fact, that's why I'm here. Dorothea said she had some more information. About the presents Kersey gave his visitors. I don't suppose you know what it is?'

'I received a package with similar gift-wrapping yesterday. Dorothea's convinced Kersey's presents must have come from the same jeweller as mine. Here.'

He opened a watch box and turned it so I could note down the address on the inside.

'There's something else,' Jules said once I'd finished writing. 'Not sure if it's got anything to do with your donkey killer, but I thought I might as well clue you in if that's OK with you.'

'Clue away. All contributions welcome.'

'We've had a visit. From the police.'

That was almost inevitable after I'd told DCI Jackson about Tina's trip to the hospice the day of her death.

'They searched Alan Kersey's room. And they asked if anyone had spoken to his visitors.'

'What did you tell them?'

'The truth. None of us had had anything to do with Kersey's friends. They seemed a trifle piqued that the hospice didn't log everyone in and out, like hired roller skates.'

'That all they asked?'

He considered for a moment and said the police had wondered whether Kersey was particularly close to anyone here. 'He wasn't, of course. And that was rather that. But there's been talk. One of the visitors thought they recognized Kersey. Reckoned he was mixed up in some murder case years back. Didn't mean nothing to me.'

'You were probably at school at the time. Don't know about you, but I only read the entertainment page and the cartoons back then.'

'Yeah, but I was telling my mum when she came over, and she knew him,' Jules carried on.

'Kersey?'

'No. The other one. The bloke who got killed.'

'Major Edwin Woolley.'

'That's him. Not that he was a real major by then, like. Mum was a typist at the council when he worked there. He was in the Environmental Health section. Pest Control mostly.'

'Just a glorified rat-catcher!'

'I suppose you could say that, yeah.'

I hadn't said it. The female with the gravitationally challenged knickers at St Theresa's Retirement Home had said it when I'd asked about Simla Woolley. At the time I'd assumed she was rambling, whereas she'd actually been trying to tell me about Edwin Woolley. She'd said something else about the late major as well. But what the hell was it?

I was still struggling to bring the disjointed conversation to mind when Dorothea burst into the room, demanding tea.

'Why didn't you tell me Smithie was here?'

'We're not allowed to wake you, you know that,' Jules said, moving round to allow her to sit down.

'Round spherical objects,' Dorothea snapped, lowering herself with the help of the carved staff. 'I've got important information to pass on.'

'We passed it,' Jules said, pouring more tea.

'Thanks for tipping me off,' I quickly interjected, seeing the disappointment on her face. 'Good lead.'

'Don't patronize. Where's the biscuits?'

'Edna's feeding a donkey with them.'

A nasty thought occurred to me. 'Did Edna tell the police about Kersey's "presents"?'

Restrapping her turban, Dorothea shook her head. 'Edna's easily intimidated by anyone in authority. The sergeant who was asking the questions was a bit on the brusque side. By the time he got to Edna she could barely open her mouth. To tell you the truth, he rather irritated all of us.'

It sounded like the charmer who'd 'invited' me in for a chat with Jackson the other night. 'Could we keep it that way?' I said hopefully. 'I mean, there's no need to mention the jeweller's boxes to the police, is there?'

Dorothea was delighted with the prospect of concealing possible evidence; Jules, however, proved to be irritatingly moral, but finally compromised by agreeing that he wouldn't actually tell unless the police made contact first.

'What about Edna?'

'I'll sort Edna out,' Dorothea promised. 'Now where's this donkey?'

Lana proved, in Edna's words, the best visitor they'd had since the Mayor came to unveil the new sluice room. Practically the whole hospice had to have a ride around the drive. Dorothea went one better and persuaded December to let her take the reins.

We all watched as she decorously trotted down the drive and guided Lana around for her return trip. Halfway along the return route, she suddenly stood upright, screamed, "Yeee-ha!" at the top of her voice and sent Lana careering towards us at full gallop. Before anyone could gather their wits, she'd belted past, the unravelling turban streaming in the breeze and the wooden staff raised like an ancient spear. It was a performance that wouldn't have disgraced Boadicea.

It's the way I like to remember her.

By the time December had retrieved his cart, driven the tired-out donkey home and dropped me off, I didn't have time to change into a suit and get back to the jeweller's shop before it closed. So I managed to persuade Annie to give me a lift and prudently didn't tell her about Plan B until we'd parked.

'Dream on,' she said. 'Do it yourself.'

'Be reasonable. Do I look like a solicitor's clerk?' I spread my arms wide to give her the full glory of crumpled tracksuit and hay adornments. 'Go on, Annie. I'll do the same for you some time.' I pushed into her hand one of the business cards I'd swiped from Spinnaker's car, and flicked her door open.

She was gone so long I was getting really nervous that they'd called the police. The car park had nearly emptied and most of the shops were showing "Closed" signs before she re-emerged and clipped briskly back to the car.

'I thought you'd been nicked,' I remarked as she slid into the driver's seat. 'Did they ring Spinnaker?'

'They tried: no dice; answerphone. Eventually they got the hospice administrator to confirm that Spinnaker was dealing with Kersey's estate.'

'Good. I was hoping Georgie-boy wouldn't be back from Holland yet.'

'Hoping! You told me he definitely wasn't.'

'I lied. What did you get?'

'I've a good mind not to tell you.' Releasing the handbrake, she executed a U-turn and headed back to Marine Parade.

Eventually she relented and handed me a copy of a receipted bill. Proof for the benefit of Kersey's executor that the several hundred pounds missing from his account had been duly paid to the jeweller for work undertaken.

Skimming through the details, I had to admire Kersey. Whatever else may have been lacking, he certainly had a pretty diabolical sense of humour.

CHAPTER 22

'Drop me off at the flat, would you?'

'I'm not your bloody chauffeur.'

Her knuckles gripping the steering wheel were white. 'Are you OK?'

Cutting up a bus, Annie asked why wouldn't she be?

'Well, for starters you wouldn't normally let me sucker you into that performance at the jeweller's.'

'So you got me in a weak moment.'

Belatedly I recalled I'd caught her crying this morning. 'Want to talk about it?'

'No. Yes. What are you doing this evening? Do you fancy a drink?'

Now I'd got the SP from the jeweller's, I'd planned to confront Judy.

'I'll meet you afterwards. How long is it going to take?'

'Depends how long Judy holds out on me.' Then I remembered Bella's invitation to pizza. 'Tell you what, you could come. Don't suppose Bella would mind.'

In fact I suspected she'd be only too pleased. Evenings chez Parker, especially if Warren was out hitting the arcades, were probably pretty grim.

'There's no need. I'll catch you in the morning.'

'Yes, there is. You might pick up on something I miss with Judy,' I urged. Besides, my car was going to be immobile for some time until I got the starter motor sorted out.

Annie let herself be persuaded. 'I've got a couple of things to do back at the office. I'll pick you up at seven thirty. Give you time to bath and change.'

'You think I need to?'

'Definitely. You smell like you've spent the day in a stable.'

'Really?' Scrunching a handful of tracksuit, I sniffed. 'Are you winding me up?'

'Hadn't you noticed all the car windows were open?'

'I thought it was another diet: fresh air and grapefruit or something,' I explained, scrambling out as she pulled into the kerb.

I seemed to have hit a raw nerve. At any rate, she moved away so fast I barely had time to shout through the passenger window: 'Can you pick up some wine for this evening?'

The telly was back on the blink. I tried the radio news, but there was nothing in the reports about the fire at Olly Colville's flat. It was probably too mundane to rate a follow-up beyond the initial report.

Now that I was on the look-out for it, I could detect donkey aroma on the jeans and shirt I'd worn on previous visits to December. Why had no one mentioned it before? Did they imagine I had some form of exotic BO?

My stand-by jeans had been picked up in Oxfam; blue denim flares with orange-patterned panels let into the legs. There was a matching blouse in the same design. Suspecting that Judy skimped on the heating, I added a big sloppy-weave pink sweater.

The bell rang whilst I was trying to decide whether the whole effect was a bit OTT seventies-revival. What the hell? I figured. Grabbing my bag, I flung open the door to Annie.

'Peace and love, sister. I'm all yours.'

Mr Mouldar stood in the basement gloom. His mouth dropped and then snapped together again in the manner of a wooden puppet.

'Oh, er, evening, Mr Mouldar. This is a surprise.' It was

more of a bloody inconvenience actually. Standing back, I invited him in.

'Thank you, miss.' Stepping inside, he carefully wiped his feet on a non-existent door mat. 'I do hope you don't mind my calling at your home.'

I did actually. I was even more worried that someone at the office had given out my home address. That was a definite no-no that not even Janice, the receptionist from hell, would breach.

Mr Mouldar reassured me. 'I saw you actually, miss. Coming out this morning. You were taking physical exercise.'

'Oh, right, sure.' He was lurking like a spare coat stand. 'Did you want something?'

He proffered a folded sheet. 'My Monday report, miss. All up to date. I wrote it up not half an hour ago.'

'Thanks. You really shouldn't go to all this trouble.'

'No trouble, miss. A pleasure.'

'How's the job-hunting? Seen the security company yet?'

'Not so far, miss. But I'm optimistic, very optimistic.'

'Oh. Good.' I didn't want him here. For no better reason, I had to admit, than that he was boring and dreary, which was pretty mean of me, but there you are, nobody's perfect. 'Hand better?'

'Yes thanks, miss.' He flexed the relevant limb.

'You should have reported that beast to the police, it's dangerous.'

'I'm afraid the poor thing's dead. They think he picked up some poisoned bait from the fields.'

Go, my subconscious screamed. *Please go*.

The door behind him was still open. I edged round him and took the handle, half inviting him to step back through it.

'I had hoped you might drop by the caravan, miss. Perhaps you'd let me cook you a meal.'

'Lovely.' What was I saying?

'Tonight.'

'Sorry, I'm fixed up.'

'Is that just an excuse, miss? If you don't mind my saying so, I can't help feeling that you don't always say exactly what you mean.'

Who did? I thought his assumption was a bit personal and I told him so.

'I didn't mean to offend, it's just that I wouldn't like you to get the wrong idea. I don't expect an intimate relationship. Just someone to chat with. Have a bit of a crack, isn't that how the Irish put it? It's not easy, you know, to admit you're lonely.'

'No. Of course it's not.' I felt a niggle of guilt. After all, the bloke was putting himself out on my behalf. With considerable relief, I saw a familiar set of wheels manoeuvring into the kerb. Annie gave two blasts on the horn.

'Look, my lift's here. But we will get together soon, promise.'

By the time I'd switched the lights off, locked the door and run up to street level, he was disappearing round the corner.

Annie must have seen him coming up the basement steps. 'That another tenant?'

'No. An acquaintance. He wants to be my friend.'

'Well, aren't you the lucky girl? Get all the class acts, don't you?'

'We can't all be lucky enough to hook computer buffs with designer label fetishes.'

The car accelerated abruptly, bringing a telltale "chink" from the carrier on the back floor.

I'd pushed the right button all right. Plainly Jonathon was behind her odd behaviour.

We were driving along the front: too fast. Reflections of the pink, green and red neon lights slid over the car windows in liquid chunks. Two boys stepped casually from the promenade side and strolled unhurriedly across the speeding traffic. Blaring horns were met with blank stares and obscene gestures. Annie pumped her brakes, which thankfully were in a better state than mine.

She slowed down a bit after that, but even so, by the time we drew up outside the Parkers' house I found my fingers were aching from the pressure of gripping the seat.

Bella fell on our necks (metaphorically speaking).

'Go through to the lounge. I'll put the pizza in. You want salad or oven chips?'

'Both,' Annie said firmly. 'And a corkscrew.' She opened the bag for inspection. 'Chardonnay. The litre bottles were on special offer at the supermarket. I got two.'

'Me too. I can see we're going to get on, girl. Here, I'll put yours in the fridge, get mine out.'

She'd made subtle changes to the house. Nothing too obvious, but the furniture had been rearranged to give it a cosier feel, the wood had a wax sheen and the gilt and silver glistened. Additionally there were flowers in the hall and dotted around the lounge.

Judy saw me looking at a tulip display. 'Magnolia's bad conscience. Who's your friend?'

'A colleague, Annie. How are you, Judy?'

She claimed to be better. And in actual fact, she looked it. The brighter complexion was make-up, of course. But there wasn't the sense of defeat that had hung over her in hospital.

Bella bustled in and flicked a tablecloth over the dining table. 'Be about half an hour. Judy tell you the police been round again?'

'Any special reason, or just more snooping?'

I'd half expected to be told they'd made the connection between Olly Colville and Tina via Kersey's tea-party.

But apparently their only purpose had been to turn down Judy's request for her niece's personal effects.

'Said they needed to retain them for a while longer. Can they do that?'

'Oh yes. Is it important?'

I had a fair idea what Judy was after, but I wanted her to tell me.

Instead she tucked her feet up behind her bottom and muttered that it was the principle of the thing.

'Don't do that,' Bella instructed, whisking back with table mats, cutlery and glasses. 'It's gonna make it tough for the blood to get past your butt and reach your heart.'

'For God's bloody sake,' Judy murmured. 'You aren't my mother.'

Nonetheless, she straightened her legs.

Clamping the bottle neck, Bella drove the corkscrew in with vigorous twists. The muscles bulging in her neck would have looked appropriate in Frank Bruno. 'You can have half a glass, Judy.'

'I'll have what I want, you cheeky cow.'

She got half a glass. The rest of us sipped appreciatively at the gooseberry-tinged crispness.

'See the news about Olly Colville?' I asked.

Chardonnay burst from Judy's glass in a fountain.

Direct hit, kid, I congratulated myself.

Licking the dripping hand, she said: 'Sorry, the news about who?'

'Oh come *on*, Judy. Colville was an ex-con who suddenly saw the light and started going straight about the time of the robbery. Murder too strong for him, was it?'

'How would I know? Ain't that pizza ready yet, Bella?'

'Fifteen minutes. Anyone want a top-up?'

Refills were accepted all round. We were going to be sloshed before nine at this rate.

'What about this Colville bloke?' Judy said abruptly. 'You said something was on the news?'

'He's dead. Fire at his flat. They're treating it as a suspicious death.'

'Oh God.' The contents of her glass went down her throat in one convulsive moment.

Bella threw me a filthy look and even Annie mouthed, 'Take it easy.'

I tried again. 'Look, Judy, I'm only trying to help. You could be in real danger here. Isn't it about time you came clean? If it helps, the coppers *know* Des was in on the robbery. And I know what Kersey gave Tina.'

'How?' Her eyes widened, the blood quickening in her cheeks.

'I'm a detective. How about a trade of information?'

'Let me get the food first,' Bella said.

She dressed the table with flowers and candles in saucers. With the lights lowered, it looked quite classy.

Tears glistened in Judy's eyes. 'Do you know, this is the first dinner party I've ever had in this house. Isn't that odd?'

Sad, more like. I tried to imagine what her life must have been like, isolated in here evening after evening after evening with the drooling wreck of the man she'd once loved.

The whole scenario gave me the creeps.

Bella dished out wedges of seafood pizza and placed two bowls on the table. One held mixed salad and the other was piled high with an enormous mound of golden chips. Invited to help ourselves, we did so with a vengeance.

Annie's diet had plainly been booted into touch. A sure sign that Jonathon was history.

'So, Judy,' I mumbled, sloshing down pizza crust with wine. 'Give. Did you know what Des and Kersey had planned for the galloping Major?'

'No. Honestly. If I had, I'd have put a stop to it. He was supposed to be going straight. He promised me. Last chance, I warned him.' Grabbing the Chardonnay before Bella could stop her, she tipped the dregs into her glass. 'Get us another one, there's a good girl, Bella.'

'You shouldn't.'

'Will you stop treating me like a kid, you black bitch.'

'I'll go,' Annie offered, nipping from the table before Bella could react.

'Sorry,' Judy muttered. 'I get so—' She waggled a hand at the paint-flaking walls. 'It could have been so nice.'

''S'all right,' Bella said. 'Go on with what you were saying. 'Bout the robbery.'

Basically Parker had picked up Kersey as a fare a few months before the murder. They'd both been shocked to come across their old cell mate and it probably wouldn't have gone any further if Kersey hadn't seen a chance of making some easy money.

'He asked Des to find someone to do the job. Bit too nice to know any common blaggers, was our Mr Kersey.'

'And Des found Olly Colville?'

'And Barken Billy. God help us.'

The plan had been simple enough. Barken and Colville would ambush the car, grab the statue and pass it on to Kersey, who'd sell it and give them a cut of the proceeds.

'They were supposed to knock Des out. I mean, he weren't daft, not then, he knew the police would be on to his record. He thought a bit of a pasting would throw the coppers off.'

'I doubt it,' Annie remarked, tipping more chips on to her plate. 'What went wrong?'

'Billy. He's a nutter. Sweet as a lamb one minute, and totally off his trolley the next.'

Edwin Woolley had put up more of a fight than they'd anticipated. Enraged at the resistance and frightened that another vehicle would come along, Billy had lashed out in a frenzy, smashing the old man's skull to pieces.

'Then he hit Des,' Judy said dully. 'Too hard.'

Fired up by adrenalin and excitement, Barken had delivered a blow far beyond that necessary to cause temporary unconsciousness.

'Hang on,' I objected. 'The witness statements spoke about two men hanging around before the robbery. If Barken and Colville carried out the murder, where was Kersey?'

'Him,' Judy snorted. 'He was safe at home, of course. Oh, he loaned them his car, and pointed them in the right direction. But he wasn't going to get his hands dirty.'

'Then why didn't he tell them that at his trial? Everyone assumed he was one of the attackers.'

'Who sodding cares?'

'It probably wouldn't have made much difference,' Annie said quietly. 'Even if he took no active part in the robbery he was very much the instigator. He must have been intelligent enough to realize how the court would view his part in a murderous assault on an old man. He'd have got the same sentence either way.'

And in Kersey's case, of course, he'd been playing the innocent victim of circumstantial evidence. A pose he'd have had to keep up while his case went to appeal. But why hadn't he said anything later, when he'd known he was well and truly banged up for the next ten years or so?

Loyalty? Fear? Or perhaps he was just smart enough to reason that time would have obliterated most of the evidence. It would have been his word against Barken and Colville.

'What happened after they'd ambushed Woolley?' I asked Judy.

Barken and Colville had delivered the statue to Kersey as planned, together with other items such as the jewellery and wallets that he'd told them to take in order to make it look like a chance mugging rather than a specific attempt on the statue. Whether they'd actually told him Woolley was dead was unknown. In any event, he was in too deep to do anything other than replace the car in his garage and act the concerned friend to the Woolley family.

His accomplices had returned to London. After a week of silence from Kersey, they'd made an unannounced call on his cottage.

'He was all packed up. Had a boat ticket for Spain. Billy went spare,' Judy explained, her eyes glazed as if she were seeing the picture unfolding in her mind. 'He reckoned Kersey was trying to skip with his share of the statue.'

'That right?' Bella asked, dispensing more Chardonnay with a pleasingly generous wrist.

'Kersey said he was gonna sell the statue in Spain. He said he was coming back and he'd let them have their share in a couple of weeks, soon as the sale went through.'

Then he'd ordered them out of the cottage. It was all the provocation Barken had needed. Seizing the nearest weapon, the discarded locking device for Kersey's car, he'd laid into the schoolteacher with a murderous enthusiasm.

'Trouble was,' Judy giggled, 'they couldn't find the statue. When it wasn't in his luggage, they turned the bloody cottage upside down. Zilch.'

'Can I ask something?' Annie enquired.

'Shoooot,' invited Judy, who was trying to replace her wine glass on the table and having a bit of trouble with the trajectory.

'How do you know all this? I mean, it couldn't have been your husband who told you. He was out of it.'

'Trrrooooo . . .' Judy agreed. 'Billy come to see me. Wwwai . . . ing when I come back from seeing Des. Warned me. Keep trap shut, know what's good fer me. Did too. Scares me, Billy. Fucking bloody terrifies me. See him comin' for me in dreams. Even com' haunt me in hospital. Alwa's there, in dark. Any more chips?'

We gave her the last and divided the salad out amongst us. Somehow in all the confusion of passing plates and juggling servers, the glasses got filled to the top again.

'I got rum and raisin ice cream, if anyone wants?'

We wanted.

'What about Des?' I reminded Judy. 'They'd turned him into a vegetable. Didn't you figure they deserved to be behind bars?'

'Thought get betta,' she mumbled. Either her metabolism was unused to coping with alcohol, or she was on medication that was speeding up the effects. 'Des get betta. Not be like . . '

The sentence was left unfinished. But we got the gist: she couldn't shop his mates without shopping her husband too. And she hadn't admitted to herself for a long time that Des would never be in a fit state for prosecution.

I guess by the time she'd acknowledged the truth, she was, in her own words, 'Too bloody tired to do anything about it.'

'Your turn. Tell . . . 'bou' Tina. Poor lillel cow. Not my niece. Des sista's girl. Allwa's trouble. Couldn' manage, not her and Des.'

'Tell me about Alan Kersey first. Why did he contact you?'

Bella had fetched a plastic tub of ice cream from the freezer and was now running a metal scoop over the pale-brown surface. We were all watching her covertly, checking that no one got more than their fair share.

'Wrote,' Judy drooled. 'Wrote Des. Said give him a chance. Said he was ill. Was 'e ill?'

'He's dead.'

'Good ri . . . ance.'

'What chance was he going to give Des, Judy?'

'Get statue. Said tell him where it was. I thought . . . my old man . . . 'titled. Go in Des's place.'

'What *exactly* did he say, Judy?'

With an effort, Judy tore her eyes from the rum and raisin and fastened them on me. Swallowing, she took a visible hold on her vocal cords and managed to tell us more or less coherently that Kersey had told Des to come to the hospice at exactly six o'clock on the previous Friday. If he was late, or failed to show, he'd lose his chance to get the statue.

'Tried,' Judy said. 'All ready.'

'But you felt the heart attack coming on?'

Judy sniffed. 'Knew wha' was. Had warnin', last year. Come to town, did the clubs, remember?'

'I remember,' Bella agreed, her face shining with alcohol and

241

the effort of digging out the dessert. 'You didn't say you were ill though.'

'No poin'. No one bloody *cared*. Thought, jus' my sodding *luck*. Pass ou' on bus, get carted off to hospital.'

Knowing that she might collapse at any minute, Judy had phoned Tina and persuaded her to go to the hospice in her place. 'Tol' her. Go home firs', might not keep me in. Then come up hospital. Didn' come. Thought lillel cow 'ad double-crossed me.'

Unscrewing the cap of a plastic bottle of chocolate sauce Bella had added to the table, Annie poured a brown lava flow over the mountain of ice cream in her dish.

'Wow, girl,' Bella said admiringly. 'You and me's definitely going to get on.'

'Cheers,' Annie said.

'Yo' turn,' Judy insisted. She was sitting next to me and her grabbing hand shook my share of the sauce over the table-cloth. 'Wha' Kersey give her? Was it the statue?'

'Not exactly.' Extracting the jeweller's receipt from my back pocket, I unfolded it with my teeth and read out the details.

To each of his four visitors Kersey had presented a gift-wrapped, three-inch-long silver model of the car-locking device that Billy Barken had used to beat him within a whisker of death twelve years previously.

'It was a final joke,' I explained to Judy's blank face.

'Was it?' Annie asked, emerging from behind the melting mountain.

'You don't think so?' I didn't see what else it could be myself, except the malicious revenge of a dying man.

'Somebody is going to a lot of trouble for a joke,' Annie said, licking the back of her spoon. 'First Tina, then Colville. What's the point of the two murders if it was just an elaborate gag on Kersey's part?'

I had to admit I didn't know.

Annie dropped the spoon with a contented sigh. 'You give one hell of a dinner party, Bella.'

'Well, thanks. We ain't the Ritz, but we aim to please. Coffee?'

She refused our offer of help. Coffee was served in real china cups with an oriental design and gold rims.

'Where'd you fin' those?' Judy asked suspiciously. We'd steered her back into the armchair, and she showed no objection to lolling amongst the cushions.

'In the attic. In a cardboard box.'

'Forget 'em,' Judy giggled. 'Job in Shepherd's Bush.'

'Great,' Annie said without any real heat. 'Now we're drinking from nicked china. What else around here is hot?'

'Only me,' Bella shrieked. 'An' it's all going to waste. There ain't a half-passable bloke in a thousand miles of here.'

'Two thousand,' I sniffed.

'Four zillion,' Annie contributed.

'All bassssstarrrrds.'

We opened the third bottle to toast all the hopeless blokes in the world.

Between us we knew so many that Annie and I ended up sleeping at the Parkers' house that night.

Since neither of us fancied the bed in which Des had expired, we ended up in the lounge. After a toss-up, I got the couch and Annie got cushions on the floor.

The Chardonnay acted like an alcohol cosh. We both slept soundly, if not well. I have a hazy recollection of staggering to the loo once and waking again when Warren crashed upstairs at some time in the early hours.

The next time I swam back to consciousness, the room was washed with grey light, my legs had stiffened into a half-bent position and my skin was tingling with goose-bumps.

I knew I'd been thinking about something vitally important. It took a minute for me to locate the half-finished dream that was sliding out of the back of my subconscious, like a hamster escaping under the skirting board. I grabbed the little critter's back leg and hauled it back just in time.

Replaying the scenes in my mind's eye, I felt my heart start thumping in time with the steam hammer in my head.

Leaning over, I shook Annie awake and told her we had something important to do tomorrow. 'I mean today,' I corrected.

One eye emerged from the blanket. 'What?'

'Dig up a dead donkey.'

'I'd have thought of that eventually.'

The eye disappeared again.

CHAPTER 23

We finally woke at nine, disturbed by rattling milk bottles and gulls with the lung power of feathered Pavarottis.

Nobody wanted breakfast. Dying quietly in a darkened room was a pretty popular choice for the morning's activity programme.

'No more booze, ever,' groaned Bella, resting her head on her arms and lying across the breakfast bar. On the whole she didn't look too bad: the multi-plaited style didn't muss like other hair, and the grey jumper and leggings weren't designed to be *haute couture* anyway.

A shower had fixed my hair, and if the seventies outfit hurt to look at, at least it went with the hungover ambience.

Annie had come out worst. She'd taken her business suit and blouse off and slept in her underwear. But yesterday's work-and-play creases were evident in the mustard wool. Coupled with a face bloated and blotchy from sleep and Chardonnay, and frizzy hair sticking out like a fuzzball, the whole effect was faintly sleazy.

Judy was still in bed.

Warren swaggered in, surveyed us and told us we ought to be ashamed. 'What kind of example d'yow think yow're setting for me, eh?'

Taking a carton of milk from the fridge, he flicked out the spout and bounced off swigging the drink to the beat of a tune that only he could hear.

'I can't go into work like this,' Annie moaned, peering short-sightedly into a handbag mirror. 'I'll have to go home, change.'

'You can't, you're giving me a lift this morning, remember?'

'You must be *joking*. The way I feel, I don't expect to be under the legal limit until some time next September. I'll have to leave the car out front, Bella.'

'What am I going to do?'

'For God's sake, Grace, same as me. Walk home.'

'I'm not going home. I've got something to do.'

Annie was gulping down glasses of tap water with the concentration of a shipwreck survivor. When she finally emerged, gasping for air, she panted: 'Do I remember you saying something about digging up a donkey?'

'Marilyn. Oh go on, Annie, come with me. It'll take ages on my tod. I'll do the same for you some day.'

'Grace,' Annie flopped down opposite me, 'I can confidently predict that there will never, *ever* be a time when I want you to assist me in disinterring a bloody donkey's carcass! God, I feel lousy. I'm getting under a cold shower.'

Bella and I listened for a few minutes to the sounds of squealing and groaning from the bathroom.

'I'm just slipping round to December's for a tick. Don't let her go without me.'

Her face pillowed on the formica, Bella mumbled: 'Stick the empties out as you go.'

I didn't remember us opening the fourth litre, but the mute evidence was staring me in the face. Scooping four necks between my fingers, I headed for the plastic wheelie bin in the back garden.

My feet seemed to be having trouble lining up one in front of the other. I stopped at the bin by the expedient of lurching into it. Annie was right: we were still three parts drunk.

I'd intended to take the front route, but since I was halfway there, the back way made sense.

Dropping to my knees, I went through the hedge tunnel on all fours. The branches caught in the woolly jumper, snagging and prodding like spiteful claws. Halfway along the packed earth I found something I remembered from my last quick exploration. Pushing it into my back pocket involved straightening up slightly.

The claws caught hold of my hair and hung on. Letting rip with a few expletives, I wrenched myself free and scuttled into the open at the back of the stables.

'Gotcha.'

My nose hit the cobbles and a large, knobbly knee was rammed into my back.

'Go ahead, punk, make my day: struggle.'

'Get off, Col.'

'Oh, it's you.' I was hauled up bodily by my jumper. 'Fought I'd got me first intruda.'

'Sorry to disappoint.' I was covered in straw again. Picking little slivers from the grip of the hairy jumper, I explained I wanted a word with December.

'You missed 'im. 'E's gone down the beach, ain't he?'

Of course he had. By now the lack of donkey noises had penetrated the skull steam hammer.

'How come you're here then, Col?'

'Bin 'elping with the mucking-out, ain't I? The birds what usually do it is sick. I'm securing the premises. Then I'm off. Tell you the troof, I'm glad to see ya. Give me a chance to say ta-ta.'

He thrust a meaty hand into mine and I shook it automatically.

'Got annuver job, ain't I? Bouncer down at TED's.'

'Crowd control personnel,' I corrected.

'Whatever. Still get to check out the best-looking birds.'

'I went there the other night.'

''Spect they 'ad to let ya in. What wiv ya knowin' Mr Drysdale's dad.'

'Hope the second lesson in Teach Yourself Diplomacy arrives real soon, Col.'

'Ya what?'

'Never mind. Best of luck with the new career.'

'Yeah, ta.'

He gave me a helping push up my backside by way of farewell as I retraced the tunnel route.

When I got back, Annie was bundled into a grubby towelling gown, drying off her mop of frizzy hair.

'We could get a cab,' I suggested.

'You get a cab, I'm going home. Then I'm going into the office.'

'Look, honey, I don't want to tell you your business,' Bella interrupted, spinning the tap and sending a Niagara into the kettle. The sound made my teeth ache. 'But I wouldn't want nobody looking like you on my case.'

Annie emerged from the towel, her skin damp and water trickling down the creases of her nose. 'That bad?'

'And how,' Bella confirmed.

I took my opportunity to recommend healthy outdoor exercise. 'Like digging.'

'Where is this donkey? And why do you want it? You're not going in for black magic or anything kinky, are you?'

'That's Thursday nights. Look what I found under the hedge.'

I smoothed out the crumpled Fry's wrapper. 'I think Tina dropped it the other night. December said she always had chocolate peppermint creams for the donkeys.'

'Clutching at straws, metaphorically and literally,' Annie said, removing a few slivers of the same from my rear end and flicking them in the sink.

'No. Listen, think about it. Somebody's waiting for her here, in the dark, when she comes in after visiting Kersey. She manages to struggle free and runs down the garden and through the tunnel. Maybe he can't figure out where she disappeared to. Or maybe he was just too big to get through. Whatever, I think she had a few minutes' head start. Enough time to hide what Kersey had given her, at any rate.'

Colour was returning to Annie's face as the water took care of the dehydration. 'So you think the model car lock was important too, do you?'

'Well, like you say, somebody's going to a hell of a lot of trouble to get it back.'

'Where she hide it?' Bella asked.

I waved the wrapper. 'She mashed it in the chocolate and fed it to Marilyn.'

No doubt she'd imagined it was the perfect hiding place. A sort of warm-blooded deposit box from which the article would emerge in the due process of nature and the alimentary system. But her killer had tortured the secret out of her before he'd killed her. And then he'd returned to collect Marilyn.

'That's bizarre,' Annie said.

'It makes sense of the timings,' I pointed out. 'And it explains the way Marilyn was treated. Throat slit to knock him out and then he starts to make a cut in the abdomen.'

At which moment Rosco and Rawlins had arrived for a bit of on-duty nookie and scared him off.

After that there had been a police car parked by the warehouse until December arrived to collect the carcass and take it to his mate's farm.

Annie said: 'So where is this farm?'

I had to admit I wasn't sure. 'We can go down the beach on the way back. Ask December. Or better still . . . Can I use the phone?'

'So *she* gets asked,' Annie murmured *sotto voce*.

Kevin wasn't at the club. But they put a call through to his home whilst I hung on, and checked it was OK to pass on his personal number.

'Hi,' he said, picking up on the first ring. 'Enjoy the cart ride?'

'Unforgettable.'

'I'm not sure how to take that.'

'It means the jury is still out.'

'Fair enough. We could try the same route in the BMW some time if you like.'

'Sure. Some time.'

'So what can I do for you?'

'I need the address of this farm where your dad buries his dead donkeys. And I want to dig up Marilyn, if that's OK?'

'Whatever turns you on. I'll give them a ring, tell them you're on your way.'

I love people who don't demand involved explanations for unreasonable requests. After issuing directions to the farm, he rang off with a casual: 'Call me back when you've time for that ride.'

Would I? I'd always steered clear of married blokes before. My life was complicated enough as it was.

The cab company quoted me thirty minutes. After examining her reflection again, Annie agreed that perhaps a rescheduling of the morning's appointments might be sensible. 'But we'll have to go past my place first. I can't do any earth-shifting in this suit.'

'Borrow my jeans if you like,' Bella invited. 'I'll just take this breakfast tray up to Judy, then I'll fix you up.'

Clad in blue denims, a black *Miss Saigon* T-shirt and a fleecy lined jacket, Annie joined me in the hall just as the taxi announced its arrival with a horn that played "John Brown's Body".

'Where to, girls?'

I gave him directions. 'How much, you reckon?'

Sucking his dentures, he tutted: 'Out the area, that. Unsocial mileage, you might call it.'

'Fifteen quid's worth is what I'd call it,' Annie said tartly. 'Take it or let us out here.'

'Sold, darlin'.'

'I take it you had no plans to pay?' Annie remarked as we headed out past the warehouse estate again.

'No cash. Sorry.'

With a sceptical grunt, Annie tightened the leather belt around the jeans another notch. 'I like Bella,' she said out of the blue. 'She's fat.'

'I thought you didn't have a hang-up about your weight, you liar.'

'I don't. I just don't like it.'

'I like a bit of meat on a woman meself,' the taxi driver shouted over his shoulder.

His eyes, like hard-boiled quail's eggs, were framed by the rear-view mirror.

'Oooh, so do I.' I snuggled into Annie. 'You won't see Bella again, will you, darling? We can work it out, promise.'

The eyes bulged and the dentures dropped. We made him turn the radio on.

'So,' I said, putting some space between me and Annie's thighs again. 'What happened with Jonathon? Has he dumped you?'

'No he bloody well hasn't. He didn't get the chance. I dumped him first.'

She got her lips closer to my ear. The quail's eggs were transfixed again. I mouthed a kiss and he looked back to the road.

'You know it was his weekend to have the kids? Well, he was supposed to drop them off at his ex's place Sunday afternoon, so I thought I'd give him a ring, invite him for supper. Only his phone was off the hook. I drove over there.'

'And?' I prompted, guessing the next act. I'd played it several times myself.

'He hadn't even had the good manners to draw the curtains.'

'Anyone we know?'

'That cow from the Electronic Daffodil. She's a fast worker, I'll give her that.'

'Sorry, which particular bovine are we talking about here? The barmaid?'

'No.' Annie shot me an exasperated frown. 'The oversexed plonk.'

Jonathon had pulled Gina Rawlins? I was just wondering whether anyone had broken the good news to Terry Rosco when Annie disillusioned me.

'Not Gina. I wouldn't mind so much if it were *Gina*. At least she's thin. It was the fat thing with the big thighs. Miss Butter-wouldn't-melt.'

So Jane Mullins had hidden depths after all. Well, they say blokes always fall for the same type, don't they? I guess Jon just wanted a younger model.

But I couldn't tell Annie that. 'Sorry.'

'Don't suppose you are really,' Annie said. 'You thought he was a pompous prick anyway, didn't you?'

'Like you said, I didn't really know him.'

'I did. And you were right. Only I wanted him to be OK, so I made him right in my head and sort of ignored the reality, if you see what I mean.'

I did. Only too well. 'Good riddance then.'

'Yes. Good riddance. Old thunder-thighs is welcome.'

Having consigned Jonathon to the depths of WPC Mullins' inadequately buttoned waistcoat, we returned to the subject of Marilyn.

'What exactly is your plan here? I mean, if he's been buried for a week, he's going to be in a pretty foul condition.'

I had to admit I hadn't really thought it out that far. 'Cut the body open, I suppose.'

The car jerked violently as the near wheel hit the grass verge.

Looking up, we caught the quail's eggs bulging out of their sockets.

'Turn that radio up a bit louder, can you, mate? We're having a private conversation on grave-robbing back here.'

Annie put an arm round my shoulders. 'Now are you sure you wouldn't find the bondage more exciting?'

'No, darling. It's necromancy or nothing.'

We were definitely still three parts cut.

Thinking of cutting, I asked Annie if she thought the vet would do the dissection for us.

'Don't know. Mind you, I'm not even sure you're entitled to do any cutting. Doesn't the body still belong to Drysdale?'

It was a moot point. And neither of us had the faintest idea of the answer. We were still arguing technicalities when we arrived at the farm.

The twentieth century had caught up with this place. Forget any preconceptions of oak-beamed farmhouses, cobbled yards and wooden barns filled with strutting hens, rotund pigs and doe-eyed cows.

The farmhouse was a modern, detached, slightly tatty affair that probably wasn't more than twenty years old. The "barns" were corrugated-iron sheds. In between was a stretch of concrete bare as an airport runway except for a couple of iron drums and a roll of barbed wire.

In answer to a blast on the driver's horn, a man in jeans, wellington boots and a bright-blue shellsuit top emerged from a small door in one of the sheds.

'You the ones Kevin rang about?'

'That's us. Mr . . . em?'

'Fred Pilkington.'

'Pleased to meet you, Fred. I'm Grace. This is Annie.'

Fred wiped something off his hand and extended it. Annie prudently paid off the driver, leaving me to bite the bullet and shake.

'Kevin said what you wanted. I dug 'im oop for you. This way.'

Surprised, but pleased not to have to deal with the exhumation, we followed him round to the back of the house.

Concealed round here was a one-storey brick and concrete structure much like the stables in Drysdale's yard.

In the adjoining field a white donkey was watching the

world over a barred fence. When it spotted us, it raised its head and emitted a long, low, mournful bray.

'Shaddoop,' Fred bawled back. 'Lonely,' he added with a jerk of his bald head. 'Used to 'ave a pensioner in with him. Turned oop his hooves a month back.'

'Maybe December could use him. Seeing he's got a vacancy.'

'He is December's. No good for beach work, though. Tried it. Chooked some kid in t'sea.'

Remembering December's version of the incident, I warmed to Snowy and gave him another wave. He brayed even harder.

'Will you shaddoop? Taking 'im down t'coast later,' he added, leading us to the far end of the stable building. 'Can stop with t'string till we get 'im a new pal. Here you are then.'

A small area had been wired off to make a cemetery. There were about thirty graves, each mound marked with a properly engraved stone giving the occupant's name, date of birth and date of death.

Fred pointed to a newly excavated pile of earth. 'There you are . . . there's Marilyn for you.'

We both stared in silence for a moment.

'I think,' Annie said finally, 'you could have a problem here.'

CHAPTER 24

Fred gave us a lift back to town. His horsebox was the 747 of horseboxes. Whilst Snowy brayed his lonely head off in the cavernous back, Annie and I perched on the high front seats.

I carried Marilyn's mortal remains on my knees. It wasn't difficult. He'd been reduced to the size of a large jar of pickled onions.

Well, how was I to know they cremated animal carcasses?

Fred was still chuckling at the thought of someone trying to dig a pit big enough to bury a carthorse as we rolled up outside Judy's house again.

Snowy bawled even harder, probably suspecting a plot to abandon him.

'Hold your racket,' Fred admonished, slapping the side of the van with the flat of his hand. 'Beach's t'next stop.'

'I'll walk him down for you,' I offered. 'Save you trying to park along the front.'

Fred rubbed a bristly chin, drawing a rasping sound with thumb and forefinger. 'Dunoo aboot that. December's particular, see, aboot who minds them.'

'They're very close,' Annie put in. 'I mean, Kevin doesn't invite just anyone to dig up their nearest and dearest, you know.'

I mouthed, "Cow". She grinned back.

'I suppoose it'll be hookay-dokay. Give oos hand with t'back then.'

We released Snowy and saw the van out of the turning.

Snowy examined his new surroundings with interest. Then he reared up and tried to climb the bonnet of Annie's car.

'Oi, get him off.'

'What do you think I'm doing?'

Trying to shift a donkey that doesn't want to shift is not an easy task. Eventually, with Annie pushing and me pulling, we got him back on to the pavement, into the Parkers' back garden, and tethered him to the drainpipe.

'What's this?' Bella demanded from the doorway, her arms akimbo. 'A miraculous resurrection?'

'Not quite. This is another beast. *This* is Marilyn.'

Bella stared. Then burst into raucous guffaws of laughter. Snowy reciprocated with enthusiastic brays.

'For Gawd's sake, shut that soddin' racket. You sound just like one of them bleedin' donkeys!'

Stepping into the garden, Bella called up to the open bathroom window above the kitchen: 'Sorry, Judy. Lunch'll be ready in 'bout half an hour.'

'Not soddin' likely.' The window banged shut again.

'You want some?' Bella asked us.

Actually I was with Judy on that one. Bella must have the constitution of an ox with dipsomaniacal tendencies. She seemed to have recovered from last night's blow-out already.

'I baked a quiche,' she demonstrated, drawing the bubbling creation from the oven. 'Real stuff. Not shop-bought.'

That was true. The washed-up mixing bowl and sieve were still on the draining board.

'Can I borrow these?'

'I guess. You want to cook too?'

'Not exactly.'

'It will have melted in the furnace,' Annie said, reading my mind.

'You never know. Might as well check since we've got him here.'

Bella took exception to my sieving Marilyn through her kitchen utensils.

After a bit of arm-twisting she produced a browning plastic

colander and washing-up bowl. With the aid of a chopping knife, we levered up the encrusted lid and tipped the black ash out in a steady gravelly stream.

It produced nothing except a grubby film on the table and a violent sneeze from Annie that sent a leg's worth of cremated donkey into the atmosphere.

'Sorry,' she apologized, sniffing into kitchen roll.

We swept up the table, but the urn was still only three-quarters full when we'd finished. In the end we superglued the lid back in place and prayed December wouldn't want to check up.

Annie glanced at her watch. 'I've got to go. It's been a fascinating morning. We must do it again, preferably in the next millennium. OK if I change upstairs, Bella?'

'Sure you don't want no lunch?'

'Not till hell freezes over. See you later, Grace.'

'I'm off too, Bella. Thanks for everything. Including the hangover.'

'My pleasure. Call round again, OK? Me and Judy's always here. Worse luck.'

'You're not going back to town yet then?'

She set the plaits bobbing with a violent head-shake. 'Somebody's got to sort Judy out. Reckon it's gotta be me, don't you? Ain't nobody else.'

'You're a nice person, Bella.'

'Yeah, well don't tell nobody. You'll ruin my image.'

I headed for the beach with Marilyn under one arm and Snowy trotting along on the other side.

He seemed to remember the route. The nearer we got to the sea, the faster he trotted. Handicapped by the metal urn, I tried to slow him one-handed, but just succeeded in pulling his head to one side. Objecting vociferously to this treatment, he swung round and started backing down the road, pulling me along with him.

By the time we reached the slipway down to the beach, no

fewer than four old ladies and a Hare Krishna follower had threatened to report me to the RSPCA.

Bellowing his hellos, Snowy succeeded in dragging the rein from my sweaty fingers and set off across the sands at a gallop to join his long-lost buddies.

Clasping Marilyn to my chest, I floundered after him. He beat me to the corral by several lengths.

December stayed seated whilst the herd milled round Snowy, exchanging sniffs and nuzzles.

'Fred dropped him off,' I puffed, flopping down beside him.

'I gathered. He's been moping. They like a bit of company. Mind, they're not usually that bothered once they're dead.'

'What? Oh yes, this. Er, we dug Marilyn up.'

I settled the pewter-coloured urn in the sand, twisting the base to fix it securely. We gazed in silence. A gull padded over and circled the metal container with suspicion, raising half-challenging wings when it spotted its own reflection.

'So? Aren't you going to ask me why?'

'I thought you'd get around to it in your own time, lass.'

Snowy's arrival had attracted a fair bit of human interest. I had to wait whilst December took the customers on a plod along the sands and back before I could tell him about Kersey's 'little presents' and my theory regarding Tina's hiding place.

'Not possible, lass,' he said, calmly unfolding his *Financial Times*.

'Why not?' I demanded indignantly. Hadn't he told me himself the donkeys would eat anything? In fact, hadn't I been virtually choked to death in the middle of a practical demonstration of said donkeys' alimentary abilities?

'Oh, aye. He'd have swallowed it all right. Appetite of a gannet, had our Marilyn. Only trouble was, he weren't there.'

'Weren't where?'

'In the stable. I went out that evening. Told you that.'

'So?'

'Had the trap out. Marilyn was in the shafts. Didn't put him back in the stable till gone ten.'

It had been such a beautiful theory. I'd been proud of it. A perfect example of original thinking. 'Oh sod it!'

'Language, lass.'

'Don't tell me how to talk. I don't even work for you any more.'

'Speaking of which, what happened to that final account you was doing for me?'

'I've been busy. I'll do it later.'

I kicked out a heelful of sand, sending it pattering over the gull, which was still fascinated by the urn.

It retreated in a hop and flutter and pattered into the corral. Lana lowered an interested head and nearly got nipped on the nose. With a startled snort he reared back, setting his harness bells jingling, and barging the others out of the way with his rump.

Something December had said at our first meeting crept from my subconscious.

'Did you say Lana and Marilyn were brothers?'

'Full brothers. Same sire and dam.'

'Did they look alike?'

'Dead spits, except for a bit of marking in the mane.' Refolding the paper, he looked down at me, understanding what I was suggesting. 'He took the wrong beast?'

'Why not?' I said excitedly, warming to my new theory. 'Tina tells him she's fed it to the big grey donkey. It's dark in there. He's not likely to have started flashing a torch around drawing attention to himself. Soon as he finds the grey donkey, he gets it out of there. It makes sense, doesn't it?'

'Yes.' He pushed the folded paper into his satchel and stood up. 'Lana favours the far end of the stable. Marilyn, now, he always had the spot near the door. Always first out in the mornings, was our Marilyn.'

And the first to trustingly greet his killer when he opened up the stable that night.

'How long would it take to go through, from mouth to butt?'

December raised the scouring-pad eyebrows. 'Hard to say. About forty-eight hours normally. If it's come out, it's spread over the fields by now. Muck's picked up regularly.'

I opened my mouth to swear again, saw his expression and swallowed my annoyance.

'Mind, I'd have thought one of us would have seen it when we mucked out.'

'Perhaps it's still, you know . . . '

December's face split into a huge smile. He handed me the bucket. 'Best follow close then, hadn't you, lass?'

He relented in the end and agreed to an X-ray. Fred was called on again to bring the horsebox down the following day and transport Lana to the nearest veterinary practice with facilities for X-raying large animals.

The veterinary surgeon questioned December over Lana's placidly chewing head.

'Any presenting signs of colic?'

'None.'

'Sweating, belly-kicking, rolling?'

'Not a one. Fit as a flea. And an appetite to match.'

The vet ran her tongue round inside her cheek, then gave her opinion. 'Doesn't sound like there are any foreign bodies in the gut. I'll do a rectal palpation if you like.'

'What about the X-ray?'

Instead of answering me, she talked over my shoulder to December. 'X-rays don't seem called for in this case. I think we should wait and see.'

'I want to see without waiting, thanks,' I pleaded with December. 'Whoever killed Marilyn might work out what happened and come after Lana. If there's anything in there, it's best that we have it than he carries it around.'

'X-ray him please, Doc.'

The vet raised resigned shoulders. 'I'll do lateral chest and abdominal shots if you insist. How big is this object?'

'Two to three inches long, by three-quarters of an inch wide.'

We took our seats in the waiting room, drinking coffee from the drinks machine and reading months-old copies of the *Reader's Digest*.

I'd just finished all the 'Life's Like That', and was wondering whether to increase my word power, when a nursing attendant beckoned us through to the consulting rooms.

The vet was pleasingly embarrassed. 'I owe you an apology, Mr Drysdale. It would seem that Lana has got more than his lunch on board.'

She tapped on the illuminated negatives of Lana's digestive system. 'See that?'

We couldn't really miss it. Amongst the milky swirls of gut and curving contours of bone was a solid black geometric shape.

'I think I can feel other matter impacting behind it,' she explained, tracing sweeps and curves over Lana's internal system. 'It will cause distress soon.'

December sucked his bottom lip. 'Operation?'

'As a last resort. Since it's well along the system, I'd like to try and dose him first. See if we can get the gut to do the work for us. I'll admit him immediately if that's all right with you?'

'I'll stop with him. Fred will see you home, lass.'

The animal hospital weren't keen, but December could be as stubborn as his donkeys.

'What about the others?' I asked as December gave me a boost into the horsebox. 'Do you want me to sleep round your place tonight?'

We'd left a temporary replacement for Colin pacing the cobbles this morning.

'That's kind, lass, but there's no need. I've made other arrangements.'

'Kevin?' My stomach tightened in an involuntary spasm of excitement.

'Noo. I'm stoppin' round t'stables. See t'mooking out in morning if needed, December.'

'Thanks, Fred. I'll call later. Afternoon, lass.'

Since he'd only ever contacted me at the office, I scribbled my home address and thrust it into December's hand as Fred crashed into gear.

'Call me too,' I shouted from the open window. December raised a lazy hand in acknowledgement.

The whole business with Lana had taken longer than I'd realized. By the time Fred dropped me off at the office it was late afternoon.

'Luscious thing,' Vetch greeted me as I stepped into the lobby. 'Interesting mode of transport. Is this the "in" vehicle of the moment? Should we expect the supermarket car parks to be packed with rows of horseboxes instead of four-wheel drives?'

''Lo, Vetch. You wearing that bow-tie for a bet?'

'Sarcasm, sweet thing, does not become you. Have you a moment to step into my parlour and discuss the distressing absence of your rent and shared facilities payments?'

'Facilities my arse: one grotty fax machine that doesn't work half the time.'

'You are forgetting Janice.'

'She doesn't work the other half.'

'Nonetheless . . . '

I scratched my midriff vigorously. 'I'm sure that damn van has horse fleas.' Wriggling my shoulders against the staircase newel, I sighed blissfully. 'God, that's better.'

'Perhaps we might delay our chat for a while, sweetness. I do have to get away on time tonight.'

'Whatever you say.'

Sauntering upstairs, I found Mr Mouldar's Tuesday report

on Supermarket Sal's progress on my desk and faxed it through to the solicitor.

Annie was out. Helping myself to coffee and biscuits, I stretched out on her sofa and listened to the sounds of the building closing down for the night.

After a while the echoing footsteps and slamming doors ceased and the pervasive "shush-shush" of the sea filtered through on the approaching night.

Tracing the cracks in Annie's ceiling with my eyes, I tried to work out where I went from here.

Once we got the model car lock from Lana's guts, what then? Did it leave us any nearer catching Barken?

It was, I realized, the first time I'd put a name to Marilyn and Tina's killer. I'd been saying 'the killer' or 'the murderer'. But when you came down to it, who else could it be but the fourth member of that little tea-party at Kersey's bedside, the elusive Billy Barken?'

Ring DCI Jackson, my inner voice urged. *Let the police take it from here.*

Annie's phone still had the electronic block on; I returned to my own office and was reaching for the receiver when the telephone bell shrilled into the silence, making me jump with a frightened yelp.

I'd half expected it to be December, but a strange female voice asked for Miss Smith.

'Speaking.'

'This is the supervisor of St Theresa's Retirement Home. I believe we met briefly a few days ago.'

I recalled to mind the frosty-faced female who'd caught me arguing through Simla Woolley's keyhole. 'I remember. What can I do for you?'

'I wondered whether it would be possible for you to call at the home?'

'Sure.' Maybe she'd lost a patient; I mean 'guest'. 'Tomorrow morning?'

'I meant right away, Miss Smith. We have had . . . an unfortunate incident.'

'Could you be a bit more specific?'

The silence on the line went on for so long, I thought we'd lost the connection. Finally she said with obvious reluctance, 'A break-in. Mrs Woolley has been attacked. She insists on speaking with you.'

CHAPTER 25

I was nearly at the flat when I remembered the car was out of action. Without Annie's motor or Fred's horsebox to call on, I was stuck with the local mini-cabs.

Unless?

When I explained my problem on the phone, Kevin said laconically: 'Fifteen minutes, OK?'

'Terrific.'

'I know I am. And modest with it.'

As I broke all previous records for dressing and applying make-up, I wrestled with my moral dilemma *vis-à-vis* married men.

On the other hand, asking for a lift was hardly the same as a date. Was it?

By the time the bell rang I'd wriggled into a black wrap-round skirt, yellow body, black jacket and four-inch heels. The sort of little number, in fact, that I usually slipped into when interviewing bad-tempered, snobbish old bats.

Kevin had thrown a tan leather jacket over the designer suit.

'Hi. Thanks for coming.'

'My pleasure.'

'Is it all right? I mean, you won't get into trouble for leaving the club?'

Kevin grinned. I decided I could eat his smile. In fact, I could have fancied all of him spread on toast.

'No. The owner and I have a pretty elastic arrangement. Anyway, I'll be back in ten minutes.'

'Oh.' I'd been rather assuming I'd get a lift both ways.

Preceding him up to street level. I asked if he'd heard from his dad.

'Briefly. Nature is taking its course, apparently. You've got great legs, you know.'

The slit skirt and open iron staircase had given him plenty of scope to judge. I was glad I'd scored maximum marks but a little put out by the practised ease with which that remark had been tossed away. Being a bit on the side would be tricky. Being another bit on the side . . .? No thanks, mate.

'Yes, it had been mentioned before,' I heard myself saying off-handedly. The BMW was parked three houses down. Feeling strange in unfamiliar heels, I wobbled over and tried the handle.

'Other side.'

'Sorry?'

'Driver's door,' Kevin said.

A motorcycle swung round the corner and he stepped from between the parked cars to raise an arm in greeting.

The biker slid to a halt and peeled off the helmet, revealing the oriental features of TED's cloakroom attendant.

She shook out long blue-black hair and winked at her boss. 'Hey, mister. You looking to get picked up?'

'Be right with you, Zizi.' Reaching into the BMW, Kevin fished out another helmet.

'You're not coming?' I felt relieved and disappointed at the same time.

'Sorry. We've got a private function booked into the club tonight and I have to be there. Drop the car back when you're finished. See you, Grace.'

Swinging himself into the rear seat, he wrapped his arms round Zizi's waist and they disappeared in a roar of unfettered Suzuki.

So much for my moral dilemma.

I was finally living the private investigator fantasy: powerful car; quadrophonic speakers; sexy outfit. I let myself wallow in the dream as I roared in the direction of St Theresa's.

Roger Woolley's yellow Metro was parked outside the main entrance and I could hear voices raised in argument as I stepped into the entrance lobby.

'For heaven's sake, Roger, if she doesn't want to go then I think it's down to you to persuade her, not me.'

'She won't listen to me, Elaine. She never does. Couldn't you try . . . ?'

'No, I could *not*. I'm sick of being the one who's left to cope. This is the first night out I've had in ages and I don't intend to miss it.'

'I can't just leave it at that, Elaine. Mother isn't responsible for her actions.'

'Neither will I be in a minute. For heaven's sake, make a decision for once, Roger. You make me bloody sick.'

They were facing each other in the main lounge, the supervisor's disapproving face framed by their angry profiles.

Her sour expression melted into something resembling approval as I appeared. 'Ah, here's Miss Smith. Perhaps she can talk some sense into your mother.'

The Woolleys swung round and glared at me, united in resentment at my supposed ability to achieve where they had failed.

Roger's hair had receded whilst his Adam's apple had become more pronounced, but otherwise he looked much like the newspaper photo taken at the time of his father's death. Elaine was at least ten years younger. Whatever prettiness she'd once possessed had faded under the worries of being the lifeboat that kept the rest of the Woolley family afloat.

'Are you social?'

'Well, you know, I'm pretty friendly most of the time, Roger.'

His thin face flushed. 'I meant, are you a social worker? We don't require that sort of interference. I take care of my mother's needs.'

'She doesn't think you do. And anyway, I'm not a social worker. I'm . . . a friend of the family.'

'How can you be?' Roger's eyes narrowed behind his spectacles. '*I* don't know you.'

'Gee, I'm sorry about that, Rog. We really must get it together some time.'

I was beginning to take a real dislike to Roger. I suspected both father and son had been promoted to their levels of incompetence.

'You could always ask your son Eddie for a reference for me.'

'You know Eddie?'

'For heaven's sake, Roger, what does it matter who she knows? If your mother wants to talk to her, that's her business. The curtain goes up in fifteen minutes. Are you coming or shall I call a taxi?'

Wrapping her coat round her, Elaine swept past me. Roger muttered: 'I'll leave it to you then, Miss Smith,' then half walked, half ran to the front door.

I turned inquiringly to the supervisor. 'Where's Simla?'

'In her room.'

She led the way into the corridor. From the back of the house the sounds of a frantic television commentator interspersed with maniacal bursts of studio-audience laughter filtered into the depressing gloom.

'An intruder, you said. When?'

'Just after six. The residents were having their evening meal. Mrs Woolley returned to her room early. When I went to speak to her a few seconds later, I found her lying on the floor.'

'You didn't see anyone?'

'Someone ran out through the front door as I came into the corridor. But as I've already explained to the police, I only caught a glimpse of their back. I was more concerned with attending to Simla. I'm afraid by the time anyone got outside, he was well away.'

'You're sure it was a he?'

'Yes . . . yes. I think so.'

'Is anything missing?'

'Not as far as we can tell. It's always difficult to say for certain: a lot of residents are very forgetful.'

We'd reached Simla's room by now. The supervisor rapped loudly on the door panels. 'Simla. Miss Smith is here.'

'Tell 'er to 'ay 'omething.' The words were oddly truncated, as if Simla was having trouble pronouncing her consonants.

The supervisor saw my expression. 'She's been struck across the mouth. There is also some damage to her wrist. She refused to speak to the police which, of course, she is perfectly entitled to do. However, I'm obliged to see that all injured guests receive medical treatment, and Mrs Woolley refuses to go to hospital.'

I saw why I was suddenly flavour of the week. My allotted task was to persuade the old bat to see a doctor so that the supervisor didn't get a black mark on her performance record.

'I've got some news about Kersey's tea-party, Simla,' I yelled through the keyhole. 'Open up.'

The door opened far enough to admit one: me.

'Si' down,' Simla ordered.

Her back was to me as she hobbled to the chair, her gait uneven because she was only using one stick.

Sitting down with a grunt of exhaled breath, she glared up at me. I clicked on the overhead light.

It shone brightly on the red and purple bruising surrounding the twisted and swelling lip.

I didn't waste any time on sympathy. 'So what's this all about, Simla?'

'You were 'ight. 'E came a'ter me.'

'Billy Barken?'

'Don't know who he was. He 'ad scarf round 'is face.'

'Could he have been one of the blokes from Kersey's tea-party the other Friday?'

''Es.'

'One of the blokes who killed your husband, in fact?'

269

'I 'uppose 'o.'

'Perhaps you'd better start from the beginning. Kersey contacted you from the hospice, I assume?'

'Few 'eeks ago. 'Old me to come that Friday. Said not to tell.' She winced, holding the bruised mouth.

'Hang on,' I instructed.

The supervisor leapt back like a startled rabbit as I whipped the door open.

'Got any frozen peas?'

'I beg your pardon?'

'Veg,' I explained. 'Ice bag. For the swelling. And a tea-towel.'

She surrendered a catering pack of petit pois with reluctance.

Once it was wrapped and pillowed on Simla's shoulder I prompted her: 'So Kersey sent you an invite. Did he say why? Apart from this desire to confess and receive absolution,' I added.

She coloured at the sarcasm. 'He said he'd give me the bronze back. Said he'd 'ell me where 'e'd hidden it. It's mine by rights.'

'So why not just tell the police?'

'What good would that 'ave done? 'Ow could they 'ake a dying man tell if 'e didn't wish to?'

Good point.

'So what happened when you got there?'

'Those men were there. And that 'irl. The Parker 'oman's niece.'

'Did you know they were the killers?'

She shook her head, working her jaw where the cold had numbed it. 'Not at first. 'Ater, worked it out.'

'What happened with Kersey?'

''E was unpleasant. Polite but sort of teasing. 'Ike he was enjoying 'imself. 'E talked about all sorts: 'Ow I'd been 'eeping; 'ow Roger was; that 'ospice 'e was in.'

She shuddered suddenly and looked me straight in the eye for the first time since I'd come into the room. "E was mad, you know.'

'Do you think he always was? Before the attack?'

'I 'ont know. 'E was Roger's friend. We only saw 'im on brief occasions.'

'You knew him well enough to help him rob your husband.'

The bag of peas dropped to the floor. We both ignored it.

'I 'on't know what you mean!'

'Keep your voice down,' I advised. 'Walls and supervisors have ears.'

'You've no right to 'ay, you wicked . . . '

Even the tears she was trying to squeeze out looked unconvincing. I don't suppose she shed many on the late Major's behalf when he turned up his toes, so it was hard to fake a few now.

'Oh come on, Simla. Kersey's other three guests were connected to the robbery in some way. And he didn't invite them out of a belated desire to atone. His agenda was quite simple: he wanted revenge for a near-death experience and years in the nick. So it stands to reason he had something against you too. Like rather more involvement in his little antique heist than the boys in blue suspected?'

As I was talking, details of my previous visit to this hole were rushing out of my subconscious. Snippets of conversation danced round my brain ('Gives herself airs. Just a fancy rat-catcher, that's all he was. My father gave them half a crown to clear the barn. Not surprised he lost his money. Takes them like that sometimes. My cousin Rose's boy would wager on two raindrops sliding down a window. They lost him in Malaya.') and joined themselves into a logical motive for Simla's involvement.

'Your husband had a decent job in local government. Your kids were long off your hands. You must have had a house? Savings plans? Pensions? Something put by for a rainy day? So how come you're living in this dump, eh?'

The tears that coursed down her cheeks were real enough now. After all, they were for herself. 'The bastard,' she hiccupped.

'When'd you find out he was a compulsive gambler?'

'I knew by our second anniversary. Too late by then. In my 'ay you married and you sta'ed married. Had no choice once you had children. Wasn't loyalty, just practicalities. Nowhere else to go. I hated him,' she spat out with surprising vehemence. 'Hated him.'

'How did Kersey know you'd play ball?'

"E was there. That morning. I opened the 'etter from the bank by mistake.' Tears filled her eyes again. "E'd borrowed against the 'ouse. All of it gone.'

'So you figured you'd take out your own little pension plan?'

The eyes flashed like chips of jet. 'I was enti'led. O'er forty years I put up with that 'elfish old bore. And what was 'e going to leave me with?'

Not a brass rupee, judging by where she'd ended up.

'Years I scrimped and made do. Keeping up appearances, living up to the standard that 'e expected.'

'Did Roger know? About his dad's problem?'

'Not when he was younger. In 'act, Edwin blamed it on me. Your mother's too extravagant, she spends too much on the 'ousekeeping, that's what he told them. Once, when Roger asked for money for a school trip to France, Edwin 'ook 'im upstairs, showed 'im a dress I'd bought for the Rotary's Christmas dance. "That's why you can't go, old boy," he said. "Because your mother fritters away our money on new outfits".' A tear of anger spilled down her cheek. 'It was the first new thing I'd had in five years.'

'Surely they caught on later?'

'Do your parents discuss their financial arrangements with you, Miss Smith? Believe me, by the time the children had grown up, the myth of a spendthrift, extravagant mummy had been well established. Never mind there was nothing to show for it.' Brushing the tears away with her knuckles, she stifled an exclamation of pain as the bone scraped over the swollen lips. 'I was *glad* when Alan asked me to help. I wanted to take something from Edwin. I wanted to hurt him.'

'What was your contribution to the plan? Keeping Kersey up to scratch on your husband's movements?'

''E knew those. Edwin told 'im 'bout appointment in London. I 'ad to arrange the taxi. Parker was going to 'ake sure he was at the dispatcher's office when I rang. It 'asn't difficult. Edwin always 'ad to 'ave someone wai'ing on him.'

'Wasn't that a bit risky? I mean, supposing the police had checked? Found out you specified Parker?'

Something like pride flitted across the bruised features. 'I t'ought of that. Didn't ask for 'arker. Just asked to speak to the driver. Asked questions 'bout 'is insurance and experience. If it wasn't Parker, I was going to say I wasn't satisfied and ring back again in a few minutes.'

'The Major didn't drive?'

'Hadn't for some years. He *said* it was due to declining road standards. Load of nonsense, of course. It was the expense.'

'So Des Parker knew you were in on the job?'

'Yes.'

'Didn't that bother you?'

'Alan had arranged to pay the man. I can't see that he would have gained any advantage by reporting me to the police.'

Her naïveté was almost frightening. Had her vulnerability to blackmail really not occurred to her?

'Did you know Kersey planned to take the ferry to Spain?'

'Naturally. He said it would be safest to sell the bronze abroad. 'E'd have preferred America, but he thought it might be too risky 'etting it out of this country and into the States. That's when he decided on the Santander ferry.'

'Why not the French ferry? Calais or Boulogne?'

Her jaw was loosening again, her speech becoming more fluent as she explained that Kersey's decision had been based on the lack of co-operation between the British and Spanish police forces. 'I mean, they had all those dreadful bank robbers living there for years and never did a thing about them. So why should they bother to put themselves out for one statue?'

'And a murder.'

'That wasn't meant to happen! Just the robbery.'

Kersey had already visited his doctor a couple of times, planting the idea he was suffering from stress. As soon as the initial dust had settled from the robbery, he'd planned to take sick leave from the school, transport the statue to a Madrid dealer and arrange a private sale.

'He said even if the British police eventually traced the sale, the dealers wouldn't want to return their commission or upset future customers by passing on the details of the statue's buyer. And if the statue turned up in someone's collection later, Edwin would have had to prove it was *his* bronze, which would be nearly impossible. And he didn't have the money to start legal action in foreign courts.'

'Speaking of money, what was your cut?'

'Half. Alan was going to pay those men two thousand pounds each, and then we would split the rest. A'an was going to open Spanish bank accounts for us both. We hoped to get thirty to forty thousand pounds each, depending on the dealer.'

'Not enough to retire on.'

'There are plenty of houses packed with antiques a'ound the country. Owners probably haven't looked at the articles in years. I said to Alan, if this works out, there's no reason why we couldn't take a few more. Provided we weren't too greedy, who would suspect a schoolteacher and a respectable little old woman?'

She was dead serious too. Kersey couldn't have known what he was unleashing when he'd made that tentative suggestion to a frustrated, bitter woman facing a frighteningly insecure old age.

Now she'd started, she seemed to be taking an almost gleeful pride in boasting of her involvement. 'He wanted to pull out, you know? When he heard abou' Edwin and the taxi driver. Said he'd dump the statue somewhere the police could find it. I had to make the worm go on with the original plan.'

'What for? You'd have got the statue back anyway. As the Major's widow.'

'Edwin left his estate split equally between me, Roger and our daughters. By the time I'd have paid off his creditors and split everything four ways, I'd have been lucky to see a thousand pounds.'

So she'd insisted Kersey take the berth on the Santander ferry.

'His accomplices thought it was a double-cross. That's why they attacked him.'

'Ignoran' fools.'

'But deadly.'

'Yes. That was unfortunate.'

'You must have been sweating after Kersey's arrest. Weren't you scared he'd turn you in?'

'Initially. Although of course I should have denied everything.'

'Why d'you think he didn't? Old-fashioned chivalry, protect-the-woman-at-all-costs sort of thing?'

'Good heavens, no.' She seemed genuinely amused by the idea. 'He wanted to torture me. I went to see him, you know. After his conviction. He wrote and asked me to come, so that he could assure me he'd taken no part in Edwin's death.'

'But you knew he had!'

She drew a sharp breath of impatience at my stupidity. 'He needed an excuse. To get me to the jail. To tell me what he intended.'

'Which was to make you sweat out every day of his sentence

275

with him? He had the statue but you weren't going to see a peseta of the profits until – and if – he was released? You served your sentence in St Theresa's while he disintegrated in Parkhurst, was that the idea?'

She looked at me with something approaching respect. 'That was precisely his plan.'

'What did you do with Kersey's present?'

'How did you know about that?'

'I told you I had informants.'

She was cradling the injured arm across her lap. Now she attempted to move and winced with the pain.

'Shouldn't you go to the hospital? I'll come with you if you're worried about running into Barken.'

'He's wasting his time.'

'You mean you haven't got Kersey's gift?'

'What does it matter?' she snapped back. 'It wasn't the right box.'

'Sorry?'

We stared at one another.

'What are you talking about?' I demanded.

'I thought you said you knew.'

'I know Kersey gave each of you an identical package.'

'Not all. One was different.' Dribble was running from the injured side of her mouth. Impatiently she fumbled a screwed-up tissue from her pocket and dabbed at the bruised lips. 'One had the location of the bronze. We had to choose. One lucky winner, that's what Alan said. I didn't get it, just the horrid 'ittle model of the car lock. It wasn't fair. It was Edwin's statue. Those others had no right.'

A light was beginning to dawn. 'So you told Eddie and sent him to search Judy Parker's house, in case Tina had chosen the box with the details of the statue's hiding place.'

Simla pouted. 'It was his idea. Said it was worth a shot. He's a good boy, Eddie. Got more spunk in his li'tle finger than his father ever had.' She leant forward, the dribble swelling out in

276

bubbles of spittle now. 'Had she? Had that girl got it? Tell her, tell Mrs Parker I'm entitled. Half and half, that's fair.'

I broke the news that Kersey had ordered four identical models. 'All the packages were the same,' I elaborated, in case she hadn't got the message.

'No. You're lying.' A cunning expression crept into the glittering eyes. 'She's offered you a share, hasn't she? I'll match it. Whatever she's saying, I'll give more. Ten per cent on top.'

That's the trouble with deceivers: they allocate the same standards to everyone else.

It took a while to convince Simla I was telling the truth, but finally it penetrated her self-obsessed brain.

'But . . . but why?'

'Revenge. Kersey plotted this for years. He's set you all at each other's throats. Colville's dead, probably murdered by Barken; Tina got what was rightly intended for Parker's widow; and you've been beaten up. You want to tell me about that, incidentally?'

'There is nothing to tell. I left the dinner table early. They were serving 'ish fingers. I loathe the wretched little horrors. I told the supervisor I intended to report the standard of catering to the board and I came back here. He was 'earching the room.'

'How did he get in?'

She shot a triumphant smirk at the door, raising her voice slightly so that anyone outside would be sure to hear. 'He took the pass key from the supervisor's office. It was still in the door. The security here is dreadful. People 'ust come and go as they please.'

'So what happened when you came in?'

'He struck me.' Her voice rose in indignation as she touched the swelling jaw. 'Nobody has ever hit me before.'

'Lucky you. Did he ask about the package?'

'No. She called out she was going to speak to me. And he ran off.'

'In which case it would be sensible to come clean with the police. Give them a statement and let them pick Barken up.'

'I shall do no such thing. I have no intention of letting the whole world know I was involved in Edwin's death. And I shall deny this conversation if you attempt to repeat it, Miss Smith.'

My patience was rapidly running out. If she didn't want my advice, why had she sent for me?

'I want the bronze,' she said simply. 'And you're a detective. I've decided to hire you.'

'You'll get it anyway, if it turns up. As soon as it goes on the market, you can claim it back as stolen property.'

'I can't.' She slapped the good hand down open-handed on the chair arm. 'Haven't you been listening, you stupid girl?'

'Listen, Simla, you're in no position to start flinging insults around. Why can't you?'

For the same reason that Edwin Woolley would have had difficulty in proving ownership once the bronze had been sold on the international market. Quite simply, the statue had no provenance. There were no pictures of it, it had never been insured, and for nearly thirty years it had gathered dust in the Woolleys' attic.

'I couldn't even describe it to the police after Edwin's demise,' Simla said. 'It was just an ugly rider on a horse, that was all I remembered. And after Alan 'old him it might be worth a 'ortune, Edwin buried it.'

'Pardon?'

''E buried it. He'd dug a hole in the back garden for some rose bushes, so he put the statue in there instead. He said thieves would never think of looking there. It's why we couldn't take it from the house. Alan said it would be obvious it must have been someone who knew about the hiding place. Hijacking the taxi was our first opportunity.'

'Where did it come from in the first place?'

'Edwin brought it back. He was stationed in France for a short time after the war.'

'It's French?'

She shook her head and winced. 'According to Alan it came from one of their African colonies. A place called Dahomey. At least it used to be when he wrote his thesis on it. It's something else now. Any'ay, sixteenth-century bronzes from there are very valuable.'

'How come the Major didn't flog it years ago?'

'He didn't know it was valuable. It was in a box of other bits and pieces. Silver mostly. He sold that, of 'ourse.'

'Looted spoils?'

'Such terms are relative after a war, Miss Smith.'

'You mean the original owner was probably dead or in no position to object if Edwin helped himself?'

'I resent your tone.'

'Tough. What makes you think I'd want to help you get it back?'

She seemed genuinely surprised by this query. 'I'll give you a share; five per cent. Why shouldn't you help?'

No reason at all that I could think of. After all, I had no client now. On the other hand the old bat made my skin crawl. 'Thirty per cent.'

'Ridiculous. Five and a half.'

We settled on ten.

'We might have to cut Judy in,' I temporized.

'That would be acceptable.' She leant forward eagerly. 'You'll do it?'

'On condition that you keep Eddie out of my face.'

'Of course. I'll speak to him.'

'And I'll need the model car lock Kersey gave you.'

'What for?'

I wasn't too certain myself. But I had faith in Annie's theory that Barken wouldn't have gone to all this trouble to retrieve a practical joke on Kersey's part.

'Have you still got it?' I asked, ignoring her puzzled frown.

'It's o'er there. In the junk drawer.'

It wasn't. Simla tipped on to the bed a jumble of tangled threads, cotton reels, loose buttons, crochet hooks, cards of fasteners, boxes of pins, thimbles, single earrings, old circulars and envelopes, library cards, washers, playing cards, mismatched cutlery and chewed and broken biros and pencils.

'It must be here,' she said, scattering articles over the bedspread. She raised a frustrated face to mine. 'I know I put it in here.'

We pulled out all the dresser drawers and squinted into the dusty hollow: our haul amounted to a couple of pairs of old tights, a single glove and an address book.

Kersey's 'little present' had vanished.

CHAPTER 26

We turned the room inside out, but it was no show. The model car lock had vanished. Finally, seduced by the promise of a lift in the BMW, and spurred on by the obvious pain she was now experiencing from her injuries, Simla agreed to let me take her to the hospital.

'But I shall not 'peak to the police,' she said rebelliously as I led her out of the front door.

'Whatever you think best, Simla dear,' the supervisor said.

'Mrs Woolley to you.'

'Yes. Of course.'

The woman raised her eyebrows at me over Simla's head in an effort to engage my sympathy for her rotten job.

I didn't respond; I had a rotten job of my own.

We were stuck at the hospital for two hours. I read ancient magazines whilst Simla was prodded, X-rayed and cleaned up.

Eventually she was delivered back to me complete with a sling, foam-rubber padding and pain-killers.

On our return to St Theresa's the supervisor attempted to confiscate the pain-killers.

'We like to issue their medicines,' she explained to me across Simla's head. 'They got confused and take the wrong doses.'

I felt a tiny twinge of sympathy for Simla. It couldn't be much fun being forced back into a second childhood. At least in the first you have the consolation of plotting the revenge you'll wreak on adults once you've grown up – unaware that by the time you get there, their behaviour will seem perfectly reasonable.

It proved to be wasted emotion. Simla had her own methods of dealing with patronization. Under the pretence of regaining her balance, she brought the tip of her single crutch down heavily on the supervisor's foot.

'Bugger off,' she ordered, her diction returned to normality.

With my hand under her injured arm, she hobbled to her own doorway. Panting slightly with the exertion, she peered up at me. 'We have a bargain, Miss Smith?'

'Are you certain you want to do this? If Barken gets wind that you've got the statue, you'll be in real danger. It might be smarter to let the police handle things. Split the statue with your daughters and Roger.'

'No. The girls are provided for. And I despise Roger.'

'For taking after his father?'

'Oh no. For taking after me, Miss Smith. I was weak. I let other people, my parents, my husband, dictate my life. Joining up with Alan Kersey was the first positive decision I had ever made for myself. When it all went wrong, I thought my chance had gone. But now I've been offered another one. I want something better than this. I want privacy, respect. I want to be able to climb into a bath that doesn't have to be scoured clean of others' bodily odours. I want that statue, Miss Smith.'

'Fair enough.'

Nodding her satisfaction, she shuffled inside.

I turned, and through the open door next to Simla's room, saw the refined one, dressed in a diaphanous nightie, sitting cross-legged on the floor in a yoga pose. My arrival in the doorway didn't seem to have any effect. Serene as a Buddha, she sat unmoving, a slight smile on the long-nosed face which was framed by knots of grey hair twisted around multicoloured curling rods. The only sign of life was the gentle rise and fall of her skinny breasts, like two used condoms, against the thin ribcage.

I'd rather expected the refined one to go in for watercolours and china model crinoline ladies. Instead her walls and surfaces were crammed with abstract collages and sculptures formed from an assortment of miscellaneous items.

The supervisor materialized by my side and I felt compelled to comment.

'Nifty. Is it art therapy or something?'

'Not at all. Lady Violet was a well-known artist before she . . .'

'Flipped?'

'I suppose so,' she sighed, abandoning politically correct medi-speak for a brief moment.

I walked over to a structure consisting mainly of old chicken wire, ring pulls, jewellery chains and picture hooks. It was extraordinary, but as I stood staring at its bizarre eccentricity, my heart gave a little flip of excitement.

I tried thrusting my arm into the wire, but the jacket sleeve caught fast. In the end I was forced to discard it and wriggle a bare arm amongst the sharp-ended metal.

By the time I'd extracted my quarry from the clutching wire, I had an armful of grazes.

The supervisor didn't share my triumph. Looking blankly at the twisted lump of metal, she asked: 'What is it?'

'Something she took from Mrs Woolley's room,' I panted, rubbing a wet thumb over the smudged silver model of a car lock.

'Oh Lord, not again.'

'Bit sticky-fingered, is she?'

'It's called kleptomania when you've got a title.'

Stowing the car lock in my pocket, I advised her not to worry about it. 'Simla was going to give this to me anyway. I wouldn't mention it unless she does.'

'If you say so.' Raising her voice, she wished the refined one good night.

There was no response, so we both left. As the door was

shutting, a well-modulated voice announced in crystal-clear tones: 'It wasn't kleptomania, it was nymphomania. But there are no bones worth jumping in this dump.'

I couldn't decide where to go after I left St Theresa's. By rights, since I'd finished my errand, I should have returned the BMW to its real owner. But I didn't want to trade in the fairy carriage just yet.

So I compromised by going via the office in the hope that there would be somebody working late. There wasn't, but Mr Mouldar had delivered his inevitable daily update on Supermarket Sal. Thankfully there was also a fax from the solicitor who'd commissioned the surveillance in the first place, calling off the pursuit. Sal's presence was no longer required: his client had decided to plead guilty.

Apart from that, the only person trying to get in touch was George Spinnaker, who'd telephoned several times in response to the message I'd left on his answerphone when I'd been trying to locate Olly Colville's address.

Dialling his number, I left yet another message on the tape, telling him not to worry. 'It's all sorted, thanks, George. Hope you and Jo had a really disgusting time in Amsterdam. I'll come round and see the home videos some time. Cheers.'

I wondered whether Colville's death had been reported on the European news. Probably not.

Thinking about Colville now, an anomaly in the sequence of events in this case suddenly struck me. Tina had been killed within hours of Kersey's tea-party. Assuming I was right and Barken had been after the 'little present', then why had it taken him another week to get around to Colville and Simla Woolley?

I'm good on questions; answers take a little longer.

Letting myself out, I glided back up the promenade. The lights strung between the promenade lamps were still glittering brightly, tracing the outline of the curving front, but most of the neon lights above the arcades had been switched off and the familiar rumbles and squeals from the funfair were stilled. Local nightlife, such as it was, had limped to a close. The only people about were a group of yobs, daring each other to walk along the top of the promenade balustrade. As I drove past, one yelled something obscene and flung an empty lager can at the car.

I drove round to Pepi's, but Shane had locked up for the night.

Annie's flat was in darkness.

Isn't life a bummer? Just when you've got something to swank about, there's no one out there to swank it to. I headed for TED.

Kevin's BMW got me VIP treatment from the bouncers and car park staff. This party at least was still jumping as I strolled in through the internal doors and found myself in the canyons of New York.

Around me lighted skyscrapers stretched up to the roof whilst the sound system relayed techno music overlaid with screaming police car sirens, taxi drivers yelling at each other in Bronx accents and random bursts of gunfire. To complete the effect, grilles in the floor were pumping out smoke, the waiters were spinning round the dance floor on roller skates and a hot-dog stand was frying tonight.

My nose locked on to the sizzling onions and shot off like an Exocet. To avoid mutilation, I followed it.

The fryer shouted to beat the noise level: 'Hi, what can I do you for? I mean, evening, sister, what can I hit you with?'

'What's on the menu?'

'Dogs or dogs really.'

'One dog, then.'

'Mayo? Mustard? Ketchup? Onions?'

'The works.'

With the dog dripping sauce down my chin, I sauntered up to the mezzanine bar, which was littered with the debris of bar snacks and flaked-out dancers. Cindy was half hidden behind a tiered cake in the shape of the Empire State Building, iced with the legend: 'Bianca and Chris – Have a Nice Day.'

'Is Kevin in?'

'Yep.'

Jangling the car keys at the mirror wall behind her brought a buzz on the internal phone. Cindy answered it and told me to go through.

Snapping down the rest of the dog in three fast bites, I walked into the blissful silence of the rear office.

'Interesting party,' I remarked.

'It's a wedding reception,' Kevin explained, rising from the desk and moving to the couch.

It seemed only polite to join him on it.

'That's the happy couple.'

They were slumped at a table: Chris was fetching in a black satin dress, feather boa and frilly garters; Bianca looked a picture in a bloke's suit jacket, black fedora and false moustache.

I tutted. 'It'll never last.'

'You think not?'

'Definitely. He's got better legs than her.'

The flip remark echoed his compliment as we'd left my flat. Unconsciously (honestly) I'd crossed my legs as I sat down and was displaying quite an acreage of black tights beneath the slit skirt.

I went to uncross the knees, decided that looked gauche, recrossed them again, and found Kevin's arm had slid round my waist during all the leg-work.

Tightening his grip slightly, he pulled me against his chest.

'You smell of mustard. And you taste of . . .'

He did a quick test on my lips and pronounced his verdict. 'Hot dogs.'

'Terrific,' I muttered, disentangling myself. 'My love is like a hot, hot sausage. Not exactly Rabbie Burns, is it?'

'I don't fancy Rabbie Burns.'

He'd slid the jacket off my shoulders and was nuzzling at the soft hollow in the base of my throat. This was definitely the moment to remind him he was married and I didn't fool around with other women's husbands.

With a soft click the venetian blinds along the dividing wall slid open.

I'd given a squeak of alarm and tried to retrieve my skirt, which had come undone, before I remembered that the mirror was one-way. Drawing out my left leg to its full stretch, Kevin ran his fingers lightly over the ankle, up the calf, massaged the back of the knee lightly, then headed along the inside of my thigh.

'I was right about the legs; right up to your armpits.'

Given where his hand was resting at that moment, he seemed to have a weird notion about the location of my armpits.

In the darkened bar, Cindy and a couple of drunk New York coppers were staring directly at us. It was a terrific turn-on: public sex with none of the embarrassment.

Grasping my waist, Kevin lifted me on to his lap.

'I should go,' I moaned, wrapping my legs round his waist, and dragging impatiently at his shirt buttons.

'Why?'

He'd dragged one side of the lycra body down and my left breast popped out. One of the NY cops seemed to be leering at it. Somehow I couldn't resist leaning back and flashing it in his direction, even though I knew very well he couldn't see it.

The movement fired the other breast out. With a heavy groan, Kevin buried his head between them.

CHAPTER 27

No, we didn't.

Kevin's wife rang. He was still discussing the kids' school trip with her when I slipped out and cadged a lift home on the back of Zizi's motorbike.

CHAPTER 28

I rang December's number first (ish) thing. Fred answered.

'I've mucked out and fed and watered t'beasts,' he explained. 'But I've to get away now, see to my own place. December said t'call security company, get them t'send guard up here.'

'Don't do that. I'll donkey-sit if you like.'

'It's not what I'd like. It's what December would like.'

I called the animal hospital to ask him. 'I could take them on the beach. Do the rides for you.'

'No.'

I was narked. How difficult could it be to run a donkey string?

'You're not used to handling them, lass, and they're not used to you. I don't want any accidents.'

'Please yourself,' I snapped. I was still wound up after last night's aborted seduction scene and was in no mood to be frustrated by yet another of the Drysdale clan.

'I intend to. Who's put you in a bad mood?'

I wondered how he'd react to: 'Your son. We were trying to have it away on the couch when the mother of your grandchildren rang.'

'No one,' I said. 'I was just trying to help. How's Lana doing?'

'Well enough. Vet thinks we'll be home by this afternoon.'

'Good.' I told him I'd got one of Kersey's car lock models, without mentioning Simla's involvement. 'It doesn't look anything special,' I said, critically examining the twisted fragment of metal. 'I'm not sure whether it's going to be worth all this palaver.'

December chuckled. 'You would if you had it stuck where Lana has, lass.'

'I guess so,' I admitted. 'You sure you don't want me to mind the donkeys for you?'

'You can take them out, give 'em a bit of exercise. But not on the beach. Take 'em along a bridle path for a couple of hours. And you'll need a helper with you, case one of them takes it into his head to have a funny turn.'

A potential helper walked in as I replaced the receiver. All this trouble with Jonathon had put Annie off her stroke. She'd forgotten to put the block on the phone.

'Comfortable?' she enquired, as I swung my feet off her desk and dunked the last of the chocolate digestive in the coffee mug.

'Yes, thanks. D'you fancy a double date with me and a string of donkeys this morning?'

'I'm not that desperate.'

'They're charming donkeys.'

'It's not the donkeys I object to.'

'Ingrate. That's the last dinner party and grave-opening I take you to.'

'My stomach thanks you; my liver thanks you; my kidneys thank you; my head thanks you . . .'

With a demonstration of the regulation police arm-lock, Annie levered me from her chair and deposited me on the landing.

Making my way round to December's, I checked in with Fred, who was itching to be gone, and said good morning to the lads. When they all lined up to accept half a Miller from me and have their ears scratched, I felt absurdly gratified.

'We'll go for a walk in a minute,' I informed them. (Was I going seriously nuts or what?) 'I've just got to go get your Auntie Bella.' (That settled it, I *was* nuts.)

Bella cavilled at leaving Judy. 'She ain't been too chirpy since our girls' night in.'

'Who has?'

'Oh, get out of here,' Judy ordered. 'I'm sick of you looming over me like some flaming vulture waiting for me to drop dead in me tracks any minute. Go on, hop it. And take that long streak of uselessness with you.'

The long streak was stretched out in the living room watching cartoon characters saving the earth from Technicolor androids to the accompaniment of ear-shattering special effects.

'I don't want go walk no donkeys. It's bad for my street cred,' Warren yawned.

'Luckily we're going on a bridle path. Anybody know where there is one?'

Bridle paths unfortunately are rather like public phones. You just don't notice them until you want one.

In the end Judy fished out an old street map. 'Got it when me and Des was looking for this place. Bridle paths is long dashes.'

In the end we found the beginning of one leading out from the back of the roads near Vetch's offices.

Grousing under his breath, Warren was turfed off the sofa and ordered to follow us.

'Give ows a break, Bella. Sub ows a couple of quid. I'll meet me mates down the arcade.'

'No chance. Shift it.'

He drew the line at taking a leading rein along the promenade, but once the string had been dissuaded from heading down on to the sands, he reluctantly brought up the rear with Snowy.

Bella and I walked shoulder to shoulder leading Errol and Humphrey.

The road seemed oddly quiet; we particularly had the stretch between the clock tower and the funfair to ourselves. Occasionally a car would blast past and hurl itself on to the roundabout ahead, but most of the traffic was confined to the seaward side of the carriageway.

The mystery was solved by a couple handing out flyers outside the cinema. 'Weald Warriors – Say No to Road', I read as the salt-tanged breeze tried to rip the yellow sheet from my hand. 'Do you think they mean "Woad"?'

'It's the motorway extension protest,' Bella said, sweeping a handful of dancing plaits out of her eyes. 'It was on the local news this morning. Didn't you hear?'

'Telly's bust.'

I recollected that the extension had been given the go-ahead last week after five years of ding-donging between planning committees, enquiry tribunals and court actions.

'Here they come now,' Bella shouted, swinging round so that the wind whipped the plaits in the opposite direction.

At the far end of the road the beginnings of a procession was emerging from the shopping area. Flanked by yellow-jacketed police it was bearing down on us to the beat of a primitive (and unintelligible) chant and the forlorn blasts of the motorists stuck behind it.

'Wicked,' Warren said, running a glistening pink tongue over the surface of a translucent lollipop the size of a dinner plate iced with a snooker table and the message: 'Hands Off My Balls'. 'Let's join 'em. Maybe there'll be a punch-up. What yow think?'

'I think you didn't have no money, and we should get out of here before the bloke who owns them buckets of lollipops clocks the one you just nicked.'

'Yows is a right nag, Bella.'

Nonetheless, Warren shot off at a fair pace, and was only stopped when Errol head-butted Snowy back into his rightful place in the string.

'How's Judy holding up?' I asked as soon as we'd cleared the town and were ambling over roughly grassed fields.

'She ain't too cut up about Tina, if that's what you're getting at. I mean, she never knew Tina, not really. She talks about her old man a lot. She wants him back. Well, truth is, she wants her whole life back. It's like she's hoping someone's going to rewind the tape and replay the last fifteen years.'

'Don't we all? Hasn't she got any plans?'

'Not really. I thought maybe if I took that aromatherapy course, her and me could set up something together.'

'Wouldn't that cost?'

Bella paused whilst Humphrey ripped up a few mouthfuls of hillock grass. 'I got money. I weren't never like Tina, spending soon as I got. And I want out of this business, before I end up like Tina.'

'How about Amos?'

'How about him? He looked out for me, and I paid him. Anyhow, that's all finished. Amos and me is history.'

I looked behind to where the rest of the string were investigating their own snack-tufts. Warren had squatted on his bottom and was moodily lobbing pebbles at a couple of crows who had been fighting over the rotting carcass of a dead rabbit.

'Shouldn't he be at school?'

'Reckons he's sixteen. I can't worry about everyone. What you doing about nailing the bastard who killed Tina? You ain't given up on me, have you?'

Dragging Errol from a patch of nettles, I gave her a brief run-down of progress to date. I included my employment by Simla but left out her involvement in her husband's death.

'That's just between you and me, OK?'

'OK. But if you're working for the widow, where's that leave Judy? She could use some cash from that statue. And it's her clue they're flushing out the donkey.'

'Let's find it first. Then I'll make sure that Simla gives Judy a cut of the proceeds, OK?'

'Glad to hear it, girl. God, I could sure use a drink. And a lav. Let's find a pub.'

We arrived at a road that looked familiar, although for the minute I couldn't think why. Flat green fields intersected with straight-banked drainage ditches stretched in all directions. There was no sign of habitation, let alone one sporting a brewer's trademark.

'Where's those good old country hostelries when you need one? The local peasants must have died of thirst around here.'

'Or bladder overload,' Bella complained, hopping on one leg. 'I'm gonna have to use a ditch in a second.'

Warren was balancing on the top of a five-bar gate. 'There's caravans in that field. Maybe they'll let yow have a leak.'

I suddenly knew why this place seemed familiar. 'Relief is at hand. I've a friend lives over there. He's always inviting me to drop in for drinks.'

Mind you, I don't think Mr Mouldar had expected me to bring seven donkeys, a large female who practically knocked him flat as she charged for the loo cubicle and a gangling kid who turned on the portable telly without so much as a 'd'yow mind?'

On the whole he took the invasion very well.

'I'm so pleased to see you, miss,' he beamed, sorting amongst the crockery to make up four matching sets of cups and saucers. 'I have news and I wanted you to be the first to know. Coffee? Sugar?'

'Rather have a beer, thanks, sweet thing.' Warren howled at his own joke, and then howled even louder as Bella whacked him across the back of the head. 'What did yow do that for?'

'Mind your manners or get out. Three sugars, thanks.' She squeezed herself on to the bunk bed next to me.

Over refreshments, Mouldar broke his good news: he'd been accepted by the security company. 'Start Monday, miss. Isn't that wonderful?'

'Wonderful,' I echoed. Mr Mouldar seemed so chuffed by his good luck that I hadn't the heart to appear anything but thrilled for him.

'I have my uniform already.' He proudly displayed the mustard jacket and trousers hanging behind the door. 'And a cap, see?'

The red-flashed peaked cap was too large and balanced on his ears. Somehow it made the brown mottled age spots and scrawny neck seem all the more prominent. The first yob who tackled him would probably put him back in hospital for a couple of weeks.

'I had hoped for the donkeys. But I've got the all-night car park. Oh, dear me, I haven't offered biscuits, how very remiss of me.'

Fussing back to the overhead cupboard, he extracted a packed of Rich Teas, carefully overlapped them in a circular pattern on a plate and passed them around.

'Thanks.' Unconsciously I'd been using Simla's mangled model as a worry bead, twisting and threading it through my fingers. Setting it down, I helped myself to a handful of biscuits.

'This what the donkey's got stuck up his bum?' Bella asked, examining the silver bar.

'That's it.'

'Dear me.' Mouldar blinked. 'The unfortunate beast. However did that happen?'

'It's a long story. The vet's sorting it out now.' I dropped the model back in my pocket and raised my cup. 'Here's to your new career. Best of luck. Cheers.'

'I'm afraid, miss, it does mean that I won't be able to keep up my surveillance for you.'

'Surveillance?' I'd temporarily forgotten Supermarket Sal. 'Oh, that. It's off. Er, I mean, mission complete. Thanks for all your help.'

'No trouble at all. In fact, I quite enjoyed it. Should you ever require further help . . .'

'You'll be top of my list.'

The mottled cheeks flushed with pleasure. I was almost

tempted to slip him a tenner for his trouble, but luckily an angry shout from outside, followed by frantic barking, distracted me.

In fact, it distracted all four of us eventually, since the lads, having been left to their own devices in the field, had managed to kick over a couple of gas canisters, rip open a black plastic rubbish sack and were currently demolishing a makeshift washing line.

I hauled a pair of Union Jack knickers from Errol's vice-like bite, and we rounded the beasts up again.

'I'd best get them back before December gets home,' I panted, geeing the string out of the caravan site. ''Bye for now.'

'Goodbye, miss. I'm so glad you finally decided to call.'

The donkeys were enjoying their unexpected outing and saw no reason at all why they should return to a boring and entertainment-free stable. The nearer we got to home, the more recalcitrant they became.

'I feel like I've just done a full work-out,' Bella groaned, dragging a loudly braying Humphrey across the cobbles.

'Girrup, yow stupid shit-bag.' Warren slapped Snowy's rump.

With an indignant squeal, Snowy lashed out. His iron-shod hoof met Warren's denim-clad kneecap with a whack. The hoof came off best.

'Yow, yow, yow . . .' Warren hopped in agony.

'Serves you right, you little yob. You strike one of my beasts again and I'll give you a lathering you'll never forget, understand?'

'Yow can't do that, Grandad. That's assault. Anyhow, yow's welcome to them. I'm going home.'

With a wary eye on Lana, who was standing placidly behind December, Warren limped out.

'Sorry,' I found myself apologizing. 'He's been really good up until now. I didn't hear the horsebox pull up.'

'Vet brought us back. She's got a trailer.'

'Mission accomplished?'

He drew a plastic bag from his pocket. 'Mission accomplished.'

'Great. Nice going, Lana.'

Lana looked at me with deepest self-pity. Given what had just been done to him, I guess he had good cause.

'I'll settle 'em in the stable and then we'll talk.'

'Fair enough. This is Bella, by the way, Tina's friend.'

Scrubbing a hand on the back of his trousers, December offered it. 'Pleased to meet you, lass. You'll be the one seeing Tina gets a Christian send-off, will you?'

'Soon as the police release the body. I'm sure pleased to meet you too. Tina, she was always talking about them donkeys.'

December's face split in a welcoming beam. We were invited to make ourselves comfortable inside while he saw to the lads.

Bella and I hit the kitchen.

'Exercise sure makes you hungry, don't it?' Flinging the window open, she whistled shrilly and waved the frying pan. 'You eaten?'

December stuck his head out of the feed and tack store. 'Can't say I have, lass.'

'Great.'

Diving into the fridge, Bella emerged with a carton of eggs, butter, milk and cheese. While she fixed omelettes, I helped December spread extra straw for Lana's bedding.

Once he was safely installed, the rest of the lads were ushered into the stable.

'Aren't you going to feed them?'

'Later. They're not working full-time at the moment, I don't want them getting fat.'

It wasn't a problem I'd ever had. Luckily. Bella made terrific cheese omelettes.

'Now,' I sighed, wiping up the last vestige of melted cheese with a sliver of solidified egg, 'how about giving us a look at the famous gut-blocker?'

I don't know why I was disappointed. I already knew Kersey had commissioned four identical models, so to expect anything different was asking for miracles.

And the miracle fairy was fresh out today.

Lana's digestive system had done it less grief than the refined one's abstract sculpturing, but it was still an unremarkable model of an old-fashioned car lock: three inches long; hooked at either end to fit over the clutch pedal and steering wheel; a round lock in the centre of the bar.

'There's writing,' Bella said, leaning so far down on the table that her fat breasts were squeezed out sideways like whoopee cushions.

'Where?' I brought it up to eye-level and we all stared at the tiny letters.

'P' I made out. 'A'. 'T.'

'Pat?' Bella spelt out doubtfully. 'That it?'

'No, there's more.' Tilting it to the window light, I made out: 'N.' 'O.'

'It's the patent number,' December interjected.

'Sod it. Sorry. No, I'm not. I keep telling you, you've no right to tell me how to talk.'

'I haven't told you.'

'You've got very expressive eyebrows.'

Bella was twisting the mangled lock from the sculpture a few inches from her nose. 'This is the patent number too: D22206-2063. That what you got?'

I checked. 'Yep.'

Well surprise, surprise. Had I really been hoping for 'X marks the spot'? Or maybe a neatly coded map reference that smarty-pants here would solve? You bet I had!

'Sod it, sod it, sod it!'

Scooping up both the useless lumps of metal, I ripped open the back door, flung them into the plastic wheelie bin and walked out.

OK, it was childish. And I knew it. But I was so full of pent-up frustration and – worse – the miserable conviction that I was a waste of space in the private investigators' world – well, the world in general really – that I just had to work it off or I'd explode.

Returning to the office, I changed into my jogging clothes and set off for the front.

I turned right, pounding along the promenade above the beach huts, trampolining pits and miniature playground. Sweeping round the harbour, I panted up the gradually increasing gradient until I'd left the shopping area behind and was speeding past neat bungalows separated from the cliffs by a stretch of windy scrubland. A stitch like a knife was driving into my ribs and the air was burning in my lungs, but I didn't *care*. I was so mad at myself that I wanted to punish my body.

It still felt good, so I reversed my route and sprinted back.

The stitch finally did for me opposite Pepi's. Seeing it as an omen, I flopped inside and ordered coffee.

'I've got no money,' I gasped through burning lungs. 'I'll have to owe you.'

'Oh, let's twist again,' Shane hummed merrily, slapping a cup in front of me and sending a wave of liquid into the saucer.

'You sorted out December's donkey yet?'

'No.'

'Pity, that. He's a decent bloke, December.'

'Yes.'

Thanks for reminding me, I thought bitterly, sipping the coffee. I really needed that.

I knew I was going to have to apologize for my abrupt departure this afternoon. It wasn't December's fault I was such a useless human being.

I hung it out through three more cups of coffee and a belly-shaking version of 'La Bamba', which reduced a party of Japanese tourists to hysterics, but finally I wished Shane good evening and plodded reluctantly round to December's.

The front door was opened by Mr Mouldar.

He beamed. 'Hello, miss. Guess what, they changed the rota at the last minute. I got donkeys after all. Isn't that wonderful? Somehow I just feel my luck is changing at last.'

'I'm ecstatic for you. December around?'

'He's out back in the stables, miss. Go straight through.'

Unfortunately by now the four cups of coffee had done just that. For the second time that day, Mr Mouldar was shouldered aside by a desperate female. 'Tell him I'll be out in a tick,' I yelled over the banisters.

Scrambling upstairs, I shot thankfully into the bathroom and slid the bolt across.

It wasn't until I was hauling my jogging pants up that the squeals and braying from the back yard penetrated. Something had spooked the lads.

Running back downstairs, I shouted: 'Mr Mouldar? December?'

The kitchen was empty. Ditto the back yard.

I checked the rest of the downstairs rooms. They were all deserted.

One of the donkeys gave another squeal and the stable door reverberated to a persistent kicking.

I'm not particularly brave. Going for help has always seemed like a good plan to me. So I went for it.

Two steps out of the kitchen door, everything went black.

CHAPTER 29

I came round to discover that someone was attempting to drill holes in the back of my skull. A bout of violent sneezing triggered by dust tickling my nasal passages made the drill bit slip. Red-hot needles of pain jabbed at the back of my eyes.

I opened them to see if that made any improvement. It didn't. In fact, now that I could see I was lying in a bed of straw, I became aware that the sharp ends were sticking down my neck.

An anxious face with long ears and soulful eyes peered down at me.

'How are you feeling, miss?'

'Bloody lousy. Help me up.'

Attempting to lever myself into a sitting position, I discovered that my legs were reacting strangely. Peering down the length of my jogging suit, I could make out the leather reins bound around my trainers. The thick padding of the shoes was taking most of the strain and letting my circulation continue as normal.

My wrists weren't so lucky. My fingers were already going numb as the straps bit into the flesh.

Mr Mouldar pulled me up and leant me against the back wall under the manger rack. Everything swum round and I had to swallow the flow of nausea that surged into my throat.

Squeezing my eyes shut, I waited for the tide inside my head to ebb again. When the roaring stopped, I opened them cautiously.

The doors were all closed, but my eyes had become more

accustomed to the darkness. Amongst the shifting forest of furry legs, I could make out another figure slumped against the end wall.

'Get me untied. There's knives in the kitchen.'

'I have one of my own, thank you, miss.'

A shaft of bright light flooding from Mr Mouldar's torch illuminated the metal blade in his hand.

'Great.' I wriggled my legs into a bent position, presenting the leather thongs for cutting.

'I think it might be best if you stayed where you are for now, miss.'

'What! Don't be flaming daft.'

'Don't call me that. I really don't like to hear such language from a young lady. Something I believe I have in common with Mr Drysdale.'

The beam of light swung left. Uneasily the lads snickered and jostled each other away from the probing beam. In the cleared space, I saw December properly for the first time.

He was bound and trussed up like me, but had the added handicap of a handkerchief thrust in his mouth. Beneath the wiry eyebrows his eyes gleamed with frustrated rage. If December had any influence in that direction, I reckoned we were about due for a well-aimed thunderbolt any second now.

OK, I'd been slow on the uptake. I plead the thump on the head.

'It was you who hit me.'

'My apologies, miss. But I couldn't have you making a fuss in the yard. You never know who might be listening.'

Gritting my teeth, I wriggled myself into a straighter sitting position and pressed my wrists hard into the rough brickwork. In the best gumshoe novels they always manage to saw through their bonds by rubbing against a jagged edge. You try it some time. After the top layer of skin was sanded off my wrist bones, I gave up on the idea.

I decided we might as well put our cards on the table. Or stable floor in this case.

'You're Barken.'

'I don't think there's any need for that kind of language. I'm as sane as you.'

'I meant, it's your name. Billy Barken.' Then the penny dropped. It was a nickname. It wasn't 'Barken', it was 'Barking', as in 'barking mad'.

Somehow this revelation didn't fill me with confidence. Neither did the way he was running a thumb lightly over the blade of the flick-knife he was caressing.

To distract him I said: 'Are you really employed by the security company?'

'Oh yes, miss. I've never been a state scrounger. I've always . . .'

'Helped yourself?'

He missed the sarcasm, and agreed that that was indeed his motto in life.

'What about references?'

'I have several. From companies that are unfortunately out of business now. And several social security numbers, dependent on which name I happen to be using at the time. I must say, I share your concern in that matter. For a security company they do seem to have a very lax attitude to security checks.'

'Everyone's slapdash these days.'

'Yes, I'm afraid you're right there, miss.'

The donkeys had all congregated at the far end of the stable. Perhaps December's presence down there reassured them. They were still snorting uneasily, jostling each other in a cowardly attempt to keep away from a vaguely perceived danger.

Mouldar (I couldn't think of him as 'Billy') clicked soft fingers at Errol. 'Come up here then, boy. Look what I've got for you.'

He delved into his jacket pocket and offered a fragment of biscuit.

Errol snorted his derision, shaking his heavy head.

It was probably a smart choice on Errol's part, but it annoyed Mouldar. A hiss of frustration leaked from the side of his gritted teeth.

Keeping him talking until someone turned up was probably the best plan. Well, let's face it, given my situation, it was the only plan.

'All those surveillance reports you did for me. Very detailed. Almost professional. Were they on the level?'

'How do you mean, miss?'

'I mean, you didn't invent them?'

'Certainly not. That would have been most unethical. Indeed, when I visited High Wycombe, I was most particular to rise early and return at a reasonable time in order to ascertain the target's starting and resting place that day. If I agree to do a job, I hope I do it thoroughly.'

'And it let you keep in touch with me.'

I was glad I hadn't given in to my softer impulses and left him that tenner this afternoon. He'd only been using the job as cover to keep an eye on me. Something which he didn't bother to deny.

'Precisely. I felt sure you'd be a great source of information. At first, of course, I just assumed you were a friend of Judy's. But when you mentioned knowing someone who was guarding donkeys, well, I just knew that fate had brought us together for a purpose.'

How lucky fate wasn't running a dating agency, I thought bitterly. It would probably pair up Mother Theresa with Freddie Kruger.

Mouldar crouched down, bouncing on his heels in front of me. The quarter-light made it difficult to see his expression clearly, but his voice continued in the same mild tone. He could almost have been discussing the weather as he invited me to hand over Simla's car lock model, plus the one that had been recovered from Lana's digestive system.

'I assume I chose the wrong beast the other week. Another example of fate intervening on my behalf.'

'How'd you work that one out?'

'A case of one bit of bad luck cancelling the other out, miss. My sudden illness prevented me from following the first corpse and finding out the location of its grave.'

'Urn.'

'Pardon, miss?'

'Marilyn ended up in an urn. They cremated him.'

'Then I have been doubly fortunate. Triply, in fact. I had intended to call on you after I'd recovered the lock which I assume is now in Mr Drysdale's possession. But your call means I can kill two birds with one stone, so to speak.'

And not just 'so to speak', I decided. He was hardly going to let either of us go after that confession.

'I know you don't have Mrs Woolley's lock on you, miss. I searched you whilst you were unconscious. So if you'd be kind enough to tell me where you've put it?'

The idea of those brown mottled hands poking and prying over my body made me want to heave again. I tried to keep the revulsion out of my face. 'I don't have it any more.'

'I don't wish to use force.'

Well, that was something we had in common. 'Did you want to use it on Tina?'

'Certainly not. I am not a violent man, but sometimes other people drive me to it. Had the young lady handed over Mr Kersey's package in the kitchen, none of the resultant unpleasantness need have happened.'

'Even though she could identify you to the police?'

'Given that the statue we both wished to recover was stolen property, it would have been foolish of her to report the loss of Kersey's directions to the police, wouldn't it? If only she'd simply let me take the bag it could have been all over in a second.'

But life on the streets had at least sharpened Tina's reactions. She'd lashed out with the bag, broken free and fled down the garden and into Drysdale's stables.

'You must have been choked when you realized you'd lost her. How'd you get her back?'

'Do you know, miss, that was the most extraordinary stroke of luck. It's what I mean about fate being on my side. I'd actually given up searching for her and decided to drive to High Wycombe and tackle Olly first, when what do you think?'

'Surprise me.'

'There she was by the roadside, miss. With her thumb stuck out. Such a dangerous practice these days. You never know who will stop.'

There wasn't a trace of irony in his voice. It was as if he was describing a separate man, some other persona who sliced people up.

Poor Tina. Too scared to go back to the house and retrieve her money and return train ticket, she'd thumbed a lift with the one person on earth who had most cause to do her harm.

'Didn't she recognize your van?'

'Not at all. I don't believe she'd ever been in the car park at the hospice. Not until she bent to get in the passenger door. Then I'm afraid she tried to run away. Fortunately the road was deserted at that moment.'

So he'd run Tina down and dragged her into the back of the van.

I knew, with absolute certainty, that if I hadn't had Bella, Warren and a herd of donkeys with me this afternoon, I'd have died in that caravan.

The knife had appeared in his hands again. Straightening up, he walked to the far end of the stables and placed an arm over Errol's neck, caressing the mane. Without warning, he drew the blade down the brown coat. With a squeal Errol swung

306

away from his tormentor, crashing into the other lads. They jostled back, catching Errol's panic. Over the tapping hooves and frightened whinnies, I heard December's low moan as a sharp metal shoe stamped on his leg.

'Now I'm sure one of you will tell me where you've put the final two models.'

Keep talking, my mind urged. Someone may come.

'You've got Colville's model then?'

'Ah yes, Olly. He'd been trying to go straight, you know.'

'And he didn't want to hand his model over?'

'Oh no, miss. He didn't mind that at all. In fact, he was more than pleased for me to find the statue. Well, he'd never have worked it out himself. Never one of life's candidates for Mensa, was Olly.'

'Then why the hell kill him?'

Why can't I learn to put the brain in gear before engaging the mouth? A spasm of anger twisted the thin mouth. 'Language, miss.'

'Sorry. But it did seem a bit unnecessary. I mean, I thought Colville was your mate.'

'Not for some years.' With relief I saw the tense lines between nose and mouth relaxing. 'But I shouldn't have wished him harm. He forced me into it.'

I just stopped a facetious crack. Mouldar's life did seem strangely full of people pulling the wrong bells.

'You see, miss, having given the matter some serious consideration, it seemed to me that since I was required to undertake the major share of the work, I should have the major share of the spoils. I mean, I do think that is an entirely reasonable assumption, don't you?'

'Oh, absolutely.'

'I'm so glad you agree, miss. Regrettably Olly insisted on fifty per cent rather than the twenty I proposed to give him. A labourer is worthy of his hire, Olly, I said to him. And I have laboured a great deal more diligently than you have.'

'And what did he say?'

'I won't soil your ears with his precise words. But I'm afraid he even went so far as to threaten to destroy the model if I didn't agree to an equal division.'

'Ridiculous,' I croaked. 'After all, twenty per cent of something is better than one hundred per cent of nothing.'

'My precise words, miss. Unfortunately Olly would not see sense. You'll get it over my dead body, Billy, he said.'

So Mouldar had killed him and set fire to the flat.

His face remained serenely relaxed as he admitted the murder. He was, I realized, truly amoral. He believed he had a perfect right to eliminate those who frustrated him.

Other pictures swam into my mind. Janice, stumbling off the crossing the day after she'd made fun of Mouldar; the dog at the caravan park that had supposedly died from poison bait the weekend it had bitten him.

I felt sick. And this time it had nothing to do with the whack on the skull. A quick flick of Mouldar's knife and I'd be choking out my last moments of life.

'Now if you could tell me where you've put the lock models, miss, I'll be off to retrieve the statue. My buyer *is* becoming rather impatient.'

'You've already got a buyer lined up?'

He preened. I sounded impressed and he liked that. 'Yes indeed. You see, that's where I feel I went wrong last time. Relying on Kersey to sell the statue was a mistake. This time I have planned more carefully. Indeed, I started to make my preparations as soon as Alan Kersey became eligible for parole. The particular collector I have found is very keen to acquire such a piece. And extremely discreet.'

'Nifty. But you'll never get away with it.'

'Oh, I think I will. As I say, this time I've given it most careful preparation.'

'Don't be daf— Er, I mean, the police are bound to start looking for Mr Drysdale's missing security guard as soon as

308

they discover the . . .' somehow I didn't fancy 'bodies', '. . . the, er, mess.'

'I fear I lied about that detail. My colleague will no doubt be reporting for duty as usual in . . .' he flicked the torchlight on to his watch, '. . . two hours. But by that time I expect to be long gone. I shall return over the fields, the way I came. I doubt if anyone will notice me. People don't, you see.'

I could believe that. He had the sort of looks that you could lose in a crowd of three.

'As soon as I'm finished here, I shall retrieve the statue, pack up and be off. I'm sure you're right about the police. No doubt they'll work it out and start issuing descriptions eventually.'

But we both knew the police would have to be damn lucky to catch him once he'd slipped the net. His description would fit a thousand grey, sad little men in any town in Britain. Once he was safely away with his money and one of his other social security numbers, it was unlikely he'd be caught unless he did something in the future that warranted the taking of his fingerprints.

'Do you know,' I said, trying to control my voice, which was showing signs of rising a couple of octaves, 'I wondered why there was a week between that business with Tina and the visits to Colville and Simla Woolley. Now it all makes sense. You were laid up in hospital.'

I sent a mental apology to Judy Parker. She'd actually told me she'd seen Barken in the hospital and I – and she – had put it down to drug-induced nightmares.

'Yes indeed. Most inconvenient. I do hope the health authorities intend to prosecute that wretched kebab establishment. I could have died.'

'Pity you didn't, you godless devil.'

December had managed to spit his gag out. I couldn't see his face beyond the milling donkeys, but his tone indicated he wasn't about to make conciliatory chitchat with Marilyn's murderer.

I intervened quickly, remembering the vomit in the heavy machinery pit. 'It looked to me like you were taken ill up at the warehouse.'

'I was, miss. Most dreadfully ill. By the time those police officers arrived, I could scarcely stand upright.'

'Must have been tricky driving the getaway van.'

'Incredibly so. I had hoped to dispose of the young lady in the sea. Fortunately I'd already loaded her into the back of the van.'

'Very lucky, that. Delayed the connection between Tina's mur . . . death and Marilyn's.'

'Exactly, miss. Anyway, ten minutes along the road, I just knew I'd have to dump her before I blacked out. After that, I barely managed to steer into the pub's car park. The host was most kind. Called an ambulance and stored the van for me until I was able to pick it up.'

And if only someone at the pub had looked inside the back of the van and seen the bloodstains, Mouldar would probably have been arrested in his hospital bed and the past week would have turned out very differently for us all.

December and I wouldn't have been minutes from death, for a start.

'Now, if you could tell me where you put the model, I am in rather a hurry.'

Nobody was going to come. If they did, they'd go away again when they received no answer at the front door. The only person likely to try round the back was Kevin. And he'd be overseeing the preparations for opening TED at this time of the evening.

I tried one more stall. 'What good are four model locks? I mean, they won't tell you anything. It was just a joke on Kersey's part. A way of setting you all at each other's throats.'

'Oh, I don't think so. He said he'd give us a chance and I believe him. It was just a question of working the matter out.'

'And you have?'

'I am confident I have. Now, the model, miss . . .?'

'Don't tell the devil, Grace.'

Shouldering the donkeys aside, Mouldar retrieved the kerchief from the straw, shook it once and stuffed it back in December's mouth. It left me in darkness for a few seconds.

I considered wriggling across to the doors, kicking the lower half open and screaming my head off. Since they all bolted from the outside, the one Mouldar had dragged me through must still be unlocked. I'd hardly levered myself into a flat position before Mouldar was back.

This time he was holding Snowy's headstall. 'Now, miss, I shouldn't like to hurt this poor animal.'

Placing the lighted torch on the straw, he took the knife from his pocket again and slashed the donkey's soft muzzle. Snowy snorted and sidled his hindquarters away, his hooves scrambling on the hard floor. Blood spattered in the cleared spaces.

The blade arced up again at the same time as my feet.

My kick caught him in the crotch. The knife dropped with a clatter. Snowy broke free and trampled over the torch, demolishing it in a crunch of broken glass.

Attempting to roll for the door, I got a noseful of straw dust and donkey hairs, causing a paroxysm of sneezing.

It made it easy for Mouldar to locate my position. In fact, he was bending over me when he flicked the lighter on.

'You'll have to pay for that, miss. You really will.'

Twisting one hand in my hair, he dragged me round. My bottom swivelled in response to the tug. Tears sprang to my eyes as he started hauling me back to my original position. I tried to jam my heels against the floor, but it was useless. Anyway, what difference did it make where I was when he killed me?

I found myself hoping that death was what he had in mind. I didn't want to think about what had happened to Tina.

'Now, miss.' The knife handle was protruding from the straw pile. Mouldar drew it free, running the lighter flame almost caressingly over the steel. 'Now, miss,' he repeated, turning back to me.

Snowy had retreated to the comfort of the rest of the herd. Now, with a shrill whinny, he charged forward. The sound made Mouldar turn. His last sight was of Snowy, rearing up to his full height.

For a moment the stable was plunged into darkness again. Squeals, snorts and scrabbling hooves echoed all around me. I knew I had to move and was scared. What if I rolled straight under those sharp metal horseshoes? What if Mouldar had just been stunned? Perhaps he was there now, knife blade raised, waiting for me to move.

Outlines crept from the shadows. The edge of the manger; an amorphous shape lying prone on the floor; two restlessly shifting furry legs retreating into the blackness that already concealed its hindquarters.

Bending my knees, I levered myself forward, using my heels for purchase. Mouldar didn't move.

A bit closer and I could see the pool of darkness spreading around his skull like a halo, the deep redness twinkling with internal lights.

It was the light that jolted my brain into gear again. It was out of place. There was no light source in the stable. So how come I could see?

Twisting my neck sent a sharp pain down my spine, but I didn't have much time to worry about it. Mouldar's lighter had failed to close promptly when he'd dropped it. Before the metal cap had snapped down, the probing flame had caught on a few strands of straw.

It was spreading even as I watched, the liquid flames creeping along the dried grasses with a gleeful crackle.

Spinning over like a felled skittle, I got close enough to thump my feet up and down on the blaze. All I succeeded in doing was scattering a shower of burnt chaff in a wider circle.

My whole body might smother the flames, but the jogging

suit had picked up a second skin of straw during my perambulations across the floor. If that caught, I'd be in big trouble.

Frustrated, I struggled to sit up. The smoke was stinging my eyes and an unwary breath sent me into a fit of choking.

A thump in my shoulder nearly gave me a heart attack. I turned, expecting a vengeful Mouldar, but found December had managed to make his way up the stable.

I used my teeth to drag the handkerchief out of his mouth.

'Get out, lass. Get help.'

'Water trough,' I coughed. 'Turn over. Help me.'

'Do as you're told. Go. Door.'

The flames had found a damp patch of straw, which reduced the heat but increased the dense smoke. Down here at floor level, the air was still fairly clear, but I knew December was right. If we passed out from smoke inhalation, we'd both be dead by the time anyone spotted the flames and alerted the fire brigade.

Lying on my back again, I raised my legs and kicked hard at the lower door. It flew open, letting a delicious stream of cool air into the stable. It also served to feed more oxygen to the flames.

They were growing higher as I manoeuvred myself into the yard, wriggling like a side-winder.

I'd half hoped Mouldar had left the top door unbolted as well. If December could drive the donkeys in this direction, their weight would push the door open and let them escape into the yard.

In the evening gloom, I saw the drawn silver bar and could have cried. Inside the stable the donkeys' squeals of alarm were rising by the moment. One of them started kicking the far door, its hooves sending reverberations round the enclosed space.

'Come on,' I called to December. 'Come through.'

'I'm trying to get this trough over. Go over to the gate, lass. Shout your head off.'

I started across the cobbles, then stopped. December's house was at the end of the row. No one was likely to walk past here.

Reversing direction, I bowled myself into the gap between the stable and feed store and along the beaten track at the back. It was harder going on the mud, without the ridges of the cobbles to help me. When I reached the tunnel under the hedge, I used the back wall of the stable to thrust me the first few inches into the hole. Then I took December's advice. I yelled my head off.

I'd wriggled halfway along before an answering shout asked where the hell I was.

'Down here, under the hedge. Help me, for God's sake.'

'What yows doing in there?'

'I haven't time to explain, Warren. Listen . . .'

I gave him a brief résumé of the situation. I assume he dashed off. I was too whacked out to do anything but lie there watching a couple of beetles scuttling along twigs two inches from my nose and listening to the sounds of shouting, braying and sirens coming from beyond the hedge.

Eventually someone hauled me out by my feet and untied me.

CHAPTER 30

Two fire tenders and an ambulance were lighting up the street outside. An interested crowd had collected to watch the entertainment. December was sitting on the ambulance steps with a blanket round his shoulders and a stubborn expression on his face.

Apart from smoke-blackened skin and a dressing on one hand, he seemed all right.

'You OK?'

'Fair enough, lass. You?'

'OK. Oh, shit.'

I sat down quickly. 'What's the matter? He didn't cut you, did he?'

'No.' I gasped and thrust my fingers into my armpits. The blood was flowing back and it was sheer agony. 'What's happened to Mouldar?'

'They carted him off in an ambulance five minutes since.'

'Alive?'

'If he wasn't, they were making a powerful fuss over a corpse.'

The donkeys had been tethered to the fence at the end of the road by a variety of scarves and belts. They huddled in a defensive cluster, eyeing the crowds and bustle uneasily. Occasionally one dropped its head and let go a mournful bellow.

'Are they all right?'

'Should be, God willing. Vet's on his way.' Reaching over, he put an arm round my shoulder and hugged. 'Thanks for what you did, Grace. Kicking out like that.'

'I didn't do anything except annoy Mouldar and start the flaming fire. It's Snowy you ought to thank.'

'Who?'

'The white donkey. The one you reckoned was too feisty to carry the kids. I call him Snowy. What's his real name?'

December's strained face suddenly showed a gleam of the old amusement. 'Don't know what his mum called him, lass, but I named him after that American actor, Ladd, who was in *Shane*.' He nodded over to where Snowy was wearing a lint dressing like a noseband. 'That's Alan.'

The pain hit me just after that. I was leaning against December's shoulder, quietly crying and wondering whether passing out would be the easiest option, when Kevin's car drew up in a screech of tyre rubber.

'Dad! Are you OK?'

He ignored me. Which, given the embarrassment associated with our last parting, was something of a relief. There's nothing like a fire and an attempted murder to get the social mores in perspective.

'How did you get here?'

'One of the neighbours rang me. Why the hell didn't you?'

'Language,' December and I chorused.

'I couldn't exactly reach the phone, Kevin.'

'Don't give me that. Are you hurt? How did the fire start?'

The ambulance medic interrupted to ask if he was Mr Drysdale's son. 'Perhaps you could get him to see sense. We need to take him to hospital. You too, love,' he added, flinging a blanket round my shoulders.

'I'm not going until the lads are seen to,' December remonstrated with his son.

'Are you mad? I'll stop with the donkeys. You get in that ambulance.'

I left them arguing and crept quietly away before the ambulance crew could hijack me.

They'd run hoses through to the back and jets of water were playing over the stable and feed store. The fire appeared to be out, although the air was still full of the stink of acrid smoke and drifting fragments of burnt straw.

A fireman blocked my way. 'Can you go back outside please, miss, until the area's safe.'

'Sure. Sorry.'

As soon as he turned his back, I shot over to the rubbish bin and pulled it over. Bundles of soggy peelings, empty tins and old papers tipped on to the cobbles.

'Oi!'

I grabbed what I wanted and fled as the fireman advanced.

Kevin and his dad were still having a loud ding-dong when I got to the front gate. I toyed with the idea of asking to borrow the BMW again, but thought better of it as another flashing blue light turned the corner of the road.

'Grace.' Bella thrust her way through the pavement gapers. 'You OK?'

'Sure. Never felt better. Don't I look it?'

'You look like shit. Come back to the house, I'll fix you a drink. If you don't want to go up the hospital?'

'Not unless they're serving double vodkas too.'

Using Bella's bulk and the curious crowd as a shield, I hurried past the two officers who were just emerging from the parked police panda.

'Judy and me was down the bingo. Warren just come down to tell us, otherwise I'd have been round sooner. You was dead lucky the little shit had come back to see if he could nick any more money for the arcades.'

I had to grab her arm as another wave of nausea surged up. When I'd crawled into that tunnel, I'd blithely assumed all three of them would be home. If Warren hadn't . . .

'You sure you don't want the doc?'

'Dead sure. Get me inside, Bella.'

She was a terrific nurse. After a triple vodka on the rocks, I started to feel better. Drunk, but better.

Judy joined me. 'Muscle relaxant,' she said mulishly when Bella tried to object. 'Have a shot yourself.'

'My muscles is relaxed enough already.'

'Can I use your phone?'

'Help yourself.'

I dialled Annie's home number.

'Listen,' I said as soon as she answered. 'Don't ask questions, just pick me up at Judy Parker's right now. And don't mention it to anyone. Especially Zeb. He's not there now, is he?'

'No. Am I going to regret this?'

'Come round and find out.'

As we headed for the caravan park, I gave her a brief run-down of my evening so far.

'And what exactly are you planning to do out here?'

'Search Mouldar's caravan for the other two car locks. I figure we've got about half an hour before December makes a statement to the police and they find out who Mouldar is and start turning his place over.'

'*We?*'

'Stay in the car if you like. But I've got this far, and I'm going to find this damn statue if it kills me.'

'It appears to be killing everyone else instead.'

She turned the car into the lane I'd crossed with Bella and Warren – was it really only this morning?

The spring growth was becoming lusher with each passing day: I could hear the long grass swishing against the chassis as Annie bumped up on the verge by the gate.

'Can you park along a bit?'

'Out of sight, you mean?'

'That's the idea.'

'I know I'm going to regret this.'

Nonetheless, she left the car on the side round the next bend, and came back with me to Mouldar's caravan which, predictably enough, was locked.

'What now, Sherlock?'

Only a few of the caravans were showing lights. Including the owner of the poisoned dog, who was still addicted to the pirate radio station.

Creeping across the overgrown grass, I banged loudly on the tinny side and shouted: 'Oi, keep the noise down, will you?'

A square of yellow light flashed on to the field, as the curtain was whisked aside. After a second it disappeared again and the music shot up several decibels.

Rooting amongst the debris under the van, I found a flat piece of rusting metal and ran back to Annie.

Masked by the blaring acid house rock, it took us about ten seconds of levering the metal back and forth under the end window to break the lock and scramble in.

'We'll have to risk the lights. Start down that end and keep your ears open for police cars.'

'How am I supposed to hear with that row going on?' Annie grumbled, feeling along the made-up bunk.

Since Mouldar had had no reason to expect a search, we tried the more obvious places first, such as drawers, clothes pockets and the top of the wardrobe shelf. We drew a complete blank, and every moment was bringing DCI Jackson and his merry minions closer.

'Think,' I urged Annie. 'Where would you hide two lumps of metal?'

'Search me. Water tank?'

'Might be tricky if he needed to get out quick.'

'There's a car coming down the lane. I can see its headlights. In fact,' Annie stood on tiptoe, 'there's blues as well. Let's get out of here.'

We both dived back out of the end window. 'Hang on.'

'What now?' Annie hissed. 'Come *on*.'

On my knees I shuffled through the wet grass, running my hand under the base of the caravan. A foot in, behind the rear wheel, I encountered the taped package. I sacrificed two nails to rip it free and sprinted after Annie.

Police were pouring in the gate as we pushed our way through the hedge at the far end of the field.

'My stuff's ruined,' Annie complained, picking twigs off her jumper and trousers whilst she drove one-handed back to the main road.

'Mine too.'

'Yours was disgusting before we started breaking and entering and stealing evidence.'

'We haven't stolen it. We've just borrowed it.'

'Somehow I don't think DCI Jackson will appreciate the finer nuances of that argument. Where to now?'

'Home, James.'

It proved to be a bad choice. Luckily I spotted the blue and white parked outside as Annie turned into the road.

'Back out,' I hissed, diving down. 'Go for the office.'

'You don't think they might have worked that one out too?' Annie asked, calmly executing a U-turn.

'Any reason we can't use your place?'

'You are covered in straw. You stink of donkey dung. You are wanted by the police. Perm any two from three.'

We ended up at Pepi's. Even Shane stayed upwind of me.

'What's your pleasure, girls?'

Annie ordered: 'Double All-Day Breakfast, double chips, double coffee. I don't know what she's having.'

Will Carling would envy the way Annie could kick a diet into touch. I had the same.

Using Shane's cutlery, I sliced the package open, tipped out the final two car lock models and added the ones I'd rescued from Drysdale's wheelie bin.

'Do they say anything to you?'

Annie poked the four strips of metal. 'Basically that Alan

320

Kersey got the last laugh. Face it, it's all a con on his part. A way of getting his revenge on those he blamed for his prison sentence.'

'Eat your chips.'

I turned the models over, making them twinkle in the neon lighting. Mouldar had been certain he'd cracked the meaning behind them. And I couldn't bear the idea that that murderous, unctuous, morally challenged apology for a human being was smarter than me.

Informing me that I was sixteen, beautiful and his, Shane delivered the coffee and picked up a model. 'I got one of them.'

Between his meaty finger and thumb the silver bar looked like a toothpick.

'Got one on the wife's Beetle. Don't know why I bother, mind. You'd have to be colour-blind or out of your skull to steal it.'

'Can I have a look?'

'At the car?'

'At the lock.'

'Please yourself. It's parked out back. You can't miss it.'

That was an understatement. It was bright pink with lime-green squiggles and an interior upholstered in fake leopard skin.

Sprawling across the front seats and holding the door open with one foot to keep the interior light on, I held one of my models against the real thing.

They were identical apart from the patent number. It might not mean anything, of course. The number could simply have been selected at random by the engraver. And since the numbers were identical anyway, it was hard to see why Mouldar would have needed all four models.

I was wriggling into a sitting position again when I glimpsed an unwelcome sight in the rear mirror. Thankfully the passenger door had already closed far enough to extinguish the light. Diving flat, I watched the top of the WPC's helmet bob past the window.

The opening back door of the café released more light and the delicious scent of frying onions into the yard.

I caught the murmur of Shane's wife. 'Two coffees to go and two bacon rolls, same as usual. No charge. That all right, love?'

'I shouldn't. I'm really on a diet.'

Jonathon must have that effect on all his conquests, viz., putting them off their food. It was WPC Jane Mullins' voice.

'Go on, you look like you need cheering up, love.'

'I do a bit. I've just been to a fire up the donkey man's place. Those poor animals were terrified.'

'No? Any casualties?'

'Only one. But it's OK, it wasn't a donkey. Just a bloke.'

If she hadn't done the dirty on Annie, I could get to like Jane. Staying low, I waited until her car's engine had died away before relocking the Beetle and making my way back to Annie.

'The local boys in blue mump their supper here,' I informed her, sliding back into my seat.

'So do you. Did you find anything useful out there?'

'No. Except the patent number isn't right. Only I don't see that that helps, since they're all the same.'

'These two aren't.'

'What!' I snatched the bars unceremoniously out of her hand. Because the first two were identical, I'd only glanced at Mouldar's two and registered the first few numbers. 'D22206-2066.' The other one read: 'D22206-2063.'

'Same here,' Annie said, appropriating the other two.

It didn't feel like a significant breakthrough. Instead of four identical models, we now had two pairs.

'You OK?' Annie asked, peering into my face. 'You look a bit odd. Odder than usual, I mean.'

I wasn't, actually. The combination of triple vodka, double breakfast and single murder attempt had finally caught up with me. I made it to the loo with seconds to spare, and heaved up the contents of my stomach into the pan.

Annie found me snivelling on the floor, shivering from delayed shock.

'Hospital,' she said, hauling me up.

The red and white tiling was showing an alarming tendency to whirl round in a pink kaleidoscope. 'Hang on.'

Clutching the hand-basin, I scooped up a handful of cold water and splashed it over my face. With droplets dripping from my fringe, I sniffed away a tide of self-pity. A smell that nudged a memory tickled elusively at my nostrils.

'Have you caught that pong?'

'I was trying to be tactful and not mention it more than necessary.'

'Not *me*. The other thing.' Leaning closer to the plughole, I sniffed the white porcelain vigorously. 'That smell.'

Annie twitched a delicate nostril. 'It's the scouring powder.'

'I know. Mouldar used the same brand.'

'Hold the front page. Come on.'

I let myself be led away to the car. I didn't mind: Shane forgot to charge us for supper. And anyway, I now knew what Mouldar had worked out.

The hospital car park was half empty, but two ambulances were unloading their charges by the doors marked "Emergency Vehicles Only".

Annie had insisted on driving round here with all the car windows open. 'I don't want you throwing up in here,' she said uncharitably. 'You've given my upholstery enough grief for one day.'

The short ride along the promenade, battered by salty, seaweed breezes so strong they bent my eyelashes back, blew away the worst of the nausea and dizziness.

'I think this is a bit of a waste of time. They'll only tell me to go home, lie down, keep warm and call my own doctor if I get any further symptoms.'

'You're going in,' Annie insisted.

There was an hour-and-a-half wait in Casualty. I spent it watching the wall-mounted telly, listening to two tossers discuss their love life, which had resulted in one having his teeth knocked out, and watching an endless procession of screaming kids who'd jammed things in strange areas of their anatomy being given priority on the waiting list.

After ninety minutes I got to see a tired house officer.

'Go home, lie down, keep warm and call your own doctor if you get any further symptoms,' she advised.

'Cheers, Doc.'

I swung my feet over the side of the bed.

'You do have a home to go to for the night, do you? If not, our social worker might be able to fix a temporary place of shelter.'

Great. Now I looked like a dosser. I declined her kind offer on the grounds that I'd got a reservation on a park bench. 'There's a waiting list, you know. I don't want to miss my turn. 'Bye.'

I went in search of Annie, who'd disappeared ten minutes into the soap opera on the telly. She was sitting on the wall outside, staring into space with a vacant expression.

'What you doing?'

'Listening to the sea. It's peaceful, isn't it?'

I concentrated, retuning my ears to a sound that familiarity had filtered out a long time ago. The powerful, rhythmic "hush-whoosh" of the waves filtered over the traffic and everyday noises of the hospital.

'Mmm. It's sort of . . . ageless, isn't it?'

'How are you?'

'I'll live.'

'They don't think Mouldar will.'

'How do you know?'

'I went up to Intensive Care whilst you were being seen to. They've a police guard on him. I know one of the blokes.'

I was alarmed to hear Annie had been fraternizing with the enemy. 'He wasn't looking for me, was he?'

'I shouldn't think anyone is – apart from Bag-Ladies-R-Us.'

'You know what I mean.' I dug my fingers into her wrist. 'I'm so close, Annie. I just got to get this right.'

'And stick one over on the force?'

'You sound like Jackson.'

Jackson led, by a logical thought progression, to Jackson's current case. The building behind me was a blaze of light. If Tina had come here when she'd got away from Mouldar in the house, she'd be alive and well today. But the hospital meant Judy. And Judy had let her down before. So instead she'd tried to hitch back to the person she trusted most in the world: Bella.

I just hoped Bella never worked that one out.

I slid off the wall. 'Let's go. I need to find a map.'

CHAPTER 31

The car park was packed, with latecomers prowling like jackals waiting for the telltale glow of a reversing light.

As soon as Annie touched her accelerator pedal, a dark shape slid into view in the passenger mirror, its right indicator blinking out its claim on our spot.

'Hang on.'

Wriggling out of my belt, I flung open the door with an abandon that said this wasn't my car paint and ran across to the hovering BMW.

The electric window slid down as I approached.

'Hello, Grace. They're not keeping you in, then?'

'No. How's your dad? And the donkeys?'

'Donkeys are fine. Fred's taken them. They're keeping Dad in overnight for observation. Possible smoke inhalation. I've just picked up his stuff. Come up the ward with me. He was worried when you just took off like that. We both were.'

'Were you?'

'I've just said, haven't I?' My fingers were resting on the edge of the open window. Kevin put his hand over them. 'You're pretty hot on disappearing tricks, aren't you, Grace? Is there any chance we might have a whole uninterrupted conversation some time? Even if it is only across my dad's sickbed?'

'No. Em, I mean. I'll visit later.'

Out here in the dark I could kid myself my dishevelled appearance wasn't too obvious. Inside he was going to get the full glory of the straw, dung and grass stains. I was suddenly glad that he'd seen me in my seduction gear the other night, even if the whole thing had degenerated into an embarrassing scramble back into said gear when it came to the point. Or rather, didn't come to the point. I pulled my fingers free of his.

'Come on. Just show your face. Dad's fretting over you nearly as much as the flaming donkeys.'

'Honest?'

An irritated pumping of horns reminded us we were both blocking the car lane.

'Has he spoken to the police? It's just I'd rather avoid them for a couple of hours.' A thought occurred to me. 'You haven't got a local map in there, by any chance?'

'I have. And it's yours if you come up and see Dad.'

I gave in.

They'd already taken December up to the ward. He was perched in the chair next to his bed, swathed in a large blanket.

'Thank heaven you're back. How are you, lass? Seen the doc?'

'Yes. Thanks.'

Swishing the curtains closed, December starting changing, leaving me to hiss the rest of my questions through the flower-printed material.

'Have you spoken to the police?'

'They left half an hour since.'

'Did they mention me?'

'Well of course they did. They want a chat. You'd best get round to the station and see Jerry Jackson.'

The curtain parted with a flourish. I blinked. December's pyjamas were a natty pattern of thick black and white stripes. It looked like he'd sewn up a couple of deckchairs.

'Silk. Christmas pressie from the daughter-in-law.'

Thanks for reminding me you have one, my *alter ego* muttered rebelliously.

'Jermyn Street's finest. Minnie likes the better things in life,' Kevin said over his shoulder. His head was currently buried in the bedside locker as he stowed towels and shaving gear. 'Well, she chose me, didn't she?'

Obviously the dutiful husband role was being called into play here in front of his father. It was time to leave.

'I'm glad you're OK. I'll pop in again. And I'm real sorry your stable got blitzed. I guess it means you'll be out of business for a while.' Taking a deep breath, I made the supreme sacrifice. 'I'll work out your bill and let you have what's left of the advance as soon as poss. OK?'

'No. You keep it, lass. I reckon you earned it. And don't worry about me being on the breadline. I got one or two other business interests that'll see me right.'

'Like what?'

'The Electronic Daffodil for one.'

'Sorry?'

'Dad owns TED.'

'Sorry?'

I was aware I was beginning to sound like a jammed talkie doll, but the connection between my brain's electronic circuits and my vocal cords seemed to be temporarily missing.

'Diversification, that's what they call it, lass. No profit in donkey rides, so I started investing my dad's savings forty years ago. Got a few bingo halls and a share in the casino too.' Beneath the wiry eyebrow, the right eyelid dropped in a fleeting wink. 'Keep it under your hat, though. Don't want everyone knowing. They might expect me to drop the price for the rides.'

I recalled the earlier impression I'd had that December wasn't the amiable eccentric he purported to be. If only I'd listened to my instincts.

'I was spot on,' I moaned to Annie when we finally drove away from the hospital. 'I knew there was something odd about him. And I never followed it up.'

'You sure he's not winding you up?'

'No. I mean, yes. I'm sure.' Who else but the owner could

have wandered into Kevin's office at TED and started helping himself to the files as December had done? I'd been too busy unscrambling my pheromones from Kevin's to make the right connection. 'Do you realize what this means?'

'What?'

'I've undercharged him!'

'Oh, for heaven's *sake*!' Crashing into fifth gear with a wrench that probably took six months off her car's life, Annie put the pedal to the metal.

I hadn't wanted to look at Kevin's map in the hospital car park, since it would involve putting on the interior light, and there was always the chance that officers arriving to relieve those on Intensive Care or further question December might spot us.

We drove out on the road I'd trotted along in December's donkey trap until we reached the next bay. It was far smaller than Seatoun's beach, no more than a narrow crescent of sand backed by a line of bright wooden beach huts and a couple of cafés. At this time of night they were all shuttered up and we had the place to ourselves.

Parking up on the slipway, we switched off the engine and extinguished the headlights. The sea suddenly sprang into focus, its black surface gilded by unexpected bursts of phosphorus. The hungry swish and slap of the tide against the wooden breakwaters filled the silent car.

'We probably look like a courting couple.'

'Wish we were,' Annie sighed. 'Not us,' she added hurriedly. 'I meant, I wish you were someone else.'

'Same here.'

There were no neon signs to reflect in the water here. The ocean swooshed and teased and whispered its secrets to shingle as it had done for a million years. It all looked very deep and achingly lonely.

'Sorry things didn't work out with Jonathon.'

'Thanks. What about you and Kevin? You an item?'

'He's married.'

'Aren't they all? All the ones you'd want to share a duvet with, anyway.'

'Sod 'em all then.'

'Absolutely.'

'Let's have a look at that map.'

We folded it out over our knees and used Annie's torch to peer at the tiny writing.

'You sure you're on the right track?'

'Kersey had this map and local guidebooks in his room. And Mouldar had the self-same lot in his caravan. I had to shift them to get to the scouring powder, that's how come I remembered.'

'It's a bit tenuous.'

'It's all we've got. And I'm right. I know I am. Kersey wouldn't have made the clues too difficult. He *wanted* them to work it out and to know that they needed all four models to find the statue. The idea was to set them at each other's throats, not to send them barmy trying to decipher obscurely clever indicators. What's the first number?'

Holding the engraving an inch from her nose, Annie read out: 'D22206-2066.'

'Maybe it's the grid reference? Find twenty-two and two tenths.'

'That's one fifth to the rest of us.' Annie's square finger traced the thin blue lines. 'Got it.'

'Now zero six on the other grid. Where does that put us?'

'About two feet off the bottom of the map.'

'Damn.'

'How about if the first numbers are a road?'

We tried scanning for the A222, the A2220 or any permutations thereof. No show.

'It could be just the A2.'

'Then what are the rest of the numbers for? Fold it back, will you?'

The map, which had been perfectly well behaved up to that point, now started to fight back. We struggled to match folds to creases.

'Hang on, that way. No. I think perhaps it's . . . Annie, that's it. It's there. I've got it.' Grabbing the laminated cardboard cover, I twisted it up. 'There, see? D22206. It's part of the bar code.'

'Hardly Mensa material, is it?'

'Neither are the people it was aimed at. What about the rest . . . 2066.'

'Two-oh-six is the map number.' Annie kindly indicated the large black and white number we'd been skipping over for the past ten minutes. 'The only maverick is the six.'

We lined up the four bars.

Pat. No. D22206-2066
Other Rights Applied For

Pat. No. D22206-2066
Other Rights Applied For

Pat. No. D22206-2063
Other Rights Applied For

Pat. No. D22206-2063
Other Rights Applied For

Taking away the bar code and map numbers, we were left with two sixes and two threes spare.

'Intersection of the thirty-six easting and thirty-six northing?'

Annie consulted the sheet. 'If it is, he slung it over the side of the cross-Channel ferry.'

'Sod it.'

'Sixty-three by sixty-three is out. There's no sixty-three on the eastings.' She showed me the row of blue numbers running along the top of the map.

'Sixty-six by thirty-three,' I suggested without much hope.

Somehow the Channel ferry trick sounded like something that might have appealed to Kersey.

'Well, it's dry land at least.'

I checked the circle of white paper under Annie's index finger. It was the intersection of a small track that headed south-west from Seatoun before joining a B road about a mile out of town.

Annie flicked the torchlight up and down the length of the road. 'Do you know where this is?'

'It's the intersection of a small track—'

'Yes, I can see that, stupid. I mean, do you know what's going on out there now? It's the beginning of the new bypass route.'

I couldn't believe it. After all that, the wretched statue was about to be ploughed under by a bulldozer.

'Drive,' I yelled, reaching across Annie and switching on the ignition.

'We haven't got anything to dig with,' she protested, edging back up the slipway.

'I don't care, just go.'

We sped down country lanes and along tracks I didn't recognize. 'You sure this is the right way?'

'We're coming up on the B road now,' Annie said, squinting into the dark, hedgerow-lined patch caught in the undipped headlights. The white stop lines approached and disappeared under the bonnet as she swung right on to the wider road.

'We should be coming up on— Oh hell!'

A police road block was slung across the road in front of us. In the field behind we could make out a wire compound full of the bulky shapes of earth-moving machinery, their black silhouettes like crouching dinosaurs under the battery of white security lights.

On the other side of the road a straggle of protestors were huddled round a makeshift bonfire. Occasionally one waved a placard in a desultory fashion at the deserted equipment compound. Between them and the road, a line of police officers in fluorescent yellow overjackets were chatting, stamping their feet and generally filling in time until they could knock off for their break.

'Talk about overkill. What now?'

'The track intersection must be past this lot. Keep going forward slowly.'

Huddling down in the passenger seat, I watched the officers until I could see the whites of their eyes.

'Try to look respectable.'

'I don't have to try.' Sliding down the window, Annie smiled sweetly. 'Is it OK to go on, Officer? I'm trying to get home.'

The constable was new, or transferred from another area. In any event he plainly didn't recognize either of us. 'Quite safe, miss. Just a few demonstrators. They shouldn't bother you.'

With a snappy salute, he backed away and waved us imperiously forward. We rolled into no-man's land.

A dozen protestors watched apathetically from the field as we glided past. Some of them looked like they wished they were in this nice warm car with us.

The track intersection was about a hundred yards further on. It was little more than a mud path straggling away into the fields. But luckily a kink in the B road hid us from the watching police officers.

Or so I thought. Until Annie reminded me that the car headlights would be visible above the hedgerows. 'They'll have seen we've stopped. Might decide to come over and check out we aren't a rearguard attack.'

'Let me out then, and you go on a bit. Where's the torch?'

'Back pocket.'

There was another road bend about a quarter of a mile further on. Once Annie's tail-lights disappeared round it, I made my way along the track. The two compass references crossed just on the left-hand corner of this track and the B road. At the point, in fact, where a small copse of trees had been left in the corner of a roughly ploughed field. Either because the farmer was ecologically minded or because it just wasn't feasible to get the tractor right into that tight turn. Whatever the reason, it was a good place to do a spot of unobserved digging.

I plodded on, looking for a way into the field. The path sloped gently downwards towards the coast. The left-hand side was bounded by a three-wire fence, but the right-hand side still sported the remains of an ancient hedgerow. It looked about four feet thick and far too densely packed for me to force my way through.

Rustlings in the ditch by my feet and the occasional glitter of small yellow eyes reminded me I wasn't alone. An uneasy, primitive fear started to make my skin crawl.

The logical part of my mind said I was being daft. But I couldn't help it. If I'd turned round and found Alan Kersey's ghost following silently in my footsteps, I shouldn't have been surprised.

After a while I could actually hear his footfalls on the packed mud of the path. A few more yards and the rhythm of his breathing was gently inhaling and expiring with my own. My neck became stiff with the effort of keeping my eyes to the front rather than glancing over my shoulder.

The damn hedgerow seemed to be going on forever. What little moonlight there had been was now obscured by clouds, forcing me to use the torch. I was practically at the far end of the field before the hedgerow suddenly thinned, the slashed and mutilated branches showing stark white in the artificial light.

Somebody was in the process of dredging up this eight-hundred-year-old hedge and replacing it with fence posts and wire. No doubt I should have been shocked by the sacrilege, but I have to admit my only thought was 'Thank heavens for that' as I forced my way through a gap.

Dropping into the ploughed field and adding a few brown

stains to the assorted pattern on my tracksuit, I couldn't resist a quick flash of the torch beam on to the track I'd just left. It was empty.

I retraced my route back along the other side of the hedgerow, stumbling over newly planted furrows. About halfway down the field the terrain changed. The furrows were hard and unyielding: frost-cracked earth that hadn't been sown this season. Presumably this was the extent of the land designated for the road-widening.

The copse of trees lurked in the corner like a bunch of sulky trolls. I was hopeless at biology at school, but even I could see that these were probably as ancient as the hedgerow they were huddled against. Short, gnarled and squat, they hugged the earth with their twisting roots and dipped heavy branches over to touch the soil with exploratory tips.

Even with their leaves just unfurling, the umbrella of boughs was dense enough to form a wooden wigwam shielding anyone inside from curious eyes. Dropping on my knees, I crawled inside.

The earth had been disturbed recently. Crumpled lumps of sod had been carelessly thrust back, their haphazard mounds still containing the dead remains of grass and weeds that had been torn out when the soil was turned over. Don't tell me somebody had got here before me?

Twisting a trailing twig from the branch above me, I tried pushing it into the dirt, feeling for an obstruction. The pliant wood bent and curved under the pressure.

Annie had been right. I needed a spade.

Frustrated, I sat back on my heels. And became aware that something else was in here with me.

CHAPTER 32

In the windless night the branches behind me clicked and rustled. At the same time a vile and nauseous smell filled the air. Frozen, I felt hair on the nape of my neck rising.

Something brushed my hand softly. It released me from my paralysis. With a scream of fright I hit out at this shade from hell.

Yowling its annoyance, a large feral tom-cat retreated in a huff to the ditch until I'd finished messing around in its own private loo.

When my heart had finished bouncing between my stomach and the back of my throat I considered my options.

Annie hadn't reappeared. I could sit it out and hope she'd come back for me (and remember to bring a shovel). Alternatively, I could hike back to town, borrow a shovel and get a cab back out here.

Hugging my knees and feeling the cold dampness of the earth (at least I hoped it was the earth) seeping into the bottom of my tracksuit, I weighed up the two ideas.

Returning to town would be the most sensible plan. But I had this terrible conviction that something would go wrong, I'd be delayed by some malignant gremlin and by the time I returned the whole of this corner would have been ripped out by the bulldozers.

I needed a shovel. And who was most likely to have one around here?

Dragging the hood of my tracksuit over my fair hair, which

would be a dead giveaway if the moon came out again, I made my way quietly across the fields.

All the police attention was concentrated on the protestors on the other side of the road. No one was watching the back of the equipment compound.

The chinks in the wire fencing were just about big enough to accommodate the toes of my trainers. Gripping with all ten fingers I started to haul myself up. Luckily the compound had been hastily thrown up and didn't have any refinements such as contact alarms.

Getting down the other side was trickier. For one thing I was going to be under the full glare of the security lights, and if anyone glanced this way they could hardly fail to spot me hanging like a spider in the middle of a metal web.

In the end I just dropped. I landed with all the wind knocked out of me but shielded by a huge dumper truck. Lying flat, I peered under its belly and spotted a stash of picks and shovels leaning against the far wheel.

It was easy enough to wriggle forward and extract a spade from the pile. Getting it over the fence wasn't so simple. Eventually I took a chance and slung it in a curving arc. It landed with a thump that I was convinced could be heard in Seatoun, but no one came to investigate.

Easing myself away from the shelter of the dumper's huge wheel, I started to cautiously haul myself up the fence again.

I had no choice but to risk being seen this time. But I comforted myself with the thought that the worst they could do was charge me with trying to nick a shovel.

I was wrong.

I'd actually reached the top and was lying full length preparatory to scrambling down the other side when they spotted me.

'Oi!'

The yell startled me so much I lost my grip and fell awkwardly on to my right shoulder.

Staggering to my feet, I saw half a dozen yellow jackets hurtling towards me. The sensible thing would have been to stand quietly and explain. But the same deep-seated instinct that said the night was a time for fear made me turn and run instead.

It was all the encouragement they needed. The violent demonstration they'd been wound up to expect had fizzled into a damp protest; the action and excitement they'd anticipated had turned into eight boring hours wandering around in the middle of nowhere protecting lumps of metal from those with anorak-angst. They wanted action, and I'd just provided the excuse.

Stumbling over the uneven earth, I looked behind and found that twenty other officers had joined in the chase. With whoops and yells of exhilaration they were pouring after me like a pack of hounds that had just spotted the fox.

I was doing pretty well, if I do say so. They'd been standing in artificial lighting, whereas my eyes had become accustomed to the dark and I'd already traversed this terrain once. My feet instinctively knew how to avoid the ruts. By cutting diagonally across the fields, I made it back to the mutilated hedgerow well ahead of them. If I hadn't got snagged up on the nails in the new fence post, I think I might have got clear.

As it was, I'd taken three steps down the track when a ton weight hit me full in the back and slammed me face down on to the dirt.

My nose hit first. It was gushing tides of gore when my hood was pulled back to the instruction to 'Hold still, mate.'

With a sense of inevitability, I twisted round and found myself looking into Terry Rosco's ugly mug.

They kept me in the back of the police van, handcuffed to a WPC, despite my protests, until DCI Jackson arrived.

'Grace,' he beamed. 'Good of you to wait.'

'Der's doe deed to be tarcastic,' I sniffed, dabbing my dripping nose with a pad of dressing from the first-aid kit.

He climbed into the van and sat beside me on the bench seat. A jerk of his head released the cuffs and got rid of the WPC.

'Well, we have been anxious to interview you, as I'm sure December will have told you. There's the small matter of a violent death in the stables, for a start. You are an important witness to the incident.'

I raised my head from the lint. 'Mouldar's dead?'

'An hour ago. He never regained consciousness.'

'They won't put Alan down, will they?'

'Who's Alan?'

'The donkey that did it.'

'You have a strange sense of priorities, Grace.'

'He's worth ten of Mouldar, or Barken, or whatever he was called.'

'His full name was William Ernest Smith; a.k.a. Barking Billy; a.k.a. half a dozen other aliases. Known associate of the late Oliver Andrew Colville. Although not listed as an associate of the even later Desmond Parker. If he had been, I suppose the original investigating officers might have collected a full set for Edwin Woolley's death instead of having to be content with Kersey.'

'Kersey wasn't there, you know, when the Major was murdered.'

'December said. But he was guilty of setting those two on the old boy, wasn't he? Personally I can't feel much sorrow for Kersey. He probably got what he deserved.'

'Dow who's dot a funny sense of priorities? You're supposed to care, aren't you? Truth and justice and all that.'

'You're mixing me up with Superman. I just do what I can to hold the tide back a bit. I leave saving planets to the Met.'

He'd opened the back doors of the van. Possibly to avoid the need for a chaperon, although I had a nasty feeling it might be connected to the current state of my personal hygiene. The police presence was being scaled down and a coach had just bumped on to the verge to collect the surplus officers. A ragged cheer went up from the demonstrators at what they saw as a moral victory.

'Do you know,' Jackson said suddenly, 'I took a look at their records: Parker's, Colville's and Mouldar's, I mean.'

'And?'

'And I reckon that if they'd just settled down to a regular job, nothing fancy, just a normal factory shift or something, they'd have made ten times as much money in their lifetimes than they ever did by thieving.'

'It's not for the money though, is it? Not just the money. It's for the high. The buzz from whipping the system.'

'That why you do it, Grace? Do you get a buzz from acting like a total prat?'

'I am not a prat!'

'You withheld information that nearly got you and December fried.'

I sniffed cautiously. The nosebleed appeared to have stopped. 'I was going to call you. Honestly. I just wanted to get the statue back first. I'm employed to do so,' I offered as justification. 'By Mrs Woolley.'

'If she's the old boy's heir, she'd get it anyway.'

I managed to dredge up just enough loyalty to my client to withhold the information that she had been hoping to defraud the rest of the beneficiaries of Edwin Woolley's will.

'She was a bit worried someone else might get there first.' I tried to look appealing. 'I've found it. At least, I know where it is. That's what I wanted the spade for. It's only a few yards up the road.'

He doesn't bear grudges, I'll say that for Jackson. With a sharp whistle he called over a uniformed sergeant and asked if anyone had the keys to the equipment compound.

'Yes, sir. Contractors left a set in case.'

'Good. Issue half a dozen volunteers with digging implements and follow us.'

The last six in the queue for the coach were 'volunteered'.

With picks and shovels over their shoulders they trooped in a file up the dark road. I bit my tongue and refrained from whistling 'Hi-ho, hi-ho'.

The cat was turfed out again. It stalked away in a huff, tail held erect to indicate its displeasure, and sat down a few yards away, giving the impression of a pair of disembodied tangerine eyes hovering a foot above the earth.

As it turned out, we didn't need six officers. The crumbling earth came away easily and the first shovel hit an obstruction a few inches down.

Under half a dozen torch beams, the soil was removed inch by inch to reveal a dirty black plastic sack.

'That's never been down here twelve years odd,' Jackson remarked, squatting on his heels. 'Look, earth's still loose all round the sides too. It should be packed hard after twelve winters in the ground.'

'Kersey probably dug it up to check. They said at the hospice he used to go out for long walks on his own when he first came. He even hired a car once.'

Jackson crumbled the earth in his fingers. 'Probably. I'd guess it was hidden somewhere else and only shifted here a couple of months ago.'

'Where?'

He straightened up, brushing down his trousers. 'We'll never know now, will we? Get it out, lads.'

With some heaving and grunting they pulled the parcel clear. It was drum-shaped, about two feet high. A few knife slashes disposed of the sack, revealing a plastic bucket. The lid was sealed with waterproof tape but through the opaque sides we could just make out a solid dark shape surrounded by some opalescent material.

We were crouched in a rapt circle, like some ancient sect worshipping at a pagan altar.

Slitting the securing tape, Jackson eased the lid off and reached inside.

The opalescent material was transparent plastic sheeting. The torchlight reflected its shiny newness. Jackson was right, the statue had been repackaged very recently.

Carefully he unrolled the protective sheets until finally the heavy metal core was revealed.

Reversing the drum, Jackson set the statue on the base, reinforcing the impression of a pagan god. Which I suppose it was in a way.

I'd expected bronze to be warm and coppery in texture. But this metal was dark and cold, almost iron-like in its appearance. The rider's stocky body was clad in a short dress-like garment and his smooth round head was topped by a headdress that resembled a stylized pineapple.

The plump, shoeless legs were clamped round the horse's rotund body. Only it wasn't a horse: from its stringy tail to its long floppy ears, the beast was all donkey.

I stared at the head. There was no mistaking it. With his lip curled back and his teeth displayed in a sneering laugh, the statue was the spitting image of Snowy, a.k.a. Alan.

Epilogue

First the bad news.

The statue was a fake. A twentieth-century copy probably produced in France sometime in the nineteen twenties, according to the experts.

It went for three hundred pounds at auction. December bought it. It's got pride of place in his sitting room.

Thinking about it now, I'd lay bets that Alan Kersey had discovered it wasn't genuine. If it had been, I think he would have dropped it off that cross-Channel ferry. Leaving it where the survivors of his nasty little plan for revenge could find it was his final piece of vindictiveness.

Simla refused to pay me a penny. She blamed me for her failure to escape from St Theresa's. Which struck me as damn unfair, given her late husband's contribution to proceedings.

(However, at the time of writing, the refined one's sculptures have suddenly become very collectible again. I ran into Eddie, Simla's house-breaking grandson, in TED the other evening, and he tells me his gran has plans to move into a bungalow with 'the old bird whose lift don't reach the top'.)

I didn't mention her involvement in her husband's murder, but from something Jackson said, I rather suspect the police had worked it out for themselves. However, nothing ever came of it. Let's face it – the only person left who could have provided them with evidence for a charge was Simla herself.

Dorothea Springle died a few days after her Ben Hur performance with Lana and the donkey trap. She left me her carved walking stick.

Now the good news.

They didn't bring any charges against me in connection with the Mouldar/Tina business.

Bella gave Tina a terrific funeral. She had the works: cars, choir, running buffet and sparkling wine. December brought the lads, all suitably draped in black-edged blankets, and contributed a donkey-shaped wreath in white carnations.

A week later Bella and Judy flew out to stay with Bella's gran in Trinidad. They sent me a postcard of waving palms and golden beaches.

I figure you never know when your time's going to be up. It's time to stop planning and start doing, honey – Bella.

And believe me, I'm doing anything that's on offer – Judy.

On a hunch, I checked Warren out on the missing persons register. His description matched that of Michael Tobias Bennett, a thirteen-year-old runaway from Birmingham. His dad was offering a three-thousand-pound reward for information.

I turned him in and got my car fixed.

December rested the lads for a couple of weeks, but now they're back plodding their patch on the beach as usual. He has a new replacement for Marilyn: a brown donkey with melting toffee eyes called Bette Davies.

And Kevin turned out to be separated from his wife.